SECRETS OF IVY GARDEN

Catherine Ferguson burst onto the writing scene at the age
of nine, anonymously penning a weekly magazine for her
five-year-old brother (mysteriously titled the 'Willy' comic)
and fooling him completely by posting it through the
letterbox every Thursday.

Catherine's continuing love of writing saw her study English
at Dundee University and spend her twenties writing for
various teenage magazines including *Jackie* and *Blue Jeans*
and meeting pop stars. She worked as Fiction Editor at *Patches*
magazine (little sister to *Jackie*) before getting serious and
becoming a sub-editor on the Dundee *Courier & Advertiser*.

This is her fifth novel. She lives with her son in
Northumberland.

By the same author

Humbugs and Heartstrings
Green Beans and Summer Dreams
Mistletoe and Mayhem
Four Weddings and a Fiasco

Catherine Ferguson

The Secrets of Ivy Garden

avon.

This novel is entirely a work of fiction.
The names, characters and incidents portrayed in it are
the work of the author's imagination. Any resemblance to
actual persons, living or dead, events or localities is
entirely coincidental.

AVON

A division of HarperCollins*Publishers*
1 London Bridge Street,
London SE1 9GF

www.harpercollins.co.uk

A Paperback Original 2017

1

A catalogue record for this book is
available from the British Library

ISBN-13: 978-0-00-825335-6

Set in 8/10pt Minion by Palimpsest Book Production Ltd,
Falkirk, Stirlingshire

Printed and bound in Great Britain by Clays Ltd, St Ives plc

Find out more about HarperCollins and the environment at
www.harpercollins.co.uk/green

For Ian and Krysy

Prologue

We stood on the dusty railway platform, Ivy and I, saying our goodbyes.

The August sun burned down, making my hangover worse. (It turned out that Ivy's home-made rhubarb and ginger wine was rather more potent than even she had realised.) I thought longingly of the cool interior of the train, imagining myself sinking into a seat and closing my eyes to ease the ache that was pulsing at my temples. My journey from the Cotswolds up to Manchester involved several changes with a long wait between connections, but it had to be done. I was due back at work in the café next day. Not to mention the fact that I was keen, as usual, to escape the countryside and get back to my home in the city, even though I hated leaving Ivy.

'Will you get a taxi at the other end?' Ivy looked worriedly at my weekend bag, which was stuffed so full, the zip was in danger of bursting. 'That looks really heavy.'

I nudged her affectionately, hoisting the bag further up my shoulder. 'I'll survive. Don't worry. I'm a big girl now.'

She smiled, forget-me-not blue eyes crinkling at the corners, her face tanned golden brown and etched with lines from a summer spent in the garden. 'You might have just turned the ripe old age of thirty, but I'm always going to worry. Show me a grandma who doesn't.'

'Especially one who's a mum and dad to me as well.' I pulled her into a hug, which was a little awkward because of the bag.

'I'll phone you when I get back to Manchester,' I added when she didn't reply.

Pulling back, I realised she hadn't even heard me. She was staring directly over my shoulder at the opposite platform, and I turned, wondering what had caught her attention. Around a dozen people with bags and suitcases – some in little groups – were standing waiting for their train to arrive.

'What is it?' I asked, not recognising anyone.

The intensity in her eyes took me by surprise. 'There's something I need to tell you, Holly,' she murmured.

I felt a twinge of apprehension but disguised it with a laugh. 'That your rhubarb and ginger wine is at least thirty per cent proof? It's all right. I already know that, to my cost!'

She gripped my forearms. 'Can you take a later train?'

I shook my head. 'This is the last one of the day.'

'So go back tomorrow.'

The Manchester train appeared round the bend. We watched as it glided to a halt and passengers began alighting on to the platform. Panic fluttered in my chest. Ivy and I didn't have secrets. We knew everything there was to know about each other.

What was it she needed to tell me?

My heart fought with my head. 'I'd love to stay another night, but I'm back at the café tomorrow morning, remember? And Patty's already short-staffed as it is, with people off on holiday.'

Ivy nodded, seeming to recollect herself. 'Of course. I'm being silly.' She forced a smile and let go of my arms. 'You have to get back.'

People were climbing aboard the train now, and the guard was walking along the platform, getting ready to blow his whistle.

2

I took her hand and squeezed it gently. 'I'll phone later and we can talk then?'

She kissed me on the cheek and shooed me into the carriage. 'Quick, quick, or it'll leave without you.'

I found a seat and sat on the edge of it, still gripping my bag, full of uncertainty. Ivy had held my arms so tightly when she asked me to stay. Perhaps I should slip off the train and phone in sick tomorrow?

But when I looked out on to the platform, she was smiling and waving, back to her normal self, and I thought maybe I'd imagined the flash of despair in her eyes when she begged me to change my plans. Ivy was forever saying the times we saw each other went by far too quickly. Perhaps she simply wanted to prolong our precious weekend together

At the exact same moment, we both realised she was waving with a paper bag full of chocolate orange cupcakes that were meant for me. A speciality of the village bakery in Appleton, where Ivy now lived, they were our all-time favourite cakes and Ivy brought some for me whenever she came to visit me in Manchester. So then, of course, I had to rush to the door and grab the bag before the guard blew his whistle and all the doors closed.

As the train drew out of the station, we were both laughing – me flopped back in my seat, breathless and giggling, and Ivy on the platform covering her face with her hands in mock horror.

She blew me a kiss as the train drew out of the station.

I never saw her again.

Eight months later

Spring

'You can cut all the flowers but you cannot stop spring from coming'

— Pablo Neruda

ONE

I know I've cocked up again when Patty abruptly abandons the milk she's frothing, and puts her arm around me.

I swivel my eyes at her in alarm.

My boss showers her *dogs* with love. But I've worked with her long enough – fourteen years to be precise, from being a Saturday girl at sixteen – to know that she's fairly reserved when it comes to showing affection for actual people.

'Oh, God.' I bite my lip and throw a glance at the queue of lunch-time customers. 'What did I do this time?'

Patty's mouth quirks up at the corner. 'You've just given poor Betty spicy tomato pickle with her fruit scone.'

I glance over in horror.

Betty, one of our elderly regulars, is removing her coat and settling herself at a corner table, clearly relishing the prospect of taking the weight off her bunions and tucking into a delicious home-baked scone with strawberry jam and cream.

She's in for a nasty surprise.

Patty grabs me before I have a chance to charge over, and the empathy in her eyes almost floors me.

Ever since Ivy died, I've been walking around in a sort of stunned daze, doing things on autopilot. Which is why, I suppose,

7

I gave Betty spicy tomato pickle instead of strawberry jam. And burned my hand on the coffee machine last week. As well as carefully spreading a mountain of rolls with gloopy baking fat before Patty noticed and stopped me. 'Not sure our customers would appreciate the irony of having lard with their healthy salad sandwiches,' she remarked dryly.

In all that time, I haven't broken down in public even once, but all of a sudden, I'm perilously close to losing it in front of the entire café.

I dig my nails into my palms, which is meant to distract you from the emotion that's threatening to knock you flat. It seems to work. And it's also slightly less weird than crossing your eyes or rolling them around, other suggestions I found online.

I solve most of my practical problems online. Ivy was hopeless at DIY so I grew up tackling all the odd jobs around the house to save us money. I even fixed a leaky tap once with one of those step-by-step Wiki guides. As a result, I tend not to be daunted by tasks that other people would run a mile from.

My independent streak seems to baffle men. When they discover my parents died when I was four, they first of all think I must want to talk about it (which I absolutely don't) and then they try to look after me and protect me from the big bad world. I should probably feel grateful. But instead, it makes me feel suffocated. That's probably why my romantic history is peppered with fledgling relationships that I've ended because the guy wouldn't give me the space I craved.

My latest doomed romance ended last summer after Adam, who I actually really liked and thought I might even be in love with, started hinting – after only three months – that we should move in together. He obviously took it as an affront when I said it was a little too early to think about that – because two weeks later, he left me for a glamour model he'd met at his local gym. I told myself I was fortunate to have found out about his shallowness so early on, and I tried not to mind when they got engaged a month after they met. Perhaps I was meant to be alone.

Ivy once told me I never gave romance a chance and she asked me if I thought I was running away from commitment. It would be natural, she said, after losing my parents so young, to fear the people I love might be snatched away from me.

Privately, I thought this was simply daft psychobabble. The guys concerned were just not for me, that was all.

'Go and sort Betty out,' Patty says. 'And then go away and sort *everything else* out, okay?'

'But . . .' I glance at the queue of people, all staring at us expectantly.

She shakes her head, gently holding my wrists. 'No buts, Holly. You were back at work the day after the funeral. *Much* too soon. And yes, I *know* the last thing you want to do is make the long journey back down to the Cotswolds and go through Ivy's things . . .'

I swallow. 'And get Moonbeam Cottage ready to sell.'

Just saying it makes my insides quiver. Moonbeam Cottage, in the heart of the Cotswolds, was such a huge part of Ivy's life.

'It has to be done.' Patty's tone is gentle but firm. 'And the sooner the better, don't you think?' She pauses. 'What would Ivy be saying to you now?'

I smile, tears filming my eyes. I can hear her in my head, speaking with that lovely West Country burr: 'Don't you stress yourself, my lover. Everything will be fine. Sooner you get down there, the sooner you'll be back home again.'

I always trusted Ivy's good sense above anyone else's – except perhaps during those turbulent teen years when we fought as much as any parent and kid. She was a great mix of gentleness, modesty and steely inner strength, and I knew her better than anyone alive.

But now she's gone . . .

I dig my nails into my palms until it hurts.

My grandma was special. I was so lucky to have had her in my life.

Actually, I never thought of her as 'Grandma'. I always called her Ivy because, in reality, she was far more than just a grandmother; she was Mum, Dad and grandparent all rolled into one.

She scooped me up when I was four years old, after my parents died, and took us off to live in Manchester. Goodness knows why she chose Manchester. I once asked her why on earth she abandoned her beloved Moonbeam Cottage in the tiny village of Appleton to bring me to a big city where we knew no-one at all. She just laughed, tweaked my nose and said, 'Isn't that what fresh starts are all about, my lover?'

Ivy missed Mum so much – I'd hear her crying at night when she thought I was asleep – but she never ever dwelled on the day of the accident, at least not in my presence. She always said she preferred to look forward, taking me with her on our exciting ride into the future.

As a child, I piggy-backed on her zest for life; she never let fear get in the way of having an adventure – even though, on a supermarket check-out/school cleaner's wage, the height of her walk on the wild side was our annual trip to the lights and magic of Blackpool.

Patty takes hold of my hands. 'You don't have to feel guilty about selling Ivy's cottage, you know.'

I nod, unable to speak.

'Would you *want* to live in Appleton? In the heart of the countryside?' she asks gently.

'No!' My insides shift queasily at the thought. Visiting Ivy there occasionally I could cope with. But *live* in Appleton? With all the painful associations I've spent most of my adult life trying to push from my mind?

'Look, love, Ivy just wanted you to be happy. She would be right behind you, whether you sold the cottage, rented it out or turned it into a refuge centre for cow-pat-hating city girls like you.'

I attempt a smile. It's not the cow pats that are the problem, but I know that, in essence, Patty's right. Ivy would have loved me to go with her when she moved back to the Cotswolds after she retired. But she understood that my fear of the countryside ran too deep for that. Ivy knew, as no-one else does, that the reason I cling tightly to my life here in the city is because I need to block out the past. It was why Ivy came to visit me in Manchester all the time. She wanted to make things easier for me. (Only rarely did I summon up the courage to go back to Appleton to visit her, and when I did, I could never totally relax.)

Selling Moonbeam Cottage really is my only option. I can't drag my feet any longer. It's now April, four whole months since Ivy died, and I've been putting off my trip down to the Cotswolds for far too long.

'And don't worry about leaving us short-staffed,' Patty murmurs. 'Olivia's finished at uni and, as always, my delightful daughter is absolutely desperate for cash. So she'll happily fill in while you're away.'

'She'll do a much better job than me right now,' I croak, feeling the familiar fears trickling in at the thought of returning to the countryside.

'Maybe. But listen, Holly.' Patty grips my shoulders and makes me focus. 'Promise me you'll take care of yourself? Take some time to get that beautiful head sorted.' Gently, she brushes back a strand of honey-blonde hair that's escaped from my ponytail.

She glances apologetically at the waiting customers. 'Sorry, folks. Staff crisis. Be with you in a sec.'

'Go,' she hisses, handing me a ramekin of strawberry jam. 'Your job's here whenever you decide you want to come back, okay? Whether that's in a month or even in *six* months' time.'

Her kindness is too much. I have to get away before I break down and make a complete fool of myself.

'Thank you,' I mouth. Then I rush over to Betty with the jam, collect my coat and bag from the cloakroom and step outside into the blustery spring day. It's a wrench leaving the cosy warmth of the café behind, and as the bell on the door jangles behind me and a cool breeze lifts my hair, I wonder with a pang how long it will be before I cross the threshold again. With her daily dose of light chit-chat and practical good sense, Patty has almost single-handedly kept me sane.

Ivy died on 14th December from a massive heart attack.

My memory of the run-up to Christmas and beyond is a bit of a blur, but I do remember refusing to leave my flat, despite offers from my best friends, Beth and Vicki – and also Patty – to spend Christmas with them. After the funeral in early January, I went straight back to work, even though Patty told me I needed more time to grieve. I convinced her that work was good therapy. And so for the past few months, I've slipped into a safe routine: keeping busy all day at the café, going home to eat and mindlessly watch TV, then sitting in the darkened kitchen, with just the pool of light from an Anglepoise lamp, to do my sketching, hour after hour, often until well after midnight when my eyes are stinging. I know if I go to bed too early, I'll only end up lying there, staring into the darkness, fretting about the future.

I've always loved painting and sketching, and now it's proving to be an absolute life-line. Ivy's big dream for me was to study art at college when I left school. She used to say being an artist was my 'calling' because my paintings made people think about life and gave them pleasure. But however much I might have wanted to pursue my art as a career, I knew it was never going to be a practical option because we didn't have the money. When Patty offered to promote me from Saturday girl to full-time staff when I was sixteen, I jumped at the chance, and I'm still there.

I still sketch, though, especially now. When I'm focused on drawing the perfect foxglove, it's easier to keep the dark thoughts at bay.

I've always been the sort of practical, clear-headed person people can count on in a crisis. But since Ivy died, I've felt vulnerable and far less sure of myself. My insides shift queasily every time I think of making that long train journey south, leaving behind everything that's familiar. Even telling myself it's just for a few weeks, and then I'll be safely back home, doesn't seem to make any difference.

How can I bear to stay in Moonbeam Cottage if Ivy's not there?

And then suddenly a memory blazes into my head.

Ivy and me on the waltzer in Blackpool.

We booked the same week every year, staying in the same guest house and reuniting with some other families we got to know who did the same. I loved it when I was a kid because there was always someone to play with.

No holiday in Blackpool was complete without several rides on the waltzer. Spinning round and around, clutching on to each other as the blaring fairground music swallowed our squeals. Laughing helplessly at the thrill of it all.

Scream if you wanna go faster!

Ivy always went on it with me, even though I knew it scared her. I think she worried I'd slip out of the safety belt. When we got off, she'd exaggerate her wobbly legs, staggering around to make the little kids laugh. The other mums and dads stood watching, smiling at their children and waving.

I remember feeling really proud of my fearless grandma for not letting nerves stand in her way.

Now, hurrying for home, I mentally open my wardrobe and start picking out clothes to pack. I'll catch the train tomorrow.

I can be brave, too.

TWO

Whenever I think of the Cotswolds, where Ivy lived the last decade of her life, I think of the row of pretty golden stone cottages skirting Appleton village green and the gnarled old oak tree by the cricket pavilion. In my mind, it's always summer there and the sky is always blue.

But when I step off the train at Stroud – the nearest station to Appleton – I'm faced with a rather different view of the Cotswolds. Storms have been raging all week, causing destruction right across the country, and today appears to be no exception. I peer out of the station entrance at people scurrying for shelter from the steady drizzle and gusty wind.

I can't afford to hang around. There's only one bus to Appleton every two hours – and the next one leaves in ten minutes.

Grabbing a firmer hold of my suitcase, I start running for the bus station, dodging passers-by and puddles of rainwater. As long as the bus doesn't leave early, I should just about make it.

And then it happens.

I round the corner a little too briskly, step to one side to avoid a man with a briefcase, and instead, cannon right into someone else.

Momentarily winded, I register the black habit and white veil the woman is wearing and my heart gives a sickening thud.

Oh God, I just nearly decked a religious person!

But worse is to come.

The nun, who I notice is remarkably tall, stops for a second to regain her balance. But she lists too far to one side and ends up staggering off the pavement into the water-logged gutter.

To say I'm mortified is a vast understatement.

'I'm so, *so sorry!*' I reach out to her, then draw back my hand, just in case she's taken some kind of vow that forbids any form of physical contact during high winds. 'God, are you all right?'

Shit, why did I have to say 'God'?

She's bending to retrieve her glasses, which mustn't fit very well because they seem to have gone flying when she over-balanced. Her attempts at picking them up are failing miserably – so, flushed and overcome with guilt, I dive in, swipe them off the ground then rub them clean on my coat before handing them back.

She puts them on, almost stabbing herself in the eye, and that's when I notice something odd. The glasses are attached to a large, false nose.

She sways and I grab her arm to steady her, wondering what on earth is going on.

'Seen a bunch of people dressed as monks and nuns?' she slurs in a voice that's surprisingly full of gravel and several octaves lower than I was expecting. 'Disappeared. And it's my turn to get the beers in.'

Stunned, I shake my head. So not a nun, then. Not female either, come to that.

I glance at my watch.

Bugger!

Thanks to this stag-do buffoon, I've now missed the bus to Appleton and there won't be another one along for at least two hours.

An arm snakes round my waist. 'Hey, why don't you come along? Join the pub crawl?'

Actually, how it sounds is *Heywhydntcmlongjnpubcrawl?* I stare

16

up at his stupid false nose and black-rimmed glasses, the lenses of which are like jam jar bottoms. I'm amazed he can see through them. No wonder he charged right into me.

He sways closer and the booze on his breath almost knocks me flat.

I feel like weeping. Today's long journey from Manchester has been emotionally exhausting, to say the least, and now – to cap it all – I'm being propositioned by a drunk disguised as a *nun*?

It can't get any worse. Oh hang on, apparently it can.

His hand just slipped lower and is clamped so tight, there seems to be no escape. The rest of him might be listing like a yacht in a force nine, but there's nothing flaky about that firm grasp.

I try to move away but the pavement is packed with people and I just keep getting pushed back against him. Then when I do manage to put a small distance between us, he staggers a bit and lurches forward. That's when I realise he was probably just grabbing on to me in an attempt to remain upright.

He grins and the cheap nylon veil slips down over one eye. 'Dirt on your coat,' he mumbles helpfully.

I glance down. Sure enough, there's a big splodge of muck from where I wiped his joke glasses on my otherwise pristine beige coat. The one I had dry-cleaned last week.

'Sorry,' he mumbles, catching my look of horror and attempting to look contrite.

'So you should be,' I snap, thinking miserably of the two-hour wait ahead. 'Pretending to be one of God's holy sisters and making me miss my bus!'

'Youdon'tapproveofmendressed'snuns?'

Quick translation while leaning away to avoid beery breath. 'No, I *don't* approve of men dressed as nuns. Especially if they're rat-arsed. If I were a nun, I'd be absolutely horrified.'

He snorts, apparently finding it all very funny indeed. 'Butyou-aren'tanunareyou?'

I grit my teeth.

A six-foot-two fake nun is using me as a prop to remain standing and people are staring. Plus, I have a two-hour wait for a bus and a lovely reminder of my unholy encounter in the form of a nasty black stain on my coat.

Just then, to add insult to injury, the bus to Appleton swooshes past, hurling a litre of gutter rainwater at me. Tears prick my eyes as I watch it accelerate off into the distance.

'No, I am *not* a nun,' I growl, and Maria von Trapp on growth hormones sniggers like a schoolboy. I fix him with my sternest look. 'Not *yet*, anyway.'

He blinks several times at me behind his glasses. At least, I assume that's what he's doing because I can't actually see his eyes through the stupid joke lenses.

'In fact,' I add, enjoying his confusion, 'I'm actually training to become a nun.'

He snorts, nearly overbalances, then starts convulsing with laughter.

'It's true,' I say, feeling ridiculously offended on behalf of nuns everywhere.

He's laughing so much, he's having to lean against some iron railings for support. 'You off to the convent now, then? Didn't know there was one in Stroud.'

I give him my haughtiest stare. 'Actually, I'm – erm – having a last long holiday in the Cotswolds before I start my training up in Manchester. And if you weren't so pissed, you'd be wishing me luck instead of acting like an utter moron.'

I walk off, nose in the air, fairly impressed with my spontaneous put-down. When I turn a moment later, he's leaning against a lamppost, arms folded, staring dazedly after me.

Me? A novice nun? Ha, that's a good one!

My triumphant smile slips when it occurs to me that a vow of chastity isn't exactly a stretch for me right now. It's been well over six months since I did anything even remotely horizontal and non-nun-like.

I can't face waiting for a bus, so I decide to treat myself to a taxi. It's expensive, but I'll get there much faster. Luckily, the taxi driver seems to sense that I don't want to chat and leaves me alone with my thoughts as we wend our way towards Appleton.

We drive through a string of pretty villages and I try to stay calm, telling myself everything will be fine. But the trouble is, I know what's coming. I know that in a minute, we'll be driving into open countryside without a single house or village pub or any sign of civilisation to reassure me. It's the wide open spaces that scare me the most.

I squeeze my eyes shut so I don't have to look at the fields on either side that seem to stretch away to infinity. I'd thought that with the passage of time, the terror would begin to subside. But here I am, my heart pounding in my ears as if it happened only yesterday.

I want Ivy so much right now, I feel as if my heart will break.

Last time I saw her, she was waving me off on the train back to Manchester.

I remember thinking how elegant she was that day. Normally, Ivy lived in casual trousers and tops. Life was too short, she said, for feeling like a trussed-up goose in the name of fashion. But she'd taken me for an early supper at a nearby pub before driving me to the station in Stroud, which was why she was all dressed up. Right then, on that station platform, she could have passed for a woman in her late fifties. Hard to believe she was seventy-two.

Actually, the way I usually remember her now is in the old gardening garb she used to wear, or in her hiking gear, fresh from walking in the country lanes around Appleton.

A painful lump wedges in my throat.

This is how it happens. I'll just be starting to think I'm doing okay, coping well, beginning to make plans – then boom! The thought that I'll never be able to see Ivy or hug her ever again sends a flood of grief washing through me.

Hot tears prick my eyelids. The nails-in-palms trick isn't

19

working. Then something Ivy used to say zips into my mind: *Worry's like a rocking chair: it gives you something to do but never gets you anywhere.*

I swallow hard, picturing her giving me one of her no-nonsense pep talks. It's almost as if she's sitting right here next to me, a twinkle in her eyes, on the bench in her beloved Ivy Garden. Telling me not to worry because things are never as bad as they seem and I'll figure it out somehow.

Of course! That's where I need to be.

Ivy Garden.

Her favourite place in the whole world.

With my eyes still closed, I picture Ivy Garden the last time I saw it, on that final weekend I spent with her.

It was a hot August day. We wandered over the road and squeezed through the gap in the hedge, to the dappled woodland clearing that, over the years, Ivy had transformed into a sanctuary of peace and tranquillity.

She discovered the place years ago, when she was newly married to Peter, my granddad. He died long before I was born, when my mum was only three years old. Ivy never talked about Peter much, except to say he was 'a good man'. She said that a lot whenever I asked her what he was like, so I still only had a rather hazy impression of him. He was a self-employed accountant and I got the impression he worked really hard. I think Ivy liked to escape the house and leave him in peace with his calculations. More than once, I heard her say laughingly that her 'secret garden' had kept her sane during her marriage.

The clearing in the trees was on public land, on the edge of a wood, and Ivy nurtured it into a lovely woodland garden. She planted shrubs, flowers and grasses for every season, so there was a rolling show of colour all year round, from the banks of snow-drops and crocuses as the frosts of winter melted into spring, to the glorious russets of autumn. Many of the villagers knew about the garden and would pop in for a chat while she worked. She often lounged on the old wooden bench reading the blood-curdling thrillers she loved, her feet up, with an old cushion at her back. She never seemed to mind being interrupted.

Someone once referred to it as 'Ivy Garden' and the name stuck.

We were there that blisteringly hot afternoon to pick lavender so that Ivy could make her perfumed drawer sachets to sell at the Appleton summer fete. She would run up the tiny white muslin bags on her old sewing machine and then fill them with the evocatively scented dried herb, tying them up with silky pink ribbon. The proceeds would be donated to the village hall community fund.

After we picked the lavender that day, she set her old gardening trug on the mossy ground and we sank on to the wooden bench under the dappled shade of an oak tree, and drank chilled pear cider straight from the bottle. It was a relief to be out of the sweltering sun and we lingered there a long time, soaking up the birdsong and the buzz of nature, as Ivy Garden weaved its magic around us.

To our right, the glorious banks of aromatic lavender nestled close to a stone bird bath Ivy had discovered long ago in a local antique shop. Opposite the bench where we sat, on the far side of the little clearing, the tall privet hedge that bordered the road had been 'scooped out' to provide a shady place for a little wooden love seat that was Ivy's pride and joy. She'd had that love seat for years and it was looking a little battered now. But it fitted perfectly in the space, as if it had been designed specially. Back then, at the height of summer, drifts of scented lilies and white foxgloves took pride of place in the garden.

The taxi slows and I hear the swish of rainwater as we drive through a flooded part of the road. I open my eyes. It's getting dark, rain still lashing down outside and we're motoring through another village, past a row of pretty cottages built from golden sandstone.

Moonbeam Cottage itself sits in a little row of properties just like these, directly opposite the gap in the hedge that leads to Ivy Garden. And in a lovely example of serendipity, the cottage came up for sale at exactly the time Ivy was thinking about selling the big house in Appleton, after my granddad died, and downsizing to a smaller place. She must have been so excited when Moonbeam Cottage, right over the road from her woodland garden, came up for sale. It probably seemed as if destiny had taken a hand.

During my last visit, she was keen to show off her new garden shed, a very pretty creation in shades of white and peppermint green. Fixed to the side of the door was a wooden placard with a verse carved into it:

> *If you long for a mind at rest*
> *And a heart that cannot harden*
> *Go find a gate that opens wide*
> *Into a secret garden.*

Ivy laughed and said the poem was a bit cheesy for her taste, but she wholeheartedly agreed with the sentiment, so it was staying put.

I stare out of the taxi as the fields and houses flash by. When I get to the cottage, I'll dump my bags and go straight over the road and through that gap in the hedge. If my grandma's spirit is to be found anywhere, it will be there. In Ivy Garden.

It's almost May, which is when the bluebells bloom.

A little stab of reality hits. I'm planning to clear the cottage and get it on the market in double-quick time so I can get back to Manchester as soon as I can. So I probably won't be here when the bluebells come out.

A chill cloud passes over. But I shake it off and check my phone for messages. I can't afford to be sentimental about Ivy Garden or Moonbeam Cottage or bluebells. They represent Ivy's past, not mine.

The signs for Appleton are becoming more frequent now; I draw in a deep, slightly shaky breath. We're almost there.

And that's when my heart plummets.

Oh, bugger! I came prepared for a bus journey, not a taxi. *I don't have enough cash on me to pay the fare!*

When I break the bad news to the driver, he says he thinks there's a cash point outside the village store, and to my relief, when we draw up outside it, so there is. The driver escorts me to the hole in the wall, clearly worried I'm going to run off into the gloom without paying. And then, joy of joys, the bloody machine isn't working.

I turn in a panic, as the wind swirls an empty crisp packet around my feet. 'I'm *so* sorry.'

Oh God, what do I do now?

His arms are folded and he's wearing a resigned expression, as if he doesn't believe a word I'm saying.

Then a voice says, 'Can I help?'

I swing around and a man steps out of the alleyway that runs alongside the village store. He arches his brows expectantly.

'No, no, thank you, it's fine,' I tell him, although it quite obviously isn't.

The taxi driver sniffs. 'She can't pay the fare.' From his tone, this is obviously not the first time it's happened.

'No, I can!' I protest. 'It's not that I don't have the money. It's just I need a cash machine and this one isn't working.' I glance at the stranger. He's slightly taller than me, probably around five foot nine, with a wiry build and fairish hair. 'Is there another one nearby?'

'We're not exactly awash with facilities here,' he murmurs regretfully. 'The nearest is probably five miles away.'

The driver hitches his sleeve and looks theatrically at his watch. 'I have another job so I don't have time to drive around looking for a frigging bank.' He must be wearing hairspray because his crowning glory is standing upright in the wind at an unnatural angle.

'Look, here's the money,' offers the stranger, drawing his wallet from his pocket. 'I'm Sylvian, by the way.' He holds out his hand to me and after a second's hesitation, I quickly shake it.

'You can pay me back tomorrow if you feel you need to,' he tells me.

I glance at him to see if he's joking. 'God, no, I couldn't *possibly* let you do that. I mean, you don't know me. I could be any old confidence trickster.'

'She seems all right to me,' pipes up the taxi driver. (Even if I was wearing a devil mask with a bag over my shoulder marked 'stolen property', he'd probably still give me a nice character reference, just so he could be on his way.)

'Look, it's fine,' says Sylvian with a shrug. 'Really. Money's nothing to me. I don't even care if you pay me back. It's the love and the trust that are important, right?'

I stare at him. *Is he serious?* He's smiling, so either he really *is* that laid-back about money or he's a mad psychopath, just biding his time until the taxi drives off and leaves us alone next to this conveniently dark alleyway.

When I still look anguished with indecision, the driver heaves a weary sigh. 'Look, just take the money,' he says to me. 'Give him your watch as collateral.'

'That's a good idea,' I say, perking up and slipping off my watch.

Sylvian chuckles. 'Thank you, but I don't need that.' He rifles in his wallet and draws out some notes. 'Keep the change, mate.'

The taxi accelerates off and, feeling like a complete idiot, I stand there on the pavement opposite Sylvian, who I can't help noticing has a rather attractive smile.

THREE

I hold out the watch again as the wind whips at my hair.

'I really wish you'd take it. I'm staying just along the road at Moonbeam Cottage for a few weeks. Do you want me to write my address down?' I scrabble in my bag for a pen and paper.

He smiles down at me, arms folded, the nearby street lamp picking up the vivid green of his eyes. He's wearing a sweatshirt in the same shade. It bears a slogan that reads: *Minds are like parachutes. They only function when they're open.*

'Stop worrying,' he says. 'It's no big deal.'

'But it *is*!'

'Tell you what, you can buy me a drink some time.'

'Dinner at a good restaurant, you mean,' I correct him, thinking of the eye-wateringly expensive taxi fare.

'Well, if you absolutely insist.' He raises an eyebrow and I find myself blushing. *Bugger, I wasn't asking him out!*

'So do you live here? Just so I know where to bring the cash,' I add hurriedly, in case he thinks I have another motive for asking.

He nods, digging his hands into the pockets of his jeans. 'Temporarily. I'm poet in residence here for a year so I've moved into the flat above the village store.' I follow his gaze as he glances up at the windows. 'The council's paying me to encourage talent and stimulate folks' interest in poetry. I'm running a series of workshops.'

'Wow. What sort of poems do you write?' I gaze at him in awe. He looks so young to be a successful poet – early thirties, at a guess.

He grins. 'Well, I have a feeling this year's output will feature sheep, orchards and idyllic cottages fairly heavily. The Cotswolds is certainly great for creative inspiration.'

'Yes, it certainly is,' I murmur fervently, while what I'm actually thinking is: *Help! I'm a city girl. Get me out of here!*

'I'm giving a poetry reading in Hayworth next week,' he says, mentioning a neighbouring village. 'Why don't you come along?'

'Oh. Thanks, it sounds great, but English wasn't exactly my strongest subject at school.'

'No?'

'I never really understood poetry.' I attempt to smooth my wind-blown hair behind my ears. 'Maths and art. That was me.'

'So you're creative, too? Did you study art at college?'

'No. It's always been my dream, though.'

He shrugs. 'You should go for it.'

'Maybe I will.' I smile shyly at him.

'Well, if you change your mind about the poetry reading, give me a shout.' He grins. 'We newcomers should stick together.'

I nod, liking the notion that I'm not the only stranger here. 'Right, well, I'll drop that money in tomorrow. And thanks again.'

'No problem. Need help with that case?' He glances along the road in the direction of Moonbeam Cottage.

'No, no, it's fine. It's got wheels. Thanks, though.' I manoeuvre the case around, ready to go.

'Right, well, lovely to meet you, Holly.' He lifts a hand and disappears through the door.

I walk the last few hundred yards of my journey feeling much lighter in spirit. Sylvian seems lovely. Open and friendly. And really very trusting.

I push open the gate and fumble for my key. And at last, I'm standing in the familiar little hallway of Moonbeam Cottage, taking in the silence as memories start flooding in.

Actually, it isn't the complete silence I was expecting. I can hear a drip.

I cock my head to one side.

To be more precise, it's a steady drip, drip, drip.

Alarmed, I flick on the hall light, push open the door to the living room and stare in dismay at the devastation before me. The ceiling in the far corner of the room is sagging and water is dripping down on to the wooden floor.

I glance upwards.

The bathroom?

I drop my bag and race up the narrow stairs, almost knocking several pottery plates off the wall in my haste.

The bathroom is, indeed, a disaster area. The floor has partially caved in, and I stand there, staring in horror, remembering what Ivy's next-door neighbour, Bill, told me at the funeral. She was apparently getting out of the bath when she had her fatal heart attack.

Looking at the scene where she died, a whole host of emotions rush through me and I have to hang on to the doorframe because my legs are suddenly no use at all. As I fight to control the panic, my brain takes in the marks on the wall in the corner where water has been obviously been dripping all the way down from the ceiling and pooling on the floor. Over time, it must have soaked into the floorboards and brought part of the living room ceiling down.

I glance up in dismay. There must be a leak in the roof. Oh God, I could have done without this!

But it's probably my fault.

The house has lain empty for over four months. When I came here for the funeral, I booked myself into a local B&B because I couldn't bear to even set foot in the cottage. It was all still so painfully raw. The memories would have knocked me flat. If only I'd thought to at least check things were okay.

What am I supposed to do now?

Bill's cottage next door is in darkness and it's too late to think about calling a tradesman. Tomorrow I'll find the number for Mike, who was Ivy's go-to handyman when she needed work done on the cottage. I'm too tired to even imagine what patching up the roof might cost. I'll face that after a night's sleep.

For now, I need some heat. Unoccupied for months, the cottage is absolutely freezing. And luckily, when I flick the boiler switch, the system groans into life. It sounds just like a monster is waking up in the spare room. Hugging myself through the sleeves of my coat, I go downstairs in a daze into the compact country-style kitchen. Thankfully everything is fine in there. I find a bucket under the sink and take it into the living room, placing it to catch the drips.

Back in the kitchen, Ivy's hideous teapot in the shape of a ladybird catches my eye. A hot cup of tea is just what I need.

The teapot hasn't been emptied from the last time Ivy used it. With a pang of sadness, I tip the contents into the sink and squeeze out the teabags to put in the bin. Then I look at the teapot with its ladybird spots and grinning clown face and find myself smiling.

Ivy loved ladybirds; they're all over the cottage. Ladybird coasters, ladybird mugs, ladybird ornaments displayed all along the windowsill. I always used to joke that her ladybird teapot was a step too far.

I pick it up with a wistful smile. Life is strange. I don't know how many times I've laughingly threatened to have the thing recycled at the charity shop.

But now I know I'll never part with it . . .

I'm about to put the kettle on when it occurs to me that the electrics might have been affected by the structural damage. Is it safe having the power on? I've no idea so I decide I'd better play safe and switch it off at the mains. I'll just have to pile on extra

28

layers. But I'm determined to stay in the cottage. There will be no more B&Bs because it's time I stopped avoiding the bad stuff.

A feeling of isolation engulfs me. I trail through to the living room and sit on the chair by the window, staring out into the darkness. How can I bear to stay here, all on my own, without Ivy to talk to and laugh with? Even a few weeks feels like forever.

And then, as I gaze forlornly at the trees over the road, a milky full moon suddenly breaks through a gap in the rain clouds and shines down its silvery beams, illuminating the hedge opposite. I stare at it, and a little burst of hope breaks through the gloom.

Here I am in Moonbeam Cottage and a moonbeam is actually showing me the way! I can't see the gap in the hedge from here but it's definitely there. Suddenly, I know what I need to do.

The storm has abated slightly. I run to the front door and slide my feet into Ivy's well-worn moccasins in the hall. They're a size too big and they flap a bit but I reason they'll do the job. Then I grab a torch that's lying on the hall table and venture out again, through the creaky garden gate, pausing to give Ivy's old silver Fiesta, parked right outside the cottage, a quick once-over. It's ancient and getting a little rusty but last time I spoke to Ivy, Florence the Fiesta, as she called it, was still going strong.

I dash over the road. Then I stop short.

The gap in the hedge isn't where I remember it. In fact, it isn't there at all.

It seems that in the short time since Ivy died, the prickly twigs have somehow locked themselves together, obscuring the gap. As if the entrance was there purely for Ivy. And now that she's gone, it's no longer needed.

I'm just about to switch on the torch when the moon slides into view again, and in the feeble light, the gap magically reappears. Holding my breath, thorns scraping at my hands, I divide the woody tangle, determined to get to the tranquil, mossy-floored haven with its bench and bird table, love seat and cute garden shed that I know lies on the other side.

29

A second later, I make it through – and my feet land squarely in a pool of ice-cold rainwater.

What the hell?

The shock makes me yelp out loud. Stepping gingerly out of the muddy pool, I flick on the torch and shine it around. And my heart sinks into Ivy's sodden moccasins as I take in the utter chaos that confronts me.

The recent storms have truly done their worst. A tree has splintered almost in two and the top half is hanging right across the centre of the little woodland glade. With a pang of horror, I realise it's crash-landed on to Ivy's little wooden love seat, which now lies in bits in the mud. The jolly garden shed lies on its side, no competition at all against the strength of the recent gales, and the mossy floor is flooded with muddy puddles that float with twigs and all sorts of debris.

It looks as if a giant ogre has lost its temper and rampaged about the small space, wrecking everything in sight. The only survivor of the storm seems to be the bird table, which lies at an angle against the trunk of the broken tree, but is miraculously still in one piece.

I can hardly believe what I'm seeing. A mix of anger and grief surges up inside me. I thought when I got here, I'd feel closer to Ivy. But instead, all that confronts me is ugliness. I'm just glad she didn't have to see it like this.

When I try to reverse my way back through the hedge, the heel of my moccasin slides in the mud and I feel myself falling. Frantically grabbing for the nearest support, a handful of hedge thorns slice deep into the tender pad of flesh near my thumb, and I yelp and let go, then land on my bum in a squelchy mass of mud.

For a few seconds, I sit there stunned, experiencing the weird sensation of cold water seeping into my pants. And then I start to laugh. A giggle at first that escalates into wails of laughter, but then gradually turns into wails of a different kind. For the first time since I got the news about Ivy, I lose it completely. Great, anguished, gasping sobs, as if I'll never be able to stop. I'm competing with the angry roar of the wind, which has started up again, and I'm grateful for that because it means I can cry as loudly as I want and no-one will hear me.

I sob until I'm soaked through with tears and muddy water. And all the time, the wind goes on raging as if it, too, is incensed by the train of horrible events that has led me to this broken wreck of a place.

After a while, my sobs lessen and some sort of stoic survival instinct kicks in. I feel slightly better having let it all out. It even seems a little comical now. But when I try to lever myself up, I promptly slip right back down into the smelly, muddy sludge. A second try also fails.

Then the rain starts again, peppering hard against my face, driven sideways by the wind, and I sit there shivering, wondering what other indignities the universe can possibly have in store to hurl at me.

I hold my face up to the rain in helpless surrender.

Then I yell at the broken tree. 'So what the bloody hell am I supposed to do now?'

Its branches shake in the wind. But as a reply, I can't help thinking it falls a little short of helpful. I wipe my face roughly with wet hands and anger surges up. I'm angry at my mum and dad for dying when I was only four. I'm angry at Ivy for buggering off and leaving me all alone in the world. And I'm angry at life in general for delivering this latest cruel blow.

'This is supposed to be a frigging *magic* garden, isn't it?' I croak. 'So *where's the magic*? And tell me what the *hell* I'm supposed to do!'

No answer. Obviously.

I scramble up and push my way back through the hedge and over the road, just wanting to put the desolate scene behind me. Lifting the latch on the gate, I glance towards the row of shops, thinking of my gallant rescuer, Sylvian, in his flat above the village store. It gives me an odd sort of comfort to know he's there. A friendly face.

Back in the cottage, I fumble for my mobile and dial Ivy's number, pressing the phone to my ear as her message kicks in.

Hello, my lovers. Ivy's answering machine is sadly broken. You're currently talking to the refrigerator. Please speak very slowly and don't mention power cuts.

I smile at her message – even though I've heard it a hundred times before – and a familiar warmth spreads through me. It's the best I've felt all day.

A heartbeat later, I dial the number again.

When Patty first worked out what I was doing a few months ago, she took me to one side in the café and said, very gently, 'Holly, love, isn't it time you let the phone company know?'

She was right, of course. But the idea that I might never again be able to listen to Ivy's voice? That was just too terrible to imagine.

I climb the stairs, still listening to the message. When it's finished, I throw off my outer layer of clothing and get straight into bed, shivering and pulling the quilt right up to my chin. Then I decide I need another pair of socks so I get out again with the quilt still wrapped around me.

I peek through the open curtains.

The storm is passing over and stars are beginning to appear. I watch a wisp of cloud wind itself around the milky white moon, thinking back to the day of the funeral.

I felt numb, as if all the chilly formalities were happening to someone else and not to me at all. It was almost as if I sleep-walked through it – waking in the B&B, dressing carefully and opening the door to a kindly man dressed all in black, who guided me into the car to drive me the short journey to the church in a neighbouring village; seeing Ivy's friends and acquaintances at the church; receiving their kind words and touches in a daze.

For some reason, I can only remember fragments of the day,

as if I wasn't completely there. The handsome elderly woman, her skin deeply grooved, who gently cupped my face and told me Ivy always said that I was her sunshine. The kind, white-haired man who shepherded me to a chair when I was feeling wobbly and pressed a clean handkerchief into my hand when I couldn't find my tissues. The fresh-faced vicar, who talked about Ivy as though she were a friend, when I knew full well my grandma hadn't been to church in years.

I keep thinking how odd it is that I can remember in vivid detail the intricate web of lines on the woman's face and the kind man's freshly ironed handkerchief – which I must still have somewhere – and yet, however hard I try, I can't recall the drive back to the B&B. I suppose I was in a daze of grief.

Now, as I stare at the moon, emotion swells in my chest until I can hardly breathe.

I might be selling the cottage and returning to my life in Manchester, but I have a precious connection to this village, through Ivy. I will always think of Moonbeam Cottage and Ivy Garden with such huge affection.

I swish the curtains closed and climb back into bed, and in the darkness, I dial Ivy's number again. But this time, all I get is silence; my phone has no signal. A single tear leaks into my pillow. The lump in my throat feels as big as a tennis ball.

Then after a while, I hear Ivy's voice in my head.

Sleep tight, my love. Everything will seem brighter in the morning . . .

FOUR

I'm woken early by the sound of someone being murdered.

As the bloodcurdling wails continue, I clutch at the duvet in fright – before realising it's a cockerel, straining its vocal cords in an attempt to wake the whole of Gloucestershire.

I glance at the clock. Four-thirty in the morning.

Really? I mean, *really?*

Naming him Colin, I lie there listening to him busting a gut and thinking I'll never get back to sleep now. Then I promptly doze off, and next time I wake, it's light outside. I swim slowly to full consciousness, aware of a vague panicky feeling inside.

I'm in Ivy's spare room.

I've thought about this moment many times; how I'd feel being here in Moonbeam Cottage, without her to shout through that she's making some tea, or coming to sit on the bed to chat. And now that moment is here, and the place feels horribly empty without her.

I take some deep breaths and start to feel calmer. Then a farm vehicle rattles past the cottage, shaking the very foundations and making my heart race at ninety miles an hour. I hug myself, rubbing my arms hard. It's not going to be easy, this enforced stay in the country, but it has to be done.

With the bathroom wrecked by the leak, I don't want to risk the shower until I know it's safe, so I have a quick wash in cold water at the sink, then dive into some warm clothes, clean my teeth and apply a little make-up.

It's after eight by then. The village store is sure to be open, and maybe the cash machine will be working again so I can repay Sylvian. Every time I think about how he saved my bacon last night, handing over all that cash to the taxi driver without even taking my mobile number, I'm amazed all over again.

I pull on my coat and head out into a calm but chilly April morning. There's a definite feel of 'the morning after the night before'. The storms that raged have passed over but there's a reddish tinge to the sky, which isn't a great omen.

'Red sky in the morning . . . shepherds' cottages on fire,' I say aloud, since Ivy isn't there to say it.

'Hey, talking to yourself is the first sign of madness, didn't you know?' calls a voice.

A group of teenagers are languishing in and around the bus shelter just ahead of me. One of the girls, presumably she of the 'witty' comment, is staring at me as if I'm completely insane. The thick, ghostly pale foundation she's wearing contrasts sharply with her heavy black eyeliner, and her asymmetric hair style looks like she's hacked at it herself, while no doubt costing a fortune in some trendy salon. The short side is bleached blonde and the longer side dyed black.

Drawing level with them, I remark casually, 'If you ask me, madness is highly under-rated.'

'I guess you *would* think that,' the girl quips, glancing quickly at a blond Adonis-type who's standing nearby. He's concentrating on his phone, and doesn't notice. The others all watch me walk by, blank-eyed, except one of the lads – a cocky, dark-haired boy – who treats me to a fake grin and blows smoke from his fag in my direction.

'Thank you,' I call back, and they snigger.

The cash point is working again, so I draw out the money and walk round to the side door which I assume leads to Sylvian's flat above the village store. My stomach swoops as I ring the bell.

He greets me at the door in tracksuit bottoms, bare-chested except for a striped blue towel slung round his neck. The sheen of sweat on his brow and finely muscled upper torso makes me think I must have interrupted a work-out.

He smiles. 'Thought it might be you,' he says, flicking a catch on the carved wooden box he's holding.

'Yes, hi,' I launch in. 'I want to thank you again for rescuing me last night. It was so good of you. I honestly don't know what I'd have done if you hadn't come along at that precise moment.'

I'm aware I'm babbling, but he's caught me unawares. It's not often a handsome man greets me in the semi-buff at eight in the morning, looking so . . . well, *buff*.

Unlike me, Sylvian seems completely at ease with his semi-nakedness. I hardly know where to look, but eventually settle on his startlingly vivid green eyes. When I hold out the money, he gives it a cursory glance then balances the box under his arm so he can stuff the notes in his jeans pocket.

'You're very welcome, Holly. I hope you had a good first night in the cottage?'

'Thanks, yes, it wasn't exactly relaxing, though.'

'Oh?'

I shrug. 'Oh, you know, unpacking . . . new surroundings. It's a bit unsettling.' I'm not about to bore him with a run-down of my disaster of a night.

'You did seem a bit stressed yesterday.' He hands me the open wooden box. 'Can you hold this for me?'

Surprised, I take the box, glancing at it curiously. It has about twenty small compartments inside, each containing a tiny brown glass bottle. It's like something you might find in an old-fashioned apothecary shop.

Sylvian locks eyes with me and hovers his hand over the box.

Then he looks down and selects a bottle, unscrewing the lid. 'Try this one.' He wafts it under my nose.

Cautiously, I sniff. The scent is subtle yet sharp at the same time. 'Lemons?'

'A great mood lifter.' He holds out another bottle and I lean forward to smell it.

A powerful floral scent fills my nose. I inhale then breathe out slowly. 'Lovely.'

'Ylang ylang. Good for relieving stress.'

I laugh. 'Bring it on.'

'It's also an aphrodisiac,' he murmurs and when I look up to see if he's joking, he winks at me. 'It's true.'

Heat rises in my cheeks. Am I imagining the frisson between us? I'm not sure, because Sylvian is already moving on, giving me a comprehensive run-down on the health properties of sandalwood – also great for stress, apparently – and wafting it under my nose.

The woody smell is heavenly, like a forest after it's been raining. 'Mmm, that's my favourite.'

He smiles. 'That's the one, then.' He screws on the cap and hands it to me.

I hold up the bottle with a bemused look. 'But I can't . . .?'

He shrugs. 'Of course you can. Tip a few drops in your bath or on a handkerchief when you need to relax.'

'But I need to pay you for it.'

He gives me an amused look and says nothing.

I smile, already knowing there's little point arguing. 'Well, thank you, but you're too generous.'

He brushes it off. 'Look, I'd invite you in but I'm giving a talk and I have to prepare for it.'

'Of course. No problem.' I start beating a retreat. 'Don't let me hold you up.'

'I very much like you holding me up, Holly,' he says seriously. 'In fact, I propose you hold me up again while I cook you dinner some time.'

His invitation takes me by surprise. 'Gosh. Well, maybe . . .'

'I'm counting on it,' he smiles.

I raise a hand and scuttle off around the corner.

I've been here less than twenty-four hours and already a caring and generous man has offered to cook me dinner! He also happens to be very fit and easy on the eye.

A vision of Sylvian opening the door naked to the waist flashes into my mind, but I tell myself to get a grip. I'm in Appleton to concentrate on Moonbeam Cottage, for goodness' sake, not a man. Even if that man *does* have hard abs and a giving nature. *Phew, is it me or has the temperature suddenly soared?*

Feeling more than a little discombobulated, I glance at the label on the bottle I'm clutching and unscrew the top. Sandalwood essential oil. Known for its calming properties.

A good sniff of this should do the trick . . .

Back at the cottage, I phone Ivy's odd job man, Mike, and he says he'll be round to look at the roof and the damage inside the house as soon as he's dropped his daughter off at playgroup. He sounds genuinely cut up about Ivy and describes her as 'bloody marvellous', which brings a lump to my throat. I love him already!

While I wait, I unpack a few more things then sit in the living room, eating the banana I brought for the train journey and wondering how I'm going to pass the time in the evenings while I'm here. There's a small digital TV and a DVD player that's so old, it was probably the original prototype, but nothing fancier than that. Ivy loved reading, so her shelves are full of gardening books and thrillers. A cook book would have come in handy while I'm here – I quite like getting creative in the kitchen – but Ivy hated cooking with a passion, so there aren't any. I smile, remembering. She preferred to just ignore the scales and throw into the pot whatever she felt like, which was usually a recipe for disaster. (She only made the beetroot and nettle omelette once, thankfully.)

Mike arrives, whistling up the path, and having looked at the roof and the bathroom, says he can fix it no problem, with a little help from a roofer friend of his. I hold my breath and ask what it will cost, and actually, it's not as bad as I thought. But when he mentions the additional cost of re-tiling and painting, I swallow hard and suggest we just stick with the repair work for now.

I've laid bathroom flooring before. And done lots of painting. Surely I can throw a few tiles on the wall? I mean, how hard can it be? It doesn't have to be perfect. This is the countryside, for goodness' sake; the land of all things rustic. People round here laugh indulgently when they accidentally tread in a cow pat; and they practically *expect* whiffy manure smells with their freshly laid chucky eggs in the morning. Ergo, a little 'rustic tiling' is sure to be a big hit among potential buyers.

Mike says he has a job to finish but he can start work on Monday. My heart sinks because that's five whole days away, but I smile and tell him that will be perfect. Actually, I have lots of clearing out to do, so the time will probably fly by. I stand at the door, watching him walk cheerily down the path to his white van.

I have a feeling that with the repairs to do and the cottage to paint, my estimate of a fortnight to get the place on the market was way too optimistic. And then there's Ivy Garden to sort out. My heart sinks into my boots. It will probably take a month at least . . .

Mike's jolly whistle as he climbs into his van attracts the attention of two people locked together just inside the bus shelter over the road. They see me peering over and break apart. It's that Adonis boy I saw earlier with one of the girls from his group of mates. The one with the extraordinary half-blonde, half-black hair. She stares haughtily back at me as if to say, *You shouldn't be looking – and anyway, it's perfectly normal to be performing tonsil tennis at a bus stop in full view of the entire village!*

Adonis just smirks at me.

I retreat inside and go straight upstairs to start on the job I've been dreading the most. Sorting through Ivy's wardrobe.

By the evening, I'm drained, physically and emotionally – and facing a long night with nothing much to do. I can't even summon up the energy to start sketching.

It's been on my mind that I need to contact Ivy's old school friend, Olive, who she used to meet up with from time to time. She wasn't at the funeral because I couldn't track down a contact number for her among Ivy's belongings or even on her phone. I found Ivy's old address book today but there's no Olive in there, either, and I went through it page by page.

I haven't made as much progress as I'd have liked with Ivy's clothes, either. Almost every blouse or jacket of Ivy's that I took out of the wardrobe, I couldn't bear to part with because of the memories, so the 'keep' pile is like a small mountain. The 'charity' pile consists of a scarf Ivy never liked and a jumper that still had the tags on it. So basically, it took me all day to move Ivy's clothes from the wardrobe to the bed, with some tearful reminiscing over old photos in between times.

At this rate, I'll still be here at Christmas . . .

I sink on to the sofa, on the verge of tears, and stare at the blackness beyond the windows. Then out of the corner of my eye, I catch something move.

I whip around and the biggest spider I've ever seen in my life comes into view, moving at a fair old speed. Its legs are so long, it literally scampers towards me, before stopping suddenly, changing course and scuttling back through a tiny opening in the skirting board.

My legs are shaking. I'd forgotten about the wildlife that rampages about the countryside. I never see spiders in my modern, second-floor flat.

I eye the skirting board nervously. A book would be a good distraction, but I don't fancy Ivy's thrillers – it's spooky enough just being alone in the countryside at night without wanting to deliberately scare myself. A thick blanket of darkness has descended beyond the window. I can see nothing except impenetrable blackness and my own reflection staring back at me, and I get that panicky feeling you have when you're driving in a snow storm and suddenly it's a total white-out.

I keep peering out, determined to see *something*, but it's no use.

King Kong could be beating his breast on top of the Empire State Building out there and I'd be absolutely none the wiser . . .

When Mike arrives on Monday morning, I practically *fall* on the poor man with the sheer relief of having another human being to talk to. I make him a cup of tea and ask about his family, and it's only when he starts edging apologetically out of the room that I remember the purpose of his visit is to fix the bathroom. Seconds later, his roofer friend arrives so I leave them to it.

After my false start, I've made a determined effort over the past five days to sort through the kitchen, putting all the stuff I want to keep in the spare room ready to be boxed up for removal. Ivy, bless her, was never great at throwing things out, and by the end of the second day, the dustbin was already filled to bursting. The only time I've been out is to the village store for groceries. (I always tidy myself up, just in case I happen to bump into Sylvian, but so far there have been no sightings. He's probably busy with his poetry workshops.)

The best thing about the village store is – pause for effect – you can rent DVDs!

I know. Exciting!

Later, after Mike has gone, I make scrambled eggs and push my latest movie into Ivy's old but reliable machine. Tonight's entertainment is *Castaway*, starring a very young-looking Tom Hanks. It's all about someone cast adrift miles from anywhere, with no way of getting in touch with the outside world, and who, in fact, makes a friend called Wilson out of a coconut husk just to have someone to talk to.

I don't think they sell coconuts in the village store.

I keep thinking about Sylvian and wondering what he's doing. It would be nice to see a friendly face. Looking on the bright side, though, the village store's collection of movies isn't bad at all, if a little limited by the shelf space. There's a few classics I've never got round to watching. Of course, there's also some real dross; several truly awful low-budget horror movies with titles like *I Know What You Did Last Hallowe'en*, and – my particular favourite – *Slasher Santa's Coming to Town*.

I mean, you'd have to be *really* desperate to resort to that . . .

FIVE

Mike is causing me problems.

Don't get me wrong. He's not eyeing up the silver or anything, and he definitely seems to know what he's doing. He's done an enormous amount in a week, and the rate at which he's working, he'll probably be finished the entire job inside a fortnight.

It's just he's so goddamn cheerful all the time.

He *never stops whistling*. He whistles from first thing in the morning right up until he packs his jolly haversack at five and heads jauntily off down the path to his van. *Whistling*. And you can tell it's not embarrassed or awkward whistling. He just whistles because he's *happy*! And it's driving me barmy.

Also, nothing seems to be the *least* little bit of trouble.

I swear if I asked him to clean out all the hairs and gunk that's blocking the shower plughole, he'd actually enjoy doing it. He'd pull it all out – every nasty glistening clump – and dispose of it all while whistling a happy tune.

I mean, there's just no need for it.

He packs up at five on the dot and his face appears round the door. 'Family night tonight.' He rolls his eyes cheerfully. 'Pizza and a movie. Probably *Toy Story again*. Take my advice, pet. Enjoy the single life while you can.'

And he's off, leaving me to relish my single life with a vast array of enchanting possibilities at my disposal. Embroidery night class in a neighbouring village. Cinema twenty miles away. Or another night in front of the telly.

I settle for the telly.

The spider pops out, clearly tempted by the *Coronation Street* theme tune, and I nod approvingly. A spider with taste. He has a bit of a scamper around, then he stands stock still, presumably having just clapped eyes on the giant and wondering whether to play dead or make a run for it.

Slowly, slowly, I rise from the sofa and we eye each other. Then, quick as a flash, he streaks back into his hole.

I feel quite disappointed. And definitely not scared.

'It's okay, Fred,' I say out loud. 'As giants go, I'm pretty harmless.'

Then I laugh at myself for talking to a spider and giving it a name. He probably doesn't even speak the same language as me. Perhaps the girl at the bus stop was right and I really am going insane, being here all alone with only a friendly arachnid to converse with of an evening.

I picture Mike driving back to the bosom of his family, the kids dancing to the door to greet him. Cherry, his wife, smiling from the kitchen, face flushed from pizza-making, telling him to hurry up and shower because they need to get the film under way if the kids are going to get to bed at a decent time . . .

I need to get out!

Grabbing my coat, I escape from the cottage, slam the door behind me and start walking briskly towards the shops.

The teenagers are gathered at the bus stop and, as I pass, I can't help noticing Adonis has his arm around a very pretty girl with long strawberry-blonde hair. The girl with blonde-black hair is nowhere to be seen. He sees me and brazens it out, treating me to a very sarcastic smile.

I frown to myself. *Little scumbag!* He's obviously the sort who enjoys spreading his favours around.

The lights of the deli-café up ahead are warm and welcoming and I decide to pop in for a coffee. Passing by the village store on the way, I hear voices in the little alleyway that runs alongside it and turn to look. There are a couple of garages along there, and I spot Miss Blonde-Black leaning against one of them, talking urgently to a man.

I do a double-take.

It's Sylvian.

Curious, I stop and lurk by the post box, pretending I'm reading the postal times, so I can observe the two of them together. (Boredom makes people act in very weird ways.) They're deep in conversation and something in the way they're angled towards each other makes me think they must know each other fairly well.

Sylvian hands the girl a small package. She glances quickly behind her, then she takes it and stuffs it into her shoulder bag. They do a quick thumbs up at each other and she walks away quickly without looking back.

As she passes me, I nod wisely at the post box times then straighten up and smile as if I've only just recognised her. She gives me an uncertain look, as if she can't quite place where she's seen me before, before marching over the road to join her mates at the bus shelter. As she joins them, I notice Adonis quickly withdraw his arm from Miss Strawberry-Blonde's waist and shuffle away from her along the rail.

I feel a pang of sympathy for Miss Blonde-Black. She obviously has no idea she has a rival for his affections.

As I approach the deli-café, something in the window catches my eye.

Oh my God, *of course*! This is where Ivy used to buy her gorgeous chocolate orange cakes. I stop for a moment, smiling wistfully at the single cupcake in the cabinet. There's only one left and it definitely has my name on it. I slip into the shop and a girl behind the counter with a swingy brown ponytail looks up, smiles and says, 'Hi. What can I get you?'

'Can I have a chocolate orange cake, please?'

'Just the one?' She glances over. 'Oh, there *is* only one.' She grabs a bag and pops in the luscious-looking sponge cake. 'Anything else?'

I shake my head. 'No, just that, thanks.'

She seems familiar somehow, but she can't be because I hardly know anyone here I must have seen her on one of the rare occasions I came down to spend the weekend with Ivy.

She frowns. 'Pardon me for asking, but are you all right? You're as white as a ghostly apparition.'

'I'm fine, thanks.'

She groans. 'Sorry, have I put my foot in it? You're probably just naturally pale, are you, with that lovely translucent skin? I'm always putting my foot in it. My mum says I should never, ever get a dog of my own because then my feet would be permanently in the shit, if you get my drift.'

She hands over the paper bag. 'They're my mum's favourite, those chocolate orange cakes. Every time I go home to Cirencester I have to take her half a dozen.'

I try to smile, but tears well up.

'Oh, what's wrong?' She looks horrified. 'Have I put my foot in it *again*?'

'No, no, not at all. It's me. It's the cake.' I stop and force myself to take a slow breath in and out. 'Memories,' I say eventually, in a calmer voice.

'Ah, yes.' She nods. 'They can pounce at the most inopportune moment.' She glances across at the only occupied table, where a dark-haired woman in a gold jumpsuit and heels sits nursing a cup, glancing from time to time at the door. 'Listen, I'll be closing up in twenty minutes or so. Why not have a cup of tea? On the house.' She holds out her hand. 'I'm Connie, by the way.'

'Holly.' We shake hands rather formally then, for some reason, we both laugh.

Frankly, I'm all tea-d out. It'll probably be a decade from now and we'll have had five new prime ministers before I have my next real urge for a cuppa. But I'm sensing the tea is not the point.

'That would be lovely, thank you.' I smile at Connie and she ushers me through a panel on hinges to her side of the counter. 'Is this your shop?'

She nods. 'Sort of. It's a family business that my granddad started up about – ooh, a million years ago.' She grins. 'And now my mum and dad manage it. They've left me in charge while they tackle the tax return.'

'Well, I think it's lovely.' I glance around, admiring the décor. 'So cosy and welcoming.'

Connie looks pleased. 'Thank you. You've just moved into Moonbeam Cottage, haven't you?' She hands me a cup of tea and a little jug of milk. 'I'm so sorry about Ivy. She was such a lovely woman.'

'Thank you. Yes, she was. I'm only staying in the cottage temporarily.' Then I grin. 'The grapevine's certainly alive and well, then. Does the whole village know who I am and when I moved in?'

She laughs. 'Absolutely everyone.'

I assume she's joking. At least, I *hope* she is. The door opens and we both turn.

A woman in a cute pink dress with long, shiny chestnut hair and enviably slim, tanned legs steps daintily over the threshold and glances around her. She spots her friend, breaks into a relieved smile and clacks over in her cream skyscraper shoes.

'Selena? Are you all right?' The gold jumpsuit woman peers up at her. 'You look . . . *harassed*, if you don't mind me saying?'

'It's *Sel*ena. Emphasis on the first syllable, remember?' She gives a little tinkly laugh, as if it doesn't really matter.

'Oh God, of course. *Sel*ena. Sorry. I've been calling you Sel*eena* for ages. You should have said.'

'No matter.'

'What's her name?' whispers Connie in my ear.

I grin. 'Plain old Selena, I think, but pronounced differently?'

49

*Sel*ena brushes something off the chair and sits down gingerly, as if it might be about to fall apart. 'Moira, you just wouldn't *believe* the nightmare I've had.'

Moira groans and crosses her eyes comically. 'I have nightmares every day living in cute-village-land. The boredom levels – *God*! I said to Roger the other night, *As soon as the smalls have buggered off, we're upping sticks and moving back to civilisation!* I mean, it's all right for him, escaping to bloody London every weekday, but it's me who's stuck in this hellhole twenty-four-seven.' She pats her perfectly teased and lacquered hair-do. 'Anyway, you were saying. Nightmare . . .?'

Selena nods. 'Well, I was *told* there was a shortcut through the park –– via someone's makeshift garden, weirdly.' She glances frostily back at us, and Connie and I – standing at the end of the counter – instantly become fascinated by the dregs in our cups.

'But with my sense of direction being so appalling, I ended up in a bloody field, didn't I? *In these shoes.* So then I was chased by a herd of frigging *sheep*!' The last word comes out as an exasperated squeak. 'Had an entire *field* of the little woolly fuckers running at me, baa-ing.'

'God. Yes. Been there.' Moira shakes her head. 'It's not "baa", you know. It's more like "brains", if you really listen.'

'Is it?' Selena cocks her head to one side. 'Oh yes, I see what you mean. Brai-ai-ains. Ha! And they all look the same, don't they? Like little woolly zombies. Had to kick my shoes off and run like hell.'

Moira sighs. 'I don't mind the sheep so much. But the cows.' She shakes her head. 'They are *evil* bastards.'

Beside me, Connie snorts and quickly turns it into a cough. I dig her in the ribs and she picks up her notepad and pen and goes over to take their order.

As she assembles a tray of peppermint teas, she motions to me to top up our cups. 'Then we can hear what else they think of the village,' she murmurs with a wicked grin, glancing over at Selena, who's examining her nails while her friend is in the Ladies.

I raise my eyebrows in mock disapproval. 'Do you listen in to *all* the customers' gossip, then?'

'Oh, absolutely.' She points at her nose. 'I blame *this* for my nosy tendencies. What's the point of having a big one if you can't make it work for you?'

I laugh and study her as she stands at the drinks machine, watching boiling water hiss into a white teapot. She's about mid-twenties with huge expressive brown eyes and an impish smile. The nose in question is what some people might term 'handsome'.

'It suits you,' I say truthfully. 'Your nose, I mean.'

'Thanks.' She flares her nostrils and gives me a profile pose. 'There's a fair few hooters like this in my family. We got them from my darling granddad, who still gets "Beaky" from his friends, bless him. Actually, we like to call them "strong" noses.'

Laughing, I point at a small mole just below my breastbone. 'I got this from Ivy. Apparently my mum had one in exactly the same place. We like to call them "beauty spots".'

Connie laughs and carries the tray of drinks over.

I touch my 'beauty spot' wistfully. My family might be gone, but it's a sort of comfort to know that in hundreds of little ways, they still live on in me. They will always be a part of me.

Moira bursts out of the Ladies. 'So whose garden is this shortcut through?' she asks Selena, continuing the conversation where she left off. 'I must say, I've never heard of it and we've lived here – ooh, nearly a whole sodding year now.'

Selena shrugs. 'No idea. Never found it. Belongs to some old biddy with a gap in her hedge, apparently.'

My heart misses a beat.

I glare at Selena's slender, lace-clad back. How dare she describe Ivy as 'some old biddy'.

Tears spring to my eyes. 'That's Ivy she's talking about.'

'The *cow*.' Connie throws her a murderous look, which makes me feel a whole lot better. 'Does she mean the shortcut through Ivy Garden?'

I nod. 'You should see it. It's a disaster after the storms.'

'Really? Oh, what a shame.'

'Does *everyone* call it Ivy Garden now?'

'Oh, yes. It's well known in the village. People still pop in there, mainly to remember Ivy and have a quiet moment on the bench.'

My heart swells with emotion at this.

Connie touches my arm. 'Listen, I fancy a hot chocolate with whipped cream. Why not make one for each of us while I wipe those tables? If you can't work the machine out, give me a shout.'

I nod gratefully and go over to investigate.

'I'm sure you'll have Ivy Garden looking gorgeous again in no time,' she calls.

I shake my head sadly. 'I've never gardened in my life. I wouldn't know where to start.'

'Then you'll just have to learn,' smiles Connie. She turns to the two women and says pleasantly. 'Can I get you anything else? No? Oh, and by the way, there's *loads* of interesting things going on in the countryside.'

I swivel round with interest.

Moira snorts at Selena and murmurs, 'I thought we all made our *own* entertainment around here.'

Connie puts her hands on her hips. 'I bet you didn't know that the Women's Institute organise a film night once a month. With a DVD and a *really big* TV.'

I realise she's joking, but the two women just stare at her in amazement as if she's one of the woolly zombies.

Connie turns and winks at me. Then she bustles back behind the counter. 'Let me know what you think of this shortbread. I baked it this morning; it's so full of butter, it's probably against the law. Go on, you know you want to!'

Moira and Selena leave soon after, but Connie and I linger over our hot chocolates. By the time we've finished, I've found out all about Connie's desire to become an infant school teacher – she's very excited about starting her course in September – and she knows all about my disastrous relationship with my ex, Adam.

A car draws up outside just as I'm thinking about leaving.

Connie peers out. 'It's Dad. He's going to be looking after the shop while Mum and I are in Spain.'

'You're going on holiday?'

'Day after tomorrow.' She grins. 'A bit of sun will set me up nicely. Even better, Mum's paying!'

'You lucky thing!'

'I know. It's for my granddad, really. He used to go off on walking holidays all the time but he's been feeling a bit under the weather recently, so this is Mum's plan to revitalise him.'

'What about your grandma? Does she go, too?'

Connie looks sad. 'Oh, she died years ago when Mum was really tiny. I never actually knew her.'

My heart swells in sympathy. I know how that feels . . .

'So it's the three of you?' I paste on a smile. 'In Spain for a family holiday? How lovely.'

Connie laughs. 'Sharing a room with Mum who likes to be lights out and asleep by ten won't exactly make for a riotous time – and then there's all the walks we'll have to go on to keep Granddad company. But yes, I'm looking forward to it.'

'It sounds like heaven to me,' I admit, hoping I don't sound too wistful.

I'm smiling so hard to show I'm pleased for her that my jaw is starting to ache. It's just I can't help thinking about my holidays with Ivy in Blackpool. We could never afford to go abroad but it didn't really matter. We had fun anyway.

I knew she also loved the times she spent with her old school friend, Olive, who lived in London. They'd arrange a weekend break somewhere at least once a year, but it was never any more exotic than Bournemouth. Ivy had simple tastes . . .

How amazing to be able to take a family holiday totally for granted, the way Connie can . . .

The door opens as I'm putting my cup in the dishwasher and three people walk in.

'Hi, folks,' smiles Connie. After introducing us all, she grabs her mum and granddad, linking her arms through both of theirs and doing a smiley pose for my benefit. 'Now you can see *exactly* where I get the, er, *handsome* nose from.'

'Fortunately, she gets the rest of her good looks from me,' quips Martin, her dad, who's over doing something technical with the coffee machine.

Connie's mum, a pretty, dark-haired woman called Helen, pretends to be annoyed at their remarks but I can tell she's not put out at all. Connie's granddad, who's tall and rather distinguished-looking, is a bit more reserved. But when Connie says, 'Holly is Ivy's granddaughter. She's staying at Moonbeam Cottage,' he immediately steps forward to shake my hand warmly and murmur his condolences.

As I leave, Connie and her mum are chatting about their holiday wardrobes and planning a girls-only shopping trip, and Martin is groaning good-naturedly at the bashing their credit cards are likely to take.

I walk slowly back to the silence of Moonbeam Cottage, thinking what lovely people they are, and trying to shrug off the weight of sadness that has descended on me after listening to their happy family banter. It was lovely to meet them all, but paradoxically, I don't think I've ever felt so totally alone in my life . . .

I glance at my watch. Five hours to while away before I can sensibly go to bed. Food is my usual time-filler these days, but I'm too full of shortbread and hot chocolate to face dinner.

There's nothing else for it.

With a sigh, I switch on the TV and slip *Slasher Santa's Coming to Town* into the DVD machine. It will provide welcome background noise, if nothing else – because Moonbeam Cottage suddenly seems more deathly silent than an undiscovered Egyptian tomb.

Then something weird happens. One of those great big ironies in life.

No sooner have I had this thought – about the Egyptian tomb – but the air is suddenly split with a great cracking sound that makes me jump a foot in the air.

It happens again.

And again.

I go to the window and look out. It sounds like someone is chopping down a tree – and the noise appears to be coming from the woods over the road.

Ivy Garden!

Quick as a flash, I'm over the road to investigate, and as I squeeze through the gap in the hedge, my mouth falls open at the sight before me.

Someone *is* doing a spot of tree-felling. A tall man in jeans and lumberjack boots. He's wielding a large axe, shirt sleeves rolled up, aiming his swings at the base of the fallen down tree, apparently completely oblivious of the rain that's started to fall.

A feeling of indignation rises up. That's *Ivy's* tree. Surely the decision as to whether it stays or goes is up to me?

Of course, it's not really Ivy's tree at all. But since she devoted so much love and care to this little corner, then surely it belongs to her in *spirit*, if not altogether legally. But anyway, that's beside the point. What right has this man to muscle in and knock that bloody tree down without a by-your-leave?

'Er, excuse me!'

He carries on flexing his muscles and whacking at the poor thing.

'I said, *excuse me*!' I start picking my way gingerly across the mud slide. 'Can I ask what you think you're doing?'

But my protests are drowned out by the now steady splish-splash of rain on the leaves and the manly grunts as axe slices into tree trunk.

Mindful of having landed on my bum in the mud last time, I concentrate on my feet, and by the time I glance up, the man is looking over at me, axe down by his side. He doesn't look terribly pleased at the interruption.

I swallow hard, rooted to the spot for a moment, and he stares back at me, squinting slightly as rain drips into his eyes. His dark hair is glistening with moisture, and his soaked shirt clings to the muscles of his upper body.

A big rumble of thunder followed swiftly by a crack of lightning makes me jump and brings me back to my senses. I look at the poor, capsized tree and suddenly remember why I'm there. Who is this man? And what on earth does he look like, posing with that axe! It's like a scene from a Jane Austen mini series. Any minute now, he'll be leaping on his horse and thundering off into the woods, watched by a puzzled and distraught heroine who's yet to realise it's all down to a massive misunderstanding.

'What are you doing?' I ask calmly.

He looks at me like I'm several twigs short of a complete branch. 'It needed felling,' he says dryly. 'So I'm felling it.'

SIX

'But I might not have *wanted* it chopped down.'

He continues to study me with a slight frown, as if I'm some sort of interesting plant life he'd thought was extinct.

'You really think we should leave it standing?' he asks at last.

'No, of course not. I'm not saying I *wouldn't* have chopped it down . . . eventually.'

His mouth quirks up at one corner.

'I *meant* I'd like to have made the decision to chop it down myself.' My cheeks feel so scorched, the raindrops are probably evaporating on landing. I shrug awkwardly. 'This was Ivy's special place.'

His expression softens. 'You knew Ivy?' He drops the axe on the ground and walks towards me.

'She was my grandma. And I can't imagine what she'd be saying if she could see this . . . *mess.*'

He looks down at me, his dark hair plastered wetly to his forehead. 'I'm sorry. You must be devastated. Ivy was one special lady.'

I can't trust myself to speak, so I just nod.

'I'm Jack Rushbrooke, by the way.'

'Holly Dinsdale.' I hold out my hand and he grips it. A funny little shock runs along my arm, I guess because when you shake hands under normal circumstances, it tends to be rather less cold and wet than this.

'Are you staying at Moonbeam Cottage?' he asks.

'Just till I get it on the market. Then I'll be gone.'

He nods. 'You're selling up. Of course.'

I glance at him, puzzled. Why 'of course'? Has he heard through the grapevine that I hate the countryside?

'You won't need Moonbeam Cottage, I suppose. Not where you're going,' he says.

'You mean Manchester?' Wow, news certainly gets around.

But he's looking at me in slight confusion. I have a feeling we've got our wires crossed somewhere, but I haven't the faintest notion how.

'Right. Well. Do you mind if I finish the job?'

I shrug, still feeling stupidly emotional about the tree. 'Yes, why not?' I say flippantly, as if I really don't care. 'You're already half way there.'

I can't help noticing how tall Jack Rushbrooke is. In his jeans, lumberjack boots and heavy duty waterproof, he looks as solid and immovable as the trees surrounding the clearing. He just shouldn't be here, that's all, in my private place, making decisions about what happens to Ivy Garden. What if him chopping the tree down alerts the local council, who own the land, and they decide it can no longer be used as a public garden?

Emotion is making me illogical, I know, but I'm suddenly desperate for things to stay exactly as they are, just the way Ivy left them.

'In future, I'm going to do the gardening myself if you don't mind,' I announce.

He nods slowly as he walks back to the tree and picks up his axe. 'Okay. I'll just get this done.' He pauses then holds out the axe. 'Unless you'd like to . . .?'

I stare at the axe for a panicked second. Does he really expect me to . . .?

Then I notice the gleam in his eyes. 'Tell you what,' he says. 'I'll see to the tree, then I'll leave the rest of the gardening to you. All right?'

'Whatever.' I give a nonchalant shrug, while privately thinking, *Thank God for that!* At the risk of sounding horribly un-feminist, I'd probably end up chopping off something vital if I so much as picked up that ferocious-looking implement.

Jack gets on with the job, wielding the axe with power and precision, as I stand by admiring his – um – technique. Well, I'd be silly *not* to watch closely, wouldn't I? Garner a few gardening tips, that sort of thing.

It's really quite an *art*, this tree-felling stuff, I reflect, admiring the muscular flexing motion of Jack's shoulder and back, clearly visible through the clinging and almost transparent cotton of his shirt . . .

He's looking over at me.

Bugger. He's obviously asked me a question but I was too busy concentrating elsewhere.

'Sorry?' Blushing, I tap my ear. 'Can't hear a thing with this rain.'

Jack frowns skywards. The rain has stopped.

'I was saying if you need help tidying this place up, I'll probably be around at the weekend,' he says.

I shake my head. 'Thank you but I'll be fine.'

'You can manage?'

'Definitely.'

He grunts, not looking at all convinced, and I feel my hackles stir.

'You're welcome to borrow gardening tools. Have you got a strimmer to get rid of these thistles and nettles? Because that's a big job,' he points out, axe balanced over his shoulder, long muscular—looking legs planted in the ground like twin oaks.

'I've got the tools,' I tell him shortly. 'At least, Ivy will have. Somewhere.'

'I could speak to Nick Wetherby. Local gardener. He'd have it whipped into shape in no time.'

I clench my teeth. Why is he so doubtful about my gardening skills? Do I look that clueless? I could be Monty Don's second cousin twice removed, for all he knows, with green fingers by the shed load.

'Right.' He shrugs. 'I can see you're determined to do it yourself.'

'Yes, I am actually. I'm a really good gardener, if you must know.' *Well, I will be, once I look up 'strimmer' in the dictionary. I'm absolutely certain of it.*

He nods. 'If you're stuck, go to the garden centre and ask for Layla,' he says, before turning back to the task in hand.

I watch him a while longer. Then he shouts, 'Stand back!' and with one more hefty stroke, the tree starts to capsize. It falls to one side with a crash and the birds flap noisily from their perches.

'Thanks for that,' I say, as he bends over to examine the tree stump that's left.

'No problem. I can take the tree away,' he offers. 'Unless it's something you'd rather do yourself, of course?'

I glare at him as he rises up to his full height. Then I catch the tiny flicker of amusement in his blue eyes.

'Thank you,' I tell him pleasantly. 'That would be wonderful.'

'You don't need the wood?' he asks.

I shake my head. 'Gas fire.'

He grunts. 'Mind if I use it?'

'Be my guest.'

He nods. 'Right, I'm off. We live in the big ramshackle of a place over there,' he says, nodding in the direction of the woods. 'Rushbrooke House.'

We? Who's we?

Perhaps there's a Mrs Rushbrooke and two point four adorable kids.

He picks up the axe and swings it over his shoulder. 'Ivy was a wonderful woman,' he says, and we exchange a look of understanding. On this, at least, we're in complete agreement.

'Well, see you, Holly.' He raises a hand and strides off through the woods, presumably back to Rushbrooke House. He turns and looks back at me with a slightly puzzled expression, as if he's trying to work me out.

I look away quickly and pretend to be examining the tree stump in an Alan Titchmarsh, highly professional sort of way . . .

SEVEN

Colin the cockerel has been preparing since I arrived for his *X Factor: The Birds* audition. This morning, his enthusiastic practice begins at prompt five-fifteen.

Sometimes I can roll over and go straight back to sleep, but this morning, the smell of freshly painted walls tickles my nose and starts me thinking about how much work I still have to do in the cottage. And then, of course, I'm wide awake.

Two weeks have passed since my encounter with Jack Rushbrooke and his magnificent axe. But although the roof has been made water-tight and Mike has finished the repairs on the bathroom, I'm still no nearer heading back home to Manchester.

I spent a couple of days painting the bathroom after Mike left and it's looking great. But I've shot myself in the foot, in a way, because the gleaming bathroom now stands out like a sore thumb and I can no longer ignore the fact that the rest of the rooms in Moonbeam Cottage are in urgent need of a make-over. I'll need a fair few coats of magnolia to cover Ivy's eye-catching teal blue and terracotta walls in the living room.

But actually, redecorating the cottage is the least of my worries.

I nip downstairs to boil the kettle. Then I bring my tea back to bed and sit there sipping it, trying not to think about Sunday

May 15th, which has always been one of the most important days on my calendar. I've been trying to ignore it, but it's only a week away now and I'm dreading it.

I sigh. Colin the cockerel isn't the only thing stealing my sleep right now.

It's Ivy's birthday next Sunday.

It looms large and scarily empty, and I haven't a clue how I'm going to fill it. I never imagined I'd still be here in Appleton in the middle of May. I thought I'd be safely back home, with Vicki and Beth to help me get through the 15th. But then, I hadn't banked on a leaky roof and a cottage in need of updating.

My blossoming friendship with Sylvian seems to have come to a grinding halt. I keep thinking I'm bound to bump into him in the village store but, so far, our paths haven't crossed. And Connie is still away in Spain, although she's due back tomorrow. I'm really looking forward to catching up with her and finding out if she's had any romantic adventures, which she assured me she fully intended to do.

Another note of interest: I see Jack Rushbrooke, he of the impressive axe-wielding skills, most nights.

Now, that sounds a lot more interesting than it actually is.

What happens is that Jack sprints past Moonbeam Cottage most evenings about eight o'clock. In fact, it's happened so often since I've been here that I now hold off drawing the curtains until I've seen him flash past. Not that I wait by the window. I'm really not *that* bored. (Although I *am* bored enough to have spent a rather disproportionate amount of time wondering where on earth he goes every night.)

Three weeks into my self-imposed exile, I am so starved of human contact, I've actually started musing aloud about life to Fred the Spider, aiming my pithy observations at the crack in the skirting board. (No come-back as yet, but I'm pretty sure he appreciates my dry wit.)

I spend the day in the local DIY store, buying paint, then

attempting to obliterate the burnt orange walls in the kitchen with a neutral shade of beige. It feels sad and disloyal, as if I'm painting away Ivy's personality.

Later, I'm just out of the bath, face scrubbed and gleaming, when I realise I'm out of milk, so I throw a jacket over my pyjamas and run along to the village store, hoping to catch it before it closes.

I'm just about to go in, when I spot Sylvian walking towards me.

'Where have you been?' He greets me with a smile. 'Hibernating?'

'Actually, I was thinking the same about you,' I admit, feeling ridiculous in my stripy PJs and trainers.

He studies my face. 'You know, your chakras are well out of whack.'

'They are?' *How can he tell? Should I be worried? And where are my chakras anyway?*

'I was just off to my yoga class,' he says, 'but I can skip that for one night. Come up to my place. I've got just what you need.'

His flat is just how I pictured it. All lovely calming blues and pale greens, a huge squashy sofa covered in cushions, and an amazing display of crystals in a glass-fronted cabinet. It smells delicious, too. A cross between some kind of lemony essential oil and . . . chocolate. Yes, definitely chocolate.

'What's that gorgeous scent?' I ask, hopeful there might be a family-sized bar of Cadbury's Dairy Milk lurking under one of his many cushions.

He whisks something off a side table and wafts it under my nose. 'Chocolate-scented candle. Lovely, isn't it?'

'Is it edible?' I've never really been one for lighting candles everywhere. I always think I might set the place on fire.

He chuckles. 'No, I'm afraid not.' His face lights up. 'But wait a minute . . .' He disappears into the kitchen and I hear him opening the fridge.

'I've got some kimchee, if you're hungry,' he calls through.

'Kimchee?' I wonder what that is? A kind of yummy Japanese cake, perhaps?

'Fermented cabbage,' he shouts. 'It's delicious and very good for you. Like to try some?'

'I'm fine, thanks. Just eaten,' I shout, rather too quickly.

He returns with a bowl of what I assume is the aforementioned 'kimchee' and starts tucking in. The smell of it is so rank, my eyebrows shoot up involuntarily. It puts me in mind of a burst sewage pipe.

'Where do you live?' I ask, while he eats his revolting snack. 'When you're not here, I mean.'

'I've got a house in Cornwall, right by the beach. Big windows so the light pours in.'

'It sounds lovely.'

'It is. Being so close to the sea is good for the soul. I'll take you down there some time.' He rises to his feet from a cross-legged position in one smooth movement and takes his bowl into the kitchen.

My mind is whirring. Did he just offer to show me his house in Cornwall?

'Now, a spot of meditation, I think,' he says, coming back into the room. 'For your chakras.'

'Er, great!'

Five minutes later, I'm lying on the floor with my eyes closed, breathing slowly and deeply, trying to empty my mind of all thoughts. Sylvian's voice is soft and hypnotic in my ear: 'Any time a thought finds its way into your head, see yourself blowing it away, like a dandelion clock. Pfft! Off it goes, leaving your mind beautifully tranquil.'

I'm trying my best but I keep getting a whiff of kimchee, which makes the 'deep breaths in' slightly nerve-racking, to be honest. Then I open one eye to find Sylvian lying on the floor next to me.

Thoughts pour in and I'm powerless to blow them away: *Is*

this an elaborate chat-up line? Let's meditate together. Ha! Good one, Sylvian!

But peering over at him, I decide his motives are probably pure. He has his eyes closed and he's meditating with me, his lean diaphragm moving up and down with his deep breathing. It looks like the only reason we're lying on the floor together is to get peaceful. On the other hand, he did offer to take me down to Cornwall. I can't decide if I'd be disappointed or relieved if it turns out he only has friendship in mind.

After our meditation, he makes nettle tea and sits cross-legged on the floor while I try out the vast sofa and admire Sylvian's suppleness. Any other bloke who sat like that I'd quite frankly think was a bit weird, but Sylvian manages to carry it off and look really rather sexy.

I tell him I feel much better for the meditation – which actually, I do – and he looks pleased. 'You should try and do it every day if you can,' he says. 'It takes discipline, of course. Abby and Sara both found it really hard to apply themselves at first but they quickly got the hang of it.'

'Abby and Sara?' I ask, puzzled.

He looks perplexed himself for a second. Then he says, 'Oh, I haven't mentioned them, have I? They live in my house in Cornwall.'

'Oh. Right.' I can't help feeling surprised at this. I'd imagined him living on his own in his lovely beach-side retreat. 'So you have housemates, then.'

'I suppose I do, yes.'

'That . . . must be nice.'

'It is. They're lovely girls. You'd like them, I'm sure.' He smiles warmly. 'And I know they'd like you.'

I smile back, flattered he's even thought about how I'd get on with his friends.

He tells me about the poetry workshop he's doing in nearby Cirencester the next day and I take this as my cue to thank him for the tea and therapy and leave him to his preparations.

He comes down to the main door and leans round me to open it, and when I turn to thank him again, his nearness takes me by surprise. We're squashed up close in the small space and his eyes are burning into mine. Then he leans forward a fraction and kisses me, full on the mouth.

It's an attractively confident kiss. No messing about. His lips are firm and warm, and as kisses go, it's a good one, breaking my current drought very satisfyingly. Very satisfyingly indeed, in fact. The whiff of kimchee is barely noticeable.

I'm just about to lean in and kiss him back, when he says, 'Do you like vegetarian food?'

'Er, yes, I . . . vegetables are *great.*' I stick up both thumbs for emphasis.

'Good. I'd love to cook for you, Holly. What are you doing on Saturday night?'

'Oh, well, nothing,' I tell him honestly. 'If you like, I could bring dessert.' I glance at his lean frame. 'That's if you eat puddings . . .'

He smiles. 'Oh, I eat puddings.' He says it in a way that makes me think he's definitely flirting with me . . . or maybe I'm imagining it. It's all very confusing.

But as I walk back to Moonbeam Cottage, clutching a carton of goat's milk Sylvian gave me, I'm feeling much lighter somehow and less stressed.

It must be the Sylvian effect.

Or the fact that Ivy's birthday on Sunday won't be nearly such a hurdle if I've got a lovely evening with Sylvian on the Saturday to look forward to.

On the way home I peer into the window of the deli-café, hoping Connie is back from Spain, and sure enough, she's there. The café is empty of customers. Connie waves madly and beckons me in.

'I wish I had time to chat,' she says, whipping up a sleeve to show off her tan. 'But Mum's collecting me and I need to get finished here.' She charges off to clear some tables. 'Talk to me!'

'I take it the weather was good, then,' I call from the door.

'Fab. We had a brilliant time. A few interesting episodes, mainly involving a Spanish waiter and a donkey, but I'll tell you about all that over a glass of sangria some time!'

'Brilliant. Can't wait.'

'Tell you what, how about we make a day of it?' she says, pausing for a minute and resting her stacked tray on the table. 'I'm not working at the weekend so what about Saturday?'

My thought processes whir into action. I'm having dinner with Sylvian on Saturday night. And anyway, Sunday would be better. *So* much better . . .

'What about Sunday?' I wince inwardly, hoping against hope it's fine.

She shrugs. 'Sunday? Yes, perfect. In fact, Sunday's probably better for me now I think about it.'

A feeling of blissful relief floods through me. 'Fantastic!'

Connie nods, completely unaware of the torrent of emotion that has just rushed through me like water from a leaky gutter. 'How about we take a drive out into the country? We can take a picnic if the weather's good or call in for a pub lunch somewhere.' She winks. 'And I can fill you in on Pascal.'

'Sounds great. Do you mind if we take your car, though? Ivy's ancient Fiesta can just about manage a trip to the DIY store but only if the wind's in the right direction.'

Connie laughs. 'Suits me fine. I'm not too good at being a passenger in someone else's car. Far too fidgety.'

'Applying the invisible brake and clinging to the sides of the seat with clenched teeth? Gotcha!'

I walk back to Moonbeam Cottage, lighter in spirit and more optimistic than I've felt for a long time.

Some families aren't so bothered about celebrating their big days. But for Ivy and me, birthdays were a highlight of the year; dates to be circled on the calendar and planned weeks in advance. It was probably because our little family *was* Ivy and me, that we were intent on ensuring we each had a brilliant day.

I've a feeling Sunday will be fine now with Connie to keep me entertained.

Then I remember what we'll be doing – *a drive out into the country* – and I feel a stab of anxiety. What if Connie's car breaks down, miles from anywhere?

I give myself a little shake. Of *course* nothing bad will happen. The countryside is *not my enemy*.

Everything will be absolutely fine . . .

EIGHT

The next day is Wednesday and I'm feeling full of get up and go. This feeling is increased ten-fold when I arrive at Ivy Garden to tackle the nettles and find a surprise waiting for me.

A carpet of bluebells has transformed the little woodland clearing.

The ground is dotted with little clumps of the tiny lilac-blue flowers. They peep out from between the trees, like tiny precious jewels, and the scent of them brings back so many memories.

I thought I'd never see the bluebells again – but here they are!

Feeling inspired, I don Ivy's old gardening gloves and set to work pulling up nettles.

As I work, it occurs to me that once all the nettles and weeds have gone, there will be a large expanse of earth available for planting, all along the hedge. An idea takes shape in my head. Before she died, Ivy kept talking about wanting to plant a wildflower meadow. Perhaps I could have a go myself? It can't be that difficult. I seem to remember reading in one of her gardening books that wildflowers actually prefer soil that isn't very fertile. In other words, they'll probably grow anywhere. Sounds like my kind of plant . . .

By tea-time, I've cleared a large patch of nettles, and I head back to the cottage feeling tired and very grubby. As I sink grate-fully into a hot bubble bath, I think about my life back in Manchester. Apart from watering my fairly indestructible umbrella plant, I've never gardened in my life. But I've just spent a whole day in the open air, getting all hot and sweaty, and aching every-where, but actually rather enjoying it. Or at least enjoying the sense of accomplishment after a job well done.

Later, feeling ravenous, I'm hunting around in the fridge when the phone rings. I rush to answer it, chewing rapidly, having just popped a large piece of quiche into my mouth.

'Hi, only me,' says Connie. 'Listen, I'm really, really sorry but I'm afraid we're going to have to postpone our day out. It's Dad's birthday on Sunday.'

I actually stop breathing for a second.

'Mum's cooking a special meal and she'll absolutely kill me if I'm not there for it. She's always been big on family birthdays. Holly? Are you still there?'

'Yes.' I draw in a gulp of air and a piece of quiche lodges itself in the back of my throat. I cough and splutter, trying desperately to swallow down the remains of the pastry, but my mouth feels dry as dust.

'Are you okay?'

'I'm fine,' I gasp. 'Bit of quiche went down the wrong way, that's all. I just need to get some water.'

'Off you go, then. Are you sure you're all right?'

She sounds as if she feels really guilty for cancelling, so I force myself to say in an upbeat tone, 'Actually, I'm planning a wild-flower meadow at Ivy Garden. So now I'll be able to do it on Sunday.'

'Oh, good.' Connie sounds relieved. 'Because I felt terrible.'

She hangs up, and feeling oddly light-headed, I walk through to the kitchen and mechanically gulp down some water. Then, remembering what Sylvian told me, I sit down, close my eyes, draw in a deep breath and blow my worry away like a dandelion clock.

Perhaps it's fate that Connie cancelled. Maybe I was *meant* to plant a wildflower meadow on Ivy's birthday. It would certainly be a lovely tribute to her. And at least I'm busy on Saturday night, at Sylvian's, which will mean I won't have much chance to brood.

Later, I'm poring over Ivy's gardening books, researching which wildflowers flourish best in a shady, woodland setting, when the doorbell rings.

It's Sylvian in his yoga gear.

'Hi, hope I'm not disturbing you,' he says with that lovely, tranquil smile of his. 'I just wanted to give you this.'

He dangles a delicate pendant necklace and I cradle it in my hands.

'Rose quartz,' he says. 'It's the stone of universal love. It opens the heart and promotes deep inner healing and feelings of peace.'

'Oh, it's gorgeous.' I hold up the tiny, pale pink sliver of crystal, admiring its beautiful luminosity.

'And don't say you can't take it.' He smiles. 'It's a gift.'

I flush with a combination of awkwardness and pleasure.

I'm a little perturbed that he thinks I'm in need of 'deep inner healing'. Is it really so obvious that my life is a wreck? Still, I very much like the idea of 'feelings of peace'.

I've never met anyone like Sylvian; he's so calm and giving and . . . *spiritual.* He has this mysterious aura of being at one with the universe which is really very attractive. I can't imagine anything fazing him. Anything at all. If the roof were to suddenly slide off the cottage, Sylvian would probably step nimbly aside in a bendy yoga sort of way then prescribe a calming 'downward dog' pose, followed by a cup of herbal tea.

'Do you want to come in?' I ask, hoping I haven't left any underwear drying on the radiators.

'Tempting. But no.' He looks genuinely regretful. 'I need to be up early.'

I nod. 'Let me guess. You're going out at dawn to commune

with nature?' I say, thinking how wonderful to be so at peace with everything.

'No, the gas man's coming round.'

'Oh.'

'Here, let me . . .' He takes the rose quartz pendant and slips it around my neck. His fingers are cool against my neck and I give a little involuntary shiver of pleasure.

He fumbles with the catch, clearly having trouble fastening it, and at one point, I turn and catch his eye. We smile at each other and it feels suddenly very intimate. His face is so close to mine, I wonder if he's going to kiss me again.

Then he says, 'Listen, I'm really sorry, Holly, but I think I might have to take a rain check on our dinner date.'

My heart drops like a stone. 'Oh. Why?'

'I'm booked to do poetry workshops at the weekend apparently. They got the dates wrong, so I've only just found out. I've asked them to try and rearrange but I doubt they'll be able to. I'm really sorry.'

I fix on a smile and give my head a little shake. 'Hey, no problem. We can do it some other time, right?'

He nods. 'It might still be okay for Saturday. I'll let you know when I hear from the organisers, okay?'

Chain fastened, he turns me round to face him, slipping his hands behind my neck and lightly massaging the tops of my shoulders. 'If we can't do Saturday, I'll make it up to you some other time,' he says, looking deep into my eyes. 'And that's a promise.'

A noise distracts me and I glance along the road. A tall figure is running towards us. It's Jack on his nightly jog.

He sees me and slows to a standstill at the gate. Then, observing that I'm otherwise occupied, with Sylvian's arms draped around my neck, he raises a hand and walks on, with that same slightly puzzled expression, probably imagining far more than is actually happening.

'See you, Holly,' murmurs Sylvian, brushing my forehead with his lips. At the gate, he turns, touches his lips and sends me an imaginary kiss. 'Love and light.'

'Yes. Thank you.' I pat the crystal. 'Er . . . love and light!'

I watch him as he walks off along the road. He's staring up at the moon, and I can't help having a look myself. It's probably an ancient source of spiritual inspiration – or something . . .

I could certainly do with my spirits lifting tonight. My weekend is once again looking as empty as a fairground in a force nine gale.

Listlessly, I watch as Jack sprints along the road then turns down the next street. I glance at my watch. He's early tonight. Perhaps the woman whose husband works in Dubai, and who Jack visits under cover of darkness because they don't want the neighbours to catch on, got home from work early today? This is my latest theory on why he flashes past the cottage most evenings. (These long nights in the country play havoc with your imagination.)

Retreating slowly inside, I pick up the phone to call Vicki, and amazingly, I get a signal first time. She's getting ready to go out with Beth and some other friends.

'Why not come and stay for the weekend, Vick?' I say it nonchalantly, as if I've only just thought of it, when what I *really* want to do is throw myself to the floor, weep copiously and plead with her to please, please, *please* come and rescue me.

'A whole weekend? In the country?' She laughs. 'Love, you know me. I'd totally die of boredom. Come back to Manchester. We miss you so much. *Please, Holly!*'

'You miss me?' Tears well up.

'Of course we do. When are you coming back?'

I can hear her rushing around getting ready as she talks into her phone, excited about her forthcoming night out with the girls.

'I can't yet. I'm doing up the cottage, and Ivy Garden's in a hell of a state.'

I pause then try again. 'Why don't you just come down for the day?'

She sighs. 'But you know I absolutely *hate* sheep, right? It's definitely a phobia.'

'So I'll give Shaun his marching orders. I promise, you'll have the bedroom all to yourself.'

'Shaun?' She perks up. 'Have you got yourself a new man already?'

'No. I mean Shaun the sheep . . .'

'Oh . . . Tell you what, Hols, I'll get myself some wellies then we'll see . . .'

My heart dives into my slippers.

Message understood.

No-one wants to visit me in the back of beyond. And seriously, who can blame them?

'But listen,' she says, 'I was talking to Beth yesterday and we decided that when you get back, we're going to have this *amazing—*'

The phone goes dead.

The stupid phone has actually cut me off!

I slam around crossly in the kitchen, making tea. Honestly, I'd probably get better reception if I moved to Mars! I carry my tea upstairs along with one of Ivy's weightier gardening encyclopaedias, deciding to bury myself in wildflowers to take my mind off everything.

I snuggle under the duvet for a minute, giving in to gloomy thoughts, then I glance at my phone which I've thrown onto the pillow on the other side of the bed. I grab it and find Ivy's number in my contacts. Then I click and wait, with a lump in my throat ,for her familiar message to begin.

I know I probably shouldn't do it, but it makes me smile every time.

I toss the phone back on the pillow and start flicking through the huge hardback encyclopaedia. It has a musty smell and the pages are stuck together in places.

Something slips out.

It's an old blue exercise book, like the sort we used at school. There's nothing on the cover, but when I open it at the first page, I see the familiar handwriting and my heart lurches. Ivy must have written it a long time ago because the ink has faded. With hands that are trembling slightly, I flick through the pages. About a dozen have been written on and the rest is blank.

It looks as if it might be a diary of some sort.

Heart pounding, I begin to read.

NINE

21st September 1965

I escaped to Ivy Garden again today.

Peter's foul mood was casting a black shadow over the house, making me so on edge, I couldn't settle to anything. I had to get out, otherwise in trying my best to placate him, I might have unwittingly said something wrong and made him even angrier. And his temper is starting to really scare me. It used to happen only when he'd had too much to drink, but since he lost his most important client, the moods have become darker and more prolonged. I try to say the right thing, so as not to upset him, but when he's in that mood, nothing I say is right.

As I was putting on my shoes, I heard the study door open and held my breath. But luckily, he didn't object to me going. Just demanded to know when dinner would be ready, then retreated into his study and slammed the door. I found myself remembering what it was like between us when we were first married three years ago. If only it could be like that still.

But I know we can never reclaim that all-too-brief happiness. I've spent the past two years walking on eggshells, doing *everything I can to make Peter happy, but it doesn't seem to matter what I do, it's never enough. Being childless doesn't help, of course. We never talk about it, but it can't have been easy for Peter to find out that the problem lay solely with him; that it was highly unlikely he would ever be able to father a child. The news must have been devastating, his pride crushed. It was hard enough for **me** to accept the fact that I'd never have the child I so longed for. The consequences for our already shaky marriage didn't bear thinking about . . .*

Stunned, I put down the notebook.

Why didn't I know about all this? It's as if I'm reading a diary written by a complete stranger. Not the person closest to me for most of my life.

Granddad's moods scared Ivy? But she always spoke warmly of him; never in any great detail, but the impression I'd got was of a happy marriage. She never told me they had trouble conceiving . . .

It must have seemed like a precious gift when my mum was finally born in September 1967. My granddad had been warned he was never likely to be a father and yet the miracle had happened! Had it made a difference to their marriage? Made things better between them perhaps?

My granddad died of cancer in 1970, so they'd had just three years together, bringing up the baby they'd longed for.

That baby was my mum.

I go back to the diary entry, eager to discover more:

I was all tensed up as I walked through the village, past the shops, hoping I wouldn't bump into someone and have to stop and chat. (It's so hard to keep up the constant pretence among our neighbours that Peter and I are just like any other normal, happily married couple.)

But I made it safely out the other side and with the hedge

and the woods now on my right, across the road, and the pretty
little row of Cotswold sandstone cottages on my left, I felt I
could breathe properly again.

I glanced at the windows of Moonbeam Cottage, the way I
always do. I just can't help myself. There's something really
special about it.

Then I crossed over the road, found the little gap in the
hedge and squeezed through into my little woodland clearing
– it lifts me every time! – and straight away, I could feel my
whole body relaxing.

I put down the notebook and stare into space.

Ivy's marriage had clearly been anything but blissfully happy,
thanks to my granddad, who seemed to have been a bully. I never
knew him because he died long before I was born, when my mum
was just a toddler.

But how terrible for Ivy, marrying a man she never realised had
such a temper. In those days, you tended to stick with your marriage,
no matter what, and that's obviously what Ivy had done . . .

I continued reading:

Sheila from next door popped her head through the hedge
while I was busy pulling weeds, and six-year-old Alice ran into
the clearing and asked if she could help me, bless her. I showed
her which were the weeds and she set to work with such fierce
concentration!

It's at times like these that I most long for a child of my
own. But maybe the fact that Peter and I can't make a baby
is a sign that we were never meant to be together. And in any
case, would I really want to bring a child into such a desperately
sad, destructive marriage? Peter loves me in his own way, of
that I'm certain, but he's made no secret of the fact that he's
had affairs while he's been away on business. He doesn't even
attempt to hide it from me either. He tells me they mean nothing

and that it's me he loves – but if you truly love someone, you don't cheat on them like that, do you?

But then, following that logic, I suppose that means I don't love Peter any more. If I did, my heart wouldn't beat faster every time I'm in darling Bee's company, would it? Not that I'd dream of being unfaithful to Peter.

To be honest, Bee is probably the only reason I haven't walked out on my marriage already. He keeps me sane. Makes me laugh. Gives me a shoulder to cry on. And he gives me something to look forward to. The highlight of my life these days is sitting talking with Bee in the garden. (I used to call it my secret garden until Bee said no, it should be called Ivy Garden because I'd single-handedly transformed the little clearing into something so special.)

It's a big cliché, I know, but Bee understands. He worries about me and he wants to confront Peter, tell him what he thinks of him – and this, from someone so gentlemanly and mild-mannered! – but I keep telling him it's not Peter's fault the way he is. Not entirely. He had a terrible upbringing, deserted by his mother when he was five and brought up by an alcoholic father who was bitter about life and much too handy with his fists. It's no wonder Peter is terrified I will run out on him, too. It's all so horribly sad.

I can't leave Peter, however much Bee's silences tell me I should. (Isn't it funny how a silence really can speak louder than words?)

I married Peter. I promised to love him – in sickness and in health. And Peter is sick. His early experiences have damaged him. I'd never forgive myself if I left him and he did something terrible. I only wish he would agree to get help, but the times I've dared to hint at this, his furious reaction has made me wish I'd kept my mouth shut. His rages scare me so much but I can see no way out.

I thank God for Bee . . .

Stunned, I stop reading.

Bee?

Who was Bee?

I never knew any of this. Ivy had obviously chosen to keep it to herself – that she'd fallen in love with a man she nicknamed Bee.

Bee must have been a pet name. It didn't sound like the sort of name you'd be given at birth. A real name. Ivy had obviously given him a codename, I suppose because she wanted to keep him a secret.

But what had happened to Bee? Is he still alive? Does he live in the village? Did he and Ivy stay friends until the end?

Why didn't she tell me about him?

So many questions.

And only Ivy could answer them . . .

TEN

When I wake the next morning, my first thought is: *Did I really find Ivy's old diary last night? Or did I dream the whole thing?*

The blue exercise book is lying on the bed. I pick it up and flick through it, as if to make myself believe it, because it all feels unreal and I'm having trouble getting my head around it.

All the astonishment from the previous night floods back.

Ivy had another life she never told me about!

In a daze, I go through the motions of getting ready, then I sit in the kitchen with a piece of toast in front of me going cold and inedible, just staring into space. Thinking about Ivy and Peter's troubled marriage. And the man who seemed to have brightened up Ivy's life.

Bee.

Is he still alive? Does 'Bee' mean the letter 'B'? In which case, am I looking for a Brian or a Bill or a Barney? There's Bill next door but he's nearly ninety, almost twenty years older than Ivy. She was twenty-two when she wrote the diary, so Bill would have been around forty at the time. But maybe he was kind to her, listened to her troubles and she found herself drawn to this under-standing, mature man who made her feel safe. Helped her feel good about herself again.

I'll have to talk to Bill. But what will I say? 'I think Ivy might have been in love with someone other than her husband, and I was wondering if it was you?'

Bill has been married for nearly sixty years to Sheila, who has dementia. He takes the bus into Stroud several times a week to visit her in the home where she's being cared for. He has quite enough on his plate without me asking awkward questions. And anyway, there's no mention of Bee having a wife in the diary. Knowing Ivy as I did, she'd have felt really guilty if she'd found herself in the role of 'the other woman'. She would have mentioned Sheila, I'm certain, even if it was just to say how bad she felt about taking up so much of Bee's time. But there's no mention at all. Her only guilt in the diary seems to be over Peter.

But if it isn't Bill, who can it be? Someone in the village? The trouble is, I don't know anyone in Appleton well enough to talk to about it. Jack Rushbrooke seems to have known Ivy fairly well. It's possible she may have confided in him over a cold beer in Ivy Garden one time, I suppose.

But no, why would she tell Jack – or anyone else for that matter – about the feelings she had for Bee, if she never even told *me* about him?

My head is spinning with random thoughts that aren't making a whole lot of sense. I need to do something. Otherwise I'll end up sitting here all day, staring at the wall and driving myself mad dreaming up all kinds of theories about the mysterious Bee.

Wildflowers.

I need to buy wildflowers so that I can plant a meadow on Sunday.

Garden centre it is, then. Let's hope Florence is up to it.

Driving into the car park, I'm surprised at how big the garden centre seems to be. Most things round here tend to be on a doll's-house scale – as in limited stock in the village store and scant-bordering-on-mythical public bus service (I've only sighted it twice since I've been here). Then there's the *one* taxi (and that's only on days Eric the taxi driver isn't doubling as Black Bull pint-puller in a neighbouring village or cleaning at the local school).

But this garden centre is *huge*. I suppose in the absence of a reliable broadband signal, people in the country spend an awful lot of time in their gardens growing things.

I start wandering curiously through the plant section, up and down the rows, admiring shrubs and flowers of all colours and varieties. They even have mini trees, which are obviously not necessary for me since mine is a woodland garden. There's a whole section devoted to Grecian urns, statues of Buddha and semi-naked people. A whole new world to me. Fascinating!

The only time I've ever been in a place like this was the time Ivy and I bought our Christmas tree from a gardening emporium near where we lived in Manchester. (We were so rubbish at tying the tree to the top of the old Mini she had in those days, this great Norwegian spruce ended up slewed half across the windscreen, and Ivy, in hoots of laughter, had to put her foot to the floor and drive at a gear-burning fifty miles an hour to evade police.)

After a while, I decide I'd better get some advice so I look around and spot an assistant, slouched over a book at one of the tills. I'm about to walk over to her when I find myself distracted by the garden furniture and take a detour to where it's all on display.

There's a wooden bench very similar to Ivy's – which was destroyed beyond repair by the storms – and I pause for a moment, picturing it in the exact spot where the old bench used to be. It would look perfect there, I think, sitting down to try it out and running my hand dreamily over the arm rest, admiring the lovely grain of the wood. It's reduced in price, too . . . very reasonable . . .

A logical thought struggles to the surface.

What on earth am I thinking?

I'll be heading back to Manchester soon. I definitely do *not* need a new garden bench!

Rising swiftly to my feet, I leave the furniture area behind and head over to safer territory – a rack full of packets of seed, each bearing a colourful picture of a flower in full bloom. Some of the packets seem to contain a mix of wildflower seeds.

Perfect! Call off the dogs. This is exactly what I need.

Five packets, maybe, or a straight half dozen, to be on the safe side? I glance at the instructions on the back. They seem fairly straightforward. I go to the till with my spoils, feeling pleased with my choice. Apparently all I need to do is prepare the ground then scatter these seeds all over it and Bob's your uncle! A wild-flower garden!

The girl on the till is deep in her well-thumbed book, which has a gory image of a glinting knife and lots of blood spatter on the cover. I clear my throat and she glances up. To my surprise, I know her. It's the girl with the blonde-black hair who hangs around with the crowd at the bus shelter. The girl I spotted in a cosy conflab with Sylvian round the back of the village store.

She picks up one of the seed packets, turns it over and says in a bored monotone, 'Is your soil rich or poor?'

'Er, sorry?'

She sighs and holds up the packet. 'Perennials like these prefer poor soil. Otherwise the coarser grasses take over.'

'Oh, right.' *Is my soil rich or poor? Golly, I haven't the faintest idea.*

She stifles a yawn and says in the same bored tone, 'Has the land been used for gardening before?'

I nod eagerly. At last a question I can answer. 'Oh, yes. Ivy used to garden there. Ivy's my grandma – *was* my grandma. She died, you see. So I'm staying in her cottage and trying to get it ship-shape, you know, so that I can sell it.'

The girl stares at me with mild disbelief as if I've just announced I'm visiting the Cotswolds on a day trip from Mars.

'Anyway, Ivy was the gardener in the family, not me,' I gabble on to fill the awkward silence. 'Of course, I'd know Alan Titchmarsh if I saw him. Probably. In a decent light. But that's as far as my gardening knowledge goes. Ivy was great, though. You probably knew her, actually. Ivy Grainger?'

There's a moment's silence, during which the check-out girl continues to stare at me. Although, oddly, her gaze now seems to be fixed intently on my left shoulder.

I glance at it, checking for bird poop.

Then I realise she's got her beady eye on a couple of boys, who are giggling together over by one of the stands.

She gathers up the seed packets and hands them back to me. 'Right, well, you'll need the cornflower annual mix, not those.'

'Oh, okay.' I walk back over to the seed stand. 'I'm Holly, by the way. Do you live in the village?'

She doesn't seem to have heard me. Her posture has gone rigid and she's leaning forward, kohl-rimmed eyes piercing the backs of those two boys. I start to ask if she could point out the cornflower seeds. But she silences me with a raised hand and continues to watch them, on high alert, like a well-trained pet waiting to be told it can snaffle its doggy snack.

'Right, you little bastards!' Without warning, she leaps out of her seat, and before you can say, *The customer is king*, she has both boys in a firm stranglehold, yelping for mercy.

As I watch, open-mouthed, she barks, 'Well, well. If it isn't Freddy Collins and Ryan Biggs. Do you think I'm blind? Well, *do you?*'

She tightens her hold and they reply weedily in the negative.

'Excellent. I'm going to let go of you now, boys, and you're going to empty out your pockets. And there's no use making a run for it because *I know who your parents are*,' she mutters darkly.

The two boys surrender up their spoils, which seem to be a couple of small plastic water pistols.

She points at the door. '*Out*. And you're on a warning. Do it again and the police will be knocking on your door.'

They disappear faster than ice-cream on a hot day.

A dark-haired boy who looks to be in his late teens appears.

He must be staff because he's wearing a green uniform with the garden centre's logo on the sweatshirt.

'Everything okay, Layla?'

'Yes, boss.' She sticks up her thumb.

I glance at her in surprise. So this is Layla, who Jack Rushbrooke told me to ask for? What's the connection between them? Maybe it's just that in a village as small as this, everyone knows everyone else.

The boy peers at her book, reads the title and quickly dismisses it. 'A bit amateurish,' he comments, adjusting his glasses. 'Have you read *The Girl Who Walked in the Shadows*? Great thriller. I can lend it to you if you like.'

'Yeah, okay.' Layla continues reading. 'Thanks,' she adds as an afterthought.

'No probs.' The boy grins at her back and walks out.

I approach the till and Layla looks up. 'Sorry about that. Little buggers. They've bloody brightened up my day, though, I can tell you.'

'I doubt you'll have any more trouble from them,' I smile, and she gives a fierce grunt, which could either mean she wholeheartedly agrees with me or wholeheartedly *disagrees*. I really can't tell.

'Bloody parents have a lot to answer for,' she says. 'If they took more interest in their kids, this sort of thing wouldn't happen.'

She scowls and I get the distinct impression she isn't just talking about the two boys' parents.

'You're right. Family support is everything if you don't want your kid wandering off the track.'

Layla studies me for a moment, looking up through her blonde and black fringe.

'Anyway, the cornflowers?' I prompt.

She points to a metal stand nearby and gets back to her killer-on-the-loose novel.

I replace the seed packets and collect half a dozen of the cornflower variety. They look lovely. There's a picture of blue cornflowers and brilliant red poppies on the front. I remember the nettles and turn back to Layla, but she's deep in her book and I find myself hesitating, not wanting to incur more teenage displeasure. But she *is* the shop assistant, her job being to assist shoppers . . .

'Excuse me, Layla.'

She glances up.

'I've got a garden full of nettles to get rid of. Any suggestions?'

She frowns. 'Strimmer.'

'I was thinking more of weed killer for the nettles?'

'Not very organic. I'd use the strimmer if I were you.' She shrugs. 'It's dead easy once you know how.'

Great, thanks. That's really helpful.

Why do people keep banging on about strimmers? First Jack Rushbrooke and now Layla. Perhaps strimmers are to people now what fridges were to people in the nineteen-fifties. In a few years, *everyone* will possess one.

I make my purchase in silence, wondering if 'the boss' knows quite how off-putting his sales girl is with her surly manner and scary make-up.

'Holly?'

I spin round.

Layla is staring over at me and, for a ridiculous second, I panic that maybe I've shoplifted something by accident.

'I did know your grandma,' she says. 'Ivy was okay.' She turns back to her thriller.

I stare at her bent head for a second. Translated from teen speak, that probably means Layla liked Ivy a great deal.

My heart lifts as I walk out to the car.

I think about Layla on the way home and her comment about parents taking an interest in their kids. And for the millionth time, I find myself trying to imagine what it would be like to have a proper family. Of course, Ivy and I were a 'proper family' – just a very small one. And there were lots of advantages to being someone's *everything* – like I was to Ivy – including the fact that you didn't have to compete with brothers and sisters for attention.

Nonetheless, I've always secretly longed for more family. I felt different to the other kids at school. At primary school, when they saw me being collected at the gates by a woman older than their mums, I told them it was Ivy, my grandma, who looked after me. So then they would ask me where my mum and dad were, and I used to lie and say they had a café in Spain and had to be there all the time, which was why I stayed with Ivy.

I learned that it was easier to lie.

If I told people the truth, the horror on their faces just amplified the tragedy and stirred up all the horrible visions in my head. The sympathetic faces were even worse. They'd often ask hesitant questions that I didn't want to answer. Or *couldn't* answer because actually, Ivy and I didn't ever talk about the day *it* happened.

It was a taboo subject in our house.

Ivy would chat to me often about my parents – what they were like, what made them laugh, how much they absolutely adored me – but the day of their deaths was out of bounds. I sensed that early on, and I learned to keep my questions to myself. Hearing Ivy sobbing in her bedroom at night when she thought I was fast asleep made me really scared. I remember pressing my fingers to my ears and pulling the duvet over my head as hot tears of panic soaked into my pillow. There was no way I could risk upsetting Ivy by demanding to know exactly what happened that day.

I'd finally learned the full story when I was about eight, sitting at the top of the stairs, accidentally eavesdropping on a conversation between Ivy and Maureen, our next-door neighbour in the row of terrace houses we lived in when we moved to Manchester.

Later, I found myself wishing I'd never listened in. Then I would still believe the version Ivy told me when it first happened – a straightforward account of a road accident that a four-year-old would understand. That version, re-touched for my benefit, contained little of the horror and none of the terrible, graphic details. Nor did it haunt my dreams like the bald, unvarnished truth has done ever since . . .

I can totally understand why Ivy would want to protect me in this way.

But I don't understand why she didn't tell me about Bee. Unless he was simply a passing fancy, forgotten long ago, and it hadn't even crossed her mind to mention him.

Deep down, though, I don't really believe this.

Bee, whoever he was, had played a huge part in Ivy's life, I was sure of it. And the fact that she kept him a secret from me all these years makes me feel sad. And a little annoyed, if I'm honest. I used to pride myself on how close we were, but I was obviously fooling myself because in the end, there was a part of her life she chose to keep hidden from me.

And now that I know her secret, there's another question I keep asking.

Did Ivy hide anything else from me?

ELEVEN

I drive home from the garden centre and get into my painting gear. The kitchen needs another coat because the original orangey shade is still faintly visible.

But instead of decorating, I find myself poring over the diary again, dissecting every phrase in a desperate bid to wring out more meaning and hopefully solve the mystery of Bee. I also spend a lot of time lying on the sofa, staring at the ceiling.

There must be *someone* in the village who knew about Bee . . .

When Jack jogs past the window later, I decide maybe he can shed some light on the situation. Quick as a flash, I'm on my feet, pulling on my trainers and diving out into the night after him. I'm not usually so impulsive, but I'm desperate to have my questions about Bee answered. If I chicken out of asking Jack, I can always say I'd like to borrow some gardening tools. He did offer, after all.

Passing the village store, I glance up at Sylvian's windows. He's probably in some kind of complicated yoga pose. I wonder if he watches the soaps at the same time to offset the boredom? Probably not.

I turn right into Farthingale Lane, following in Jack's wake. It's eerily dark away from the main street and I'm suddenly having trouble seeing my feet. This makes hurrying along the potholed lane, while also trying to keep Jack in sight, a little treacherous. I pass a row of cottages on my left, fields on the right, and I'm just about to shout Jack's name when the gloom seems to swallow him up altogether.

Where's he gone?

There's a large house beyond the cottages, with what looks like a huge glass conservatory extending into the garden. Maybe he's gone in there. I stand by the gate, peering over. The house seems to be in complete darkness and there's no sign at all of Jack.

Suddenly, the conservatory space is flooded with light. I shuffle closer to the camouflage of the hedge. The extension houses a long swimming pool, the sort that encourages you to swim lengths (not splash around doing the odd width and trying to convince yourself this constitutes exercise, which is what I tend to do).

My eyes widen. Jack is standing at the edge of the pool, adjusting his goggles. He's stripped down to his swimwear.

I gulp, which sounds quite loud in the silence. Maybe he does a *lot* of tree chopping, then, because you don't get a taut, hard-muscled body like that lounging around watching *Castaway*.

But budgie smugglers? Dear, oh dear. Although he wears them very well, I have to admit. I cock my head on one side as he dives in and starts powering his way along the pool. Great technique. Perhaps I'll just hang around for a bit and watch . . .

'Oh, hello, dear,' says a rich, plummy voice right next to me, and I actually shout out, it's such a shock.

Oddly, when I spin around, there's nothing there except a large bush.

Next minute a woman's head pops up from its depths, attached to a set of binoculars. 'Doing your Neighbourhood Watch thing, too?' she asks in a dramatic stage whisper. 'Great minds think alike.'

'You gave me a fright,' I say weakly, grasping my chest and

staring at her in alarm. A large woman with a red-lipsticked mouth, she has lots of bright auburn hair tied up in a jolly, patterned scarf.

'Oh, did I?' She emerges fully, swishing her enormous, floral-patterned dressing gown back into place. 'Sorry, dear. I'm Henrietta. The villagers are quite used to me, popping up here, there and everywhere.' She gives a loud, throaty chuckle, and I glance in alarm at Jack, who's still front crawling up and down the pool like an Olympic athlete. He won't hear us, with the water in his ears, but Henrietta's flamboyant appearance might well attract his attention through the glass walls of the conservatory, scarily only a few yards from where we're standing.

Henrietta sways closer and murmurs confidentially, 'I'm head of the Community Watch committee.'

'Ah, right.'

She trains her binoculars on Jack. 'It pays to be vigilant, don't you think?'

A giggle rises up and I turn it into a cough. 'Oh, absolutely. You can't be too careful.'

She puts the binoculars down and peers approvingly at me. 'That's just what I say to my darling Henry when he tells me I'm *far* too community-spirited for my own good. But where's the joy in life if you can't sacrifice your time to help others?'

I nod, keeping a firm eye on Jack. The last thing I need is to be caught spying on him with the exuberant Henrietta.

'So what are you doing here, my love?' she booms, like she's voice-trained to reach the person in the back row.

'I wanted to have a quick word with Jack,' I whisper, hoping this will encourage her to lower her voice, too. 'But he's obviously busy, so—'

'Ah, yes. Jack,' she booms. 'Well, you've certainly come to the right place. Do you know, he's here just about *every night* doing his physical jerks.' She holds the binoculars aloft again.

'Pardon me?'

'His exercise. In the swimming pool? The house belongs to his friend who works abroad. Jack keeps an eye on it for him. Have a gander, m'dear.'

She pushes the binoculars into my hands, just as it occurs to me that, weirdly, I was half-correct about Jack's mysterious nightly visits: they do actually involve a man who works abroad . . .

'No, honestly, it's fine,' I say hurriedly, trying to hand the binoculars back. But Henrietta is pushing open the garden gate, apparently on a mission.

'You can't go without seeing Jack,' she announces. 'Here, let me grab his attention for you.'

Before I can stop her, she's sailing across her neighbour's lawn towards the conservatory, waving her arms about and calling, 'Coo-ee! Ja-a-ack!' Her bat-wing sleeves flap up and down, making her look like a giant, exotic bird attempting to take flight.

'What's your name, dear?' she calls back.

'No! Honestly, it's okay.' I signal frantically for her to stop – but oh God, Jack is even now emerging from the pool and appearing at the door of the glass-walled extension, rubbing his wet hair with a towel.

'I say, *lovely* Speedos.' Henrietta's throaty approval carries back to me on the cool night air and I flinch with shame. I have a violent urge to flee the scene, but it's too late. Jack has already spied his eager fan club of two and is looking past Henrietta in my direction. 'Holly? Was there something you wanted?'

'No! I mean, yes.' Oh God, I have to give him some sort of explanation for my being there. I walk over the lawn towards him. 'You kindly said you'd lend me gardening tools,' I improvise swiftly, 'and well, I need something to dig up nettles?'

He nods. 'A spade? Or a strimmer? Of course. No problem.'

'Right, well, I'll leave you two to your . . . *chat*,' says Henrietta in the nudge-nudge-wink-wink tone of a *Carry On* movie. 'Toodle-ooh!' The exotic bird gives Jack a coy little wave and starts flapping back across the lawn.

'I see you've met our most colourful villager,' says Jack, wrapping the towel round his waist.

I laugh, full of relief that the amount of taut, lightly tanned body on show has been reduced somewhat, at least to broad chest, strong arms and hairy calves. 'Does she always watch you swimming?'

His lips twist in wry amusement and I notice how different he looks when he smiles. He seems calmer and more relaxed, too. The swimming obviously does him good. 'Henrietta's lovely,' he murmurs. 'She takes her Neighbourhood Watch responsibilities a little too far, that's all.'

'But spying on you, though? I couldn't believe it!' I say, desperate for him to know I wasn't in any way involved in Henrietta's saucy antics with the binoculars. (Me? Eye up a gorgeous buff male body in sporty action? Perish the thought!)

'Oh, Holly?' Henrietta is sailing back towards us. 'I think you still have them, dear.'

I frown at her, confused, and she laughs heartily.

'The binoculars, dear. Or would you like to hold on to them for a bit longer?'

'What? God, no!' I off-load them as if they've just been microwaved then shoot a furtive glance at Jack. But he's rubbing at a mark on the conservatory door with an expression of concentration, and thankfully doesn't seem to have heard.

'Thank you!' trills Henrietta, swooshing off, her gown billowing around her. 'Good night. Sleep tight, my dears.'

Jack looks down at me, a suspicion of a smile on his well-shaped lips. 'So, anyway, a strimmer?'

I flush and laugh rather awkwardly. 'Yes. I saw you run by the cottage, so I thought, *No time like the present!* And here I am.'

He nods. 'Actually, I run past Moonbeam Cottage most nights, although usually I'm a bit later than this.'

'Do you really? Gosh, I've never noticed.' I adopt what I hope is an innocent expression.

'It's generally after seven. I don't normally get back from London till then but I managed a half day today.'

'You commute to London every single weekday? That must be at least two hours by train each way.'

He gives a curt nod. 'Look, do you mind if I just grab some clothes?' He pushes the door wide for me. 'Come in. James won't mind. And anyway, he's in Singapore.'

Ah, not Dubai, then.

I stand by the pool, breathing in the chlorine, while Jack nips into what I assume is a changing room, re-emerging a few minutes later in jeans and a black sweatshirt. He runs a hand through his hair. 'So. Gardening tools. We could go and get them now, if you like.'

'Oh, I don't want to put you to any trouble . . .' I begin, feeling a bit of a fraud. The tools were just an excuse. I really want to ask him about Ivy, but now that he's here, I'm not sure how to begin.

He shrugs. 'It's no trouble at all. Let's go. Do you mind doing the shortcut through the woods?'

'Er, no, not at all.'

We start off walking side by side, although I have to do an extra skip every now and then to keep up with Jack's long stride. I ask him about his job and his long commute, and he tells me he works in the City but that it's not practical for him to stay in London during the week. I want to ask why – does he have a wife and kids he needs to get back to every day? But we've crossed the road by then and are having to walk in single file as we approach the entrance to Ivy Garden. Once through the gap in the hedge, I follow Jack on what is clearly a well-trodden path through the woods. Twigs cracking underfoot, I breathe in the evocative scent of wood smoke as up ahead, the path opens out into a field.

Jack holds a fallen branch to one side so that I can walk through. 'The field's still a bit boggy from the storms.' He glances at my footwear. 'Sorry, I probably shouldn't have brought you this way.'

'It's fine,' I assure him, the second before stepping into a muddy pool that soaks right through to my socks.

Jack opens a gate and there is Rushbrooke House ahead of us.

It's a substantial Georgian farmhouse with a very pleasing symmetry, large windows and lots of ivy climbing up the walls. You can tell it was a handsome house in its day. Actually, it still is – except that it obviously needs a complete overhaul, including a whole new roof and window frames, to keep it from turning into the kind of dilapidated haunted house you see in old horror movies with lightning flashing behind it for extra thrills.

'Wow,' I breathe. 'It's – erm – big.'

He laughs. 'Yes, it is. But old farmhouses like these need a lot of upkeep.'

'I can imagine.' I think of my modern flat that's so easy to maintain and heat. How many rooms (and radiators) does Jack have here, at Rushbrooke House? The bills must be enormous. But I suppose if the house has been in his family for years, it would be hard to let it go.

'In reality, it's a draughty, leaky old monster that eats cash for breakfast,' says Jack bluntly, sounding anything but sentimental about his proud heritage.

Curious, I ask, 'Wouldn't you rather sell the house than have it hanging round your neck like a millstone?'

'It doesn't matter what *I* want. You can't be selfish when the happiness of people you care about is at stake.' He smiles grimly. 'Your feet are wet. Are you okay?'

'Yes, thanks.' I can tell by his expression that he doesn't want to talk about the house any more. For some reason, selling up is obviously not an option, however much Jack seems to want to. I can't help wondering whose happiness he's protecting.

We walk along a path that skirts the mellow red brick boundary wall of the house and enter the grounds at a set of wrought iron gates. A tarmac drive leads up to a gravelled parking area at the front of the house, but we veer off to the right, towards a gate that I assume leads to the gardens at the back.

Jack stops at the gate. 'Would you like a drink? Tea? Coffee? Wine?' He pauses and gives me an odd look. 'Well, maybe not wine.'

I stare at him, confused. *Maybe not wine?* Why on earth not? Because he hasn't got any? Because he's driving later? Or because I look like someone who might get overly frisky after a glass or two? Very strange.

'That would be lovely but I should be getting back. And I'm sure you've got things to do as well.'

He grins. 'With a family like mine, there's always plenty to do.'

My heart gives a funny little skitter. Perhaps he has a wife and a whole brood of kids, then. Or a live-in girlfriend who's obsessed with putting her mark on the décor and is always on at him to do DIY.

I follow him down a path that skirts an enormous, fairly well-kept lawn, to a garden shed that's in a similar state of dilapidation to the main building. Jack holds the door for me and I walk in. The delicious scent of wood shavings tickles my nose.

'It's my mother's house,' he says, as if he's read my curious mind. 'I live here with her and my sister.'

'Oh.'

'You sound surprised.' He brings a long-handled gardening implement from the dark depths of the shed. I assume it's what's called a strimmer.

'Surprised? No, not at all. That's – erm – really nice for you, living with your family like that.'

He raises an eyebrow, as if he's about to come back at me with a sarcastic quip.

Then he looks at me and his face softens. 'Living on your own has its merits, too,' he murmurs. 'No-one to please but yourself.'

'That's true.' I smile up at him. He's only saying this to be kind and my heart swells at his thoughtfulness. 'It's just sometimes I can't help wishing I'd spent more time with Ivy while I could. Talked more about her past and her memories. It's so true that you don't know what you've got until it's gone.'

We lock eyes and he nods slowly.

Now is my chance to ask about Bee. But for some reason I'm feeling a little light-headed and I've completely forgotten what I planned to say. My mouth is dry, too, when I try to swallow. It's probably nerves because I feel like I'm wasting Jack's time. And actually, I think he might be a bit suspicious of my motives for talking to him because he's looking down at me with that slightly quizzical expression again.

I draw in a deep breath and break the spell. 'Anyway, Ivy was the best. I couldn't have wished for a happier, more loving upbringing. So you see, I'm really very lucky.'

'You are,' he agrees, balancing the strimmer over his shoulder. 'We can drive this over now or I could drop it off on Saturday night when I get back from London?'

'Oh. Right.' That's when I *might* be having dinner with Sylvian. He hasn't confirmed yet whether it's on or off, but I need to keep it free in case. 'I'm – er – out on Saturday. Dinner with a friend.' Oddly, I don't think I want Jack to know about Sylvian, although I'm not sure why. 'It's not a hot date or anything,' I add quickly, while at the same time flushing to the roots of my hair. The temperature in the shed is suddenly tropical. Honestly, I might as well have tipped him a wink and joked, 'Can't wait to rejoin the ranks of the sexually-active, know what I mean?'

He's looking at me slightly askance. 'I never imagined it was,' he says calmly. 'A hot date, that is.'

'Oh. Right.' *That told me, then!* I'm clearly nowhere near attractive enough in Jack Rushbrooke's eyes to warrant a man asking me out with amorous intentions in mind!

I feel ridiculously crestfallen.

Not that I care what Jack thinks about me. It's just I've been wondering myself what Sylvian has in mind for Saturday. And now I'm thinking maybe his intentions are purely platonic.

'Let's take it round now, then,' he says, patting his pocket for his car keys.

We're about to go out again, into the night, when something catches my eye. There's a workbench at the back of the space and lying on its side on top is what looks like a wooden chair.

'That's my latest project,' says Jack, following my gaze. 'I make furniture. It's a dying art and if I could, I'd be doing my bit every day to keep it alive.' He hefts the chair off the table with one hand and sets it down in front of me.

'It's beautiful,' I tell him honestly, running my hand over the smooth, polished grain and admiring the tall, ladder-back effect. It's a simple design but very stylish.

'Another five to go, plus a matching table,' he says smiling broadly.

'Wow. How long will that take?'

He laughs ruefully. 'Probably longer than my customer would like. But the day job takes up so much time.'

'Can't you give up your work in London and do this instead?'

'If only. I need the big salary to keep this place going.' He nods in the direction of the house. 'Really, it needs a complete overhaul, but that's out of the question. And Mum refuses to even think about selling, so . . .' He shrugs and glances down at the sawdust on the floor.

I study his profile thoughtfully. He should be making furniture full-time. It's such a waste of talent.

Ivy would say working with wood was Jack's calling. When he talks about it, you can see his passion, the way he's right there 'in the zone'. His face really comes alive.

'So you're stuck in a job you don't particularly like, with a time-consuming commute to London every day.'

'Yeah. That's about the size of it.' He shrugs. 'But I guess there aren't many of us privileged enough to be working at something we really love. Not when the bills need paying, anyway.'

'How true.' I smile sadly, thinking of how Ivy always wanted me to do art, the thing I loved best. 'My grandma knew what my "calling" was even before I knew it myself. It's taken me a long time to realise I should probably stop resisting and do something about it.'

It's odd. This thought has only just crystallised in my mind, standing here talking to Jack. It suddenly seems very clear that now is the time for me to get serious and take my talent for art to the next level. Apply for college, maybe . . .

A little thrill of excitement rushes through me at the thought.

Then I realise Jack is giving me that oddly distant, assessing look of his again, as if he still can't quite work me out. I wish he would stop it. Under those watchful blue eyes, I feel gauche and self-conscious, as if all my flaws are being magnified under a microscope.

'Maybe your mum will change her mind about selling the house?' I suggest, to fill the pause in conversation.

A shadow passes over his face. 'No. She never will. When Dad died, she went completely . . .' He clears his throat. 'Well, she wasn't herself for a very long time, and she still hasn't recovered. Not really.'

'How awful.'

'Asking her to move out now would be the cruellest thing I could do to her.'

He forces a smile, as if embarrassed he's confided so much. 'Rushbrooke House reminds me of that Eagles song, "Hotel California". *You can check out any time you like . . .*'

'*But you can never leave,*' I finish. I know the song well. It was one of Ivy's favourites from the Seventies. Poor Jack . . .

On the drive back to Moonbeam Cottage, he asks me where I'm dining on Saturday night.

'Oh, we're not going out to a restaurant. He's – erm – cooking for me.'

'He?' He glances across then shakes his head. 'Sorry, don't mean to be nosy.'

'It's fine. He's the new poet in residence?'

Jack darts a look at me. 'You're having dinner with *Sylvian*?'

'Yes. Why? Do you know him?'

'I know *of* him.' He twists his lips into a scathing smile. 'I assume you'll be trying to reform him, then.'

I stare at his profile as he pulls in outside Moonbeam Cottage and switches off the engine. '*Reform* him?' What a strange, old-fashioned expression. 'What do you mean?

He grins. 'Sorry. Shouldn't have said anything. Selena heard some rumours in the village about his, erm, interesting romantic life.'

I turn curiously at the mention of Selena, the woman from the café, wondering how Jack knows her.

He shrugs. 'Even if the rumours are true, a woman in your position shouldn't have anything to worry about.'

I glance at him in confusion. *A woman in my position*? What's he saying? That even if Sylvian plays around, he's unlikely to want to play around with *me*? Well, that's charming!

'What do you mean, *a woman in my* . . .?' I begin. But he's already getting out of the car.

'Are you coming over?' He leans back in. I'm still sitting with my seatbelt on. 'Let's get this strimmer into your shed.'

TWELVE

'People always write nettles off. But they make great soup.'

Ivy's words come back to me as I stand in her garden, surveying the thriving army of nettles I still need to tackle. They've established themselves like a thick, defensive barrier all along the front of the hedge. Just looking at them makes my arms feel itchy.

They look vibrantly green and full of vitamins, and they'd probably keep me in soup for about twenty years. Free food! What's not to enjoy? Especially when you've got a whole cottage to paint and very little cash with which to do it. *Move over Hugh Fearnley-Whittingstall and make way for the new Foraging Queen!*

An hour later, I'm over-heating with the exertion of pulling them out at the roots, and I've gone off nettle soup entirely.

I sink down on the tree stump and wipe the back of my hand across my sweaty brow. I refuse to be downhearted. Ivy Garden is going to look beautiful by the time I've finished!

'Christ, this is a bit of a wilderness,' says a voice and I spin around.

It's the girl from the bus stop. And the garden centre.

Layla.

She saunters over and looks around as if she's the gaffer, inspecting my labours. 'You left your debit card.' She digs in her pocket and holds it out.

'Oh.' I stand up, pushing back the straggles of hair that have escaped from my ponytail, and take the card. 'I didn't realise I'd left it. Thank you. It's really nice of you to bring it over.'

Layla shrugs. 'No probs. It was on my way home anyway. So Jack says you're staying in Ivy's cottage?'

I nod. 'Just until I get it sorted out, painted, that kind of thing. And the garden, of course.'

'And then you're selling up?'

'Yep. Going back to Manchester, where I live.'

'Is that where your family is, then?'

I swallow hard and bend to toss another pile of nettles on the compost heap. Naturally, she assumes I have other family, aside from Ivy.

I paste on a smile. 'Yes, that's right. They're in Manchester.'

It's true, in a way. My friends are my family now.

Layla nods. 'Cool. You're bloody lucky you don't have to live in this dump forever.'

'Don't you like it here, then?'

She snorts. 'No. If I had money, I'd be off in a flash. No looking back. But the garden centre pays peanuts so I'm forced to cohabit with my grump of an older brother and a mad mother whose mission in life is to control what she calls my wilful behaviour and to hang on to a decrepit house that's practically falling down around our ears.' She rolls her eyes dramatically.

'How old are you?'

'Seventeen.'

Ah. Teen years. I remember them well. I stalked around resenting everything, including Ivy, for a long time. Thankfully, once I hit my twenties, I became normal again.

'Couldn't you get another job?' I suggest. 'Train for a profession, maybe?'

She gives a scornful laugh. 'What, without a single GCSE to my name? I don't think so! What do *you* do, anyway?'

'I work in a city centre café. My boss, Patty, is lovely. She's given me time off to come and get everything sorted here.'

'But you don't want to be here, right?'

I laugh. How does she know that? 'Well, I suppose it makes a bit of a change. It's – erm – very peaceful.'

Layla screws up her nose. 'But you still can't wait to get back to the city, am I right?'

I'm not sure I like the way she's standing there, arms folded, challenging me on what's quite a sensitive subject. But she's absolutely right so I nod. 'Patty's keeping my job open for me.'

'So is that really what you've always wanted to do?' she asks. 'Work in a café?' Her pale grey eyes are unsettlingly sharp.

'Well, it probably wasn't a *burning* ambition of mine when I was a kid,' I concede. 'But it's fine. I like it.'

'So why didn't you "train for a profession"?' she demands, doing sarcastic quotation marks in the air.

I draw in a long breath. 'Well . . . sometimes life can get in the way of your plans. And my circumstances meant I had to leave school at sixteen and get myself a job. Luckily, I'd been a Saturday girl at the café for a few years already, so Patty took me on full-time.'

Feeling like I'm being interviewed for a job, I glance around at the nettles still to be plucked. 'Any good at pulling up weeds?' I ask, just to get her off the subject.

She stares, probably wondering about the 'circumstances'. But I'm not getting into all of that with a slightly obnoxious teenager, who doesn't know when to be quiet. I know I haven't exactly achieved the dreams I had as a kid – of going to college and developing my talent as an artist – but who the hell has?

'What circumstances?' she asks.

Good grief, she doesn't give up!

'Oh, nothing interesting.' I leap up and grab my gloves which

I'd dropped on to the grass. 'Right, better get on. Thanks for bringing my card.'

'Bugger off, in other words,' she says cheerfully, seeming not in the least offended. 'Righto, no probs.'

'No, I didn't mean . . .'

'Hey, it's fine.' She grins. 'I'm used to being told where to go. Not in so many words, of course. My snobby mother is *much* too polite for that and my brother thinks he's being "supportive".' She does the quotes thing again. 'While actually never listening to a bloody thing I say. But hey, that's families for you. Love 'em or hate 'em, you're pretty much stuck with them.'

I swallow hard and turn back to the weeding, and Layla finally takes the hint and marches off.

A thought occurs to me. 'Oh, Layla?'

She turns.

'Do you know Jack Rushbrooke well?'

She pulls a face. 'Far *too* bloody well. He's my workaholic brother.'

'Oh.' I'm surprised, not least because as siblings, they look quite different. Jack is tall, with dark hair and blue eyes, while Layla has the sort of fair skin you can tell will burn easily in the sun. Mind you, it's impossible to tell what her natural hair colour is.

She scowls. 'He's worse than the police. He was thirteen when I was born, so he's much older than me and he doesn't approve of me having a boyfriend.'

I think of Adonis.

'You have a boyfriend?'

She blushes beneath the pale foundation. 'Yeah. He's called Josh.'

I nod. 'I think I've seen you with Adon – er, *Josh* at the bus stop.'

She looks a little sheepish, obviously remembering the time I saw them snogging.

'Who's the girl with the long strawberry-blonde hair?' I ask casually.

110

'Oh, that's Anne-Marie, my best mate. And by the way, you're in luck because it's my day off tomorrow if you want some help sorting this jungle out.'

My heart sinks. The work's hard enough without enduring the company of an unpredictable and bolshy teenager asking about things I don't want to dwell on.

'That's a very kind offer, Layla.' I smile politely. 'But really . . .'

'But really I'll probably end up doing more harm than good? Funny, I get that a lot.' Her mouth hitches up at the corner.

'No!' Guiltily, I rush to put her right. 'That's not what I was going to say at all. I'm sure you'd be a hell of a lot better than me at recognising what's a weed and what's not. I'd *love* your help.'

'Really?' She throws me a disbelieving look.

'Yes. Really.'

'So tomorrow, then?'

I hesitate, about to make an excuse why I can't be here.

But then I remember the yawning expanse of empty hours I'm facing over the weekend. 'Great! I'll be working in the house in the morning. But I'll be here in the afternoon.'

'Right, well, I'll see you tomorrow afternoon. I'll bring a couple of hoes to help with getting rid of those nettles and grasses. And if you don't want to talk, just tell me. Honestly, I promise I'll be as quiet as a graveyard.'

I nod, wondering about the 'hoe' bit of her speech. I thought a hoe was an American term for a 'loose' woman. And she's bringing *a couple*? I grin to myself. The mind boggles. But I suppose the work would get done faster.

I watch, wincing slightly, as she charges at the wall of thorns and forces her way through.

She yelps indignantly as nature fights back. 'Bloody stupid fucking hedge.'

Oh God, what have I let myself in for?

* * *

The next afternoon, I'm on the sofa drinking coffee and reading up on how best to prepare the soil to plant my wildflower seeds, when there's a sharp and insistent rap on the window just a few feet from me.

I nearly jump out of my skin with fright.

Layla is peering in at me, using her hands to block out the sun, a puzzled frown on her face. Sighing, I haul myself off the sofa to answer the door. She has a variety of mysterious, long-handled tools with her.

'Borrowed them from the shed at home,' she says, seeing my surprised look. 'My mother likes to *think* she's a gardener but with Prudence, it's mainly a case of *all the gear but no idea.*'

'Prudence?'

'Mum. She prefers Prue, so I call her Prudence.'

'Oh. Right.' I grin. 'That makes perfect sense.'

'We've got about half an acre of grounds at Rushbrooke House, mostly lawns, but all Prudence does is drift around, talking to the plants, like the lady of the manor. Jack does all the hard graft, like mowing the lawns.'

At once there's an image in my head of Jack labouring over the grass-cutting, shirt flung aside, sweat gleaming on his well-muscled chest, a bit like the hunk in the fizzy drink advert . . .

No, no, no! What is it with me and men wielding axes or doing sweaty physical labour? I give my head a little shake to dislodge the image.

Layla peers around me into the hallway, as though wondering if I have company. 'So are you ready? I thought you'd already be over there.'

We go over the road and Layla shows me how to use the hoe to tackle another batch of nettles, weeds and coarse grasses.

'So, Layla, how come you left school early?' I ask as we work side by side.

She shrugs. 'We can't all be mega intelligent. In our family, Jack got all the brains.'

112

I frown. 'I don't think that's true. You seem really bright and you've got an amazing vocabulary for a kid your age.'

'I'm hardly a kid,' she retorts.

'No, of course you're not,' I amend quickly. 'I just meant . . .'

'Yeah, I know. It's all relative. No offence taken.'

I smile to myself. 'It just seems a waste that you didn't stick at school.'

'Oh God, please don't start trying to convince me the sky's the limit if I bother to put my mind to it, because believe me, you won't get anywhere.'

She turns away and starts attacking the weeds with a gardening fork, driving it into the ground with more aggression than seems strictly necessary.

At that moment, someone appears through the gap in the hedge.

It's the boy from the garden centre. Tom. I recognise him from the green uniform. He looks around him.

'Hey, what a great place. I've heard people talking about it. It's awesome.'

His enthusiasm warms my heart and I smile at him. 'Thank you. Ivy would have been chuffed to hear that.'

He smiles back and glances quickly over at Layla, who's showing no interest at all in his appearance. 'Sorry to butt in,' he says. 'But can I give this to Layla?'

'Of course you can.'

He walks over to where she's wielding her garden fork like a weapon of mass destruction. The weeds really don't stand a chance.

'Shame you don't labour this intensively at work,' Tom quips, and she looks up at him, shielding her eyes against the afternoon sun.

'Joke.' He grins, holding up a paperback with a skull and crossbones on the front. 'A thriller with more gore and guts than a butcher's block. Any takers?'

Unimpressed, Layla sticks out her hand. 'Go on, then.' She

takes the book and plonks it down on the grass then goes back to her weeding.

'So are you going to Barton Fields?' he asks, looking around at the bluebells and the pink climbing roses adorning one of the oak trees. The roses are just beginning to bloom, although Layla has said she's going to prune them.

Before she answers Tom, she glances accusingly over at me. I quickly look away, to show I'm not listening, which seems to be little short of a capital offence in Layla's book.

'I'm probably going with Josh and a few of the others,' she says ultra-casually. 'So I guess I'll see you there.'

'Right.' Tom nods, taking it on the chin, and I feel his pain. 'Okay, well, I'll see you at work tomorrow. Enjoy the book.'

As he leaves, he and I exchange a look of amused frustration.

'That Tom is so nice and polite,' I murmur later, as we're taking a break, sitting on the grass, cooling down with bottles of chilled pink lemonade I brought from the fridge at home. 'He's funny, too. And he seems to like you a lot, although I can't imagine why.'

She glares at me. 'Well, thanks, I must say!'

'Don't be so sensitive, Layla.' I laugh. 'All I meant was you don't seem to give him any encouragement at all, yet he keeps on trying.'

'He's a geek.'

'Right.'

She sighs heavily to indicate I really haven't a clue, then tips her head back and drains her lemonade bottle.

I stare at her thoughtfully as she runs her hand over the grass at her side. 'My best subject at school was art. I can do a mean caricature. I'll do you if you like.'

Layla looks up. 'You can draw?'

I nod.

'Can you paint as well?'

'I like doing watercolours. Ivy wanted me to go to art college but we couldn't afford the fees.'

'That's a shame.'

I shrug. 'Maybe. But my point is, everyone is good at something. So what's your special talent? Apart from a photographic memory?'

She looks sulky again. 'I was the class clown at school. *That's* what I was good at. I made people laugh and I bunked off – *a lot* – because I hated it so much.'

'Why did you hate it?' I ask. 'Did you get bullied?'

She turns in surprise. 'No. Well, a bit – mostly because I didn't have a dad like everyone else.'

'Oh.' My heart goes out to her. I suppose I'd assumed her parents must be divorced. 'I'm sorry to hear that.'

'Thanks, but it's no big deal. He died just before I was born. It was one of those unexplained deaths. He just went to bed one night and never woke up.' She shrugs. 'William Rushbrooke. He was forty-five.'

She says it all so matter-of-factly. I wonder if she's had to grow a hard shell to cope with the fact that she never knew her dad.

'Mum was totally devastated apparently. But I never met him. And what you've never known and all that . . .'

'I know what you mean,' I murmur.

'Do you?'

I smile sadly. 'Both my parents died when I was four, in a road accident.'

Layla's mouth drops open. 'Oh God, that's *awful*.'

'Yes.' I shrug. 'But I didn't do too badly. I had Ivy to look after me.'

She tips her face to the sun. It's nearly June and the weather is hotting up. 'So have you got any other relatives?' she asks. 'Aunties, cousins, whatever?'

'I'm afraid not.' I smile brightly to show her it really isn't the end of the world. I hate people feeling sorry for me. 'I've got some great friends, though, back in Manchester.'

'Friends are sometimes nicer than your family,' she says thoughtfully. 'You can choose your mates and they *get* you.' She frowns. 'Mum and Jack think all my friends are a bad influence, especially Josh.'

I think of Adonis/Josh with his arm around Anne-Marie's waist. Mum and Jack may well have a point.

She flushes beneath the pale make-up. 'Josh has asked me to go with him to the live gig at Barton Fields,' she says nonchalantly. 'But don't tell Mum and Jack or they'll try and stop me.'

'Is that a music festival?'

'Yeah. It's sort of a small-scale one with bands from all over. I've never been before but Josh has been loads of times.'

Probably with a different girl every time.

She smiles. 'Josh says it's brilliant. It's on at the end of June. You should go.'

'I'll probably have gone by then.' As I say the words, my stomach does a funny little twist. *Don't say I'm getting attached to the place!* That's not good because I obviously can't stay. Not that I'd really want to. I'm just feeling sentimental, that's all.

Layla looks thoughtful. 'But I thought you still had loads you wanted to do here?'

'I do but it all costs money and I'm not earning at the moment. My savings have practically run out.'

'So it's just lack of money that means you'll have to go back earlier than you want to?'

I shrug. 'Pretty much.'

'Money rules our lives, doesn't it?'

'Some people are slaves to the filthy lucre, yes.'

'They're *what*?'

I smile. 'I just mean money can rule your life if you let it. Sometimes, though, you have to be brave and go for your dreams, even if it means coping with less money for a while.' I'm thinking of Jack and his furniture business.

We spend the next hour working in silence. Then I ask her if she knows which flowers thrive in shady woodland conditions and she starts reeling off a whole list of names that I've never heard of.

I hold up my hand. 'Hang on. I'll never remember all that. Can you send me a text with those flower names so I have it when I next go to the garden centre?' I grin. 'And maybe you could get me a discount since you work there.'

She carries on working as if she hasn't heard me.

Puzzled, I stare at her back. 'Layla?'

She turns grumpily. 'What?'

'A list of flowers? In a text?'

She shrugs. 'You don't need that. You can remember them.'

'Well, I won't.' I laugh, wondering what the problem is. Perhaps she doesn't want me to have her phone number? 'Could you write them down for me, then?'

She heaves a sigh as if I've asked her something really challenging. 'Yes, if I remember.'

I shake my head, bemused. 'Hey, it's no big deal. I'll bring a gardening book over and you can point them out, okay?'

She shrugs. 'Okay.'

Later, she wanders over to the trees and murmurs into her phone for a while, keeping her voice ridiculously low so I can't possibly hear anything. She finishes her call and says she has to go because she's meeting Anne-Marie.

She wanders over to the broken love seat and bends down to examine it. 'Shame about this. Are you going to get it fixed?'

'I thought I might have a go at mending it myself.'

'Oh, God.' She grins. 'I hope you're better with a hammer than you are with a hoe.'

'What are you doing tomorrow?' I ask, laughing at her gentle insult and surprising myself with the thought that I wouldn't mind her company. *Especially tomorrow . . .*

'Sunday lunch with the family,' she groans. 'Can't escape it. Jack's threatened to cut off my allowance if I don't show up.'

'Really?'

'Yeah. Unless there's a very good reason for my absence, of course. Like if my leg accidentally gets amputated.'

117

I laugh. 'You'd better be there, then.'

She grins. 'Yeah. Are you doing anything tonight?'

I shake my head. 'Someone was going to cook me dinner but they had to cancel.' Sylvian finally phoned me last night to confirm that the workshop dates couldn't be changed.

'Shame,' she says and turns to leave.

I suddenly remember the time I saw Sylvian in deep discussion with Layla, handing her a parcel. I've wondered about that a few times.

'Oh, Layla?'

'Yes?'

If I ask her about Sylvian, she'll probably just get all defensive on me, thinking I'm prying into her private life.

I smile at her. 'See you soon.'

'Yeah. See ya!'

It's Saturday night. And since I'm spending it on my own instead of being wined and dined by Sylvian, I decide to push the boat out and treat myself to a good bottle of wine.

In the village store, it's clear I'm not the only one planning a night in. As I stand in line with my bottle of red, the two rather glamorous women in front of me in the queue are squabbling good-naturedly over what flavour tortilla chips to buy with their chardonnay. I admire the long summery dresses they're wearing. They both look about my age.

'Ooh, candles,' says the taller, dark-haired woman, who's wearing deep pink. 'Do you have scented candles?' she asks the store owner.

He shakes his head. 'Sorry, ladies.'

The other woman, a blonde in a flowing turquoise dress, laughs and says, 'Honestly, Sara, you and your candles! I'm sure he'll have quite enough anyway.'

I listen to their chatter, trying not to feel envious. It sounds as if they're off to a party. If I was in Manchester tonight, no doubt

I'd be getting ready to meet friends. Or I'd be having Vicki and Beth round for a girls' night in. Take-away, wine, rom-com. Perfect!

Still, there's no reason why I can't have a good night on my own. I might even treat myself to *two* rental movies tonight!

The next morning, I raise a glass of orange juice to Ivy on what would have been her seventy-third birthday then quickly get into my gardening gear.

I'm planting my wildflower garden today in her honour.

It seems the perfect thing to do on her birthday. I tell myself I'm almost glad my plans for the weekend ended up being cancelled. I empty out the packets of wildflower seed into an old plastic box, mainly because I'm curious to see what they look like. Nothing terribly exciting, to be honest, and I find it quite a stretch to imagine that these little muesli-like lumps will transform into a colourful display like the one on the front of the packet.

During the morning, I work on preparing the ground, then I take a break, eating a ham sandwich sitting on the tree stump. I'm clapping crumbs off my work trousers, about to start trickling the seed on to the prepared ground, when I hear a car draw up and park beyond the hedge.

Instantly, I'm on high alert. No-one ever parks there. What if it's the council come to inspect this bit of their land? (Ivy never seemed to worry about this, but it was always in the back of my mind that, one day, the council might have plans for the area.)

Car doors slam and voices drift over the hedge, making me anxious. Perhaps I'll duck out of the way just in case. I don't feel up to answering any awkward questions.

Making for the trees, I keep my eye trained on the gap in the hedge, hoping these people – whoever they are – aren't heading in here. But in my haste to make myself scarce, I walk straight into the side of the tree stump, trip awkwardly and go sprawling on to the ground.

Lying there dazed, I realise the voices are drawing nearer, so I scramble up, rubbing my knee, which took the brunt of my fall.

Only then do I realise I wasn't the only thing to go flying: the box containing the wildflower seeds is now lying on the slope of the compost heap.

Damn! But at least it landed right side up. So with a bit of luck . . .

Glancing into the box, my heart sinks. It's practically empty. Most of the seeds have been lost and I'm left with about a dozen rattling around in there that wouldn't make much impression on a window box.

A voice drifts over. 'Well, you can hardly expect me to go commando-style through the park, all the way from Rushbrooke House.' It's a woman and she doesn't sound very pleased. 'Even if it *is* a shortcut.'

I'm about to dive into the trees for cover when I hear a laugh I recognise. 'I should hope you don't go commando-style *anywhere* at *your* ancient time of life.'

Layla?

I relax slightly. What on earth is she doing here? I thought she had a family lunch?

'What are you talking about, Layla?' demands the woman.

A third voice, male this time, says, 'Commando-style means to go around completely naked. That was just Layla's little joke, Mum.'

Jack!

Oh God, what is this? A family trip out?

I glance down at my tatty work wear and wipe the back of my hand across my mouth to get rid of imaginary ham sandwich crumbs.

'I still don't see why we had to bring the car around,' Layla complains.

'I'm fifty-eight. I don't want to be traipsing through forests at my age.'

'Bloody hell, Prudence, you're not exactly on your death bed,' Layla mutters. 'I should think you've got at *least* another twenty years left in you for annoying the hell out of me.'

'I beg your pardon, Madam? Just because my hearing is not what it used to be does not give you the right to name-call behind my back. And please don't refer to me as Prudence. I'm Prue to everyone else, but *Mum* to you.' She gives a little squeak of protest. 'Oh my gosh, you don't *really* expect me to crawl through that filthy hedge, do you? I could catch all manner of terrible diseases.'

Layla snorts. 'Don't be ridiculous.'

'I am *not* being *ridiculous*. It's been a long time since my last tetanus injection.'

'A sense of humour injection would be good.'

'Er, I *heard* that, young lady!'

'Hmm. Funny how you just happen to catch some things and not others. I think they call it being *selectively* deaf, don't they?'

'Sorry? I didn't hear that.'

Jack's deep voice interjects. 'Here, let me hold those thorns back for you, Mum. Then you can squeeze through easily. Just as well you're as slim as you ever were, eh?'

Prue laughs.

Jack's flattery has apparently worked because next second, a tall woman in a belted peacock blue suit and black patent heels steps into the clearing. She pats her shoulder-length, mid-blond hair and glances around her in surprise. 'Oh, my goodness. This is odd. I never even knew it existed.'

Layla, arriving through the gap followed by Jack, rolls her eyes. 'Well, bearing in mind you hardly ever leave the house for fear of running into The Dreaded Ribena, it's not surprising you don't know about this place.'

'I am *not* frightened of Robina Worsley,' says Prue sternly.

'I should hope not, Mum. By all accounts, she's just a sad old bully who you haven't seen in years. I don't know why you allow her to get under your skin the way you do. You should just ignore her.'

'Yes, well, you know nothing about it,' snaps Prue.

'If I were you,' suggests Layla, 'I'd probably go and tell her to —'

'Yes, *thank* you, Layla,' Jack warns.

She grins broadly and looks around, instantly spotting me semi-lurking among the trees.

'Hi, Layla.' I walk forward and exchange a nod with Jack.

'This is Holly, Mum,' says Layla. 'The gardening expert.'

I shoot her a baffled look. *Is she joking?*

Prue steps carefully over the grass towards me. 'Hello, Polly, I'm Prue Rushbrooke.' She looks around. 'Well, it's, erm, certainly interesting here. I'm sure it's going to look lovely when it's finished.'

'I'm helping her to clear the nettles and I'm going to prune the climbing roses,' says Layla. 'And it's *Holly*, Mum, not Polly.'

'You cleared the petals?' Prue looks confused. 'I wouldn't have thought the flowers would be dying off this early in the year.'

'The *nettles*, Mum,' shouts Layla close to her ear, which makes Prue jump. 'We cleared masses of them yesterday.'

'Well, there's no need to shout. And weren't you meant to be helping *me* by cleaning your room yesterday?'

Layla looks sheepish.

I chew on my lip, feeling guilty by association.

Prue turns to Jack, who's walked over to the shed and is now peering inside. 'What's your opinion, darling? Would Polly be suitable, do you think?'

'Definitely. She'd be brilliant,' says Layla.

'I wasn't asking you, dear,' Prue says frostily. 'I was asking Jack. Although why I'm not allowed to make my own decisions about things like this, I really don't know.'

I stare at them in bewilderment. *I'd be brilliant for what exactly?*

Jack frowns. 'You don't need a gardener, Mum. You've got me to cut the lawns.'

'Yes, but you don't know anything about roses,' she points out. 'And if we can chop those horrible leylandi down so they no longer block out the sun, I might be able to have a rose garden at last.'

Jack looks decidedly underwhelmed by this.

'Layla tells me you have *terrific* green fingers, Polly,' says Prue.

'Oh, she has,' Layla jumps in. 'Haven't you, Holly?' She opens her eyes wide at me, signalling something I'm definitely not getting. 'She could easily plant you a new rose garden, and I could help her.'

'What do you say, darling?' Prue turns to Jack, who's inspecting the strimmer he lent me that's been in the shed ever since.

He frowns at me. 'This hasn't been used. Is there something wrong with it?'

I shake my head. 'No, not at all.'

'You have used one before, haven't you?'

Behind him, Layla's nodding her head manically at me.

'Oh, yes. Of course. Dozens of times.' I force a smile. 'You wouldn't believe how many times a strimmer has – um – saved the day!'

'Right. Know anything about roses?' he asks.

'Do I know anything about roses?' I repeat, stalling for time. '*Do I know anything about roses!*'

I catch Layla in the background giving me an enthusiastic thumbs up.

Actually, by sheer coincidence, I was reading all about the darned things in one of Ivy's gardening books last night. So yes, I do know a bit about roses. Especially the sort that can climb trees. I start waffling on about dead-heading and greenfly and horse manure, while Layla tries her best not to laugh.

'Well, you sound just the girl for the job!' announces Prue, beaming at me.

I stare at her in alarm. 'What job?'

'Gardener at Rushbrooke House,' says Layla, grinning. 'I said you'd be great.'

Jack's eyes are fixed on me with that weird stare again.

God, I'm being grilled for a job I didn't even apply for!

'Actually, Layla did a lot of the work here,' I begin. 'She's very knowledgeable about gardens, so perhaps *she* could . . .?'

'So you're saying you won't do it?' Prue frets, completely ignoring my suggestion that her own daughter actually has the skills required.

Layla folds her arms and starts kicking angrily at some stones by her feet.

I really feel for her. She's a teenager and probably by definition not the easiest person to live with, but I happen to know for a fact she'd do a great job on the garden. Why won't they give her a chance?

Prue is looking expectantly at me, waiting for my answer.

'Well, I don't know,' I begin. 'I'm very busy getting the cottage sorted out to sell at the moment, so I haven't got a lot of spare time. And I'll be leaving Appleton soon.'

'It would obviously just be a very temporary job,' says Jack.

Prue frowns at him. 'Would it?'

'Yes. Holly has to – get back to Manchester.'

'Oh.' She peers at me. '*Manchester?* Whatever for?'

'That's not the point, Mum,' interjects Layla crossly. 'The point is: temporary or not, do you want to hire Holly?'

Prue smiles. 'Of course I do. I think she'll be fabulous.'

I try to smile but inside I'm feeling rattled by Jack's comment. Why was he so adamant that I'll be leaving soon? It almost sounded as if he couldn't wait to see the back of me! Even now, I can see him studying me out of the corner of my eye. I bet if I turn, he'll look away.

I swivel my head, and sure enough, his eyes flick away, caught in the act. What *is* it with him? There's obviously something about me that bothers him but I can't for the life of me think what it can be.

'All that work you're doing on the cottage must be costing a bit,' says Layla. 'I should imagine the money would come in handy?'

I hesitate. She's right. It would.

Prue beams at her son. Then she turns to me and mentions an

hourly rate that's ridiculously generous. I catch Jack's reaction and I can tell he's not best pleased.

But apparently what Prue wants, Prue usually gets.

'Weekday mornings would be best. Say nine to twelve-thirty?' she says. 'What do you think, Polly?'

'Holly,' corrects Jack.

Prue looks bemused. 'That's what I said. Polly.'

My mind is racing. The extra cash really will come in handy. It will mean I can afford to stay on here a little longer and get the cottage and garden completely finished. Trouble is, I feel bad accepting a job I'm not qualified to do.

'Are there no gardeners living in the village?' I ask, thinking they'd undoubtedly do a much better job than me. Even *with* Layla's help.

A shadow passes over Prue's face. She shakes her head. 'I don't want anyone from the village. I want you.'

I can feel Jack's eyes on me again. Why do I get the uneasy feeling he can see right through me? He probably knows I've never done a day's gardening in my life . . .

Then he confounds my suspicion by saying, 'So, Holly, will you do it?'

I'm so surprised, I find myself saying, 'Well, yes. Okay. I will.' Drawing in a deep breath, I smile at Prue. 'I'd be happy to help out. On a temporary basis.'

Prue seems delighted. We make arrangements for me to call by the house the following week so she can show me the gardens, then Prue and Jack start heading back to the car.

'I have to warn you, though,' I call, with a sudden attack of conscience. 'I've never done any gardening professionally.'

'Oh, we won't worry about that, Polly.' Prue flutters her fingers back at me. 'See you next week, dear.'

I watch her go.

'The first job I want to tackle is those dreadful leylandi things,' she's saying to Jack. 'Why on earth we planted them, I'll never know. They block out all the sunlight. But thankfully, we've got Polly to sort all that out now.'

I feel a bit dazed. I'd like to confess that 'Polly' doesn't even know what 'leylandi things' are, never mind how to get rid of them. But I doubt if it would make any difference to Prue Rushbrooke. I appear to be hired, whether I like it or not!

Layla gives me a sly grin. 'Well done. Those green fingers of yours have just landed you a job.'

I laugh. 'Correct me if I'm wrong, but I think you just engineered all of that yourself.'

She shrugs. 'Maybe. But everyone's happy, aren't they? You need the money. Plus, Mum will never employ anyone from the village and Jack will just get even more grumpy if he has to mow the lawns throughout the summer in his free time.' She frowns. 'Not that he has any free time. But that's sort of the point. So you see, it's the perfect solution all round.'

'Layla?' Jack calls from beyond the hedge.

'Wish I could stay here instead,' she mutters.

'Come *on*, Layla,' calls Prue in a sing-song voice. 'Auntie Joan will be expecting her Earl Grey tea.'

Layla rolls her eyes. 'Auntie Joan will be snoring her head off in the armchair after overdosing on triple helpings of sherry trifle.'

She tramps wearily off to the car.

THIRTEEN

The following week, I invite Connie round for a girls' night in.

She brings a bottle of champagne on the pretext of toasting my arrival in Appleton, and we end up telling each other our life stories, the good bits and the bad. (It's probably the champagne, but the bad bits seem even more hilarious than the good.)

'By the way, you'll like this,' she says, diving in her bag at one point and bringing out a copy of the local newspaper. 'Don't *ever* tell me village life is boring,' she laughs, showing me the front page.

The headline reads: *Who's Stealing Our Garden Gnomes?*

I raise my eyebrows at her, and we both burst out laughing.

'It's the talk of the village,' she says. 'Some nutter is going round pinching everyone's garden ornaments.'

'Nutter, eh? They might be no less sane than you or me.' I shrug. 'It could just be their idea of entertainment round here.'

Connie grins and takes another glug of wine. (We've moved on to chardonnay.) 'You really *don't* like the countryside, do you?'

I shake my head. 'Not much.'

'But why? We've got acres of space, amazing country walks right on the doorstep, and lovely pure air, as long as you don't mind breathing in the occasional disgusting farmyard smell. What's not to love?'

I force a smile. 'It's those evil bastard cows, if you must know.'

I tell her I like painting and sketching caricatures, and her eyes light up. 'Do caricatures of those two awful model-types who were in the café that time. Moira and *Sel*ena.' She emphasises the first syllable in a comical high-pitched voice and we fall about laughing.

I embrace the challenge and Connie goes into ecstasies over the result. Even *I* have to admit it's rather good. I've caught Selena's likeness especially well, exaggerating her mane of thick, glossy hair to mammoth bouffant proportions and making her fantastic cheekbones as sharp as knives. I'd noticed her gleaming white teeth had a tendency to protrude ever so slightly, so I give her proper rabbit's gnashers, which makes Connie laugh so much she nearly falls off the sofa.

I feel a bit bad that we're having a chuckle at Selena's expense, but I reason that the sketch is for Connie's eyes only. No-one else will see it.

When she's gone and I'm tidying up the kitchen before heading for bed, I pick up the caricature of Selena, remembering back to when I realised I had a real talent for sketching.

It was on one of our many trips to Blackpool.

I had a friend called Rhona, whose family booked the same week as us, at the same guest house, regular as clockwork. Rhona was the same age as me. If the weather was good, we'd spend our days on the beach, throwing a Frisbee, splashing in the sea and running away, squealing, from the suncream-brandishing grown-ups. We ate the packed lunch doorstep ham sandwiches and wedges of fruitcake provided by the guest house, kids of all ages huddled on the same sandy tartan rug, the adults reading their newspapers in deck chairs. If it was overcast, we went to the cinema or walked along the pier and went on the fairground rides.

One year, when I was about eleven, a big, ginger-haired girl called Jessie joined the group with her parents. Jessie took an instant dislike to me and decided Rhona was going to be *her* friend and not mine. She had bushy eyebrows and pillow-like lips, which she had a habit of hitching to one side in a sneer, especially when she was lording it over me. Rhona must have been flattered by Jessie's attention because she stopped speaking to me for a while and I remember being utterly heartbroken. I'd been so looking forward to seeing Rhona and now the holiday was in ruins.

It was a miserable grey day and Ivy took me to a café for an ice-cream to cheer me up. She said all the right things about Jessie being nothing but a bully and that Rhona would come to her senses eventually, but I couldn't so much as raise a smile.

Then Ivy pushed a pen and a white paper napkin across the table. 'Draw her.' Her eyes twinkled mischievously. 'Go on, Holly. Do Jessie.'

So I thought for a moment, then I drew a caricature of my tormentor, making her generous eyebrows look like jungles and sketching her big lips in a pronounced sneer that made Ivy's eyes widen with glee when I passed it back.

Doing that drawing made me feel a whole lot better, as Ivy knew it would.

I lay the sketch down on the table, thinking about my plan to apply for a place at art college once I've sold Moonbeam Cottage. I've been looking at colleges online and there are some really good ones. But before I can think about leaving Appleton and doing something new with my life, I need to decide what I'm going to do about Bee.

I keep thinking perhaps I should just leave it all in the past, which seemed to have been Ivy's intention. Maybe I should respect her wishes and leave well alone.

But what if it *wasn't* her intention to keep the secret from me? What if she'd been going to tell me but then she died before she had a chance? I keep remembering that last time I was with her, on the station platform in Stroud. She was waving me off on the train, and just before I boarded, she gripped my arms and said there was something she needed to tell me.

I should have stayed and talked to her. But Patty had needed me back in the café.

What if that had been my one chance to find out the truth – and I'd blown it?

What on earth do I wear for a gardening job 'interview'?

I've already been hired, of course, but even so, I feel I should make an effort when Prue shows me around for the first time.

My normal smart suit that I wheel out for formal occasions is hanging up in my wardrobe back in Manchester. But in any case, surely something more casual would be more appropriate?

In the end, I settle for my work outfit at the café – black, slim-fitting trousers, a white shirt and black loafers. Smart but casual. The trousers feel a little more 'snug' than usual, which I was kind of expecting. (All this fresh country air makes a girl ravenous for carbs. That's my excuse, anyway.) I examine my reflection in the mirror. As long as I'm breathing in, the trousers aren't *too* tight. I'm due at Rushbrooke House for ten and I plan to use Jack's shortcut through the woods.

I was up very early reading gardening manuals, as if cramming for an exam, hoping I could absorb some crucial facts that would make me sound impressively knowledgeable. Actually, that's a ridiculous hope. Just knowing a little bit more than zero would make me happy at this stage.

I'm crossing my fingers that Layla's working a shift at the garden centre this morning, well out of the way. I have a feeling my ability to blag my way through the 'interview' with Prue will be a hundred times more challenging if her teenage daughter is standing there, grinning away, thoroughly enjoying my discomfort.

I set off through the trees, knowing roughly the direction I'm going in, and after a few minutes, Rushbrooke House comes into view.

Now, should I cross the field or walk all the way round?

As I stand by the fence, debating, a squawking noise catches my attention.

Four ducks are waddling under the fence close to where I'm standing. I watch them, fascinated, having rarely been up so close and personal to wildlife – except for pigeons in the city.

Three of the ducks have flamboyant jewel blue plumage, while the fourth is plain and brown, obviously female. The male ducks are vying for her attention, in a very jostling, un-gentlemanly way. It puts me in mind of my Manchester local of a Friday night. One of the males just walks right over the female's head. I suppose that's as good a way as any to get a girl's attention. I'd love to know if her animated squawks mean, 'Come and get me, big boy,' or 'Bugger off.' But it's impossible to tell.

Still, she does have three guys – er, *birds* – after her, which can't be bad, can it?

It's pretty deflating for me, though. Apparently even Jemima Puddleduck's social life is racier than mine.

I pause by the fence to watch their antics.

'So what's it to be?' says a deep voice behind me.

I spin round.

Jack is standing there, lazily observing me, a glint in those deep blue eyes.

I open my mouth but nothing comes out.

He shrugs. 'Wriggle underneath or just go for it and clamber on top?' he drawls.

Huh?

My eyes swivel to the ducks and back again.

'At a wild guess, I'd say you were a clamber-on-top sort of person.' His wicked smile brings the colour charging into my cheeks.

Crikey. I knew the grapevine was bound to be constantly a-buzz in a small village like Deepest-Marsh-on-Bog, but is speculation about my sexual preferences circulating already?

'The fence?' He says it slowly as if any faster and my poor

over-taxed brain might be unable to take it in. 'Holly, I'm talking about the fence. You could go *under* it or *over.*'

Relief floods through me. 'Ah, yes, I see what you mean.' I laugh a little too raucously, and he says, 'Need some help?'

The thought of Jack manhandling me over the fence proves astonishingly motivating.

'No thanks, I can manage,' I squeak, before aiming my foot at the middle rung. There's a ripping sound – as a dodgy seam in my trousers parts company – but when I haul myself up, hop down the other side and turn to face him, Jack's face is poker straight, so I think I got away with it.

I stand back, expecting him to vault athletically over the fence after me.

Instead, he walks a few yards along, clicks open a gate that has mysteriously bypassed my attention, and coolly joins me on the other side.

I roll my eyes and he grins, a little sheepishly. 'Sorry. Couldn't resist.' He points ahead. 'Can I escort you to Rushbrooke House?'

I smile tightly, my cheeks aflame, and let him lead the way across the field.

With legs about twice as long as mine, Jack sets a fair old pace and I have an awful feeling I'm going to pitch up for my 'interview' sweating like a racehorse that's just won the Grand National. Not a great start.

We join Prue in the garden. She's bending over a flower bed, looking fresh as a daisy in beige linen trousers and a cool white shirt. I can see what Layla means about the lady of the manor thing. She's not exactly dressed to get down and dirty pulling weeds.

I'm so nervous, wondering what she'll expect me to know, that I accidentally cannon into Jack.

'Whoa!' he says and reaches out to steady me.

He grasps my hand for a second and I leap away immediately, as if I've collided with an electric fence.

'Ah, Polly, good to see you,' says Prue.

'It's *Holly*,' calls Layla in a bored voice, and we all turn to see her marching out of the house.

'Sorry, dear?' says Prue inevitably.

Layla sighs. 'Mum, why don't you get your ears checked out?'

Prue bristles. 'I do *not* need a hearing aid.'

'Well, you *do* because it's quite obvious you can't hear a bloody thing . . .'

'Layla!' barks Jack.

'It's fine.' Prue touches Jack's arm. 'Layla, dear, I'd like to have a little chat with Polly. Could you go in and put the kettle on, please?'

Layla holds up her hands. 'Okay, I know when I'm not wanted. I just thought I could help, seeing as I do actually work at a *garden centre* and have picked up a thing or two about horticulture. But pardon me for actually *breathing*.' She stalks off into the house.

'Oh, dear.' Prue looks upset. 'Layla is so crabby these days, I don't know what to do for the best. I blame the people she hangs around with. Especially that awful Josh boy she talks about. Have you met him?'

I shake my head. 'No. But I do get the impression he's rather full of himself.'

She sighs, looking anxiously back at the house. 'I shudder to think what she's getting up to, staying out so late. But will she listen to me?'

I frown in sympathy, thinking Prue would be horrified if she realised her daughter knew Sylvian, a mature man practically twice Layla's age. Perhaps best not to mention it. Sylvian's lovely and I've got no reason at all to think their meeting in the alley beside his flat was anything other than perfectly innocent.

'Anyway, let me show you the garden, Polly.'

'Holly,' I remind her, but she's already walking off.

We're just examining the sun-blocking leylandi, when Jack joins us.

133

'Come to spy on us?' asks Prue waspishly. She leans closer to me. 'Jack wants to make sure you're value for money.'

I bet he does!

I glance at Jack, who says smoothly, 'I have absolutely no intention of interrupting your cosy tête-à-tête with Holly, Mum. I was just going to offer you coffee.'

She frowns. 'But I asked Layla to . . .' She stops. 'Never mind. That would be lovely, Jack, thank you.'

He strides back to the house, and a moment later, a female voice calls, 'Coffee's on, Prue.'

I turn in confusion. That didn't sound like Layla.

'All right. Thank you,' Prue calls back and we start to make our way round the side of the house, to the back door.

'Have you met Jack's girlfriend?' she asks.

My heart drops like a stone.

Girlfriend?

Jack has a *girlfriend*?

'Gosh, no, I didn't realise.'

Prue nods. 'She's very ambitious. Has her own business. She's a top interior designer. Very much in demand.'

'Oh. Great.'

I'm not sure why I'm feeling so . . . shocked. It's weird. I mean, Jack is an attractive man; he probably has loads of female admirers. It's hardly surprising that he has a woman in his life. I suppose I'm just feeling a little shaken because he never mentioned her to me.

He loaned me his strimmer but he never thought to say he was attached!

'Are you all right, Polly?' asks Prue. 'You look a little . . . startled.'

'No, no, I'm fine. Does she live in Appleton?'

'Oh, no. Her parents live near here but she works in London. She and Jack met on the train a few months ago. Stunning girl. And quite the country-lover, too. She and Jack are really very well suited that way. You know how he detests London.' She smiles. 'Yes, if anything, I'd say she loves the countryside even more than he does.'

There's a tall, slim girl standing by the back door and when she sees us, she gives a little wave. I look over covertly, trying my best not to stare. She's got long chestnut-brown hair that's glinting in the sun

Frowning, I peer closer.

Hang on, I recognise her . . .

At that precise second, her smile freezes and I can tell she recognises me, too.

Oh my God, it's Selena. Emphasis on the first syllable.

'Hi, Prue,' she smiles as we draw nearer. 'I've just arrived.'

'Lovely, dear.' Smiling, Prue takes her hand and squeezes it before heading indoors.

Selena and I lock eyes. I feel totally bewildered. This can't be Jack's girlfriend.

She loves the countryside even more than he does, were Prue's exact words.

But I heard her in the café complaining about zombie sheep. This woman hates the countryside with a passion, just like her friend and the 'evil bastard' cows!

Selena's beautiful pale grey eyes narrow to dangerous-looking slits as I draw level. 'You're the gardener?' she murmurs with a scornful little smile. 'Pull the other one, sweetie. I was in that café, remember? I heard what you said.' And she whisks inside, clacking down the hall in her high-heeled peep-toes, tiny bum swaying in her tiny pink skirt.

I stare after her, stunned, as I recall my conversation with Connie. I vaguely remember telling her that I'd never gardened in my life.

Selena's message is loud and clear.

Bust my cover by bringing up the zombie sheep, sweetheart, and Jack will find out you can't garden to save your life . . .

135

Layla appears at the door, glued to her mobile phone, calling vaguely, 'I'm going out.'

She sees me and grins. 'Have you had the tour of the grounds? Did Mum show you the cottage in the woods?'

'The cottage in the woods? No, where's that?'

She points over the expanse of lawn at a little copse in the distance. 'There's a little cottage among the trees and Dad used to go there to do his inventing.'

'His inventing?' I ask in surprise.

'Yeah. Dad was an engineer by day but he loved inventing things as well,' says Layla, with a proud smile. 'He patented a new type of screwdriver apparently.'

'Wow, he must have been really clever, your dad.'

She nods sadly. 'I just wish I'd known him.'

'I bet he'd have been really proud of you,' I tell her.

She snorts. 'Yeah, right. Because I've achieved so much in my life.'

'Layla, you're only seventeen. Your life has barely started!'

She shrugs. 'Well, anyway, you should ask Mum to show you the cottage. It's amazing. She's preserved it exactly as it was when Dad was alive. It's pretty creepy, really. Sort of like a shrine. I once went there at the dead of night and—'

'Oh, you did, did you?' barks Jack, making us both start. He's standing at the door, frowning over at Layla. 'I wish I hadn't heard that. You know Mum doesn't like anyone disturbing the cottage.'

Layla looks guilty. 'Sorry. I just don't know why we're not allowed to go there. It's such a waste of a perfectly good place.'

'Well, never mind that,' says Jack. 'Just try and think about how Mum feels in future, okay?'

'Okay.' Layla nods glumly and glances at her phone. 'Right, I'm going.'

Prue emerges from the house. 'Not until you've tidied your room, young lady, and unloaded the dishwasher. And peeled the potatoes for tonight.'

'I'll do it later,' Layla gestures, without taking her eyes off her phone.

Prue marches after her. 'And what time is "later", may I ask?'

When Layla ignores her, she shouts, 'Make sure you're back for dinner at seven-thirty. Layla? *Layla!*'

But now, apparently, it's Layla's turn to have gone selectively deaf . . .

FOURTEEN

Connie and I have finally rescheduled our long-overdue drive out and pub lunch for today. When I pull back the curtains, it's to a clear blue sky and not a breath of wind.

It's late May and I've managed a whole week working for Prue at Rushbrooke House without any major calamities. Thankfully, the work has mostly involved weeding the vast number of flower beds skirting the lawn. I've made sure to work really hard and the arrangement seems to suit both of us. I think Prue enjoys having someone else to talk to. And so far, I've given Jack no reason to think I'm not good value for money.

As I head for the shower, I feel the old, familiar panic rising up in my chest. But I tell myself I'll be fine with Connie there with me.

She picks me up in her little Beetle at ten, as planned. As I slip into the passenger seat, she points behind her. 'Goodies. Lots of.'

I turn and nod my approval at the hamper on the back seat. 'Full of deli delectables, then?'

She nods firmly and I stick up my thumb. 'Good work.'

We drive out of the village, and almost immediately, the panic descends.

'Where are we going?' I ask, trying to sound upbeat.

Connie taps the side of her nose. 'Aha! You'll see. It's a surprise but I think you'll like it.'

'Is it far?'

'Not really. Ten miles or so. Why?'

'Oh, no reason,' I say lightly. 'It's just the city girl in me panicking at the thought of getting lost.'

I laugh to show her I'm joking.

I really wish I were.

Truthfully, I'd been hoping today might be the day I conquer my phobia once and for all, with Connie here to make things feel 'normal'. Make me laugh. I'd convinced myself I'd be absolutely fine. But the fact that we're a mere five minutes into the drive, and my insides are already grinding round and round, is not a good sign.

We've left the houses and the shops far behind now, and I know without looking that on all sides, stretching away to infinity, are miles and miles of fields. Nothing else. The phone signal will be weak or completely non-existent. Not a house or another person in sight.

Keeping my eyes fixed forward, I scramble in my pocket for my mobile and glance at it. One bar. We're all right for now, but what if we drive into a dead area? And something bad happens? *What then?*

It alarms me that my fear seems to be getting worse as the years go by. I really thought I was making progress in recent times, but now I seem to have regressed to my childhood days when all the troubles began.

Then it clicks.

Ivy.

Her death hurled me into a pit of fear and loneliness. Despite doing my best to fill the void with activity, I still miss my grandma every single day. There is no-one left in my world to love and cherish me unconditionally, like family do. No-one to make me feel I really *belong*. The stark truth is I'm totally alone now, a tiny craft bobbing about on a frightening expanse of ocean. I'm not sure I'll ever be able to make peace with that.

Beside me, Connie is chattering away about the village summer fete in a couple of months. She really relishes all these country events. I wish I could feel the same.

But right this minute, all I can think about is getting the hell out of Appleton, and going back home to Manchester and everything that's familiar. So I can feel safe.

Connie is saying my name. And again. Louder this time.

Dazed, I turn and she takes her eyes off the road for just a second, concern written all over her face. 'Are you okay there?'

I swallow down the nausea and try to smile. 'I'm fine. Really. Just feel a bit sick, that's all.'

'Oh. Are you a bad traveller?'

'Not at all.' I shrug. 'Maybe it's something I ate.'

'Do you need to stop?' She sounds alarmed. 'I can stop any time you want.'

'No, no, honestly, I'm fine. It'll pass.' I take a deep breath to try and relax. It seems to work because thankfully I can feel my shoulders subside.

'Okay. If you're sure.' Connie gives me a quick, appraising glance. 'Not long now, actually.'

'Right.' I smile at her. 'Fab.'

I settle back in my seat, determined to calm down and conquer this ridiculous fear of wide open spaces. If I can only focus on how illogical the phobia is. Because the likelihood of something bad happening to me is really very slim indeed.

But the trouble is, unlike a phobia of flying or spiders, which may not even have a relatable cause, my fear stems from something very real and catastrophic . . .

'Wilf, my great-uncle, is eighty-five and he grows the biggest marrows you've ever seen,' Connie is saying with a giggle, reverting to the topic of the village fete, I imagine to distract me. 'He always wins prizes for his veggies, bless him.'

Wilf. Despite feeling as if I might be about to throw up, I'm still conditioned to wonder about any new man I happen to hear about. Especially those over seventy. *Was Wilf the mysterious Bee?*

'Did Wilf know Ivy?' I ask.

She shakes her head. 'Don't think so. He's lived in Lancashire all his life.'

'I haven't told you about my new job,' I say.

She swings round. 'New job? Where?'

I grin, glad of the distraction. 'At Rushbrooke House.'

'Ooh, for hunky Jack Rushbrooke?'

She grins across at me and I find myself blushing. 'No, no, it's his mother, Prue.'

'Prue? Oh, God.' She makes a face.

'What do you mean? What's wrong with her?' I ask, alarmed.

Connie back-tracks. 'Oh, nothing. She's probably a very nice person. It's just everyone in the village thinks she's a bit of a toffee-nosed cow, to be honest, looking down her nose at everyone.'

'Really? Tell me more.'

Connie shrugs. 'Well, she's determined to hang on to Rushbrooke House, despite the fact that it's literally tumbling down by all accounts. I think she enjoys being lady of the manor. I've never once seen her in the village, mingling with the locals. She never comes into the deli, which is a bit odd, don't you think?'

I concede that yes, I do think it's weird. But I also know from Jack that she's been through tough times.

'I get the feeling there's some mystery about her past,' Connie says, 'but I've no idea what. I just remember Mum and Dad making sort of weird faces at each other if ever she was mentioned. Like they knew something but didn't want to gossip. *And . . .*' She lowers her tone and leans towards me. 'I was once in the village store and two women were chatting as I squeezed past, and I distinctly heard one of them say, "Well, of course, Prue Rushbrooke was a *prostitute* at one time."'

There's a beat of silence.

Then I bark with laughter and swing round to Connie, thinking I must have misheard her. '*Prue?* We *are* talking about the same person, are we?'

Connie shrugs. 'I know. Weird or what?'

'Lady of the manor, most definitely. But *lady of the night*?'

Connie giggles. 'It does seem a stretch, I'll admit.'

'It's probably just the rumour mill working at full throttle. These small villages . . .'

'That's such a cliché,' accuses Connie.

'What? That people in villages are all gossips?'

'Yes!'

I nod. 'I'm sure you're right. There's actually only *one* gossip in every village and she's usually called Ethel,' I joke.

I was trying – but failing – to picture Prudence Rushbrooke in a scanty get-up plying her trade in a seedy part of Cirencester. (*Was* there a seedy part?) It was too ludicrous for words.

It was as bizarre as saying, *Well, of course, the Queen was a man before she had her sex change.*

'Apparently, she was left with nothing but debts when her husband died,' Connie adds.

Now, that I *could* believe. 'Poor Prue,' I murmur, thinking how hard it must have been to find herself on her own with two young children to bring up, Layla a mere babe in arms.

We're silent for a moment, then I turn to Connie. 'Did your parents once live in Appleton? Is that why they have the deli-café?'

'Dad comes from Cirencester but Mum grew up here, in the flat above what's now the deli-cafe. It was just a plain, old-fashioned bakery in those days, run by my granddad. When Mum and Dad took over, they turned it into the bakery/café that it is today. A few years ago, they opened another deli-café in Cirencester.'

She grins. 'I think they're expecting me to follow in their footsteps – yet another generation of the Halstone family devoting their lives to feeding people!'

'Except you're going to be a teacher,' I say, desperate to keep the conversation going so I can try and forget where I am. The vast acres of fields on either side of the road are making my head spin every time I glance to the left or right.

Connie nods. 'I do love baking and making people happy with my food, though. Last week, I made up this incredibly moreish recipe for chocolate mousse cheesecake, using chocolate digestives for the base and . . .'

I stare ahead, a smile fixed to my face, as Connie talks on.

And then I see it.

Way ahead.

I have to screw up my eyes. But it's definitely there.

A tractor.

Orange with those giant black wheels.

I shudder and grab hold of my seatbelt.

It's travelling the same way as us, about half a mile up ahead. Probably doing no more than twenty miles an hour.

'You'd better slow down,' I say, interrupting Connie's description of the dark chocolate swirls on her cheesecake.

She glances at me in surprise and peers ahead. 'Oh, for the tractor?'

I nod, not taking my eyes off it.

'One of the downsides of living in the country,' she remarks. 'Farm machinery galore hogging the roads.'

My insides shift queasily. I keep clenching the seatbelt at my shoulder, eyes glued to the giant orange contraption, as Connie continues to spin along happily, eating up the distance, closing in on the tractor.

My heart rate goes into overdrive.

'Please slow down.' The words sound thick; my mouth is so dry. 'Of course.'

Connie brakes. But not enough. Not nearly enough . . .

We're sailing towards it, too close. *Far too close* . . .

'Please stop the car.'

'Sorry?'

'*Stop the car!*'

Connie gets the message, slows to a crawl and pulls on to the grass verge, cutting the engine.

I watch the tractor lumbering away from us.

Connie turns to me, her eyes wide with concern. 'Hey, what's wrong, love? You're shaking. Aren't you feeling well?'

I shake my head and release my clutch on the seatbelt, my arms slumping at my sides.

'Look at your poor hand!'

I glance down. My right hand is resting on the gear box, palm up, deep nail imprints visible from where I was gripping the seatbelt.

'Can we go back?' I whisper. 'I wasn't ready for this.'

Connie's face is full of sympathy. 'Of course, love. Let me just find a farm track to turn around.' She moves off, scanning the road ahead urgently.

We drive back in silence and I clutch my heart the whole way, waiting for my breathing to normalise. Connie keeps darting anxious looks at me. At last the village comes into view.

I stare exhausted out of the window as we drive past the little row of shops. Relief at being 'out of danger' is coursing through my veins but I'm also devastated to the point of wanting to cry my eyes out. I thought I'd cope, facing my fears head on. But apparently I'm nowhere near being 'cured'.

Suddenly, my attention is caught by a familiar figure. Sylvian. He's standing outside his flat door, talking to Layla. They're laughing about something and just as we pass, he hands a small package to her and she slips it into her bag. It's the secretive way she does it, casting a furtive look behind her, that strikes me as odd. *What on earth is in the package?*

Connie draws up outside Moonbeam Cottage and asks if it's all right for her to see me inside.

'You'd better.' I attempt a smile. 'Otherwise you never know where I might end up sleeping tonight.'

She grins at my feeble joke, gently takes the house key from my hand and walks ahead up the path to let us into the cottage.

After ordering me to flake out on the sofa, she rootles through Ivy's drinks cabinet and finds some brandy. The first swallow is like fire and makes me gasp, but it does make me feel a little calmer.

'Would you like to talk about it?' Connie asks, after a moment.

I nod, but then my throat chokes up so I can't speak.

'Was it to do with your mum and dad?' she probes gently. 'I heard they died in a car accident.'

I pick up the brandy glass and take a large, eye-watering swig.

Then, after a few long shaky breaths, I tell her the whole story.

'I was only four when they died so I don't remember much about them. I grew up believing what Ivy told me – that they'd gone for a drive in the country while Ivy was looking after me and they'd crashed into a tractor. My parents and the tractor driver all died instantly and Ivy was always extra keen to emphasise that they wouldn't have known anything about it.'

Connie's eyes are huge. 'But that's not what really happened?'

I shake my head, staring at the floor. 'I was ten when I found out the truth. One night Ivy had the next-door neighbour round for a chat. It was a school night so I was supposed to be in bed but for some reason I couldn't sleep, so I crept out of bed and sat on the top stair, thinking I'd shout down to Ivy that I was thirsty. The stairs led directly into the living room where they were sitting, so I could hear every word they were saying.' I glance up at Connie, my heart beating fast at the memory. 'They were talking about the day of the accident.'

'Oh, God,' breathes Connie. 'Poor you. And Ivy had no idea you were there.'

I take a big breath. 'Ivy said the police told her that according to the tyre marks on the road, Mum and Dad must have been driving at some speed along a straight bit of road, with the tractor up ahead. Dad must have started to overtake, still at speed because

146

the road ahead was clear. But just as he approached from behind, the tractor started turning right into a field, directly into Dad's path. Maybe the farmer didn't indicate or perhaps Dad just didn't *see* him indicating. We'll never really know. But anyway, Dad just couldn't stop in time and he smashed right into the tractor.'

'Are you okay?' Connie touches my hand. 'You're as white as a ghost.'

I nod, although I'm feeling far from okay. But something is urging me on, making me relate what had happened for the very first time. I've had nightmares for years about what I heard, sitting on the stairs, but I've never, ever talked about it. Even Ivy never knew that I'd found out the truth, listening in to her conversation that night.

'You don't need to go on,' Connie says.

'But I want to.' It's odd, this sudden, overwhelming compulsion to get it all out. I suppose it's way overdue . . .

FIFTEEN

I swallow audibly, psyching myself up to start talking about that day. Connie takes my hand and squeezes it gently.

'A spike of metal from the wreckage of the vehicles drove through Mum's abdomen, pinning her to the seat. My dad suffered trauma to his heart. He was obviously conscious for a while because he was clutching his smashed phone when the paramedics arrived nearly an hour after the crash.'

'The paramedics took that long to get there?' says Connie, horrified.

I shake my head. 'The paramedics weren't to blame. It was the fact that the accident happened on a quiet road in the middle of nowhere. It was a good twenty minutes before another passing vehicle stopped and called the emergency services.'

Connie takes my hands in both of hers. 'And all that time, your poor parents . . .'

I nod. 'I can't imagine the pain Mum must have been in, and how Dad must have felt knowing he could do nothing to help her because his phone was broken.'

'So did they die at the scene?' Connie whispers.

'No. When the paramedics eventually arrived, they were both still alive, although Mum was obviously bleeding out and in huge distress, and Dad was unconscious by that time. They both died in the ambulance on the way to the nearest hospital which was thirty miles away.'

A tear rolls down Connie's face and I swallow hard, within a breath of breaking down myself. 'Ivy said Mum died from blood loss. There was a chance she could have survived the trauma of the injury – and Dad, too – if only they hadn't been so far away from civilisation and a hospital.'

I grit my teeth. This was the bit that gave me nightmares even now. 'So because they were right in the middle of the *frigging countryside* when it happened, they never stood a chance.'

And then I *do* start to cry.

I sob noisily on Connie's shoulder, my heart breaking as if it had happened only yesterday. Connie's brilliant, hugging me hard and telling me to just get it all out.

At last, I calm down and Connie produces some paper hankies from her bag and makes me a cup of hot, sweet tea. The sugar makes me gag but I smile and tell her it's just what I need.

She wants to stay to make sure I'm okay, but I finally manage to convince her I'll be fine. I just want to curl up in bed.

'Are you sure?' She frowns, examining my face.

'Absolutely. And Connie?'

'Yes, love?'

'You've been amazing.' I smile at her. 'Thank you.'

After she's gone, I feel so exhausted, I'm convinced I'll just flake out and sleep. But I can't. No matter how many sheep I count, I just lie there, tormented by the reel of clashing images rolling by on a loop in my head. In the end, I go downstairs in my pyjamas and stare at the TV screen, not really watching. Then I lie on the sofa and try to do the meditation Sylvian taught me, thinking perhaps that might calm my mind and help me to relax.

It does the trick because I fall asleep right there on the sofa.

When I wake, it's already dark outside. Rubbing my gritty eyes,

I climb the stairs and slide between the cool sheets, my head still full of the drive with Connie.

Ivy and I should have discussed my parents' accident a long time ago, then maybe I wouldn't have built up the horror of it in my head as I have done. It all happened so long ago. Yet tonight, it feels horribly overwhelming, as if it only happened yesterday.

I catch sight of Ivy's diary, still lying on the bed. Reading it might make me feel she's still here with me. I prop up the pillows, settle myself on the bed and start reading slowly through the pages, hearing her voice in my head, still hoping to find some clue that I missed the last time.

When I'm finished, I flick through the rest of the pages. They're all empty. Every last one. I go back and read the final entry again, with mounting frustration that this is all there is.

I wish there was more . . .

Then I look more closely at the page with the last entry. That's strange. Maybe it's a trick of the light, but it looks thicker than the rest.

My heart rate quickens. It *feels* thicker, too. And that's because there are two pages stuck together.

How did I not notice this before?

Carefully, so as not to tear it, I slide my finger in to loosen the corner, where the two pages seem to be attached. And sure enough, when I prise them apart, there before me are two more sides full of Ivy's handwriting.

Heart thudding in my chest, I begin to read:

4th December 1966

What a night! Where do I begin? I should be feeling so sad and guilty this morning, but instead, I'm filled with such happiness, I think I might explode!

We rarely give dinner parties at home – mainly because I can barely boil an egg without burning the pan. It was Peter's idea. He's been doing some business with Henry Chicken, who lives in the village with his extrovert wife, Henrietta, and he asked me if we could invite them over for a meal. He seemed really keen on the idea and I hoped that it might be the start of a new, more sociable life for us, so I agreed. Then the numbers grew and the upshot was, there were eight of us (including Peter and me) sitting down for dinner last night!

This was the guest list:

Henry and Henrietta
Ben and guest (he brought the lovely Lucy Feathers)
Mr H and Penelope

I was slightly worried how everyone would get on. (Ben and Lucy hadn't met Mr H and Penny.) But as it turned out, we all had a marvellous night. Everyone loved the main course, which was quail and roast vegetables with a redcurrant sauce, and the Crepes Suzette for dessert went down very well indeed! The men also enjoyed Peter's single malt far too much! He didn't seem to mind at all, though. In fact, Peter probably drank more than everyone and ended up very drunk. (But happily drunk, for a change.) In the end, I had to help him up the stairs, which he didn't even remember this morning.

And somehow, late in the evening, Bee and I found ourselves alone together, as I knew we would. Even when I was planning the evening, I think I realised that this would be the night. That finally, we would give in to our feelings and my life would change forever . . .

I've been sitting forward, devouring every single word Ivy wrote. Now, I slump back on the pillows, stunned. The evening of December 4th 1966 had been a truly momentous one for Ivy. That was the night she finally gave in to her passion for Bee.

She must have really loved him to give herself like that while my granddad was still alive. I knew Ivy well enough to know she must have agonised for a long time before giving in to her strong feelings and starting an affair.

So now I knew the truth. Ivy's relationship with Bee wasn't simply a friendship and a flirtation. It had gone much deeper than this, starting on that night in December.

And there was more . . .

13th January 1967

I can barely believe it! But it's true! I finally went to the doctor's today and he confirmed what I already knew, but was too scared to hope was true.

Tears are rolling down my face on to the page as I write this. Our baby will be born in September! (My due date tallies with the night of the dinner party.)

It would be so incredible if only . . .

I want to run to Bee and tell him the amazing news, but more than ever now, our relationship must remain a secret. I can't do it to Peter. He's always wanted a family. Could I really deny him that now?

My only comfort is that Bee will understand.

I've never felt so emotional in my life – down one moment, high as a kite the next. I'm finally having a baby, and it's such a glorious feeling!

In a way, it feels as if it's meant to be. Even persuading Peter that he's the father should be easy.

Peter came into my room, drunk, one night before Christmas and we had sex for the first time in months. It was miserable because it's so obvious he no longer cares for me. But that coupling – desperately sad though it was – will serve a very important purpose. It means Peter can believe that the miracle he was told might never happen has come true. He will be a father. He won't calculate the dates, I'm fairly certain of that. He's always wanted a family. So maybe we can all be happy . . .

There, the diary ends.

Stunned, I flick through the rest of the pages. But this time, I know for sure that there is no more.

For the next few hours, as the sun comes up, I stare into space, thinking of the incredible ramifications of this latest revelation.

Ivy had a baby with her lover, Bee.

That baby was my mum, so Bee was her father.

And my grandfather . . .

SIXTEEN

I need to see Sylvian. His warmth and wise words about life are just what I need to help me think straight.

Despite the humid, summer night, my limbs feel chilled and stiff with sitting in the same position for so long. I glance at the clock and a little shock runs through me.

An age has passed since I found the pages stuck together in the diary. Literally hours. It's almost midnight! I really want to talk to Sylvian but will he still be up so late? Should I be disturbing him at this hour? He did say I could knock on his door any time of the day or night. Perhaps I'll just walk along there and see if the lights are on in his flat.

Jack's words flash through my mind. *Selena heard some rumours about Sylvian . . .*

But I brush them aside. Sylvian is a good person. And he's so caring and generous. If he were the sort to behave badly with women, surely he would have had his wicked way with me by now? Let's face it, he's had plenty of opportunities.

And anyway, I wouldn't trust that Selena as far as I could throw her. It's quite ironic that Jack should be warning me about Sylvian, when really, it should be *me* warning *him* about Selena. With her elegant little outfits and horror of sheep, she sticks out like a sore thumb in the countryside, whatever she might protest to the contrary. Why can't Jack see that?

A little voice in my head whispers: *Maybe he does see it, but he loves her anyway, because love is blind.*

My heart twists. But I shake off the thought and climb out of bed, dressing in my jeans and top from earlier. I pause only to run a comb through my hair. It doesn't matter that my face is scrubbed bare of all make-up. My skin is lightly tanned from working in the garden and looks healthier than it ever has. And anyway, Sylvian doesn't judge people on superficial looks. He's got much more substance to him than that.

I leave the cottage and walk along to Sylvian's flat, breathing in the balmy night air. The moon hangs over the village green, a pearly crescent set in a navy velvet sky. As I walk, the moon's presence grounds me and, at the same time, makes me think about the mysteries of life. We're like little orbs of light ourselves, going about our daily business and striving for our individual goals, but it's our connections with others – family, friends, even the stranger you exchange a smile with in the street – that make all the striving worthwhile.

All my family had gone and I was learning to live with it.

But now . . .

I'm still trying to take it all in. It seems incredible that, thanks to Ivy's romance with Bee, my mum was born – *and so was I*! I can still barely believe it. I might have a granddad! He might, even now, be staring at this moon, marvelling at how beautiful it looks.

My heart swells with emotion.

I don't know how I'll track Bee down. I don't even know if he's still alive. But I *will* find him.

Sylvian's living room window is in total darkness. Disappointed, I slow to a halt and turn to walk home. I really wanted to see him. The diary revelation has rocked the very foundations of what I thought was true, and I know for a fact I won't sleep tonight.

'*Holly?*'

156

I spin round. Someone is sprinting along the pavement towards me.

Miraculously, it's Sylvian.

'I thought it was you.' He stops in front of me, not even out of breath. 'I was on the village green, looking at the moon. I'd rather appreciate it with you, though.' He smiles and takes my hand.

He takes my hand. I smile at him. 'Lovely.'

He leads me across the green, shining his phone light in front of my feet so I can see where I'm going, and we stop beneath the branches of an ancient, gnarly oak tree. The moon sails out from behind a wispy cloud at that moment, casting an eerily delicate light over everything.

I like that Sylvian hasn't asked me what I'm doing out at this time. It's as if he just accepts this is the way it's supposed to be. Sort of serendipity at play. That's what it feels like to me, too.

'I've been lying looking up at the stars,' he says, sinking to the ground, cross-legged. 'Why don't you try it?'

I follow his lead – a lot less gracefully, it has to be said. (With Sylvian I tend to feel a bit clumsy and awkward, like a baby elephant larking about in the mud.) The grass feels cool beneath my hands as I lean back and breathe in the gloriously sweet scent of – actually, I haven't a clue, but I'm sure it's some really pretty flower with an unpronounceable name.

Sylvian is so close, our arms are touching and I can feel his body heat. He draws in a deep breath and blows the air out slowly.

'Do you know what day it is next week?' he asks.

I think rapidly. *Election day? A month to the day since we first met? Wednesday?* 'Um, is that a trick question?'

He chuckles softly. 'No. I just wondered if you realised that next Monday is Midsummer Night.' He lifts my hair and places his lips gently on the side of my neck, holding them there. His delicate touch sends little electric pulses pinging off in all directions to the furthest outposts of my body. 'The night when druids and pagans and lots of other folk gather to mark the summer solstice.'

'Do you celebrate Midsummer Night?'

He nods. 'I've been down to Stonehenge many times. It's cool to be there. But this year, I thought I'd like to celebrate it with you.'

'At Stonehenge?' I ask alarmed. I'm not sure communing with the universe is really my thing. I'd be bound to stand out like a sore thumb somewhere like that, amongst all those folk in weird costumes.

He chuckles. 'No. I thought somewhere closer to home.'

'Where?' I can't help being intrigued.

'It's a surprise.'

'Ooh!'

'So put next Monday night in your diary.'

I smile at him. 'Okay. I will. If I can squash it in among all my other exciting appointments.'

'Excellent. I look forward to it,' he murmurs, lying back and staring up at the moon.

I lie down beside him and he asks me about my past, and I find myself telling him everything, even about my parents' horrible accident. I stop short of talking about the diary, though. For some reason, it feels too soon to tell anyone about that. I need to hug it to myself for a while first. Explore how I feel about it and decide what I'm going to do.

When I talk about Mum and Dad, he takes my hand and tells me how his own parents have both died, although much more recently than mine, when he was in his early twenties. I feel even closer to him when I hear that. I want to roll over and hold him tightly and make him feel safe, even for just a moment. We can shield each other from the fears and the dark thoughts . . .

Meanwhile, it's nice to be just lying here, holding his hand.

'You'll get on well with Abby and Sara,' he murmurs. 'They'll love you, I'm certain of it.' He chuckles. 'Abby's the organiser. If I tell her you're trying to fix up the cottage, she'll be wanting to come up and help.'

'They know about me?' Surprised, I swivel round to look at him.

'Yeah. I speak to them on the phone most days.' He turns and flashes me that lovely, serene smile. 'Naturally, I talk about things – and *people* – that are important to me.'

'Oh.' I swallow hard. Sylvian talks to his friends about me? And I'm *important* to him? But we hardly know each other.

I haven't been important to anyone in that way for quite a while, though, and it feels nice.

A brief image of Adam making his gym Twiglet feel important on a deserted beach whizzes into my mind. She's welcome to him. I'd far rather be lying here with Sylvian, staring up at the stars, with that feeling that I might just be on the brink of something special . . .

'You should come down to Cornwall,' he says. 'I want to show you the house. It's incredible. And the girls would love to meet you.'

'I'd like to meet them, too,' I tell him, feeling suddenly rather shy.

'Good.' He squeezes my hand. And after a pause, he says, 'You know, family comes in all shapes and sizes. Just because we have no blood relations, doesn't mean we can't make a family of our own . . .'

'Gosh. Um, I suppose not.'

Crikey, what's he suggesting? I've only known him for a few weeks. It's a bit too soon for babies.

He suddenly swings up, on to his elbow, and looks directly into my eyes. 'Sorry. That didn't come out right. I just meant there are all sorts of family set-ups out there and none of them less valid than the rest.'

Relieved, I smile at him. 'I know what you mean.' I love that he talks about deeper issues and really *thinks* about things.

'It must have seemed as if I was coming on too strong just then.'

'No, no.'

He sighs. 'The trouble with me is I tend to accept what my intuition tells me, without question. And right now, it's telling me that it feels absolutely right to be lying here with you in this moment.' His mouth twists into a smile. 'Of course, society would probably argue that taking time to "think things through" is far more important than something as ridiculously unscientific as intuition.'

His green eyes burn with intensity as he looks down at me, and I feel a strong urge to reach up and kiss him.

'Who cares what society thinks?' I smile, feeling fired up by his passion. 'Not me!'

He nods approvingly. 'Good for you, Holly. I wish more people thought that way. People should trust their intuition more and let themselves just go with the flow. Do what comes naturally.'

'Sounds perfect,' I sigh, stretching my limbs languorously. I'm feeling deliciously light and carefree under this beautiful moon with this beautiful man, who seems to like me very much.

The feeling is mutual. I'm liking Sylvian more and more.

I knew talking to him would be the right thing to do. I should listen to my own intuition more often! My head was all over the place after reading the stunning final pages of Ivy's diary. But having spent time in Sylvian's tranquil presence, I'm feeling much calmer now. I just need to relax and things will work out exactly the way they're supposed to . . .

'There's a fantastic art college near where we live in Cornwall, you know,' he says.

I raise my eyebrows, not knowing quite how to respond to this.

'You're a free agent, Holly. You have no-one else to consider now. You can go anywhere you like in the world, and Cornwall's just as good a place as any. In fact, it's better. I know I'm biased, but it's a dream location for anyone studying art. All those beautiful seascapes and glorious scenery.'

My heart bumps faster at the thought of attending art college. Sylvian's right. Once the cottage is sold, I can go anywhere I want.

I sigh. 'It must be so lovely living right by the sea.'

He nods. 'It is. When I'm there, I do my morning yoga on the beach then I run along the edge of the sea for miles if the mood takes me. It doesn't feel like a work-out. It's pure pleasure.'

'It sounds wonderful.'

He settles back down on his back and snakes his arm around me, pulling me into his side. It feels so good lying there, breathing in the balmy night air, so close to Sylvian I can feel his heart beat. I can't think of anywhere else I'd rather be.

'By the way, how do you know Layla?' I ask, suddenly remembering I've been meaning to ask.

'Layla?'

'Yes, you know. Layla. She lives at Rushbrooke House?'

'She's nice,' he says. 'Very clever and wise for her age. She likes you a lot.'

'Does she?' I ask, pleased. 'So how did you meet her?'

He's silent for a while. Then he chuckles. 'That would be telling.'

'Tell me.'

'No.'

'Please?'

He squeezes me closer. 'Absolutely not.'

I laugh. 'No, come on. Spill. Or I'll tickle you.'

He smiles. 'Sorry, I'm sworn to secrecy. Layla's stipulation, not mine.'

'You can tell *me*, though. I'll keep your secret. You can trust me.'

He leans over and kisses me very gently on the lips, which feels heavenly. 'I'm sure I can,' he whispers. 'But I've given Layla my word. So I'm afraid you'll just have to start the tickling.'

'Right, mate. You've had it!'

A tickling session ensues and soon I'm giggling uncontrollably, while trying desperately to keep the noise level down. It is four in the morning, after all, and I really don't want a reputation for getting up to mischief on the village green at all hours . . .

Later, when we're lying all relaxed again, staring up at the stars, I start thinking about Bee again. Who is he? Where is he? Does he live here, in the village? What if he lives in one of these cottages overlooking the green? What if my laughter has woken him up and he's looking out even now at the two people lying staring up at the moon?

But that's too mind-bending a thought. There's no point fantasising about who my granddad could be. I need a concrete plan if I'm going to find him.

Perhaps I should confide in Sylvian. Being an objective outsider, he might have some constructive ideas about what I should do. Because right now, the inside of my head is about as clear and capable of logic as a muddy puddle.

But just as I'm about to broach the subject of the diary, he squeezes me closer and says, 'Holly? Have you ever heard of tantric meditation?'

SEVENTEEN

It's nearly six and already light by the time I finally fall into bed. I think I will sleep now, thanks to Sylvian.

I'd drifted off for a while on the green with Sylvian's arms around me, and I woke just as the sun started to rise. We parted with the delicious thought of Midsummer Night on our minds. He still won't tell me what he's got planned.

A banging on the door drags me from sleep less than three hours later. My head is pounding and my mouth feels dry, almost as if I have a hangover. It must be because of the events of yesterday. Finding those extra pages in the diary. Learning I have a granddad I never knew about. It was all so emotional. Then spending such a lovely time with Sylvian.

The tantric massage sounds amazing. Incredibly powerful. I've never heard of it, I must say. But I'm looking forward to exploring it with Sylvian on Monday!

Yawning, I pull on my dressing gown and go downstairs.

It's Layla, wondering why I'm not over at Ivy Garden. She's in a petulant mood, having fallen out with Prue again – over very little, as far as I can make out.

As she grumbles away, I can feel myself growing impatient. I'm exhausted after last night and I want to be on my own so

I can really think about the startling new development in my life. Bee.

But Layla keeps ranting on about Prue, following me around the cottage to make sure I hear every last shouty syllable, making my headache even worse.

At last, I cry, 'Stop!'

She halts in mid-sentence.

'Layla, your family loves you, so why not stop criticising them and start appreciating what you have! Honestly, have you any idea how lucky you are?'

She's staring at me, shocked, and I'm already regretting my outburst.

Pursing her lips angrily, she blurts out, 'It's all right for *you*. Ivy thought you were wonderful, but my family just thinks I'm a waste of space!'

'So make them proud!' I say, gently but urgently. 'Stop hanging around at the bus stop wasting time with Josh and doing whatever the hell it is you do round the back of the newsagent's with Sylvian!'

She looks alarmed. 'What? Sylvian? But it's nothing—'

I shake my head. 'I've seen you with him, thick as thieves the two of you. And I saw him hand you parcels. I dread to think what you're up to – and with a man who's almost twice your age.'

I've obviously hit home. She's glaring at me, her face flushed with anger.

'Sylvian is a nice man,' she says tightly. 'He's – helping me.'

'What about the parcels?'

She flushes scarlet. 'That's none of your business.'

'Look, I'm just saying this because I care about you and I don't want you wasting your life. You've got a brain. You could do so much more.'

'So because I like talking to Sylvian, I'm obviously up to no good?' she yells.

'You tell me.'

She laughs incredulously. 'You don't think there's actually something going on with me and Sylvian, do you?'

'Well, is there?'

'*No!* I'm hardly going to fancy him, am I? I mean, he's *really old*.'

'He's no more than thirty!'

She shoots me a puzzled look. 'Yeah, exactly. He's *ancient*.'

I decide to let that one pass.

'Look, Layla, you need to start believing in yourself. Prove to your family that you can make a real success of your life. What is it they say? The best revenge is doing well?'

She grins, liking this idea. Then her face drops again. 'Trouble is, it actually doesn't matter *what* I do or don't do because nothing is ever good enough for them.'

She folds her arms and looks sulkily at the ground, but not before I notice the slight sheen to her eyes.

'Hey, your family loves you to bits, however harsh they might be,' I say softly. 'And don't you *ever* forget that. You know what would make them happy? If you went back to college and studied for your exams then took up a proper career.'

She glares at me, her eyes glittering with angry tears. 'It's so simple to you, isn't it? But you really haven't a clue. It would take me *years* . . .'

'Of course it wouldn't.'

'Oh, believe me, it would.'

'But you're so bright! I honestly think you'd get straight As if you really put your mind to it!'

'Yeah, right.' She laughs scathingly. 'You're living in cloud cuckoo land, as my dear mother would say, if you really think that.'

We lock eyes for a moment and her chin trembles.

Then she storms off down the garden path, almost slamming the gate off its hinges.

I trail into the kitchen, exhausted, a feeling of deep sadness washing over me.

I hate myself for shouting at her and possibly breaking the delicate bond we've forged over our work in Ivy Garden.

What if she doesn't come back?

I'm surprised at how sad this makes me feel. I've got used to her moods and her daft jokes, and that wise way she has of knowing how I'm feeling almost before I realise it myself. I'd miss her a lot if she didn't come back . . .

On the other hand, I can quite see how she drives Prue and Jack to distraction with her lack of thought for others and total inability to plan for her future.

Then I think of it from Layla's point of view. She's worked wonders with Ivy Garden already and has obviously picked up a lot of knowledge working at the garden centre, so why on earth didn't Prue ask *her* to help, instead of employing me?

Reliability, I suppose. Prue wants someone who will show up when they're expected, which is not something she could take for granted with Layla. And that, of course, would lead to more family friction. Perhaps Prue just wants to avoid making things worse between her and her daughter? Still, I think I will mention Layla's green fingers to Prue next time I see her. Not that I want to talk myself out of a job, of course. My weekly wage is proving very useful indeed.

I make some tea and go back to bed, still feeling exhausted after yesterday's incredible discovery. It still hasn't properly sunk in that I have a grandfather, somewhere out there.

Connie phones and we chat for a while, and all the time I'm wondering whether I should tell her about the diary. At one point she actually asks me if I'm all right because I sound a bit distant. But I assure her I'm just tired.

I'm still not ready to tell anyone about my discovery. I need time to process it myself first and decide what to do. Because I'm not even sure where to start . . .

Just as I finish talking to Connie, there's a knock at the door. It's Layla again.

She nods across the road. 'Just been over there and the nettles are sprouting up again. I could do with some help.'

I smile at her, knowing this is her way of apologising. The storm has raged and blown itself out in the blink of an eye. Teenage hormones! I'd rather be on my own to think, quite frankly, but the last thing I want is for Layla to feel she's being rejected all over again, so I say, 'Okay. Give me a mo and I'll get dressed and join you.'

We work in the garden in companionable silence for a while, which suits me because I want to think about the diary. The mystery lover she called 'Bee'.

Layla breaks into my thoughts. 'Was Ivy really strict with you when you were my age?'

I stop digging and lean on the fork to think. 'I went through a stage of being embarrassed because she was so much older than all my friends' parents. I cringe now to think how I behaved. But I'm sure Ivy understood it was just my age.'

'It would be nice if Prudence could be understanding,' she says testily.

I sigh. 'Teenagers and parents. It's not easy. You're definitely not the only seventeen-year-old who's felt misunderstood. But you have to remember that your mum is just acting in a way she thinks is best for your welfare. And sometimes you sort of have to read between the lines of what she says to you.'

'What do you mean?'

'Well, just because she's sometimes hard on you, doesn't mean she doesn't love you. In fact, quite the opposite. Jack as well. They just want what's best for you. They think they're doing the right thing by being a bit tough with you sometimes. They want you to make something of your life.'

'I suppose so.' She sighs. 'But Mum's not exactly a great role model as far as that's concerned.'

I glance at her, puzzled. 'What do you mean?'

Layla shrugs. 'She refuses point blank to go into the village. She makes up all these excuses like she prefers to do her shopping in Stroud – but I know it's because she's terrified she might bump into her arch enemy, this witch called Robina Worsley.'

'Really?' Prue doesn't seem like the sort of person who'd be intimidated by anyone. 'Why is she afraid of her?'

She frowns. 'No idea. Won't talk about it. Classic case of denial.'

'It's sad she can't be part of the village community.'

'I know. She's never even been to the Appleton summer fete. Can you believe that?' She gives me an incredulous look. 'She loves the helter skelter and they have one at the fete every year – and all she does is stare at it from the upstairs study window. I've seen her. Of course, she'd deny it if you asked her.'

We're silent for a while, absorbed in our own thoughts.

'It's funny,' I say at last, 'you can think you know someone inside out, know everything about their life and what makes them tick. And then you discover something surprising about them that totally rocks your world and makes you realise you never knew them as well as you thought you did.'

Layla glances at me curiously. 'Oh, yeah?'

I nod, thinking of Prue. And Ivy and Bee.

'Sounds to me like you're talking about something else altogether now,' Layla says, with a sly sideways glance.

I glance across. 'No, no.'

She gives me a doubtful look.

'Fancy some lemonade?' I quickly offer. 'This is thirsty work.'

'Do you have anything stronger?' Layla perks up at the mention of refreshments.

'Such as?'

She grins. 'Cider?'

I laugh. 'In this heat? You'd fall asleep on the job. And anyway, you're too young.'

Layla shrugs. 'That's only in pubs. Obvs. I'm allowed to drink at *home*.'

I collect some soft drinks then return to Ivy Garden, smiling to myself. Layla can sound wise beyond her years at times, but then in a flash she'll betray how young she actually is. A typical teenager, really . . .

I'm itching to ask her about Sylvian again but I know I have to go carefully. She could very easily storm off again if I ask the wrong questions.

'So have you known Sylvian long?' I say, when we're sitting on the grass with our drinks.

She shrugs. 'Just since he's been living here. Why?'

It's my turn to shrug. 'Nothing really. He just seems a bit older than your other mates, that's all.'

She narrows her eyes at me. 'That doesn't mean I can't be friends with him, does it?'

'No,' I say carefully. 'I would just hate you to get yourself into trouble and ruin your future, that's all.'

'And that's going to happen because I'm friends with Sylvian?' she snaps. 'You do realise I've had this lecture already – from Mum and from my dear brother?'

'They care,' I tell her simply. 'And so do I.'

'Well, you don't need to worry about me. *Any* of you. I'm well able to look after myself.'

'I'm sure you are, I say softly. 'I just got worried when I saw Sylvian giving you those parcels.' I shrug. 'It was probably perfectly innocent and I definitely don't want to pry, but—'

She gives a harsh laugh. 'But you're going to anyway.'

I sigh, torn between the impulse to let it drop and wanting to reassure myself that she's not up to anything dodgy.

'You know,' I say carefully. 'If you're doing anything you'd rather your family didn't know about, you can always talk to me about it. You can trust me, I promise.'

She keeps staring down at the grass, her face set in a frown.

At last, she looks up. 'You really expect me to believe you're not going to just run off and tell tales to Mum and Jack? *If I tell you . . .?*

My heart starts beating a little faster. 'You have my word.'

Oh bugger, please don't let it be too bad. Otherwise it's a promise I'm going to find very hard to keep . . .

EIGHTEEN

'So what's with the terrified look?' Layla demands. 'I'm not dealing drugs, if that's what you think.'

'I didn't for one moment imagine you were, Layla,' I say, hoping I sound sincere. 'But I can tell from your face that *something's* going on and I just think that if we're going to continue working together in the garden, we need to be able to trust each other.'

She glares and folds her arms.

'Look, we can't talk here. Why don't we go back to Moonbeam Cottage?' I suggest, but her obstinate expression remains in place.

'Okay.' I shrug. 'That's a shame, though. I made some ice-cream with the wild raspberries you found the other day and I wanted you to taste it. See what you thought. I've never tried making ice-cream before and I'm sure you're more of an expert than I am.'

She sighs, relenting. 'Okay.' She eyeballs me fiercely. 'As long as you say you believe me that it's nothing bad.'

'I do believe you.'

'Good.'

We gather our things and walk back over in silence to Moonbeam Cottage. My mind ticks over nervously all the way.

Okay, so not hard drugs, then. That's a relief. But perhaps it's something else that's habit-forming? And if so, I'll have to try and persuade her it's not a great idea. Trouble is, I'm not exactly experienced in this kind of thing . . .

Once inside, I serve up dollops of the raspberry ice-cream, which luckily has frozen nicely and is a big success. Layla gives it the thumbs up. When we've finished, she clears away the bowls and I follow her through to the kitchen.

'So are you going to tell me?' I ask, keeping my tone cheery.

She leans back against a worktop and folds her arms, and for a moment, I think she's going to flatly refuse. Then she heaves a long sigh. 'Okay, but if I tell you, you've got to swear on your life you won't breathe a word to Mum and Jack.'

My heart sinks. She looks so agonised, it *has* to be something really bad, which puts me in a terrible position. How can I *not* tell her mum?

'Promise?' she urges.

'I'm not sure I *can* promise that, Layla.'

She closes her eyes in exasperation at me.

'And actually,' I tell her, hardening my tone, 'if you *don't* tell me what's in those packages, I might have to tell your mum and Jack anyway. For your own safety.'

'You think I'm smoking weed or something, don't you?'

I smile sadly at her. 'Hey, Layla, you'd hardly be the first teenager who went down that particular experimental route . . .'

'I am *not* buying *weed*!' she interrupts, flushing an angry red. 'How *stupid* do you think I am? I couldn't afford it anyway, but that's not the point.' She shrugs and says sheepishly, 'I did try it once and it had no effect whatsoever. Plus I hate real smoking. It makes me cough and I've seen pictures of what it does to people's lungs and I'd never, ever do it.' She gives a melodramatic shudder. 'Disgusting.'

Relief washes through me. I look at her quizzically, waiting.

'Okay, here goes,' she sighs. 'But I'm warning you, if you laugh, I'll be straight out of here and you'll never see me again.'

Her eyes are wary, and to my surprise, I see tears glittering on her lashes.

She tips up her chin and says defiantly, 'I write mystery stories.'

My eyes open wide with astonishment.

Mystery stories?

Is she serious? On my list of possible activities going on in the lane with Sylvian, writing mystery stories would come way down the pecking order. Her confession is *so* not what I was expecting, that I almost laugh, which I've been strictly warned not to do.

She's staring at me anxiously, her face tinged pink beneath the make-up.

I clear my throat. 'Wow. Mystery stories. Phew.'

I'm flabbergasted, and at the same time mightily relieved I'm not facing some horrible moral dilemma of whether or not to tell Prue and Jack their daughter is wandering down a dubious path in life.

She smiles shyly at my astonishment. 'They're probably not very good. But I like writing them.'

I shake my head in genuine admiration. 'And you've kept this a secret from everyone? Your mum and Jack? Honestly, Layla, if I'd written anything, I'd be so proud I'd want to tell the whole world.'

A ghost of a smile appears on her face. 'I've written about a dozen short stories.'

'Really? Crikey, I haven't got enough imagination for *one* story, never mind a dozen! I could fill a book with sketches but as for having the imagination to dream up a story from scratch . . .' I shake my head in amazement. Then something occurs to me. 'Hang on, what has this got to do with Sylvian?'

'He helps me,' she says with a shrug. 'He doesn't do any of the writing but he keeps an eye on my grammar and lets me know if he thinks something could be worded better.'

I gaze at her, feeling bad for underestimating her and thinking the worst. Just like Prue and Jack, according to Layla. She seems so grown up all of a sudden.

'So what's in the packages?' I ask. They didn't look manu-script-shaped to me.

She smiles sheepishly. 'My old phone. It's knackered really, but the record function still works, so I dictate the stories into it and Sylvian types them into his computer and puts them on a dongle for me.'

'Oh. Don't you have a computer you can use at home, then?'

Her face falls and she twists her mouth uncertainly.

'Oh, don't tell me, Jack doesn't trust you to use it?'

She looks puzzled for a second then her face clears and she laughs. 'No, it's nothing like that.'

I wait.

'No, it's just that . . .' Still she hesitates.

'Yes?'

She folds her arms and blows out her breath in frustration. 'Okay, I suppose I'm going to have to tell you. Here goes.' She closes her eyes for a moment as if drawing strength. Then she looks at me challengingly. 'I can't read or write properly. There, what do you think of that?'

My mouth opens in surprise but nothing comes out.

'Sylvian's great. He's promised not to tell a soul. People would bloody laugh their socks off if they knew I wanted to be an author.'

'No, they wouldn't.'

'Yes, they would.' Layla's brow knots fiercely. 'I'm dyslexic, you see. It takes me a hundred years to just *read* a book, never mind actually write one down. All those thousands of words.' She laughs bitterly. '*I've* never heard of a dyslexic author, have you? What an absolute frigging hoot!'

I'm still trying to comprehend all of this.

There have been clues to her dyslexia but I didn't twig at the time. There was her reluctance to write me that list of plants. I'd put it down to her being lazy or stubborn. Was that the reaction she'd faced from people all her life? Just because she was too embarrassed to admit she suffered from dyslexia?

Layla shrugs. 'I'm dyslexic but we didn't find out until I was eleven. Mum and Jack – and the teachers as well – all thought I was just a pain in the arse pupil who couldn't be bothered to learn and only wanted to be the class clown. What they didn't realise was that *I* thought I was as thick as two short planks because I couldn't keep up with the other kids, so I *made* myself not care. I got the other kids on my side by acting the idiot and entertaining them. So then they didn't laugh *at* me . . .'

She frowns. 'I've got all these stories in my head so I speak them aloud into my phone and Sylvian types them into a computer for me. I made him swear on his collection of crystals that he wouldn't breathe a word to anyone about it.'

I'm full of sympathy and admiration for this feisty, intelligent girl, who's clearly battled all her life with the thought that she must be stupid because she struggled to read and write like everyone else. I can't imagine what that must have felt like, at school, when all you wanted to do was blend in. And how challenging later on in life when even applying for a job – filling in all those application forms – is a struggle.

'Oh, Layla, I never realised. But I still don't understand the secrecy.'

She shrugs. 'When you're dyslexic, you get used to people thinking you're stupid or just a lazy arse. If I went round telling people I write books, they'd bloody laugh like drains. Mum and Jack included.' She laughs harshly. '*Especially them.*'

I shake my head. 'Of course they wouldn't.'

'Yes. They would,' she snaps, her expression fierce. 'My dear mum and brother think I'm a total waste of space and actually, I don't blame them. They want me off their hands. And that's what *I* want as well. But unfortunately, because I can't string a frigging sentence together or read properly, I can't study for exams or get a well-paid job that would mean I could afford my own place.' She shrugs. 'So I'm stuck living with them. And they're stuck with me.'

'Have you shown your stories to anyone? Apart from Sylvian?'

175

She shakes her head vehemently.

I decide to be bold. 'Would you let me read one?'

She flushes bright red and it's clear she's wavering. She wants to show me. But she's scared I'll laugh, bless her.

'Please? I'd be really honoured if you'd let me read a few pages.'

Finally, she nods. Her smile is vulnerable and hopeful at the same time, and I feel a great sense of privilege, being permitted entry into Layla's own private world. The pressure not to let her down, however, is huge.

'You mustn't tell Mum or Jack,' she begs.

'Why not? They'd be as amazed as I am that you've kept such a wonderful endeavour all to yourself.'

She shrugs. 'I doubt it. I haven't exactly made them proud so far, have I?' She says it defiantly but her chin does a tell-tale wobble that she disguises by pressing her lips together. 'So it has to be our secret.'

I nod. 'Our secret.'

Layla looks down, pursing her lips as if she's mulling something over.

When she looks up, there's a shyness there I've never seen before. 'Would you . . . would you *really* like to read one of my short stories?'

I smile broadly. 'Layla, I'd absolutely love to.'

She clearly can't wait for me to read it because she disappears off to Rushbrooke House straight away and returns less than half an hour later with a manuscript in her hand. With a shy smile, she hands it over to me and says, 'Keep it overnight.'

I nod solemnly. 'I'll read it tonight. Thank you.'

'I'll go, then,' she says with a rabbit-caught-in-the-headlights look, and she dashes off, clearly terrified at the thought of me reading her work.

I feel incredibly honoured to be the first (after Sylvian) to learn of Layla's secret scribbling – and to be allowed to read some of it, too! It can't have been easy for her to hand over that story. I settle down on the sofa as soon as she's gone to start reading. Strangely, I feel nervous, too – I'm probably almost as anxious as Layla right this minute. I know I'd be terrified to let someone else read something I'd written, in case they thought it was really bad and were too polite to say so.

Even as I open the folder filled with typed pages, I'm already composing in my head a kind and gentle let-down. Just in case her story isn't very good. But when I start to read, my shoulders – which have been positioned somewhere around my ears with the stress – begin to relax.

Half way through, there's a smile on my face – even though one of the characters has just met a grisly end. Thank God! Layla can actually write.

If you ignore the fact that almost every paragraph ends with an exclamation mark (even two, sometimes), her mystery story is really very readable. Layla's talent for writing black comedy is clear and I laugh out loud on several occasions. Before I fall asleep, I quickly text her to say how brilliant I think her story is, smiling to myself as I imagine how pleased she'll be.

Summer

'Summer was a book of hope. That's why I loved and hated summers. Because they made me want to believe.'
— Benjamin Alire Sáenz (*Aristotle and Dante Discover the Secrets of the Universe*)

NINETEEN

When the doorbell rings early next morning, I know exactly who it will be.

I open the door with a big smile. 'Your story's brilliant.'

Layla peers at me anxiously. 'You're just saying that to be nice.'

'No, I'm not. If I didn't like it, I'd say it had potential or something. But I do like it. I like it a *lot*. You have real talent as a writer, Layla.'

'No, I don't.' She frowns as she crosses the threshold, but I can see a smile fighting to get the upper hand.

'You bloody well do. Look, I don't want to give you false hope here, Layla. I'm definitely no expert on literary matters. But I know what I like – and I *very much like this!*'

I'm surprised to feel hot tears pricking my lids.

Layla lets out a girlish shout of delight. Then she clamps her lips together to hide her glee.

She sits down at the kitchen table while I fill the kettle. About to swing her boot-clad feet on a chair, she catches my eye and crosses her legs instead.

'How long have you been writing these stories?'

'Oh, since I was about fifteen, I suppose. I was meant to be studying for exams but we all knew there wasn't much point because I was going to flunk the lot. So I used to escape into my imagination instead. It seemed like a far better use of my time to be honest. And it was fun, just opening my mouth and seeing what came out in the recording.'

'But you must dream up the plot first, before you start dictating it into your phone?'

'Yeah. Of course. That's the easy bit. Choosing the right words is much more like being back at school – but in a good way.'

I laugh. 'So you have all the right words but not necessarily in the correct order?' I quip, remembering something Ivy used to say.

'You what?' Layla looks puzzled.

I shake my head. 'Don't suppose you've ever heard of Morecambe and Wise.'

She frowns. 'Are they an R & B band?'

'Comedians. From way before your time.' I reach into the cupboard for the tin of oatmeal cookies. As I arrange them on a plate, I'm smiling to myself at the whole 'suspicious package' misunderstanding. It's a good lesson for me in not jumping to conclusions, and I'm sure Prue and Jack would also be pleasantly astonished if they read Layla's work.

'What's this?' I hear Layla ask. 'Have you been writing a diary?'

Diary?

My heart leaps.

I spin round and Layla is flicking through Ivy's notebook, which I'd left lying on the worktop.

'No!' I snatch it out of her hands and she looks at me in alarm.

I shrug awkwardly, holding the diary behind my back. 'It's – um – not mine. It's Ivy's diary.'

'Wow. Should you be reading it?'

Her question makes me blanch. I hadn't thought about the moral angle. Maybe Ivy wouldn't have wanted me to nosy into her private thoughts? But then, if I hadn't read it, I wouldn't have discovered her incredible secret. And even though she never got round to telling me about him, Ivy would have *wanted* me to find my real granddad, I'm sure of that. She certainly wouldn't have wished me to be all alone in the world, like I am now.

'Are you all right?' demands Layla. 'You've gone as white as a ghost.' She kicks out a chair. 'Sit down before you fall down.'

I slump into a chair, emotion threatening to overwhelm me.

'What's going on?' demands Layla.

I shake my head, but Layla cuts me dead.

'Don't say "nothing", like I'm a child who needs protecting,' she snaps. 'I get enough of that at home. You've helped me, so now it's time for *me* to help *you*.'

I smile at her. I very much doubt she'll be able to help, but Layla is like a dog with a bone. If something's bugging her, she will not let it go until she gets answers. And actually, maybe she *can* help? I can't keep this all to myself. I've got to confide in someone or I'll go mad. And Layla seems as good a choice as any. For starters, she could probably tell me all about Henry and Henrietta Chicken. And she might even be able to shed light on the identity of Ben, Lucy Feathers, Mr H and Penelope, Ivy's dinner party guests.

So I tell her the whole story. Of finding the diary and reading all about the dinner party and Ivy's baby confession.

Layla listens intently, not saying a word.

'So there you are.' I swallow hard. 'I might have a granddad I never knew I had.'

We stare at each other, the words vibrating in the air between us.

Layla breaks the silence. 'Bugger me. It's like something out of *Long Lost Family*.'

I laugh, which breaks the tension. 'I suppose it is.'

'So when do we get started?' She rubs her hands together.

'What do you mean?' I ask, faintly alarmed.

'Well, obviously you need to work out who Ivy's secret man

was, and I'm the ideal person to help you because I'm totes into solving mysteries.'

'Yes, but this isn't an episode of *Miss Marple*. It's my *life* we're talking about. Not some exciting whodunit.'

She frowns. 'Don't you want my help, then?'

I hesitate.

'I know the Chickens, for a start,' she says, leaning forward, a gleam in her eyes. 'I think we should start there. We could go and interview them. And they'll know the others who were at Ivy's dinner party that night. I think I know who Ben is – and I met Lucy Feathers at the Appleton summer fete once. They might know who Mr H and Penelope are because I've never -'

'Hold on, hold on!' I laugh to hide the panic rising up in my chest at the very thought of speaking to these people. 'We – *I* can't just pitch up on the Chickens' doorstep and start asking questions about Ivy and prying into their personal lives. It's just not the done thing.'

Layla snorts. 'Sod the done thing. You thought you didn't have any family, Holly – and now it looks like you might! *Just think about it!*'

'Of course I'm thinking about it! I haven't actually thought about anything else since I read the diary!'

'Well, you need to act on it or you'll go mad.'

My head is spinning, and I'm not sure if it's because Layla is storming on ahead with barely a thought for how I'm feeling about all of this, or because I know my life might be about to change forever. Ivy's secret has the potential to make all my dreams come true.

I might have family!

Layla's eyes are shining. 'Well? What do you think?'

I give her a tiny smile, touched by her eagerness to help me.

Maybe Layla has a point. I don't want to barge into people's lives like a bull let loose in a branch of Collectibles. But perhaps this isn't the time for subtlety and caution. Not when there's so much at stake.

'We need to make sure we don't upset anyone,' I tell her carefully. 'After all, my real granddad might not even know I exist.'

She points at me gleefully. 'You said "we"! So we're a team!'

My heart is drumming excitedly, wondering what we might uncover, but I need to put the reins on Layla.

'You can help me figure it out,' I tell her. 'But we are *not* Inspector Barnaby and his sidekick, okay?

TWENTY

Next morning, there's a sharp rap on the door as I'm standing in the kitchen, eating buttered toast. I quickly finish the last bite and put the plate in the sink.

I haven't even made it to the hallway before the knocking resumes, much louder and with three times the urgency.

It has to be Layla. Patience is definitely not one of her major strengths.

'Got a surprise for you,' she beams when I open the door.

'A surprise?' I repeat warily.

I can't help feeling nervous. The last time she said that, she flipped over a rock with her foot to reveal the most gargantuan spider I'd ever clapped eyes on. Then she screamed with laughter at my horrified expression.

She grins. 'You don't need to look so worried. You'll like it. Come on.'

She's already half way to the gate.

'Layla, I'm not going anywhere in my pyjamas,' I point out, and she grins and says she'll wait while I get dressed, but I need to hurry because otherwise the bird might have flown the coop.

'Is this a real bird?' I ask, trying to keep up with her loping stride along the main street ten minutes later.

She looks at me as if I'm mad.

'The bird that might have flown the coop?' I prompt.

Her face clears. 'Oh, right. No. Well, *sort of.*'

I peer at her expectantly.

She shrugs. 'It's a chicken. Well, two chickens actually.'

My heart sinks and I slow my pace. 'Hang on, Layla. Please don't tell me we're heading for Henry and Henrietta Chicken's house?'

'Why not?'

'Because I'm not ready,' I tell her tetchily. 'And it really *isn't* up to you, Layla, to decide how I'm going to proceed with this.'

Her eyebrows shoot up. 'Ooh, keep your feathers on. You want to know if Henry is your granddad, don't you?' She raises her arms in a melodramatic shrug of expectancy, then stares at me as if I'm as brainless as one of her barnyard chickens.

'Yes, of course I do,' I tell her firmly. 'And I appreciate you wanting to help, Layla. But we'll do it my way, okay?'

She rolls her eyes and I take a deep breath as my heart hammers away at the mere thought of actually meeting Henry Chicken.

I suddenly realise I'm holding my breath, which might account for the feeling of disorientating light-headedness, as if I've just stepped off a fairground waltzer and can't make my legs move in the right direction.

If I'm honest, it's hard to believe I'm even *having* this conversation with Layla, discussing the best way to approach possibly finding my real grandfather. I feel like I'm in a weird sort of dream, wandering through the pages of a novel, like a less brave Alice in Wonderland.

I need to keep my feet on the ground, though, and not get too carried away. If this were a story in a book, I'd be practically guaranteed a happy ending. But what are the chances that my probings into Ivy's past will result in a happy ever after . . .?

I do want to meet Henry. Of course I do. I want to find out about *everyone* who was at that fateful dinner party.

But the truth is, I'm petrified of what I might find.

And how am I supposed to find out if Henry had an affair with Ivy? I can't just blurt it out, as in *Hey, Henry, did you and Ivy have a thing going and if so, do you think it's possible I might be your love grandchild?*

What if he actually *is* my grandfather but he's horrified at me turning up out of the blue like this? If he and Henrietta were together at the time of the affair, she could be in total ignorance of her husband's indiscretion, so he's hardly going to welcome me pitching up at his door and asking him awkward questions.

He might deny all knowledge of an affair and threaten to call the police if I harass him any more . . .

Layla is studying me, arms folded, tapping her foot impatiently. 'You don't get anywhere being a mouse,' she says. 'Come on. Let's find your family.'

I nod and she sticks up both thumbs triumphantly then leads the way to Henry and Henrietta's cottage. I've never seen her move so fast.

She strides along the main street, a girl on a mission, then takes a right turn into the unmarked, potholed road that's already familiar to me after I trailed Jack to his swimming session that night.

I'm managing to keep up, despite the fact that my legs are quaking with a mix of nervous anticipation and plain old-fashioned terror.

Layla opens the gate of the Chickens' cottage and I swallow hard, remembering Henrietta popping up out of the hedge with her binoculars.

An attack of cold feet descends and I shake my head as Layla holds open the gate for me.

'Why not?' she frowns.

'Just no.'

'But you've come this far. You can't chicken out now.' She snorts at her unintentional joke. 'Chicken out!'

'Yes, I can.'

'But don't you want to *know*?' Her face is a picture of exaggerated teenage disgust, as if I've casually remarked that dog food makes a nice change from cornflakes in the morning. 'Christ, I'd be *desperate* to find out if I were you.'

Her range of disparaging expressions is truly breathtaking. I'm learning a great deal about teenagers. Apparently you have to mentally dilute their frustration by about a hundredfold and then you might be near the truth. So in this case, I can probably assume that Layla is *mildly surprised* I'm not more eager to know if Henry is kin.

'Yes, of course I want to find out,' I tell her in an urgent stage whisper. 'But not like this.'

'Why not?'

'It's too sudden. You haven't given me any time to think. I mean, what the hell do I *say*?'

She smiles and grabs my wrist. 'Don't worry about that. You don't have to say anything. *I'll* ask the questions.'

I snatch my arm back and hiss, 'Layla, for God's sake, you're not frigging Hercule Poirot. Now will you *please* come back to Moonbeam Cottage and we can talk about this sensibly.'

A key grating in a lock makes us both flinch. We turn to find a small, balding man standing in the cottage doorway. He's wearing a maroon dressing gown and neat glasses.

'Good morning, Layla.' He looks at us expectantly. 'Can I help you, ladies?'

I plaster on a smile as my heart leaps up and down like a kid on a bouncy castle. 'Er, no, it's fine. Sorry to disturb. We, er, got the wrong cottage.' I shoot dear Hercule a warning glance. 'Didn't we, Layla?'

'Did we?' She looks confused for a second but I know it's an act. 'No, I don't think we did.' She adopts a butter-wouldn't-melt expression. 'You are Henry Chicken of 3 Rose Cottages?'

Henry looks slightly taken aback. As well he might, bearing in mind he's lived all his life in this tiny village and so has Layla.

He adjusts his glasses. 'What's this about, Layla?'

I grab the back of her jumper, hoping to subtly drag her back up the garden path but she's inching determinedly forward, detective persona well in charge.

'It's about Ivy,' she says. 'Ivy Grainger?' She turns to me. 'Holly's granny.'

Henry looks at me.

Behind the little round glasses, his eyes widen. '*Holly?* Is that really you?'

Swallowing hard, I nod.

'Well, blow me down,' Henry breathes, gazing at me as if he's just clapped eyes on the eighth wonder of the world.

I stare back at him, my heart leaping in my chest. I'm certain I've never met him before but he seems to know me.

How does he know me?

His eyes are kind. They're a blue-grey colour, just like mine. And he has the same fine hair that's impossible to handle on a damp day – except that he's lost most of his.

I open my mouth to speak but my throat is bone dry.

Have we found him? Was Henry the love of Ivy's life? Is he the grandfather I never knew I had?

He's still looking at me as if he can't believe his eyes.

Perhaps he always knew about me and has been hoping that one day, I'll turn up on his doorstep just like this?

He opens his mouth to say something, at which point Layla, unable to contain her excitement for a second longer, squeaks, 'So did you and Ivy have a secret affair, then?'

Horrified, I nudge her hard, making her squawk with indignation this time.

Then I force a hearty laugh. 'Teenagers, what are they like? Don't you want to just *murder* them at times? Ha ha ha!'

Henry blinks at Layla. 'Secret affair? With Ivy? What on earth are you talking about, my dear?'

My heart sinks a little. Of course he and Ivy weren't a couple. Talk about jumping to conclusions.

On the other hand, Henry could be denying it in order to protect his marriage . . .

Layla groans with disappointment. 'So you and Ivy didn't . . . *you know?*' She illustrates her question with a helpful shagging action.

Henry's eyes nearly pop out of his head. This is awful. I have to get her away . . .

'Yoo-hoo!' trills a voice behind us.

We both spin around. Henrietta is sailing up the street, a fuchsia pink smock billowing around her ample figure, her bright auburn curls tied back with an orange scarf.

'Layla!' she booms, panting up the path. 'To what do we owe this very definite pleasure?' She peers at me. 'Don't I know you, dear?' My eyes are riveted by a bead of perspiration snaking down between her enormous perfumed breasts.

I hesitate. What can I say? *Yes, you do know me. You were popping up out of a bush in your nightwear last time we met . . .*

'It's Ivy's girl,' says Henry. 'Holly. Remember? I couldn't quite believe it was her, all grown up. She was knee high to a grasshopper the last time we saw her.'

Henrietta smiles. 'Ah yes, of course, the Holly and the Ivy.' She lays a hand on my arm. 'Your grandmother was a delight, my dear. You must miss her terribly.'

I nod as a pang of sadness whacks me in the gut.

Layla snorts appreciatively. 'The Holly and the Ivy. I never thought of that.' She links my arm and whispers, so only I can hear, 'Aw, so in a way, that was your song, wasn't it?'

Taken aback at the contact, I smile at her. 'I suppose it was. In a way.' I give her arm a little squeeze.

Henrietta is snuggling up to her husband, towering over him by a good six inches, giving his bum a playful squeeze. Henry's hand reaches round her waist as he gazes up at her adoringly, and I get the impression they've briefly forgotten we're there.

Layla and I exchange a glance.

'Hen, my Huggy Panda Bear?' murmurs Henry.

She smiles. 'Yes, my Luscious Honey Pie?'

'Layla and Holly would like to know if I had a fling with Ivy.'

His tone is perfectly calm. He might just as easily have said, *Layla and Holly would like to know if we prefer Spain or France for holidays.*

I fill the stunned silence with a gulp, as Layla tightens her hold on my arm.

Huggy Panda Bear stares down at her Luscious Honey Pie in confusion. Then she gives a throaty laugh. 'Well, no disrespect to your grandmother, Holly – she was a perfectly lovely lady – but why on *earth* would my Henry ever feel the need to venture elsewhere for his afternoon delight?' She gives her husband a coy smile and he blushes bright red with pleasure.

'When we met, it was an *irresistible magnetic attraction*,' she booms, thrusting her bosom closer with each word, as if she's impatient to devour Henry right there and then.

Layla frowns. 'I take it that's a "no", then?'

'That would indeed be a "no",' agrees a besotted Henry.

'Not even an – erm – quick shag that you forgot about?'

'Layla!' I dig her hard in the ribs and shake my head at the surprised couple in apology.

'What?' demands Layla indignantly. 'We've got to be sure, haven't we?'

'Thank you.' I smile at them and herd Layla through the garden gate. 'Our mistake. You've been really helpful.'

'What about before you were married, Henry?' calls back Layla, as I frogmarch her away. 'Did you know Ivy way back then?'

'We married at eighteen,' Henrietta bellows cheerfully. 'And my Henry was most certainly a virgin. I realise you might find that hard to believe because he's such a *sexual firecracker* . . .'

I glance at Layla and she grimaces.

'It was always meant to be,' shouts Henrietta. 'Even our names go together.'

Layla snorts and mutters, 'Well, obviously, they *don't*. Unless you're writing a book for five-year-olds and the main characters are two naughty piglets.'

'Layla! I think they're lovely people.'

She looks a bit abashed. 'So do I. I didn't mean *they* were naughty piglets. Just that their names sound weird together.'

I turn to smile and wave, just in time to catch Henrietta pulling her husband indoors with undoubtedly a little more than lunch on her mind.

We walk side by side in silence for a bit. My mind is whirling. I've actually met two of the guests at Ivy's dinner party all those years ago. It makes the puzzle real somehow. But I definitely need to get Layla under control because she's embarrassingly unstoppable when she's on a mission. On the other hand, I can almost certainly cross Henry Chicken off my dinner party list, and that wouldn't have happened if it wasn't for Layla – however cack-handed her methods might be . . .

If Henry *was* in love with Ivy, surely I'd have spotted some sign of regret or guilt or at least *recognition* in his expression? But frankly, the poor man just looked bamboozled.

'Christ,' says Layla as we head along the main street. 'Imagine being married to that.'

'Henry? He seems nice.'

'No. I mean sex-crazed Henrietta.'

I grin at her. 'Henry looks the picture of health. I don't think he's complaining.'

She makes a vomiting face. 'I'm surprised she hasn't suffocated him by now. You can bet she'll be the one inventing the weird positions.'

'Layla! I don't want images like that in my head.' I bump her sideways and she almost falls into the hedge with an indignant shout. I smile to myself, wondering what Layla would think about Henrietta and her binoculars, spying on her brother? She'd probably consider it hilarious and go round telling everyone in the village. I'd better keep the unsavoury image to myself for now.

'Right, I'm off,' she says, noticing Josh is in the bus shelter, talking to one of his mates.

'Layla – how did you meet Sylvian?' I ask suddenly.

'Why do you want to know?' She darts a suspicious look at me as colour rises in her cheeks.

I shrug as if it doesn't really matter. 'I just wondered how you first got to know him. He's a bit older than your friendship group.'

She smiles. 'I went to one of his poetry talks, hoping I might get some tips on writing. I chatted to him afterwards and he was really encouraging. See ya!'

She saunters coolly across the road, over to the bus stop. A car whizzes towards her and I shout a warning, but she doesn't even slow her pace.

Josh is grinning over at her. I'm really not keen on that boy . . .

'Er, Layla?' I call.

'What?'

'I'd like a word, please.'

She sits down beside Josh but I beckon her over.

'Right *now*?' She looks sulky.

'Yes, right now. We need some ground rules. If you want to continue helping me, that is.'

She sighs and doesn't move.

'Of course, if you don't *want* to help me crack the case, that's absolutely fine.' I start walking away.

Three seconds later, she shouts my name.

'Yes?' I don't bother turning round.

'I've probably got ten minutes,' she yells, sounding extremely narky.

I keep on walking. 'We'd better be quick, then, hadn't we?'

Back at Moonbeam Cottage, I make us a cool drink and take the glasses through to the living room, where Layla is lounging on the floor. She gulps hers down immediately then lies flat, stretches her arms over her head and gives a huge yawn. 'That was good fun. When are we doing Ben?'

'Could you sit up, Layla? This is a serious business and we can't have meetings lying on the floor.'

'Crikey, keep your wig on.'

'Right, so you're with me in this?' I demand once she's sitting up straight.

'Yes. I told you that, didn't I?'

'Just making sure. Because if we're going to do this, we can't just go barging into people's lives asking all sorts of impertinent questions, okay?'

Layla purses her lips. 'What you mean is *I* can't go barging in . . .'

I grin at her. 'Well, you are a little on the *eager* side. Not that that's necessarily a bad thing.'

She doesn't look convinced.

'Look, I need your help. You're a smart girl. Highly intelligent—'

She gives a grunt of disbelief.

'You are, Layla. Stop underestimating yourself. Look, if it hadn't been for you marching me along to the Chickens, I'd be no further forward, would I? We just have to *channel* your enthusiasm. Make sure it doesn't get you into trouble.'

'Okay.' She stands up and gives a mock salute. 'Ready, boss.'

I laugh and she joins in.

'Right, Layla. What exactly do you know about Ben?'

TWENTY-ONE

'Ben Hart's all right,' says Layla.

'Really?'

She shrugs. 'He's *way* less of a wanker than most of the oldies I know.'

'Wow. Praise indeed,' I say caustically, as my heart rate quickens. 'Examples?'

She frowns, thinking. 'Well, he once caught me and my mates setting – erm – doing an experiment on a dead rat, and instead of threatening to call the coppers, like most oldies would, he said he remembered what it was like being a teenager. It was natural to want to experiment at our age. But it was probably best not to – erm – do what we were doing.'

I nod, liking the sound of Ben. 'And the experiment on the rat was?'

She grins. 'Seeing how fast it would burn.'

'Ah. Right. Of course.'

'But it's like Ben said.' She's immediately on the defensive. 'It's practically our *duty* to experiment. I don't know why the oldies can't see that.'

'I know. Especially since setting fire to a dead rat represents such a mammoth advance for mankind in the field of animal biology.' I grin. 'Layla Rushbrooke, Pulitzer Prize winner, here we come.'

'Okay, okay,' she says, looking sheepish. 'That was *years* ago, by the way. When I was fourteen.' She jumps to her feet. 'So shall we go and talk to Ben?'

Alarmed, I watch her pulling her jacket on, getting ready for action.

'No! We are not going to knock on Ben's door. There *is* such a thing as subtlety, Layla. We have to talk strategy.'

I sound calm and in control, but I'm actually the very opposite. I've got butterflies in my stomach at the very thought of meeting Ben.

'I do know what subtlety is. I'm not stupid,' says Layla sulkily.

I heave a sigh. 'I'm aware of that, Layla. You're actually a very long way from stupid.'

'Hmm, well, you're the only one who thinks so.'

Hoping to head off a nobody-understands-me adolescent sulk, I smile brightly. 'So. Do you know anything else about Ben? Apart from the fact that he's all right?'

Layla thinks. Then her face lights up. 'He's one of the summer fete organisers – and they're always looking for helpers. We could volunteer!'

A little spark of excitement ignites within me. I've got a good feeling about this.

'Well done, Layla! That's more like it.' I smile at her admiringly and even through her stark white make-up, I can detect a pleased glow. 'So how do we sign up as volunteers?'

She shrugs. 'No idea.'

'Community hall.' I get to my feet. 'And there's no time like the present. Coming?'

'Yeah.'

'Don't you have to be somewhere? Won't *Josh* be missing you?'

She glares at me but doesn't deign to reply.

'You don't have to come with me.'

She snorts. 'Yes, I do. You need someone brave enough to ask questions.'

I eye her warningly.

'*Subtle* questions, of course,' she relents.

'Good.' I nod approvingly. 'You're starting to get the idea.'

When we get to the community hall, it's empty apart from a woman at the far end of the room running a mop over the wooden floor.

'It's Mrs Trowbridge,' Layla hisses. 'She cleans in the village.'

'Isn't your mum looking for a cleaner?'

Layla frowns. 'Yes, but she'd *never* hire someone from the village. Perish the thought. They might be a friend of Robina's or something.'

Mrs Trowbridge stops mopping and tells us to add our names to a list in the kitchen if we want to help with the fete. Layla disappears off to the toilet – I suspect to refresh her vampire lipstick – while Mrs Trowbridge finds me a pen and chats away about the fete.

'It's usually a good day, if the weather's all right. My grand-daughter's taking part in the freestyle dance competition and I'm making a dozen of my big lemon curd tarts for the refreshment tent. They're always popular.'

'Ooh, they sound lovely,' I say politely. 'I'll have to make sure I grab a piece before it all goes.'

Mrs Trowbridge's eyebrows rise. 'I hear you're gardening for her up at the big house.'

I smile and nod.

'How's that working out, then?'

'Fine. Yes, it seems to be going – well, fine!'

She nods, her expression giving little away, and I'm left wondering what she expected me to say. I'm suddenly aware of a 'them and us' divide, which I didn't think existed any more.

'I'm not one to tell tales.' Mrs Trowbridge leans closer and I prepare myself for some juicy gossip. 'But I have heard Prudence Rushbrooke was a bit of a *one* in her younger days. If you know what I mean.' She nods conspiratorially.

'A one?'

'Yes, you know, *loose*.' She purses her lips. 'Giving away her favours at the drop of a hat. Or a pair of scanties.'

I stare at her in confusion. Prue? *Loose?* It's very hard to visualise. But the problem is, I had the same story from Connie, so they're either both listening to the same unreliable gossip or there's actually a grain of truth in their tale. But this I really can't believe.

'You must be thinking of someone else,' I begin, but her face suddenly closes up and she springs away from me. Her eyes flick across to the door, just as Layla enters the kitchen.

'What's going on? Talking about me, are you?' She laughs self-consciously.

Mrs Trowbridge gives me a knowing look and gets on with the mopping.

On the way out, Layla realises she's left her eyeliner in the bathroom so she dives back inside, while I find a sunny spot to sit down on the old stone wall in front of the hall.

It's peaceful here. The scent of summer blossom on the trees around me drifts up my nose as I turn my face up to the sun, thinking of Ivy. I'm fairly certain the love of her life wasn't Henry Chicken.

I know the oddest-looking couples can be happy together, but I just don't see Ivy and Henry as a pair of lovebirds. And in any case, it's clear Henrietta wears the pants in their relationship. She'd never allow her pint-sized hubby to stray further than the garden gate.

So it's one down, two to go. Soon, I will meet Ben Hart. My heart leaps frantically at the very thought. Ever since I read the mind-blowing entry in Ivy's diary and realised there was a whole area of her life I knew nothing about, I've hardly been able to eat a thing. And it's not only excitement at what I might discover. It's also real, gut-wrenching fear, because there's so very much at stake here.

I'm aware that the search for my grandfather is filling the huge void left by Ivy's death. I'm no longer drifting aimlessly, like a tiny boat on the ocean, wondering what use my life is if I don't matter deeply to another person. Someone who shares that precious genetic bond.

The discovery that I could possibly have family I have yet to meet has catapulted me off on a whole new journey, which fills me with a sort of breathless yearning. How I would love to be part of a family again! But the flipside of all that hope and possible happiness is almost too painful to contemplate.

What if I fail in my mission? What if I can't find Ivy's lover? Or what if I do – but he wants nothing at all to do with me? He might even deny any connection and then I'd feel even lonelier than I did before.

And what then . . .?

My return to Manchester will inevitably be delayed while I try to solve the mystery, but that doesn't bother me the way it once would have. I've grown fond of Appleton, living in Moonbeam Cottage and having Ivy Garden literally on my doorstep. I'm even enjoying the gardening and sprucing up the cottage. And then there's the people I've met, of course . . .

The sun slips behind a cloud and I shiver. Something tickles my arm and automatically I go to shake it off. But when I look down, the breath catches in my throat.

It's a ladybird.

I hold my arm very still, struck by the insect's perfect, glossy red and black symmetry. A huge lump forms in my throat.

I needed something – *a sign* – that I'm on the right track. And there it is. It can't be a coincidence. I smile, remembering the ugly ladybird teapot that's packed away carefully in bubble wrap.

'Thank you,' I whisper, as a single tear rolls down the side of my nose and plops on to the warm stone wall beside me.

Ivy's with me. I just *know* she is. She wants me to find Bee . . .

The ever-present ache in my heart seems to swell through my whole body to a bittersweet crescendo. I was *so lucky* to have Ivy in my life, loving me and helping to shape the person I've become. Anchoring me. Giving me that profound sense of belonging that equips you to go off and explore life with confidence.

I've known what it's like to be loved absolutely unconditionally, and I'm so grateful for that.

The ladybird billows its wings and takes flight, and my heart flutters with panic, watching it float away. But then it settles right beside me on the wall and I breathe easy again.

A door slams, hauling me back to reality. Layla barges out of the community centre, shouting that she's found out what Ben needs help with at the fete.

'Mrs Trowbridge says Ben's desperate for someone to organise and run a cake stall. I told her you've worked in a café for years so we'd do it.' Her eyes are shining. 'I know how to make chocolate cake.'

I open my mouth to say that just because I've *served* cake doesn't necessarily mean I'm good at *baking* the things – but I suddenly realise she's about to plonk herself down on the wall beside me.

'No!' I push out my arm to protect the ladybird and accidentally whack her on her side.

'Woah!' Layla stares down at me. 'What the . . .?'

'Sorry.' I try to smile and look normal. 'It's – um – just a ladybird.'

It sounds so ridiculous. I'm expecting Layla to accuse me of needing to get a life, or something similar, with a few more expletives thrown in for emphasis. But her eyes light up.

'Where? Oh, yeah.' She peers down close enough to scare the poor thing half to death. 'Wow.'

We both examine it for a while.

'Ladybirds are *amazing*, don't you think?' says Layla at last. 'I mean, they're so *perfect*.'

Her girlish enthusiasm cheers me.

I smile at her. 'They are, aren't they?'

TWENTY-TWO

On Friday morning, when I arrive at Rushbrooke House for my daily gardening session, Prue has some news for me. She brings me into the kitchen to tell me.

Her sister, who lives in Kent, hasn't been well and Prue is going down the next day to spend some time with her.

'Now, I trust you to keep an eye on things while I'm away, Polly,' she says briskly. 'You don't need to keep to your usual hours. Just pop over when you like and make a note of the hours you work.'

'Okay. No problem.'

'Jack's driving me down there tomorrow and he'll collect me in a fortnight.'

'That's nice of him,' I say, wondering about her pristine VW Golf in the garage.

She sighs. 'Well, I told him I'm perfectly capable of driving myself but he absolutely insists. I don't know what on earth he imagines will happen. Does he think I'd take a nap at the wheel and cause a major pile-up on the motorway?'

'I guess he's just being protective,' I soothe, stifling a yawn. It's nice the way Jack looks after his mum, but I sometimes think he might be a little *over*-protective.

'Hmm. You're probably right.' She peers at me. 'You seem tired, Polly. You should have an early night.'

'Oh, I'm fine.' I smile at her.

I'm learning to let Prue's bossiness wash over me. It's just the way she is. And actually, she's right. I'm shattered. Since discovering the stuck pages in Ivy's diary, I've lain awake a lot at night, thinking about Ivy and Bee. And I still haven't caught up properly on sleep since my lovely time with Sylvian, lying on the village green all night staring up at the stars.

'Did you know Ivy at all?' I ask Prue casually, hoping for a clue. Anything, really, that might point me in the direction of Bee.

She lifts her sunglasses and dabs carefully at her mascara. 'I knew her a little when I first moved to Appleton when I married,' she says, 'although we didn't move in the same circles. And then, years later, I heard she'd returned to the village, back to Moonbeam Cottage.'

'Can you remember who Ivy was friends with, all those years ago?' I ask, my heart beating a little faster. 'It would be – um – nice to talk to people she used to know in her younger days.'

Prue frowns. 'To be honest, my memory isn't what it used to be. I seem to recall she and Peter were great friends with the Chickens at one stage.'

'Henry and Henrietta?'

'Yes. Do you know them?'

'I've met them.'

Prue smiles. 'You wouldn't forget *her* in a hurry. Not that I've seen her for many years.'

'Did you ever bump into Ivy in the village, after she came back?' I prompt hopefully.

'Do you know, I never did.' She turns away and starts dead-heading flowers. 'Mind you, that's hardly surprising since I never have much need of going into the village. That corner shop is a total rip-off, so I do all my shopping at the big superstore in Cirencester.'

I study her back curiously. Is Layla right? That Prue is too scared of bumping into that Robina person to ever venture into the village? How sad, if it's true.

She goes off to find a list of jobs she's written for me to do while she's away, and I glance curiously around the big farmhouse kitchen. It's a complete mess. Not only is it untidy, with dishes and pans on every single surface, but it smells musty. The plaster on the ceiling looks ancient and seems to be coming away in lumps, and there's a big patch in the corner where the wallpaper is hanging loose, presumably because the wall needs treating for damp. Rushbrooke House really is crumbling around their ears, just as Jack said.

I really feel for him, having to work at a job he hates just to keep this old monster ticking over.

When I get back from my morning's gardening, I make a sandwich and take it over to eat in Ivy Garden. It's a gloriously sunny June day and I want to prune the climbing roses the way Layla has shown me. I'm hoping she'll come over later with news about Ben and our part in the summer fete. She promised me she'd find out.

Sure enough, she drops by late afternoon, straight from her shift at the garden centre.

'Ben knows we're doing the cake stall and he wants us to meet him for a chat on Tuesday,' she says, eyes sparkling at the prospect of some more sleuthing.

'Great.' I swallow hard. That's only three days away. 'Where are we meeting?'

'Deli-café at midday. Is that okay?'

'Fabulous.' I sound calm but my mind has gone into instant overdrive. Maybe Ben is the missing link and we can finally solve the mystery. Excitement and apprehension at the very thought make my insides roll over.

Unaware of all this, Layla gives me a thumbs up. 'Right. Can't stop. Meeting Josh.' And she barges her way back through the hedge.

That night, I lie awake, thinking about Henry Chicken and Ben.

I've pretty much ruled Henry out as Ivy's secret love. At first, his stunned reaction to seeing me made me think that maybe he was The One. But then I realised he was only amazed at how the years had flown by because last time he saw me I had been little more than a toddler.

But what about Ben?

My heart trips along that little bit faster every time I think about meeting him in the café at noon on Friday.

TWENTY-THREE

Midsummer Night dawns sunny and warm.

It's Monday, the day before Layla and I are due to meet Ben in the deli-café, which I'm really nervous about. Every time I think about meeting this man who could be my granddad, I feel slightly queasy, wondering what I'll say to him.

Another person who's making my heart beat that little bit faster is Sylvian. Seeing him later for our Midsummer Night date will go a long way towards taking my mind off meeting Ben.

Since our delicious night on the village green, I've been thinking about Sylvian quite a lot. The very next day, he sent me an email with details of the art college near where he lives in Cornwall, which surprised and delighted me because it proved he'd been thinking about me, too. I've never met a man who's so caring and intelligent, and has such fascinating ideas about life. I've been doing the meditation thing whenever I feel over-anxious, and I have to say, it really does work. Going to stay in Sylvian's house by the beach would probably be like visiting a spa! I'd return home so much more relaxed. I'm sure I could really get into his way of life . . .

It helps, of course, that he's also gorgeous and sexy. And I think he really likes me, too.

I can't wait to find out what he has planned for our pagan

celebration tonight. Thankfully, since I assume we're going to be somewhere outdoors, the night ahead is set to be dry, mild and rather humid.

Perfect!

What do pagans wear, I wonder? Searching through my limited wardrobe, I come across a long, silky summer dress, patterned with big red poppies that I've never worn. I slip on my gold gladiator sandals and pose in the full-length mirror. Floaty and floral is good, I think, admiring the effect. And the dress will be nice and cool for a humid night. I've blow-dried my hair and it gleams in the sunlight filtering through the bedroom window.

I keep having visions of Sylvian turning up at my door in full pagan attire. What that would be, I'm not entirely sure. As long as he's not wearing scratchy robes and a long fake beard or dressed as an ancient, gnarly tree, I really don't mind. I'd draw the line at green body paint, though.

He arrives on the dot of eight o'clock wearing, to my relief, a lovely, if unimaginative, outfit of jeans and a pale blue T-shirt. He looks gorgeous. And so does the large, expensive-looking picnic basket he's carrying.

He smiles wolfishly. 'You look beautiful, Holly. Very . . . woodland creature-like.'

I grin. 'Exactly the effect I was aiming for. Where are we going?' I lift my dress to reveal my flimsy sandals. 'Are these going to be appropriate? If we're hiking to the top of a hill, I'd better change.'

He shakes his head. 'No hills. Just a relaxed walk over the road.' He nods in the direction of Ivy Garden.

'Oh. Fab,' I say, pleasantly surprised.

He smiles. 'It's such a magical place. I didn't see any point in going further afield. Shall we go?'

He takes my hand and I lean into him as we walk over the road. He holds the hedge back at one side so I can get through the gap without snagging my dress.

'This is glorious,' I sigh, breathing in the scent from the climbing roses, as Sylvian shakes out a blanket for our picnic by the tree stump. 'After you,' he says with a flourish and I lower myself on to the rug in as graceful a manner as I can.

He places the picnic basket in the middle and sits down opposite me. 'I hope you're hungry. I've got some little delicacies that I'm sure you'll love. Champagne?'

'Ooh, yes, please.' I love champagne. I don't love the sound of the 'little delicacies' so much but maybe they won't be so bad. If I concentrate on the champagne, everything will be fine . . .

He draws a chilled bottle from the basket, pops the cork and I cheer and hold out my glass. 'To Midsummer Night,' I toast, and we laugh and clink our flutes and take our first sip of champagne. It's cold and delicious, and I smile happily, savouring the bubbles fizzing on my tongue.

There's only one cloud on our Midsummer Night horizon.

I keep taking furtive sniffs of the air around us, flaring my nostrils with extreme caution.

'Any, erm, festering cabbage in there?' I ask nonchalantly, as Sylvian starts unpacking the picnic basket. Because seriously, if the dreaded kimchee makes an appearance, I'm going home.

Leaking sewage pipes do not a happy picnic make.

'Fermented cabbage?' He smiles affectionately at my adorable ignorance of nutritional matters. 'No, I finished it off last night.'

'Ah. Shame.'

'Smoked salmon and dill salad?'

We tuck in and the food is actually delicious. Not a putrid vegetable in sight. The champagne is also going down well. Rather too well, actually. But so what, I think. Apart from my fab girls' night with Connie, this is the first time I've done anything special like this since I left Manchester. I'm just going to make the most of it and have fun.

After we've eaten and everything is cleared away, we lie on our sides facing each other on the blanket, idly chatting, our glasses with the dregs of champagne resting on the tree stump.

'So, do you think you might want to come down to Cornwall to check out that art college?' he smiles, his beautiful green eyes roving lazily over me.

I smile back, a little flirtatiously. 'Maybe I would. I'd love to see that beach house of yours.'

'Then let's get it organised.' He reaches for his glass, raises it in the air and drains it.

A little quiver of excitement runs through me.

Life is so strange. When I first arrived in Appleton, feeling as if things couldn't get any worse, I could never have imagined that a month or two later I'd be getting to know a really lovely man and planning to apply for college.

My eyes follow Sylvian as he moves the picnic basket off the rug so he can scoot closer to me. His movements are surprisingly graceful. I love watching him. It must be all the yoga that makes him so supple. What, I wonder, would Ivy have thought of him?

I think she'd probably have said that as long as Sylvian was a caring man and he made me happy, that was fine by her.

'I found out what you're doing for Layla,' I tell him. 'Typing her stories. I think it's really nice of you.'

'She has talent.' He smiles. 'I was thinking I might enter one of her stories into a national competition.'

'Oh, that would be brilliant! Will you tell her what you're doing?'

'Only if she wins. There's no point asking her to enter because she'd just say her stories weren't good enough.'

I smile ruefully. 'That's so true.'

'She needs a good confidence boost. That's why I thought of the competition.'

I nod enthusiastically. 'If she were to win, she might actually start believing in herself. You have to do it!'

'I will, then.' He smiles into my eyes and my heart does a joyful little leap.

We lapse into silence for a while. I'm thinking about Layla and how much I wish she'd have faith in herself and her abilities.

Sylvian is watching me with a lazy smile. 'You know,' he says softly. 'This is the perfect setting for tantric meditation.'

'It is?' I give him a coy, flirty look.

He smiles. 'It is. Like to try it?'

Those green eyes are mesmerising. He looks so gorgeous lying over there. How can I possibly resist?

He tells me to lie down and concentrate on my breathing. Then he kneels at my side, speaking in an infinitely soothing, hypnotic tone.

'Feel your breath moving in and out of your nostrils. That's right. Inhale and out. Now start becoming aware of the movements in your chest and belly as you breathe.'

After a few minutes, I'm right in the zone, focusing on nothing but the air moving through me and feeling completely relaxed. (Well, except for the twig that's digging into my back. And the sound of a car alarm going off somewhere in the distance. And my worry that my boobs probably look completely non-existent lying flat like this.) But apart from all that . . . it's so lovely and relaxing!

'And now we're going to work on your first chakra. So I want you to contract the sphincter muscle.'

I open one eye. 'My what?'

'Your sphincter muscle,' he repeats. 'It's the one down in your—'

'Yes, I know,' I say swiftly, as an image of a bottom swims into my mind. Cautiously, I tighten what I think he wants me to tighten.

It's not exactly romantic, this sort of meditation. I preferred it when we were just lying on the floor next to each other, doing our deep breathing. Still, Sylvian seems to know what he's doing. And *tighten* . . .

'Now we're going to introduce a chant to awaken the chakra. LAMMMMM! Try it.'

Oh, hell. I know I should take this seriously, but *really*?

Still, in for a penny . . . here goes. 'LAM!'

'That's it. But lengthen the sound. LAMMMM! Feel the kundalini energy deep in your pelvis resonating to the sound.'

'LAMMMMM!'

'Feel the vibration deep down?'

Actually, I did. And it felt rather nice. Wanting to be a good student, I practise a few times more. 'LAMMMMM! LAMMMM! LAMMMM!'

Hang on, what's happening?

Sylvian is suddenly astride me, although we're not touching. In the dim recesses of my mind, I seem to remember that's what kundalini energy and tantric meditation is all about. Not touching. Just building up the sexual energy until it reaches the most incredible pitch.

Crikey! Aren't I the sexually liberated one!

I have a sudden worry that Ivy might be looking down on me disapprovingly, which is a bit inhibiting. But I tell myself not to be so silly. I just need to relax . . .

'Now, with every breath in, charge your sexual centre with more and more vibrant sexual energy!' commands Sylvian.

I open one eye and give him a nod. *I'll give it a go!*

'Now, focus on your genitals! LAMMMM! There's a liquid melting sensation in your genitals as you bring all your awareness to this build-up of sexual energy! Allow your pelvis to move as you breathe!'

I'm doing pelvic thrusts now. Just as well I've had alcohol, otherwise I'd feel like a right plank. Still, it's all good fun. And Sylvian seems happy.

I thrust a little too enthusiastically and we actually touch by mistake.

Oooh, he's *very* happy!

There's a sudden rustling in the undergrowth.

'What's that?' I yelp. *The last thing I need is a badger charging at me when I'm in such a compromising position.* 'Sorry. LAMMMMMM! Ooh, yes, I can really feel that reverberating. Deep in my – er – genitals.'

'Lucky you,' says a sarcastic voice.

My eyes spring open. That's not Sylvian. *Who on earth . . .?*

To my horror, Jack Rushbrooke has somehow arrived and is towering over us.

The setting sun, a red ball of fire, is directly behind him, giving him a strange sort of devilish halo.

'Hi,' I squeak, scrambling to a sitting position and trying to push Sylvian away. But he's staying firm (in more ways than one) in the straddle position.

Oh, bloody hell.

What on earth will Jack think of me? *This is not what it looks like!* Although actually, it's exactly what it looks like . . .

'I'd like a word when you have a minute,' says Jack shortly, glaring down at me. Then he strides off.

I stare after him. How bloody rude! I mean, okay, we were probably about to have tantric sex in a public place, but there was no need for Jack to look quite so horrified and disapproving, was there?

I glance at Sylvian. 'Sorry, do you mind if I . . .?'

Sylvian rises smoothly to his feet. 'I'll go and get more wine,' he says, as calm as ever, not looking in the least ruffled by Jack's intrusion.

I run after Jack and spot him just as he's about to head down Farthingale Road for his daily swim. His face is like thunder. He obviously doesn't like Sylvian *at all.*

'Jack.'

He turns at the gate.

'Well?' I demand. 'You wanted a word?'

He thinks for a minute then he says, 'Look, it's probably none of my business, Holly. But you do realise Sylvian's juggling women like a Billy Smart's Circus clown?'

I stare at him. Then I burst out laughing. 'Don't be ridiculous.'

'I'm not being ridiculous. I'm just telling you what I know because I . . .' He swallows and looks down.

I stare at him as he scuffs at the ground with his foot. 'Because you what?'

He looks up. 'Because I don't want you getting hurt.'

'But I'm not *going* to get hurt. Sylvian's a lovely, caring man and we're having a nice time, that's all.'

He nods. 'So you're not bothered that when he was supposed to be cooking dinner for you a few weeks ago, he actually chose to entertain a couple of attractive women all weekend instead?'

'Sorry?' *Two women? What's he talking about?*

'I saw them with my own eyes as I was driving past, going into Sylvian's flat with wine.'

I stare at him as a memory surfaces. Two women. In the village store squabbling over tortilla chips and asking the store owner if he sold scented candles. Presumably a gift for Sylvian.

It was weird, certainly. If he had people coming round, why didn't he just tell me? Or invite me along?

I shake my head. 'Just because he had two women in his flat doesn't mean there was anything going on.'

He shrugs and says nothing.

'Look, is there anything else you're not telling me?'

He opens the gate. 'You'd better ask Sylvian. I don't do gossip.' Then he strides across the lawn and into the conservatory, slamming the door behind him.

I stand there, leaning on the wall, my mind ticking over. Jack's not a liar, I'm sure of it. So those women were definitely there.

Then I remember something. When I was listening to the women's chat in the store, I'm sure one of them called the other woman 'Sara'. Of course. Sara and Abby. Sylvian's housemates.

My shoulders relax. Of course. That makes perfect sense.

Then I think: *But does it really?* Sylvian keeps saying how Abby and Sara would really like me and that he wants us all to meet. So why didn't he take the opportunity of their visit to Appleton to introduce us?

Something's definitely not right . . .

I walk back to Ivy Garden, and Sylvian is still there, stretched out on the blanket. He sits up when I arrive and says calmly, 'That man could benefit from a good pummelling on a massage table. He needs to relax.'

'You might well be right,' I say, thinking of Jack's thunderous profile.

'I am. Now, that wine . . .' He gets up.

'Sylvian? Have you had Abby and Sara to stay the weekend? Were they there that Saturday night when you said you had poetry workshops?'

He immediately sits back down and looks directly into my eyes. 'Yes, they were.'

My heart twists. So Jack was right. I draw a deep breath, trying to stay calm. 'So why didn't you tell me? Wouldn't that have been the perfect opportunity to introduce us? You're always saying that's what you'd like.'

'Because I was waiting for the right moment,' he says simply.

'What do you mean?' I ask, puzzled. 'It's no big deal introducing friends, is it? It's not like you have to plan it well in advance.'

He sighs. 'No, but it's tricky. This situation.'

'*What* situation?' *Something weird's going on. I wish to goodness he'd just spit it out!*

'Us. You, me, Sara, Abby. I wanted you to know more about my lifestyle before I introduced you to each other. It's important for all parties to go into it feeling it's something they're perfectly comfortable with.'

'Your *lifestyle*? All *parties*?' There's a feeling of dread in the pit of my stomach. 'What are you talking about, Sylvian?'

He shrugs. 'Polyamory.'

'Poly *what*?'

'It's when you make a conscious decision to be in a loving relationship with more than one person.'

I stare at him. *More than one person?*

Seeing my confusion, he shuffles closer and takes my hand. 'It's an alien concept to many, and it might take a while for you to get your head round it. But I get a powerful sense that you're more open to exploring other ways of living than most people are, Holly.'

'So are you telling me you're already in a poly-thingy relationship with Abby and Sara?' I'm starting to feel quite nauseous. 'And you all live together in your house in Cornwall?'

'Well. Yes,' he says simply.

'Bloody hell,' I breathe. 'Unbelievable.'

'It is, actually. You have to live it to understand how beautiful it really is.'

'So basically, you can sleep with who you like?' My voice is trembling, I feel so gutted. And stupid for not seeing the signs. 'And were you intending to invite *me* to join your little harem?'

'It's not like that, Holly.'

He's so calm, I want to jump on him and shake him to make him react!

He shrugs. 'It's not as if I'm at the centre, enjoying as many women as I like. It's not like that at all.'

'So what the hell *is* it like?' God, how naïve have I been! I can't believe I was starting to think there might be something between us . . .

'Well, for instance,' he says, 'Abby also has a girlfriend who chooses not to live with us. And Sara, as well as being with me, is in a loving relationship with her ex-husband's new wife.'

'Her ex-husband's *new wife*?'

He shrugs calmly. 'They're separated.'

'Oh. Right. Well, that's okay, then,' I say testily. 'Christ, Sylvian, I'm sorry but I think it's completely bizarre. And I also think you could have let me know all this a lot earlier.'

I'm trembling with the shock of it all. I wasn't in deep with Sylvian. We barely knew each other, really. But I'd started to trust him. And so to find out that actually, I didn't really know him at all, is quite upsetting.

'I didn't want to frighten you off,' he says. 'I really like you, Holly. I was hoping it might work.'

'Well, sorry,' I say, getting to my feet. 'It might sound boring to you and very in line with *what society expects*, but I'm afraid I'm a one-man woman. Always was, always will be.'

He smiles sadly. 'I'm not sure what to say.'

'How about: "It's been nice knowing you, Holly, and good luck?"'

I hurry across the garden and through the gap in the hedge, feeling thoroughly let down and ridiculous. And sad. Really, really sad.

I manage to hold back the tears until I'm back in the cottage.

Then I spend the rest of the evening wondering why on earth I didn't spot the signs that something wasn't quite right – because they were definitely there . . .

TWENTY-FOUR

The next morning, I'm awake early, reliving the shocking moment when I realised Sylvian wanted me to be part of his 'love-in' down in Cornwall.

I can't believe I was actually considering leaving Manchester and going to college in Cornwall, just because that's where Sylvian has his house. How stupid! I realise now I knew so little about the real Sylvian because he hid it from me, knowing full well he'd scare me off if I knew about his cosy little arrangement with Sara and Abby!

Why didn't I heed the warning signs?

I remember thinking it was odd when he mentioned Sara and Abby for the first time. He seemed awkward, as if he hadn't meant to tell me about them yet. Then there was all that talk about how much they would like me. And how I was sure to love them, too. He'd obviously just been priming me for the eventual revelation that he was into polyamory!

Am I sad that things have turned out this way with Sylvian? Not really. The chief emotion I'm feeling is annoyance – at myself – that I allowed myself to be taken in by his charm and his silly half-truths . . .

To fill in the time until the meeting with Ben at midday, and so that I'm not just hanging around brooding about Sylvian, I decide to go out for one of my walks.

Ever since my disastrous drive into the country with Connie, I've been venturing out for a walk every day. Not very far. But I've been trying to go a little further each time, beyond the safety of the village, in an effort to get over my fear of being stranded.

In one direction, the road is too narrow to be safe for pedestrians. But the other way has a grass verge to walk on. So far, the furthest I've managed is about half a mile, which takes me as far as a farm with a red barn. But that seems to be my limit. I get stuck at the red barn. I start to panic and my feet just won't allow me to risk going any further into open countryside. But I'm going to keep on trying . . .

There's a knock at the door just as I'm about to go out. When I open it, Jack is standing there and my heart wallops against my ribcage.

'Sorry about yesterday,' he says, without preamble.

I shake my head. 'You've got nothing to apologise for. In fact, I'm grateful you forced me to face up to what was going on.' I smile ruefully. 'It would never have worked. Me and Sylvian.'

'Well, I'm sorry anyway.' He glances at my trainers. 'Were you going out?'

'Just for a walk.'

'Oh. Right. Mind if I join you?'

'No,' I say, surprised, glancing at his jeans and T-shirt. 'No London today?'

'Day off,' he says and doesn't elaborate.

'I don't go very far. Just to the red barn and back.'

'Fine.'

We set off. It's a beautiful sunny morning and it feels lovely to have company on my walk. Not just any old company, either . . .

Walking side by side when the grass verge allows it, we keep bumping arms, which makes my heart a little skittery.

'So you're not too cut up about Sylvian, then?' he asks.

'No, not really. It would never have worked, even if he hadn't been into polyamory. We're too different.' I laugh. 'He likes kimchee.'

'What the hell's that?'

'Believe me, you really don't want to know.' I glance at him quickly. 'I'm sorry about the tantric meditation you stumbled upon.'

He laughs. 'So that's what it was. I did wonder. It was the fact you were fully clothed that had me puzzled. It certainly cleared up one thing, though.'

'What's that?' I ask curiously.

'That you're not actually training to be a nun.' He digs into his jeans pocket and holds up a pair of black-framed glasses.

I stare at them, my brain ticking over. I've seen them somewhere before but I can't remember where . . .

He puts them on and it hits me. The tall nun barrelling into me outside Stroud station . . . the clown glasses . . . wiping them on my coat . . . 'Oh my God! You were the nun I nearly knocked into the gutter?'

He grins. 'Do you think the nose suits me?'

'Absolutely. I'd no idea that was you!'

'Well, I *was* dressed as a nun with most of my face hidden by jam jar specs and a false nose. And I was quite, erm, well-oiled if I remember rightly.'

'You were totally rat-arsed, you mean.' I hoot with laughter.

'Stag do. Terrible things.' He grins. 'You told me off for being disrespectful to nuns – and then you said you were taking a last long holiday in the Cotswolds before heading to Manchester and checking yourself into a convent.'

'Oh, God, I did, didn't I? I was just so annoyed at you for making me miss my bus. And your face when I said it was an absolute picture!'

He grins. 'When you appeared in Ivy Garden as I was cutting the tree down, I couldn't believe my eyes. I was really glad you didn't recognise me because I had a sneaky feeling I'd made a complete and utter dick of myself in Stroud, grabbing on to you so as not to fall over. As well as being generally obnoxious.'

I nod. 'All of the above.'

'And then I remembered the thing about the convent and I couldn't decide whether you were serious or not about wanting to become a nun. Obviously I couldn't come straight out and ask you, otherwise you would have realised I *was* that irritating drunk who accosted you in the street.'

I shake my head. 'Of course. I couldn't understand why you kept giving me funny stares when you thought I wasn't looking. As if you were trying to work me out. And you said a few weird things that made me think we definitely had our wires crossed somehow.'

'What weird things?'

'Oh, when I said I was having dinner with Sylvian but it wasn't a hot date, you said you never assumed it would be! Presumably thinking I was taking a vow of celibacy! I thought you meant I wasn't attractive enough.'

He smiles and bumps my am deliberately. 'Well, clearly that's not true.'

I feel myself blushing. 'And then you said I was obviously going to try and *reform* Sylvian. I thought that was weird, too,' I say, gabbling a bit self-consciously because after his compliment, my heart is skipping along like a four-year-old at nursery.

'Well, anyway, I'm glad we've sorted that out. What *is* your "calling" by the way? If it's not a religious one?'

'Art,' I tell him shyly. 'I love painting and sketching.'

'Great. I envy you. I can only draw stick men.' Then he points back along the road. 'You've gone much further than the red barn today.'

'Sorry?' I spin round and to my astonishment, so I have. I've been so wrapped up in our conversation, I didn't realise. But I feel fine. I really do. I could probably walk even further if I had the time.

We turn back and I invite Jack in for a coffee but he says he needs to deliver some furniture to a client.

'I brought you something,' he says, opening the boot of his car. He holds up a green can. 'Thought you might need petrol for the strimmer? I assumed that's why you hadn't been using it?'

My face falls. *Bugger! I don't want him to know it's because I've no idea how it works! I get paid to garden for him!*

'Oh, right. I thought it was one of those you plug in,' I mumble.

He looks at me askance as we go back into the cottage. 'An electric one? But where would you plug it in over there?'

My blush deepens.

'Where do you want it?' He carries the can through the hallway into the kitchen.

'Oh, put it on the table and I'll find a place for it,' I tell him. 'Have you been in here before?'

He nods. 'Quite a few times. Ivy made a fine mug of builder's tea.'

'She did. You could practically stand your spoon up in it.' We both smile fondly, remembering.

'A sketch of yours?' he asks, picking up something from the table, and I glance at the paper he's holding. *Oh, frigging hell! It's the caricatures I did of Selena and Moira.* My insides roll over queasily as he stares at it.

'Interesting.' He looks across at me, his mouth quirked up at one side.

I force a laugh. 'Oh, that's nothing. I was just larking about with a friend who was over the other night. She wanted me to draw something. In fact, *that* was *her* idea.'

'It's very good,' he concedes. 'Right, well, I'd better be going.' He pauses at the door and grins. 'Let me know if you need a lesson in using a strimmer.'

After he's gone, I collapse into a chair, shamefaced.

I should never have left that caricature lying around. It's my own stupid fault.

Oh God, what if Jack puts it down to jealousy? As in, I hate Selena because she's beautiful, thin and a successful career woman. (Basically everything I'm not.)

I feel thoroughly ashamed of myself. It will be a long time before I draw anyone else, that's for sure . . .

Layla pitches up far too early for our meeting with Ben, so I suggest she goes along to the café and grabs a table for us.

At exactly twelve o'clock, I cross the threshold of the deli-café, red-faced and nervous. *Breathe, for goodness sake. Breathe.*

Shaking my hair into place, I spot Layla sitting at a table in the far corner, chatting to a man with short silvery hair and the healthy-looking tan of someone who spends a lot of time in their garden. His bearing is very upright and he's wearing a smart navy bomber jacket. They're engrossed in conversation and haven't seen me. Swiftly, I check my underarms. No damp patches, so that's a good start.

I can't believe how nervous I am. Smoothing moist palms down the side of my jeans, I plaster on a smile and head on over.

Layla looks up with a grin. 'Ben, meet Holly. Didn't I tell you she looks a lot like Ivy?'

Ben rises nimbly to his feet and when I offer my hand, he takes it in both of his, holding it firmly, and murmurs, 'She does indeed.'

I smile at him, feeling instantly at ease.

Ben is average height, a few inches taller than me, which makes him about five feet nine, and his brown eyes are lively and very smiley.

He studies me for a second, his head on one side, then nods slowly. 'You have Ivy's lovely peaches and cream complexion. And that mouth I'd recognise anywhere. It's lovely to meet you, my dear.'

He blinks rapidly and I get the feeling I'm not the only one overcome with emotion.

'It's great to meet you, too,' I say, feeling suddenly shy. 'What are we having? Coffee?'

'Let me get you one,' he says quickly, squeezing my hand firmly before releasing me and heading over to the counter.

He smiles back at us. 'What will it be? The choice is a little bewildering for a man of my mature years.'

'A cappuccino would be lovely, thank you.'

I sit down opposite Layla, giving Connie a little wave as she appears from the back to serve Ben. Layla leans towards me, eyes shining. 'Isn't he great? We were chatting about Facebook and Twitter. He's really cool for an oldie. And just the kind of person you'd love to have as a granddad.'

'*Layla!*' Alarmed, I shush her, glancing nervously back at Ben. 'We're here to talk about the cake stall, remember? No interrogation of the poor man, please.'

She grins. 'As if!'

I give her a warning look and hiss, 'Think of our embarrassing chat on the Chickens' doorstep and do the *exact opposite.*'

She adopts a stern expression and zips her lips, which doesn't exactly fill me with an enormous amount of confidence.

Her eagerness to help is lovely, though – and I don't think it's purely the chance to solve a fascinating mystery that's motivating her. I have a feeling she really cares that I find what I'm longing for.

Layla joins Ben at the counter and – displaying a persuasive charm that's rarely seen – asks him for something really complicated with almond milk, whipped cream and chocolate sprinkles. I glance at the board and wince at the cost but Ben takes it all in his stride and even suggests she has one of the deli's famous triple chocolate chip cookies.

I sit there, watching the two of them. They look so relaxed in each other's company and my foolish heart swells with hope.

I obviously don't know him yet, but on first meeting, Ben seems really lovely. Such a gentleman and, as Layla commented, just the kind of person you'd want for a granddad. While I find it hard to imagine Ivy and Henry Chicken as secret lovers, I can perfectly understand Ivy finding herself drawn to a man like Ben. His gentle, caring nature would have been a complete contrast to what she was used to with Peter and his selfish, controlling ways.

Does Ben have family? I know he's not married because Layla, with her investigative hat on, casually asked Mrs Trowbridge. Does that mean he's a widower? Or divorced? What about Lucy Feathers, his girlfriend at the dinner party that night? Did they ever marry and have a family? Perhaps the reason he never married is because Ivy was his one true love and no-one else could ever measure up . . .?

Catching my imagination running riot, I straighten up in my seat and give myself a swift talking to.

Just because Ben grew a little emotional talking about Ivy doesn't mean he was in love with her. They were probably just good friends. In fact, they *must* have been friends if Ivy and Peter invited them to dinner. I'm being completely ridiculous, jumping the gun like this. Talk about setting myself up for a fall!

When they return to the table, Layla is regaling Ben about all the work she's done in Ivy Garden.

Ben smiles at me as he hands me my cappuccino. 'I hear you've both worked wonders and I'm so pleased. Ivy would be, too. When it grew wild after she'd gone, I felt immensely sad because she loved that place so much. It was her sanctuary and we had many a lovely time, sitting on that love seat in the shade, putting the world to rights.'

'That love seat was her pride and joy,' I say sadly. 'It got broken in the recent storms but I'm hoping to get it fixed.'

'We found it in a little antique shop in Bourton-on-the-Water.' He smiles, remembering. 'Actually, it was her birthday. I bought it for her.'

I stare at him in surprise. '*You* bought her the love seat?'

I glance at Layla and she flashes me an urgent, wide-eyed look that echoes just what I'm thinking: *It must be him!*

Ben lifts his coffee cup and I admire the mother-of-pearl cufflink at the wrist of his checked shirt. Before he sips, he looks at me wistfully and murmurs, 'You know, Holly, you remind me so much of darling Ivy.' Then he takes a long swallow of black coffee, sets the cup down and smiles. 'Layla tells me you're doing up Moonbeam Cottage. A costly business. If you'd like a job doing my garden, it's yours.'

'Oh!' My eyes open wide in surprise. And slight embarrassment.

Layla snorts with laughter.

Ben looks from me to Layla and back again. 'Oh, dear. Have I said something funny?'

I grimace. 'The thing is . . . can I let you into a secret?'

'Go on.'

'The fact is, I'm not very good at gardening. In fact, I'm completely clueless. As Layla will confirm.'

Ben grins at Layla. 'Is this true?'

'Oh, yes. She's pants.'

I smile wryly. 'Thank you, Layla.'

She grins. 'You're welcome.'

'I assumed because Prue hired you, you must be a talented landscape gardener, at least. She's got a reputation for – er – not suffering fools gladly.'

'Nah! She was just desperate,' says Layla. 'Mum won't have anything to do with the folk in the village, but Holly's an outsider, so apparently that's okay. She practically steamrollered Holly into doing it, but I'm her gardening advisor so it's all okay.'

'Right.' Ben arches his brows in amusement. 'Well, don't worry, I won't tell Prue. Your secret is safe with me.'

'Did my mum always act so stand-offish with people?' Layla asks him curiously.

'Erm, well, I wouldn't say that exactly.' Ben looks uncomfortable. 'You shouldn't be too hard on your mum, Layla. She – um

– didn't have the easiest time when you were born. And afterwards, she – well, I suppose she felt she wanted to keep herself to herself. We all have times when we'd rather not see other people.'

Layla frowns. 'You mean she had a bad time because my dad died just before I was born?'

'Yes. Exactly,' says Ben. 'It wasn't easy for her, bringing you and your brother up on her own. We all cope with the bad times in our own way, don't we?' He glances at our cups. 'Now, I'm having another. Anyone else?'

Curious, I watch him at the counter, passing the time of day with Connie. He seemed relieved to escape the conversation. There was definitely something he wasn't telling us about Prue, but what on earth could it be?

When he sits back down, Layla takes a breath and launches right in. 'You used to have dinner parties in the old days, didn't you? That must have been fun. Holly found Ivy's diary from way back and you were mentioned in it.'

'Really?' Ben looks pleasantly surprised.

Layla nods. 'You were at Ivy and Peter's for dinner, along with the Chickens and someone mysteriously referred to as Mr H.'

My heart is in my mouth. I glare at her, my face reddening, but Layla is deliberately not looking my way.

I will absolutely kill her when we get out of here!

Ben thinks hard. Then his face breaks into a smile. 'Oh, I remember that night.' He stares off into the distance with a slight frown. 'Yes. It was the Chickens' first wedding anniversary that day, if I remember rightly, and Ivy really pushed the boat out for dinner. We had a game casserole – quail, that was it.'

I smile wistfully. 'That was quite exotic for Ivy. She always hated cooking.'

'She had something really flamboyant for dessert as well.' He clicks his fingers. 'I remember being quite impressed. Crêpes Suzette! That's right.'

Layla makes a disgusted face. 'Ugh! What on earth's *that*?'

I can't help smiling at her expression. 'Pancakes with orange liqueur, I think.'

I look at Ben for confirmation but he mustn't have heard me. He's staring into the distance, lost in thought.

'Yes, that was some night all right,' he murmurs. 'A real life-changer.'

'Was it?' Layla leans forward eagerly. 'In a good way or a bad way?'

Her question seems to snap him out of his reverie. 'Oh – well – in a *good* way.' He gives a curiously sheepish smile and adds, 'A very good way indeed.'

'Ooh! So what happened?' demands Layla, and I kick her hard under the table.

'Ouch!' She reddens and glares at me. Then she shrugs as if to say, *Great! He was just about to tell us something important and you've ruined it!*

'All right, Layla?' Ben looks concerned.

'Fine, thanks, Ben,' said Layla sweetly. 'Holly thinks I'm being too nosy.'

I force a laugh and shake my head at her in mock disapproval.

'Of course you're not,' Ben reassures her.

Beside me, Layla heaves a sigh and stirs her cup noisily, which I know is directed at me. She'll no doubt have plenty to say later about me putting the brakes on Ben's reminiscences.

And as we chat on about the fete, moving further and further away from the topic of Ivy's fateful dinner party, I find myself wishing I'd allowed Layla free rein to ask her questions. Not because I think this mission is going to be a success for all concerned. (To be honest, I still have grave doubts, which turn into an attack of butterfly tummy every time I think about the potential for a less than happy outcome.) But I'm beginning to realise just how determined Layla can be when she gets the bit between her teeth.

Is there really any point in trying to rein her in? She's going to get answers to her questions by hook or by crook, regardless of me trying to apply the brake. And maybe that's a good thing.

The conversation broadens out as Ben starts telling us about all the different stalls and rides planned for the fete.

'Oh, I used to *love* the teacups when I was little,' Layla enthuses, eyes shining, and I smile, catching a rare glimpse of the child within the rebellious teenage body.

Then she spoils it by asking chirpily, 'So do you have any children, Ben?'

My heart slams against my ribs. I almost can't look at him.

A shadow seems to pass over his face. I wonder if it's my imagination working overtime.

He smiles. 'I'd have loved children. But sadly, it wasn't to be. And I never married.'

'Was that because you never found the right one?' asks Layla.

He gives a funny little sigh and looks down at the table top, smoothing his finger along the edge. Then he looks up. 'I *did* find the right one but things were . . . complicated. We couldn't marry. It wasn't possible.'

He's looking directly at me when he says this and my vision swims crazily for a second as my brain finds a deeper meaning behind his words. Is it possible he *was* Ivy's lover, and he's saying he couldn't marry her or have children because she was already married to Peter?

If all that is true, I can take some of his sadness away by revealing who I am.

My heart is hammering frantically.

Already, I'm picturing the look on his face when he learns we're related – natural doubt fighting with the desire to believe it. And finally, enormous delight in finding he has a granddaughter he never knew about . . .

'There are plenty of advantages to being a bachelor,' Ben says. 'I can do what I want, when I want, with no-one to please but myself. I'm healthy and I've still got all my marbles.' He taps his head. 'Believe me, girls, that counts for a lot when you get to my age.'

'You definitely don't *look* ancient,' says Layla earnestly. I catch Ben's eye and we smile.

'*What?*' Layla demands, looking from one to the other.

'Nothing,' we chime together.

She sighs. 'Anyway, kids ruin your life so you're probably better off not having any, Ben. Plus it's bloody hard work bringing them up.'

'How do you know that?' I ask, laughing.

She shrugs. 'It's what Mum always yells at me when we're having a row.'

'Oh.' Is she exaggerating? Quite possibly. I can't believe Prue would be as insensitive as that. 'Your mum *was* on her own with you and Jack after your dad died,' I remind her. 'It can't have been easy for her.'

I'm expecting Layla to argue. But for once, she just frowns and lapses into a pensive silence.

'I haven't bumped into Prue in years,' muses Ben, after a moment.

Layla sniffs. 'That's because she avoids the village like the plague.'

Ben and I exchange a glance as Layla scrapes back her chair and bounds over to the counter to sprinkle more chocolate on her cappuccino.

He reaches over and lightly touches my hand. 'By the way, I really wouldn't consider it nosy if you wanted to ask me anything to do with your grandmother. She was one very special lady, and if I can help in any way by filling in the gaps, please ask away.'

I nod but it's impossible to speak because of the lump in my throat.

'I knew her most of my life, from when we were kids at the village school.' His eyes glisten. 'I miss her, too.'

Plonking herself back down at the table, Layla catches the tail end of this and nods. 'Ivy was cool. She actually sort of understood teenagers, instead of deciding we're all yobbos like some folk around here. Including Mum.'

Ben smiles in agreement. He's just the sort of man Ivy would admire. Quietly spoken but self-assured. Younger than his years in mind and body. A *gentle* man.

Ben clears his throat. 'I suppose we'd better get down to the real business of the day, eh, Holly?'

My head swims. I'm still far away in my own thoughts about his relationship with Ivy, and just for a second, I actually imagine he's talking about the business of finding my granddad.

Layla nudges me and murmurs, 'The cake stall.'

'Ah, yes, of course.' I force a smile. 'The cake stall.'

We chat about the fete and what Layla and I can do to make the cake stall a success.

I'm really warming to Ben. He's wise and thoughtful with a lovely, dry sense of humour, and almost without realising I'm doing it, I'm analysing his face, his posture, his mannerisms, even the shape of his nails, looking for clues as to whether we could possibly be related.

When he said he missed Ivy, I could tell the sentiment came right from the heart. He wasn't just saying it to make me feel better. He really meant it.

Oh God, what if . . .?

I have to take a sip of coffee to hide the sudden surge of emotion. My hand is shaking and when I set down the cup, it rattles in the saucer.

'Do you help to organise the fete every single year?' Layla is asking.

Ben chuckles. 'It certainly looks that way. They always ask me and I never have the heart to refuse.'

I leave them chatting and slip off to the Ladies, where I lean on the basin and stare at myself in the mirror. It's ridiculous imagining Ben might be the granddad I never knew. *Isn't it?* It's just too fantastical for words – like something Layla might dream up when she's penning one of her cosy mysteries.

So why, if I don't believe it, am I examining my features in the mirror for any trace of a family resemblance?

TWENTY-FIVE

When I get back to the table, Layla is showing Ben how to work his phone.

'See all this?' Layla indicates the pile of summer fete paperwork he's generated. 'You could store the information on your phone instead. Then it would all be in one place.'

Ben nods. 'Sounds great but I wouldn't know where to start. I've only just discovered how to send a text. I had no idea what an emoticon was until yesterday.' He smiles sheepishly. 'I thought it was something to do with car theft.'

Layla grins. 'I could give you a lesson if you like. Walk you through all the features on your phone.'

'That would be marvellous.' Ben beams. 'Thank you, Layla. I'd really appreciate your help some time.'

'Hey, no problem.' She smiles a little shyly, her cheeks tinged with pink. 'I know we haven't got time now, but there are a couple of things on this phone that would make your life *so* much easier . . .'

Ben watches, genuinely fascinated by what she's showing him, and I suddenly wish Prue and Jack were here to witness how helpful and lovely Layla can be when the mood takes her. I get the feeling they get her bolshy, rather childish side most of the time, and as a result, their expectations of her are perhaps limited.

Jack works his butt off all week and Prue seems to be in her own little world most of the time. Even at meal times they all do their own thing, according to Layla. Ships that pass in the night, with no time for the kind of healthy communication that brings families closer together.

It's a slightly depressing scenario. Sometimes, when Layla is on one of her rants about her family, and declaring she can't *wait* to have a place of her own, my heart feels heavy. From my vantage point, she has family, therefore she has everything. She just doesn't realise it.

I sneakily think all three of them need their heads knocking together.

At last we get down to chatting about the practicalities involved in organising a cake stall, and Layla suggests I make notes on my phone.

She turns to Ben. 'I'm dyslexic, so I can't do it.' She laughs. 'At least, I *could*, but it wouldn't make much sense and we'd be sitting here till midnight.'

Ben nods at her revelation. 'They say there's an element of genius in a lot of people with dyslexia. Look at Leonardo da Vinci.'

'Tom Cruise and Jennifer Aniston,' I supply, having done some research. 'Not sure about "genius" but they're exceptional in their field.'

Layla nods. 'Apparently Agatha Christie had a learning disability and couldn't spell for toffee. Imagine that.'

I nudge her gently and murmur, 'You're in good company, then, especially Ms Christie.'

She stiffens, shooting me a warning look.

I know what it means.

Don't tell Ben about my writing!

'He's class. I wouldn't mind having him for a granddad myself.' Layla peers at me to gauge my reaction as we stand outside the deli-café watching Ben hurry off to his car. '*Clueless* about modern

238

technology, though. And we're no further forward in discovering if he's your granddad or not.' She sighs. 'I wanted to ask him straight out if he'd had an affair with Ivy. But I pictured your face and stopped myself in time.'

'Gosh, Layla. That was very mature of you. You sure you're not coming down with something?'

'Oh, ha, ha! Very funny. I'm not a kid any more, you know. I am learning when it's best to keep my mouth shut.'

I grin at her. 'Subtlety *and* diplomacy? Crikey, Layla, we'll make an impressive adult of you yet. Ben certainly seemed grateful for your technology skills.'

We walk in the direction of Moonbeam Cottage in companionable silence, deep in our own thoughts.

'Something happened that night at the dinner party,' Layla muses when we reach my garden gate. 'Something that was important to Ben. Do you think it might have been him and Ivy – erm – *doing it* for the first time?'

'That did occur to me – especially when he described it as a "life-changing" night.'

'I wonder what happened to his girlfriend?'

'Lucy Feathers?'

She nods. 'He obviously didn't marry Lucy. But maybe, if we found her, she'd be able to tell us whether Ben and Ivy were ever an item. I googled her but nothing came up and no-one around here seems to know where she lives.'

I stare at her. 'You've been doing detective work in the village?'

She shrugs. 'I've asked a few customers at the garden centre. I've been telling people Lucy Feathers is an old friend of Mum's and we want to get back in touch. I've drawn a blank so far though.'

I fall silent, mulling over Layla's proactive approach, as she talks on about how much she likes Ben. It makes me slightly uneasy. It was all very well when it was just the two of us, talking things over and trying to solve a mystery, but I'm not sure I want the wider community knowing all about Ivy's affair.

No-one knew that her husband, Peter, was emotionally abusive towards her. Ivy kept quiet about that, probably out of a misplaced sense of loyalty towards him and guilt at finding herself having feelings for another man.

But with my lovely grandma no longer here to defend herself, I'm worried people might judge her harshly for having an affair, without knowing the circumstances.

A little voice in my head is nagging me.

Ivy's reputation is not the only reason I'm not keen on news of our search spreading.

The fact is, Layla's detective work is making the search for my granddad frighteningly real. The more people she talks to, the more likely we are to make progress and solve the mystery.

My insides are in uproar at the very thought.

With her uncanny way of sensing my mood, Layla frowns and says, 'Look, I know you must be scared, Holly. But trust me, it'll be fine. You've got to do this. Then whatever happens, at least you'll have found out the truth and you won't drive yourself mad wondering what might have happened if you'd only been a little bit braver.'

I give her a feeble smile. 'Wise words.' I lean in to her for a second to show my gratitude.

'I know.' She tosses her head. 'I'm a genius. By the way, how did Midsummer Night with Sylvian go?'

I glance at her in horror. 'He *told* you about that?' *Oh, God, please don't say she knows about the tantric meditation!*

'Hey, relax. He hasn't told me any of the gory details. Just that he was planning a picnic in Ivy Garden.'

'Oh. Well . . . it was fine.'

She grimaces. 'Ooh, that bad, eh?'

'Let's just say Sylvian and I have – erm – different ideas about life.'

'Say no more.' She taps the side of her nose.

It hasn't taken me long to get over Sylvian and to realise that I had a very lucky escape there. We had nothing in common really. I was feeling so lonely when I arrived that I think I just grabbed on to him when he gave me encouragement. I needed to feel I wasn't entirely alone. I don't bear him any ill will at all. I still think he's a good person. It's just his lifestyle seems so alien to me.

'Now, we need to talk about the stall,' Layla says, 'so we can get things organised and do Ben proud.'

Instantly my heart goes into overdrive. I try to join in as Layla talks about the merits of whole cakes over muffins and vice versa, but I'm finding it hard when my stomach is fluttering and all I can think is: *How will our search for my granddad end?*

It will truly be a dream come true if there's a happy conclusion. *But what if there isn't?*

TWENTY-SIX

The next few weeks pass in a whirl of decorating the cottage and planning for the fete cake stall.

I'm aware I should be spending more time gardening for Prue, but I'm finding it hard to concentrate on anything. I just can't stop thinking about the whole Ivy mystery and wondering about Ben . . .

On my way back from the village store this morning, I'm so deep in thought, I almost collide with a woman walking towards me. We do the 'dancing' thing, trying to get past each other, and laugh at how silly it is.

She looks around sixty and she's dressed smartly in a floral skirt, blue jacket and sensible shoes. When she laughs, her whole face lights up. My mum would be like her, I think, as I often do.

And then, of course, I remember my brilliant idea for a matching agency, which I came up with years ago when I was in my early teens and raging hormones meant I was always wishing Ivy would bugger off and leave me alone, and I could have my real parents back. (Because, of course, *they* would have been so much more understanding . . .)

Wouldn't it be lovely, I used to think, if children without parents could be matched with parents without children? Such a simple idea but how much happiness it could bring! I'd only allow really lovely mums and dads on to my books and they'd have to pass a kindness test – possibly involving a stray kitten.

I got quite obsessed with the idea at one time. I mentioned it to my best friend at school and she gave me this really sad, pitying look. But actually, I wasn't looking for sympathy. I already had a parent, and despite the occasional tearful shouting match, deep down I knew that in having Ivy to fight my corner, I was a whole lot luckier than some.

I just thought I was on to something with the matching agency.

I smile, recalling those idealistic days of childhood when the idea was born. Things seemed much simpler then. Of course, when I was a bit older I learned all about adoption, but that seemed unnecessarily complicated, full of rules and regulations, and it took the shine off my enchanting vision.

Thinking about it now, on a purely practical level, a parent 'match' would certainly solve the problem of where to go for Sunday lunch, when everyone else is busy with cosy family plans.

My mobile rings. To my surprise, it's Prue.

'Hello. How are you?' I say. 'Is your sister feeling any better?'

'Oh, yes. Thank you. Now. Polly. I'm phoning to check everything is all right in the garden. I hope you're giving my greenhouse babies lots of love and care. The tomatoes especially need very *particular* attention.'

I wince. *Oh hell, do they?*

'Er, actually, I'm off there this afternoon,' I say quickly. 'And yes, the tomatoes are looking – um – delicious!'

'Excellent. Well, I'm expecting great things on my return. Goodbye.'

She hangs up without waiting for my reply.

I frown at the handset.

I'm fairly certain *she* wouldn't pass the kindness test. Too chilly by half. The poor stray kitten would be dismissed immediately and expected to fend for itself.

I feel a sudden pang of sympathy for Layla.

Prue is definitely no 'earth mother' . . .

Later, when I finally go over to Rushbrooke House, I'm alarmed at the amount of weeding that needs to be done. But then, it *is* July, the height of the growing season. The result is a very long session that makes me ache in places I didn't realise I had.

There are also the 'greenhouse babies' to check. In all the recent upheaval, I've been forgetting to do that, which is very remiss of me considering just how proud Prue is of her salad vegetables.

Thankfully, when I enter the greenhouse, everything looks fine. Not a greenfly in sight.

'Hi, Holly,' says a voice behind me, and I swing round.

It's Selena.

She's 'dressed for the country' in brown cord trousers, white shirt, tweed waistcoat and matching tweed hacking jacket. A brown cap perches at an angle on her gleaming chestnut hair. It pains me to admit it, but she definitely has a way with a jaunty angle. In that outfit, she could be modelling for a huntin', shootin', and fishin' catalogue.

'I was looking for Jack,' she says. 'I've got to get back to London tonight but he said on *no account* was I to leave without a kiss goodbye.' She smiles smugly, narrowing her eyes at me so they look almost feline. 'He's *such* a sweetie.'

I paste on a smile. 'If I see him, I'll tell him you're looking for him.'

'Thank you, Holly. Oh, and by the way, you'd better prune those tomato plants.'

'Really?' I swing round and stare at the plants in question. They're vibrant and green, climbing up the wooden sticks, with little orange flowers sprouting from their stalks.

'But they look really healthy,' I start to say. Then I think: *Hang on a sec, is she having me on?*

She's so sly. Can I really trust her to tell me the truth?

Selena shakes her head firmly. 'Appearances can be deceptive. If in doubt, get pruning. That was always Daddy's motto.'

'Your dad?'

She smiles sadly. 'He's gone now.' She swallows and glances down at her feet, and my heart goes out to her.

'He was a good gardener?' I prompt gently, in case she wants to tell me about him.

When someone you love dies, people often assume you'd rather not talk about them because you'll get upset, but it's not always the case. I always welcome any opportunity to remember Ivy.

When Selena looks up, she's smiling through her tears. 'Dad had real green fingers. We had an ornamental garden at Hatley Hall next to the maze, and Daddy used to insist on doing the pruning himself. He said the gardeners were never ruthless enough. I used to hold his sweater while he worked.'

'Memories like that can be a real comfort,' I murmur, surprised to suddenly be feeling such empathy towards my arch enemy.

She nods sadly. 'They can indeed, Holly.'

'And obviously with tomato plants, you have to – erm – prune away all the . . .' I wave my arm vaguely in the plants' direction, hoping she'll fill in the blank.

'Absolutely. Lop off all those beastly orange flowers. Cut them back to the wood, as Daddy would say.' She totters out on a cloud of Chanel No. 5, swatting away a wasp with a little squeal of horror. 'And Holly?' She turns at the door. 'Be *ruthless!*'

Ruthless? I can do that.

Twenty minutes later, the tomato plants are looking shiny, green and rather naked, every one of those pesky yellowy-orange flowers plucked and dropped in a box that lies at my feet.

I survey my handiwork and clap muck off my hands. A job well done, if I say so myself. Prue will be delighted.

I glance around the greenhouse, noticing a proliferation of

yellow flowers growing on another type of plant. I seem to remember Prue saying they were her prize courgettes.

More pruning!

Diligently, I set to work, nipping off the delicate little flowers. A high-pitched laugh distracts me.

Jack is walking towards me, across the lawn, with Selena running daintily beside him, trying to keep up.

'Holly? Could I have a quick word?'

'Yes, of course.' Jack doesn't usually concern himself with my tasks in the garden. Thank goodness. (If he did, I'd have been rumbled a long time ago.)

He clears his throat. 'Look, I know this is above and beyond the call of duty, but Layla's in the house trying to make a shepherd's pie and I'm worried she might set the kitchen on fire.'

'Really?' I laugh.

He grins. 'I was wondering if you could go in and supervise her for a while?'

'Yes, of course.' My ability to stop fires before they start *way* exceeds my gardening talents. This will be a breeze.

'Great. I'm running Selena to the station but I'll be back in an hour.'

They turn to leave. Then Jack swings round and stares at the tomato plants.

'Funny. I could have sworn they had blossom on them yesterday when I looked. I told Mum to expect a fine crop of tomatoes in a week or two. But I think she's going to be disappointed . . .'

Puzzled, he shakes his head, clearly fearing for his mental health.

Shocked, I glance at Selena. 'But didn't you say your father used to prune off the blossom?'

She glances at Jack with a wide-eyed look that says I'm obviously delusional. 'I don't know where you got that from, Holly,' she laughs. 'Daddy doesn't know the first thing about gardening!'

I frown. 'Your father's still with us?'

'Of course. I'm meeting him for dinner tonight.' A smug smile of victory flashes across her face. 'I'll tell Daddy you said hello, shall I?'

Speechless, I watch her trip away across the lawn with Jack. *Unbelievable!*

TWENTY-SEVEN

I find Layla in the messy kitchen, clutter on every surface. She's peering into a casserole dish on the ancient cooker top and there's an ominous whiff of burning, which is presumably why Jack asked for my help.

She turns. 'Welcome to the mad house. Think I've torched the minced beef.'

'Let's have a look.' We both stare into the dish and I swipe it off the heat. 'I think it's caught on the bottom.'

'As in "caught fire"?' Layla looks incredulous.

'Well, kind of. But if we're lucky, we could take out all but the very bottom layer that's burned and transfer the rest to another pan.' I glance around. 'Another pan?'

An assortment of pans and dishes sit on the worktop but I can't tell if they're clean.

Layla peers into them, shaking her head.

'You can't possibly have used *all* these pans for your shepherd's pie,' I laugh.

She looks puzzled. 'No. I've just used that one on the hob. The kitchen always looks like this.'

'Really? Doesn't anyone tidy up? It looks as if you've been burgled.'

Layla feigns an offended look. 'Well, *that's* rude.'

I grin, slightly shamefaced. Perhaps Layla's direct manner is starting to wear off on me. 'I mean, it's a *lovely* kitchen but just a bit disorderly, that's all,' I amend, noticing a strategically placed bucket over in a corner. The ceiling above it shows signs of a leak. In fact, the whole house has that slightly musty smell that hints at nasty surprises in the woodwork.

'It's a bloody dump, you mean,' grunts Layla. 'Look at the ceiling.'

We stare up at it and I wince. Some of the ancient plaster has crumbled away. It definitely needs some attention. But in a house this cavernous, where would you start?

'It's like a freaking haunted house,' grins Layla. She runs a large pan under the tap, swills it out roughly and presents it to me. 'Voila. One pan.'

'Great.' Trying not to notice what's been in it before, I grab a damp tea towel, wipe the bottom of the pan and tip the rescued beef into it. There's a carrot and a stock cube lying on the bench, along with a bag of sprouting potatoes.

'Does your mum usually do the cooking?' I ask, thinking Prue's absence must be the reason for the chaos.

Layla snorted. 'Not unless she absolutely has to. Like if we have Auntie Joan over on a Sunday. Usually, we all just get our own food. My favourite's Pot Noodles.'

'So you never sit down for a meal together, during the week, just you, your mum and your brother?'

'Hardly ever. If we waited for Jack, we'd starve to death. He's always back quite late. And Mum prefers to eat ridiculously early.'

'How early?' I ask, stirring the beef.

'Seven o'clock,' says Layla scathingly. 'Can you believe it? I'm never even in before eight.'

'Seven's okay. Any later and you won't be able to digest your food properly,' I point out, sounding scarily like a mother myself.

'Perhaps you should make an effort to get back earlier. Especially if your mum's cooked you something nice.'

Layla frowns. 'I don't think she's that bothered. I think she quite enjoys eating on her own. She says she likes the peace and quiet.'

I shrug. 'You might be surprised. So where do you have your – erm – Pot Noodles?'

She shrugs. 'If I'm in, I get my food and take it up to my room. Then I either record my stories or watch telly.'

She peers into the pan. 'I don't like shepherd's pie much, but Jack keeps banging on about how it's time we made an effort to eat proper food. He's paying me a tenner to do this.'

I stare at her. 'He *paid* you?'

She shrugs. 'Why not? It works for me.'

I feel a pang of sympathy for Jack. He works his butt off every day to provide for them all and the prospect of a scrap with a stroppy teenager over getting dinner on the table is probably an obstacle too far. No wonder he resorts to financial incentives.

I abandon the pan and peer in the fridge.

'What are you doing?' asks Layla at once.

I bring out some onions and an aubergine that's just this side of turning, along with a block of cheese and some milk. 'I think we can do a bit better than boring old shepherd's pie.'

I set Layla the task of digging around in the cupboards for a can of tomatoes, dried garlic and herbs, and I harpoon an opened bottle of red wine to add to the meat sauce.

'My version of moussaka,' I explain. 'Do you want to make the cheese sauce?'

An hour later, when Jack walks in, the kitchen is looking a lot tidier. The wooden table has been cleared and wiped clean and a vase of freshly picked freesias sits in the centre.

Jack looks around in mild surprise. 'You've been busy.'

I smile, feeling oddly self-conscious. 'Yes, we have. We've made moussaka.' My voice sounds weird, as if it doesn't belong to me. 'Or at least, my take on it. Layla made the cheese sauce.'

Jack grins and perches one buttock on the edge of the table. 'From a packet?'

He's changed into faded jeans and a blue checked shirt.

'No!' squawks Layla, full of indignation. 'I made it from scratch with butter and flour and everything.'

Jack nods, impressed. I'm aware of him studying me lazily, arms folded, with an appreciative smile that crinkles his eyes at the corners and brings fire charging into my cheeks. I keep breathing in little wafts of his cologne. I wish I didn't like it. But I do. Far too much.

'You can come again, Holly,' he says.

Smiling, I blush a bit more and concentrate hard on getting the moussaka into the oven.

'And I take it you'll be joining us for dinner?' he adds matter-of-factly, hopping off the table and going to select a bottle of red from the wine rack. He holds it aloft. 'Like a drink?'

'Oh, no, don't worry.' I hope he doesn't think I've been hanging around, expecting an invitation to stay. 'I'll be getting off home now.'

Layla clatters a pile of knives and forks on to the table. 'No, you won't. I'm setting you a place.' She lays the table with a flourish. 'So now you *have* to stay. It would be rude not to. Wouldn't it, brother dear?'

'Definitely.' Jack winks at me. 'And we'll need a second opinion on this cheese sauce of yours, dear sis.'

He smiles at Layla, watching her work. I get the feeling harmony in the kitchen doesn't occur terribly often here.

I laugh. 'Oh, well, if you put it like that . . .'

'Good.' Jack glances at his watch. 'Actually, I need to deliver a chair to a customer. Have I time to nip out before this incredible feast is served?'

'Loads of time,' I assure him. 'The moussaka will be an hour and we need to make dessert yet.'

'Can't wait.' He rubs his hands together. 'A sit-down dinner

252

during the week that doesn't involve peeling off cellophane. What a novelty.'

He grabs his keys from the table and goes out, whistling.

While he's gone, I show Layla how to make a crumble for dessert with some of the apples piled in the fruit bowl. We add cinnamon to the apples and porridge oats to the topping to make it extra delicious. She's never baked with Prue, apart from the messy stuff when she was little, and I find that quite sad. I learned all my baking skills from Ivy. She hated cooking and never attempted anything fancier than shepherd's pie. But baking she loved.

'We should light some candles,' I suggest, as Layla sneaks a spoonful of crumble. It's fresh from the oven, and she yelps as it burns her mouth.

And right at that moment, all the lights go out and we're plunged into gloom.

'Shit. Power cut,' says Layla. 'We haven't had one of those for months.'

'Told you we should light some candles.'

'Yeah, that was a bit spooky. Are you psychic or what?'

She pulls open drawers, presumably looking for candles, uttering a choice expletive when she can't find any.

She clicks her fingers. 'I know! Follow me.'

We leave by the back door and crunch along a gravel path in the descending gloom. It's only seven-thirty but there's a chill in the air and the sky is dark and threatening rain.

'Where are we going?' I ask.

'The cottage in the woods.'

'Are you sure?' Warning bells ring. I seem to recall Jack saying Prue doesn't like the cottage being disturbed. 'Won't your mum mind?'

Layla's charging along at a fair old pace. 'Mum's not here,' she calls back. 'And anyway, we're just looking for candles, not wrecking the place.'

A little way into the woods, there it is. A small but perfectly formed cottage. It's like a little house from a fairytale, except it has a sad, neglected air about it. The white paint is peeling off the front door and the two hanging baskets suspended from the porch are overgrown with weeds.

Layla pushes open the door with some effort as it seems to have got stuck – the wood warping over time perhaps – and we walk straight into the living room of what had been William Rushbrooke's private space.

I flick the light switch but of course nothing happens. I wonder whether that's because of the current black-out, or has the power long since ceased to reach this shabby little hidey hole in the woods?

A wooden desk in one corner holds an ancient word processor and a flask, with its black plastic cup sitting beside it. I wander over and draw my finger through the dust on the computer screen. A candle on a saucer has burned down to the wick and I notice the cup has been used and contains a film of mould from a long-ago coffee.

I shiver. When her husband died seventeen years ago, Prue obviously closed the door on his precious bolt-hole and left it exactly as it was. It reminds me of Miss Havisham in *Great Expectations*, a prisoner of the past in that ill-fated gown and veil, the wedding breakfast that was never eaten draped in cobwebs, left to go mouldy along with all her hopes and dreams.

A lump rises in my throat.

Poor Prue . . .

Layla is rummaging around in some boxes piled along one wall.

'Yes!' She holds up a church candle in each hand. 'I thought I'd find some here.'

'How did you know?'

She shrugs. 'I've been here before. Lots of times when Mum didn't know. It's cool, isn't it?'

We glance around and I nod. 'It is. I love the fact that it's hidden away in the woods, like the gingerbread house in Hansel and Gretel. It's so – romantic.'

Layla gives a little sigh. 'I think of my dad sitting there at the desk, using that weird dinosaur of a computer, dreaming up his inventions.' She pauses. 'I wish I'd known him. He sounded – I don't know – *different*. In a good way.'

I smile at her. 'A bit like you.'

Layla's eyebrows rise. 'You think so? You think I might have taken after him?'

I nod. 'Absolutely.'

She turns away, but not before I catch the glisten in her eyes.

She places the candles on the floor and opens a few more of the boxes, peering inside.

'Hey, look at this!'

She's holding an old orange folder in one hand and a glossy black and white photo in the other. I draw closer to look. It's a side-on picture of Layla, her hair dark, clearly its natural colour. Reed-slim in a black leotard, she's holding her arms in a ballet pose, laughing into the camera.

I look again.

It's not Layla at all.

'It's Mum,' says Layla, sounding shocked. 'I thought it was me for a minute.' She stares at the photo. 'I look just like her when she was young.'

'Haven't you seen these photos before?' I ask, surprised.

'No, they were in this file. I thought they must be Dad's engineering papers or something so I never looked.'

She passes me a few of the photos, all showing Prue not much older than Layla, in various laughing dance poses. She looks so happy in them, it makes me wonder who the photographer was. Her husband? William Rushbrooke?

I turn one of them over. There's an inscription on the back in blue ink.

Broadway, New York, July 1978.

I gasp. 'Oh my God. Your mum danced on Broadway?'

Layla nods, looking surprised at my reaction. 'She first met Dad in New York. He was over there on holiday with a mate and they went to a Broadway show and Mum was one of the dancers. Jack told me he fell in love with her on the spot and tried to get backstage to talk to her but he couldn't. So he waited at the side door for her and that's how they met.'

Realising my mouth is open, I snap it shut. 'Wow. How romantic. She must have been a brilliant dancer. I bet she's told you loads of tales about those days – did she ever work with anyone famous?'

Layla shrugs. 'I don't think so. Jack mentioned someone called Glenda Close?'

'*Glenn Close?* Wow! Your mum ought to write a book.' I grin at her. 'Or maybe *you* should write it!'

Layla crosses her eyes comically. 'You're joking. Mum never talks about her life in New York. *Ever.* I think she's ashamed that she used to be a dancer.'

'Ashamed? But why? She must have been a fabulous dancer to have been picked for productions on Broadway.'

'Yeah?' Layla stares at me.

I nod excitedly. 'Oh, yes!'

'So why won't she talk about it?' Scathingly, she says, 'Of course, she's lady of the manor now. Maybe she thinks she's too posh to have been in musicals.'

'But she should be proud of it! Crikey, if *I'd* been a dancer in the Big Apple, I'd be telling everyone I know and boring the pants off them.'

'Mum's not like most people. She—'

The door suddenly flies open and a torch is swung in our eyes. '*Layla?* What the *hell* do you think you're doing?'

TWENTY-EIGHT

Beside me, Layla jumps.

'I was looking for candles,' she bursts out, clearly well-practised at finding excuses for bad behaviour. Except that in this instance she is telling the truth.

Jack's face is like thunder. 'Well, get them and let's get out of here. You know the rules.'

'What rules?' Layla looks sulky.

'Don't give me that,' growls Jack. 'You know what I'm talking about. Mum hates you disturbing this place.'

'Well, I don't know why,' grumbles Layla, although she does as she's told, gathering up half a dozen candles. 'She's got a photo of Dad by her bed to remember him by. Why does she need this place as well? It's such a waste, sat here empty all the time—'

Jack turns and fixes her with a glare and she snaps her mouth shut. He glances at me and his face softens slightly. 'Sorry, Holly. It's just she knows the score.'

He marches off into the gloom and I follow him, turning at the door, just in time to see Layla quickly stuff the photos she found up her jumper with a guilty look.

Back at the house, she runs upstairs, supposedly to wash her hands but probably, I'm guessing, to escape the tense atmosphere. From what I remember, teenagers spend their whole lives in their bedrooms, and Layla is clearly no different.

I busy myself getting the moussaka out of the oven while Jack finds saucers for the candles and lights them, placing three on the table and dotting more on the counter where I'm working.

We collide at one stage, as I reach over to the rack for a serving spoon, and I feel his hand at my waist. A little shiver runs right through me, tingling all the way down my spine. I try to say a polite, 'Sorry.' But my throat seems suddenly as dry as the desert and all that comes out is an odd grunt.

Jack flicks on the music and Frank Sinatra fills the room at high volume.

'Mum's favourite,' he grins, turning it right down. 'Is it okay as background?'

I smile, bringing the food to the table. 'Yeah, great. Ivy loved Frank as well. I'm rather partial to a bit of "Moon River".'

Jack pulls out a chair for me. '"I've Got You Under My Skin",' he murmurs, close to my ear, as I sit down.

'Sorry?' I stare up at him, my heart suddenly hammering like a drum solo.

'One of Sinatra's best, I think. Along with "I Get a Kick Out of You",' Jack says, taking a seat opposite. He laughs softly. 'Sorry, does that make me sound very uncool?'

'No! No, not at all.' Flustered, I rise to my feet. 'Napkins! Do you have any?'

'Top drawer. I'll get them.'

I scurry over before he has a chance to get up, hiding my flushed face in the drawer.

What's wrong with me?

You'd think I'd never been alone with a man in a kitchen my entire life!

I take some calming breaths as I sort out matching napkins

with hands that tremble slightly. Then I turn and say brightly, 'I'll go and get Layla, shall I?'

Jack is lolling back in the chair, arms folded, long legs stretched out. He nods, grinning lazily at me, and I get the distinct impression he's been taking his time, studying my back view. Thank goodness I have on my best blue jeans and the pale green close-fitting top that always seems to attract compliments.

As another wave of heat sweeps over me, I resort to a bit of sweeping myself – out of the room . . .

Hurrying up the stairs and wafting cool air down my top, I call for Layla and she yells, 'Door straight ahead of you.'

I go in and she's sitting on her bed, the black and white photos spread out around her, staring at the one in her hands.

'Dinner's on the table,' I tell her, but she ignores me and leaps to her feet, her usual cool abandoned.

'Look at this.' She thrusts the photo into my hands.

It's a colour print this time of a slim woman in her mid-thirties. Wearing little more than a G-string and sparkly, plunging bra, she's wrapped around a silvery metal pole, head flung back in a posture of careless abandonment, which means I can see her face only in profile.

I look closer and my eyebrows shoot up.

'Bloody hell, it's Prue,' I murmur. Then I remember Layla's seeing this for the first time, too. 'Wow, your mum looked – erm – *hot* when she was younger.'

As soon as I say it, I realise it probably wasn't the best thing to point out to a teenager. *Hey, your mum was proper raunchy back in the day!*

But Layla doesn't even flicker. She's too busy staring at the photo herself with an expression of utter bewilderment on her face.

'Holly? Layla? Are you coming down? I can't wait to try this world-class cheese sauce.'

At the sound of Jack approaching, we glance at each other in shock.

'Hide them,' I hiss, wanting to avoid another scene. 'Quick.' I gather up the other photos and, pulling open the wardrobe door nearby, I virtually throw the photos inside.

'No!' shrieks Layla, and it flashes across my mind that maybe the wardrobe is broken and about to collapse.

A second later, the reason for her panicked response becomes very clear.

Out of the wardrobe tumbles a kaleidoscope of colourful objects, all roughly the same size and apparently people-shaped. They bounce on to the floor and land in a heap at my feet.

I stare at them, frozen with shock.

The locals, including Prue, have been exclaiming for weeks about their missing gnomes. And now we know where their beloved garden ornaments have been enjoying their vacation.

In Layla's wardrobe.

'Layla, what's been going on?' I find my voice. 'What on earth possessed you?'

'It wasn't me,' she says quickly. 'At least, it wasn't only me. We all did it just for a laugh. It was Josh's idea . . .'

'Oh, *Josh*. Well, that makes sense.' I shake my head wearily at her. 'And I suppose he sweet-talked you into hiding the spoils?'

She shrugs miserably. 'You're going to tell Jack, aren't you?'

I sigh heavily, not at all sure what I'm going to do. Perhaps if I make her promise to return them all to their rightful homes, I could keep it quiet . . .?

'Honestly, Layla, why on earth you think that loser Josh is so great, I'll never know.'

Well, that's not exactly true, I think to myself. I had teenage crushes on unsuitable boys at school so I know what it's like.

'Yes, yes, okay,' says Layla grumpily. 'Look, if I promise to take them all back—'

'Layla? Holly?' Jack knocks and enters the room.

He takes in the scene, Layla looking red-faced and guilty, the floor covered in small, bearded men.

'I'm sorry,' Layla bursts out. 'It was my friend's idea of a joke. It was stupid. I'll take them all back.'

Jack continues to stare at the gnomes.

Then he walks over and picks up two of them. He brandishes them at Layla. 'These belong to Mum. She's been distraught over their disappearance. You do realise they were the last gift Dad ever bought her?'

Layla's mouth drops open in horror. 'No! I never knew that. Honestly, I didn't. If I had, I'd never have *dreamed* of taking *her* garden gnomes.'

She looks so distraught, it's obvious she's telling the truth.

'You shouldn't have taken any of them,' starts Jack angrily, but Layla, fighting back tears, slides off the bed and flees out of the room.

'Layla?' Jack strides out on to the landing. 'Come back here.'

'Sorry. I really am,' she calls. 'I'll be at Anne-Marie's.' And the front door slams.

When Jack walks slowly into the bedroom, I'm picking the motley collection of garden gnomes off the floor and – for want of something better to do with them – arranging them on top of a chest of drawers by Layla's bed.

Jack stares at them for a moment, shaking his head. I catch his eye and feel a smile start to tickle at the corners of my mouth. I suppress it, though, because obviously, this is a grave matter and I'm not sure what Jack's approach will be.

At last, he heaves a sigh. 'Bloody teenagers. Her mother's going to flip when she finds out her own daughter is the mystery garden plunderer.' He comes over and picks up one of the garish newcomers – a cheery little chappy with rosy cheeks, a battered red hat and a grin that borders on the lascivious.

'Hideous things,' he murmurs. 'But they don't deserve the kidnap treatment. Or at least, their owners don't.' He frowns. 'She'll be taking every single one of them back with a big apology. If they can remember where they came from.'

'They?'

'I've no doubt it was a group effort. Layla probably just agreed to hide the stolen goods, more fool her.'

He looks at me, his mouth twitching up at one corner.

'Are you laughing?' I ask.

'No, no. This is serious.'

I eye him, not sure if he's joking. Or at least *half*-joking. 'It *is* quite funny. She does have a sense of humour, your sister.'

'Yeah, she does. But she has to learn that thoughtless "jokes" like this have consequences. She'll wish she'd never embarked on it by the time I've finished with her.'

I grimace. 'Will the punishment be harsh?'

Jack grins. 'No, but I'll be going with her when she humbly apologises to all of our neighbours – and being embarrassed by your relatives is the worst thing ever for a teenager.'

He puts the leery gnome back and picks up another two.

'Mum's,' he explains, as we go downstairs. 'She'll be so relieved to have them back.'

Jack returns the gnomes to their rightful place in the back garden, then we sit down opposite each other at the table and I serve the food while he pours me a glass of wine.

'She shouldn't have taken our gnomes.' He shakes his head wearily. 'Dad gave them to Mum as a joke. She hasn't exactly got green fingers. She likes to think she's a gardening expert but we all know better.' He grins. 'Dad bought her the gnomes the Christmas before he died, saying he thought a bit of help in the garden from those guys might improve matters. She pretended to be offended but those gnomes always had pride of place at the back door. She named them Charlie and Dimmock.'

I smile sadly. No wonder she's been so upset, thinking Charlie and Dimmock had been stolen.

We're silent a moment in the gathering gloom, sampling our moussaka.

'Layla can't have known that story,' I point out. 'Otherwise she would never have taken the gnomes.'

Jack's blue eyes are velvety dark in the pool of candlelight. 'I'm sure you're right.'

'I am. She'd never deliberately upset her mum like that, I'm certain of it.' I cross my fingers in my lap, determined to speak to her myself.

Jack nods. 'Maybe she forgot that Dad had given them as a present. It was way before she was born, after all. Layla's a pain in the arse these days,' he chuckles. 'But she's never nasty.'

'She's got a really good heart. And she's been an incredible help to me in the garden,' I tell him. *And with other things, too.* 'Your sister is a girl of hidden depths,' I add, thinking of her 'cosy mystery' stories, which apparently only Sylvian and I know about.

Jack nods. 'She's extremely bright. But she wasn't diagnosed with dyslexia until she was eleven.'

'I know.'

He looks surprised. 'She told you? That she's dyslexic?'

When I nod, he says it has to be a first because she doesn't normally tell people.

His comment makes me ridiculously pleased. 'We talked about it. I've a feeling the dyslexia won't hold her back any more.'

He raises an eyebrow. 'You two seem to be getting along incredibly well. I've noticed. She seems to have really taken to you.' He smiles and a delicious warmth steals over me. 'Not that I'm surprised,' he murmurs, his eyes searching my face. 'Not at all.'

The compliment – and the way he says it – throws me completely. Colour surges into my cheeks and I swallow, hardly able to meet his eye. When I do manage a quick, shy glance, he's sitting back in his chair, arms folded, smiling at me in a way that makes my heart beat faster.

My insides quiver. How am I supposed to force down even a

mouthful of this food now? My throat feels so dry, it would probably get stuck.

What the hell is going on with me?

I take a deep breath.

Pull yourself together, girl!

He's grateful you've managed to get through to his bolshy, adolescent sister. That's all . . .

I paste on a bright smile. 'I like Layla very much. She talks to me, I guess because I'm not family. She's a credit to you.'

'That's good to hear.' He leans forward and I feel his warm hand close over mine. A million shivers hurtle up my spine. Our eyes meet and hold, and my body starts pulsing with long-forgotten but delicious feelings that make me move slightly forward in an unconscious desire to close the gap between us . . . inching me nearer to those magnetic eyes and that beautiful mouth that I suddenly realise I so badly want to feel against mine.

An image of the candle glows in the dark depths of his pupils as we slowly drink each other in. My heart is slamming against my ribcage.

If it weren't for the table separating us . . .

Without warning, a deep 'clunk' sounds out, and suddenly lights are blazing all around us. We blink at each other in surprise. The power cut is over.

I give an awkward laugh and withdraw my hand from his to run it through my hair.

Jack does the same. Then he rises to his feet, scraping back the chair with a sound like nails down a blackboard. 'We need dessert.'

I watch him as he brings the apple crumble out of the oven. Tonight, talking and sharing a meal with Jack, has been so lovely. I don't want it to end.

Then I remember Selena and a cold hand grips my heart. However I feel about Jack, nothing can ever happen between us. He's already spoken for.

And that's when it hits me with such force, my heart practically leaps out of my chest.

I'm in love with Jack!

He turns with the crumble. 'Shall I just bring it to the table and we can help ourselves?'

I stare up at him, shell-shocked.

'Okay?' he asks with a little frown.

I rally myself. 'Yes, yes.' Then I lurch to my feet and start clearing away the plates with trembling hands. My head is whirling with the glorious shock of it, and I'm in such a daze, I end up trying to wrestle the huge marble chopping board into the dishwasher.

Smiling, he reaches down and gently takes the cumbersome board out of my hands, and the contact sends a little ripple of pleasure through my entire body,

Did he feel it, too?

Then I have a horrible thought. Maybe getting dessert was just an excuse to move away from me? Were my feelings written right across my face? When, just for a moment, I imagined a heat between us?

Oh God, what if I've embarrassed him! What if he thinks I've developed a crush on him? I couldn't bear it if Jack felt sorry for me.

We sit down for apple crumble and there's a touch of awkwardness between us that wasn't there before.

Think of something to say!

We both start talking at once. Then there's a splash as something plops into his wine.

He laughs and looks up. 'What the . . .?'

It seems a lump of plaster has fallen from the ceiling.

Grinning, Jack fishes it out. 'The whole bloody place is literally falling down around our ears.'

We look at each other and burst out laughing, which dispels the awkward atmosphere perfectly.

'Do you think Layla's okay?' I ask after a while.

Jack glances out of the window at the darkening sky and frowns. 'If you don't mind, once we've eaten, I'll walk you home then go and collect her from her friend's house.'

I nod, unable to help the swoop of disappointment inside at the thought that the night is ending. 'Of course.' I put down my spoon. 'Let's go now. I'm not really hungry, to be honest, and you can heat this up and have it with Layla when you get back.'

'You sure?' His eyes on me are full of concern, as if above all else, he doesn't want to let me down.

'Of course,' I say lightly. 'I'd feel much happier knowing Layla's all right.'

Minutes later, we're crunching along the path through the woods, the light from our torches giving the trees a bleached and rather eerie appearance. I'm very glad Jack is with me. He makes me feel safe.

Then I reflect that, depending on what happens with Ben, Moonbeam Cottage will likely be on the market soon and I'll be returning to my life in Manchester. I'll probably never see Jack again . . .

And it isn't just Jack I'll miss.

It's now early August. I arrived here in April – just four months ago – and yet there are people in this village I've already grown very fond of. The thought of leaving and never coming back makes me feel surprisingly heavy-hearted.

I'm even growing more used to the countryside.

When I first arrived, everything about it jarred, particularly the fear that I might find myself isolated and in danger, in the middle of nowhere. But since my chat with Connie, when I poured out all my grief over the horrible way my parents died, I've made a sort of peace with the tragedy. I no longer feel so haunted by it. Talking about everything was something I should have done long, long ago, instead of bottling it all up in the hope I could contain it, which of course was impossible.

In any case, it's all fairly immaterial because soon I'll be back in Manchester, where such a situation is never likely to arise. Wrapped in the cocoon of my little flat, surrounded by neighbours on all sides, I'll feel safe again, buffered by the solidity of the buildings and reassured by the constant hum and bustle in the streets down below me.

City life has always been in my blood.

But with a shock, I realise that things have changed.

Leaving Appleton for the last tme will be nowhere near as easy as I thought it would be, back in April . . .

TWENTY-NINE

Woken from a deep sleep, I fumble for the phone.

At the sound of Prue's staccato voice, I sit up straight in bed. She has that effect. 'Good morning, Holly. How is the garden?'

'The garden?' I squeak. 'Oh, the garden is in great shape. Don't worry about that.'

I rub my eyes with my free hand. Honestly, how did it happen that the morning Prue decides to phone me is the one morning I manage to sleep in?

I glance at the clock. Six-forty-five.

Six-forty-five? Is she having a laugh?

'It's just I'm coming back later today and I wanted to give you some warning,' she adds, her directness proving more effective than a bucket of cold water at dragging me fully to my senses.

'So no problems, then?' she asks.

'No problems at all. It's – um – looking marvellous.'

At least, it will be by this afternoon!

Mentally, I started ticking off jobs already done and listing those still to do.

'Excellent, Polly. Well, I'll see you later. Jack will be collecting me later this morning. Will you be at Rushbrooke House when I arrive, around three?'

269

'Yes, I will.'

She hangs up, and I dive out of bed and head for the shower. That gives me roughly eight hours to get the garden looking decent for her return.

Weeds, beware! I'm on to you!

Later, rubbing steam from the mirror, I stare at my pink-faced reflection, thinking about Jack and recalling the previous night with a little shiver of pleasure. Perhaps I'll see him later, when he arrives at Rushbrooke House after collecting Prue from Kent?

Then I remember Selena is sure to be with him and my heart plummets. She never misses a chance to monopolise him – and truthfully, I really can't blame her.

We actually have something in common, Selena and I . . .

As I clean my teeth and pull on my 'best' gardening gear, I once more analyse the exchange I had with Jack at my door.

We were walking through the woods, talking about Layla, and Jack confessed he hated having to be so hard on his sister but that he worried about her constantly. She was so bright and could do anything she put her mind to, he said, but he felt the kids she hung around with were a bad influence.

'She's a teenager, Jack,' I told him gently. 'It's her *job* to be bolshy! But she'll work through it and she'll be fine.'

I wanted to tell him about her ambition to be a writer. I had a feeling he'd be amazed in a really good way. But of course I couldn't, because I'd promised Layla it was our secret.

At my gate, I turned to say goodnight but, to my surprise, Jack walked up the path with me.

'So you're really leaving us soon?' he demanded suddenly. 'Going home?'

'Well, yes.' I stared up at him. His face was in darkness and I couldn't quite make out his expression. 'It was always my intention to get the cottage on the market as soon as possible so I could get back to Manchester.'

'It's not exactly a great time to be selling a property.'

He sounded brusque and I laughed in surprise. 'Isn't it? I thought houses were snapped up around here as soon as they went on the market.'

'If you're very lucky.'

'Well, here's hoping I will be . . . lucky.'

He nodded and looked down, stuffing his hands in his pockets. 'Right, well, I'd better go and find Layla. Goodnight, Holly.'

He walked off, clicking the gate shut and raising his hand.

'Goodnight,' I called, taken aback by Jack's sudden mood change.

I'd thought he must be more worried about Layla than I realised. It didn't help that his work routine was so punishing, it left him little time to be with his family – and not for the first time, I wondered why he didn't make the leap to selling bespoke furniture. It was obvious that was where his heart lay. Not in the City.

I'm so distracted thinking about the strangeness of that conversation with Jack that I manage to leave the house wearing my smart loafers, and have to return a minute later for my scruffy gardening shoes.

But soon – less than an hour after Prue's phone call – I'm over at Rushbrooke House, hard at work in the garden.

After a while, Layla comes out of the house to say hello as I'm kneeling on the grass, attempting to do right by a rose bed. I look up, shading my eyes from the glare. It isn't quite nine-thirty, but already the July sun is hot.

Layla grins down at me. 'Just pluck out green things and you'll be fine.'

'Oh, ha-ha!'

'And by the way, roses *like* being pruned. But tomatoes aren't so keen.'

I bark a laugh. 'Crikey, the wit is in full flood this morning. What on earth did you have for breakfast?'

'Funny you should say that. It was *Wit*-abix.' She crosses her eyes at the corny joke.

I sit back and groan. 'So I take it Jack told you. About the tomato pruning?'

'Easy mistake to make,' Layla says seriously.

I give her a disbelieving look and we both burst out laughing.

'I've just got to tidy the kitchen, then I'll come out and help,' she offers, and I give her a thumbs up.

She turns. 'By the way, I was thinking, Mum could be the dance judge.'

I frown, taking a minute to understand what she means.

'The summer fete,' she says. 'Ben's desperate for someone to judge the dancing and Mum's a dancer.'

'*Was* a dancer,' I say slowly, mulling it over. It's a great idea in principle, but I'm fairly certain Prue would refuse point blank to do it.

Watching her walk off across the grass, I find myself wishing Layla would offer to help Prue as readily as she volunteered to assist me in the garden. By all accounts, she's pretty lazy around the house – in common with most teenagers, granted – and I'm certainly not fooled by this sudden willingness to tidy up the kitchen. She's probably hoping to get into Prue's good books, to soften the blow when the truth is revealed – that it was actually Layla who 'kidnapped' Charlie and Dimmock . . .

By the time I hear Jack's car draw up at the front of the house, soon after three, I'm hot and sweaty and desperate for a shower. But at least the garden is looking well groomed.

I'm not really sure about gardeners' etiquette. Do I carry on working and let Prue come and find me? Or should I pop my head round and say hello?

In the end, I plaster on a smile and walk round the side of the house, attempting a discreet brow wipe with the back of my hand.

My heart sinks.

Selena is there, sucking up to Prue, helping her with the smaller bags. She must have gone to Kent with Jack to collect

Prue. Either that or she got the train up and Jack collected her at the station.

Whatever, it's obvious they're still an item.

When Selena sees me, she makes a great show of linking her arm flirtatiously through Jack's and whispering in his ear. I pretend I haven't noticed them walking off, round the side of the house. As Jack opens the gate for her, he turns back to look at me, and I quickly flick my eyes away and follow Prue into the house.

She seems pleased to see me. 'Polly! I do hope you've been keeping a tally of your hours. I can't wait to do a tour of the garden.'

'Oh, good grief. Someone's been cleaning,' she says when we enter the kitchen. She stares around her in amazement.

I smile. 'That was Layla.'

Prue looks around her, amazed, and Layla bursts in at that moment.

'What do you think?' She beams at Prue.

'It looks lovely, darling. Now, I'm absolutely desperate for a proper cup of tea. My sister is so thrifty, she uses teabags twice.'

Grinning, Layla fills the kettle a little too enthusiastically, managing to spray water everywhere.

'Dear, dear, nothing changes. Welcome home, me.' Prue clips over to help with the mopping process, but she's smiling as she puts her arm round Layla's shoulders.

'So what's this about a cake stall?' she asks, as we sit down to drink tea at the freshly cleared kitchen table. The flowers still sit in the centre in their glass vase, reminding me, with a little stab of emotion, of sitting here with Jack the night before in the glow of the candlelight. I'm trying hard not to think about what Selena and he are up to in the garden.

'It was Layla's idea,' I tell Prue, hoping to encourage this fragile mother–daughter bond that her absence appears to have engendered.

It's not a lie. Not entirely. It was Layla's idea to turn detective

273

and help me find my grandfather, and then, of course, she suggested we get closer to Ben by becoming involved in preparations for the summer fete.

We chat about our ideas for the cake stall and then I start bringing the topic of conversation round to other aspects of the fete. 'Ben's desperately in need of someone to judge the dancing competition,' I add, busying myself freshening the teapot. 'Layla and I think the perfect person for the job would be you.'

You could cut the stunned silence with a knife. Even Layla is quiet. I bring the teapot back to the table.

Prue is staring at me in alarm. She's gone chalk white.

'So what do you think?' I ask lightly, pouring her more tea.

Layla leans forward eagerly. 'Go on, Mum. You'll be brilliant.'

Prue manages to find her voice. 'I think you've both gone mad,' she says bluntly, before pushing back her chair and walking out of the kitchen. We stare at each other nervously, listening to the back door open and Prue's footsteps on the terrace beyond.

'Well, that went well,' I comment.

Layla makes a face. 'I might have known. She won't do it in case she bumps into that bloody Ribena. I'd like to deck that witch, I really would.'

'Violence isn't the way,' I say automatically.

'Well, yes, I know *that*.' Layla flicks her eyes at the ceiling. Her lips are pressed together and I can tell she's furious on Prue's behalf. I feel pretty annoyed myself.

'I can totally understand you wanting to protect your mum. And of *course* I know you wouldn't do anything silly,' I tell her. 'You're far too intelligent for that.'

She groans. 'Except when it comes to kidnapping garden gnomes.'

'You're regretting that?'

She nod gloomily. 'Of course I am. Mum's going to go frigging apeshit when she finds out.'

As if on cue, there's a squeal from outside and the back door

274

bursts open. 'Charlie and Dimmock are back!' Prue practically dances into the room, her eyes shining like an eight-year-old waking up on Christmas morning. She holds the gnomes aloft, one in each hand, like a victory salute. Then she clasps them both to her chest.

'Your dad bought them for me one Christmas.' She smiles at Layla, her eyes shiny with happy tears. 'I honestly never thought I'd see them again.'

Layla has slid so far down in her seat, she's almost under the table. She looks thoroughly wretched.

'Gosh, that's brilliant,' I smile.

'I know. Layla, isn't it wonderful? I actually don't care who took them, I'm just so delighted they've brought Charlie and Dimmock back again!'

'You really don't care who took them?' Hope sparks in Layla's eyes.

'No, my love, I don't. I'm just so happy to have them back.' She sets the gnomes on the table, and to Layla's obvious surprise, gives her a hug and a kiss on the cheek.

I watch in amazement. It's the happiest and most relaxed I've ever seen Prue. Even Layla seems encouraged by this display of affection. She's smiling at her mum, although I couldn't help wondering how much of it is relief that Prue doesn't seem to care about the identity of the kidnap culprit.

The door opens and Jack strides into the kitchen, his face thunderous.

'Layla, haven't you got something to tell Mum?' he demands, with a breathtaking lack of preamble.

Still smiling, Prue turns to her daughter. 'Something to tell me?'

The room falls silent, except for Layla's audible gulp.

She glances at me with the desperate look of someone who's well and truly cornered.

'Well?' prompts Jack.

THIRTY

Prue lays her hand on Jack's arm. 'What is it? You're scaring me.'

'It was me, Mum,' confesses Layla in a small voice. 'I kidnapped the gnomes. I'd forgotten Dad bought them for you, otherwise I would never have . . .' She trails off miserably.

Prue's face falls.

'I'm so sorry, Mum.'

Prue says nothing. She just calmly picks up the gnomes and walks out.

'It's not so hilarious now, is it?' barks Jack, and Layla gives a strangled sob before fleeing from the kitchen.

'She's really sorry,' I say softly. 'You could tell she was horrified that she'd upset her mum like that.'

'Yes, well, it's a bit late for sorry. I had to make sure she could see the devastation her stupid, unthinking actions have caused.' He glares at me. 'You think I was *wrong*?'

'No, of course not. She shouldn't have done what she did. It's just I don't think yelling is the answer.' I shrug. 'It's obvious she was already aware she'd messed up big time.'

'Damn right, she did. And listen, I'd very much *like* to have the time to pussyfoot around being all diplomatic and considerate with her, but unfortunately, I don't. It's a full-time job trying to keep this bloody roof from falling down on our heads – quite literally. Is it too much to expect Layla to start pulling her weight around here, instead of behaving like a spoilt brat with no consideration at all for her family? And by that I mean her *mother*.'

He's glowering at me, challenging me to argue.

'Perhaps the problem is you.' I'm struggling to keep my voice calm. 'If you gave up the job you so clearly hate and started doing the work you enjoy, you'd not only be a less stressed, nicer person to live with, but you might also have a family life. I mean, do you ever actually talk to Layla? *Really* talk?'

'She's a teenager,' he barks. 'Teenagers *won't* talk.'

'Well, she talks to me.' To my great astonishment, I find there's actually a lump in my throat. 'You never know, Jack. If you tried, you might be surprised.'

'She said yes.'

'Who said yes?' I glance across at Layla, who's slumped in the passenger seat, staring glumly ahead. She won't tell me what's wrong, but clearly something bad has happened.

'Mum,' she says. 'She's agreed to judge the dancing competition.'

We're on our way to Ben's house to talk about the summer fete and, aside from worrying about Layla, I'm desperately trying to keep Florence from stalling every time I slow down. Ben lives a little way out of Appleton but he still feels very much a part of the village community.

'Wow, well done you. How on earth did you manage to persuade her?'

She shrugs. 'We had a big discussion and I told her I was really sorry for taking Charlie and Dimmock. So then I admitted I'd been in the cabin looking for candles—'

I glance sideways. 'Gosh, you really were confessing everything.'

She snorts. 'I know. I thought I might as well be hung for a sheep as a lamb. So anyway, I told her I'd found the photos of when she was a dancer and I was really proud of her, which actually, I am. She said no, I wasn't. And I said of course I was, because, let's face it, no other person I knew had a mother who'd lived in New York and danced in Broadway shows.'

I nod admiringly. 'Well played.'

'Yeah,' she says, rallying slightly. 'So then I said it would be one in the eye for that horrible Robina if Mum was to take charge of the dance competition and show her she didn't care two hoots about the witch.' She makes a face. 'Mind you, she didn't seem too sure about that. In fact, I thought I'd ruined it at that point.'

'So what happened?'

'Well, I told Mum I'd be there with her at the fete and I'd give the witch a black eye if she as much as looked at Mum the wrong way.' She turns and glares at me. 'I will, too.'

I smile encouragingly, recognising this is all just her bad mood coming out.

'I think that last part was the clincher,' she adds, 'because she said yes after that and she even cried with relief that I was offering to sort out the enemy.'

I laugh. 'Layla, that's brilliant. Well done. But I don't think the clincher was you offering to knock Robina's lights out.'

She frowns. 'No?'

I shake my head. 'I'd say she liked that you said you were proud of her and that you'd be there to support her.'

'Oh.' She's silent for a moment. 'Anyway, whatever, she's going to do it.'

'Ben will be pleased. Unless he's already got someone, of course.'

'No-one's better qualified than Mum, though.'

'Very true.'

I've got butterflies in my stomach at the thought of talking to Ben again. Mainly because I've made up my mind to ask him if he and Ivy were ever really close romantically. I've already briefed Layla on going to the bathroom for an extended visit to give me the chance to talk to him alone. I'm not quite sure how I'll phrase my question. I'm just going to play it by ear.

I've prepared myself for a negative result. I've told myself a hundred times that it's too good to be true that a man as nice as Ben would turn out to be my granddad. (My motto recently has been: expect little and then there's the chance you might be pleasantly surprised.)

'How long do I have to stay in the bathroom?' asks Layla. 'I don't want him thinking I've got some horrible disease.'

I laugh and try to swallow down the slightly sick feeling caused by my shredded nerves. 'Just use your common sense.'

'Okay. Are you nervous?'

'Just a bit.'

'Don't be. It'll be fine. You're far too nice not to have everything work out perfectly.'

I smile across at her, grateful for the sentiment, even if it is ridiculously naïve, but she's staring glumly ahead.

'Layla, what's the matter? Has something happened?'

She heaves a sigh and slumps lower in her seat, turning away from me to stare out of the window. To my alarm, I notice her chin trembling.

'Layla?' I say softly. 'Tell me what's wrong. I might be able to help.'

'No-one can help,' she says savagely. Then she turns and gives me a sheepish glance. 'But thank you for the offer.' She sighs again. 'Josh is going out with Anne-Marie but neither of them bothered to inform *me*. They just went behind my back.'

'The bloody little toe-rag!' I burst out, indignant on Layla's behalf.

'Which one?' she snarls.

'Well, there's not much to choose between them, by the sound of it,' I murmur, my heart going out to her. I remember how terrible it was the first time I had my heart broken. I thought the world had ended. 'Perhaps you're better off without them.'

Layla turns back to the window and doesn't bother answering.

'Hey, what's going on?' she asks a moment later, when we turn into Ben's street.

My heart sinks. About a dozen cars are parked half on the pavement around number nine. This is clearly a meeting for everyone concerned with the fete, not just Layla and me. And as we walk up the short driveway, squeezing alongside the cars parked there, I realise the chances of me getting Ben alone to chat are practically zero.

We exchange a disappointed look, although part of me actually feels relieved.

It's good to meet some of the other fete organisers, though. Some of them even promise to get their baking skills out of mothballs and contribute to our stall. When we get back in the car, Layla says, 'I know you're disappointed you couldn't talk to Ben. But there is some good news.'

'Oh?' I manoeuvre the car off the pavement and drive away. 'What's that, then?'

'Guess who'll be at the fete?'

'Who?' My heart is hammering even though I haven't a clue what she's going to say.

She pauses dramatically. 'Only *Ben's old girlfriend*, who was at Ivy's dinner party with him that night. Lucy Feathers!'

'So we might be able to talk to her. That's brilliant!'

Layla sighs as if she couldn't care one way or another.

'Oh, Layla, I wish I could help.'

She barks out a laugh. 'Help? There's not much chance of that. Unless you can hire a contract killer to take out Anne-Marie.'

I grimace at the thought.

'*Joke*,' she says. 'Just an outbreak of raging acne would be fine.'

'What about Josh?'

She laughs harshly. 'What about him? That excuse for a human being is not even worth using up my brain power on.'

I nod admiringly at her. 'Hey, good for you.'

THIRTY-ONE

The day of the August summer fete dawns cool and overcast.

I set my alarm for seven and I'm showered and dressed in my newest jeans and a bubblegum pink T-shirt by the time Layla's distinctive knock sounds on the front door.

As I pass through the hall, I catch my reflection in the mirror.

I'll see Jack later, at the fete.

This thought fills me with a sort of breathless anticipation, mixed with the anguish of knowing that he'll be with Selena. I'm going to just put on a brave face and get on with selling cakes. And with Layla on the stall with me, it certainly won't be boring.

I paste on a smile in the mirror. And what I see gives me hope. I look nothing like the sad, frightened person I was when I first arrived in Appleton. My skin glows from being outside in the sun and fresh air and I've spent time twisting my hair up and adding a touch of lipstick. The pink T-shirt sets off my gardener's tan very well. I've come a long way in a short time. I've made friends and grown to actually enjoy living in Moonbeam Cottage. And now I'm entering into the community spirit of the village by manning a stall at the summer fete!

I will have to return to Manchester at some point soon because my life is there – my flat, my friends and my job, which Patty is so generously holding open for me,

But I get a weird sinking feeling in my gut these days when I think about leaving Appleton.

Today, I brush it determinedly aside. I've got too much to do . . .

Layla and I have spent the last few days baking up a storm. She's really cut up about Josh, and I think losing her best friend, Anne-Marie, is proving even harder to bear. I suppose it will just take time . . .

Anyway, she's been pouring all her hurt and aggression into whipping up cake mix with the result that twenty large Tupperware containers – on loan from the village hall kitchen – are sitting on the worktop, filled to the brim with goodies, waiting for us to bear them off in Florence to the village green.

Layla comes into the kitchen and starts peering into the containers. 'Double chocolate cookies. Yum.' This seems like a good sign. Perhaps she's on the road to recovery.

'Don't start on them yet,' I warn. 'Right, let's get going!'

Loaded up with boxes, we head out to the car and the nerves in my tummy ratchet up a level. They're not just over Jack and Selena. I'm also feeling very nervous about speaking to Ben and Lucy Feathers. I haven't been able to face breakfast – although as I'll be stationed behind a cake stall all day, there'll be no shortage of food if I get hungry later.

'Are you all right?' demands Layla. 'You were miles away. Are you worried the cakes aren't going to sell?'

I shake my head. 'I was thinking about Lucy Feathers.'

'Ooh, yes, I can't wait to talk to her about Ben.' Her eyes shine at the prospect. 'She might provide exactly the clue we've been looking for.'

I glance sideways. 'Er, *I'll* be doing the talking if you don't mind!'

She makes a sheepish face and I grin at her, glad of her company.

Her determination to uncover a happy ending for me is touching and I don't want to quash her excitement – but Layla's optimistic approach is led by youthful enthusiasm and a very vivid writer's imagination.

Yet this is no fairytale. This is real life.

And in real life, getting your hopes up so often leads to crushing disappointment.

'It's a big day for your mum.' I glance across at her, keeping my eyes peeled for a parking space by the village green. 'Is she okay?'

'Not sure.' Layla pulls a worried face. 'She keeps saying she wants to go on the helter skelter.'

'Well, that's a good sign, isn't it?'

'I'm not sure. I think she might chicken out and then she'll feel worse.'

I pull up alongside the green, which has been transformed over the past few days into a truly magical scene.

Dominating the view is Prue's old-fashioned helter skelter, painted in glorious reds, blues and golds. It towers over the round-about rides, which range from the sedate giant teacups to the rather more bone-shaking rides that will appeal to the older children. Stalls are ranged around the edge of the green, and already, the delicious aromas of the fairground – toffee apples, hot dogs and candy floss – are drifting over, mingling together on the breeze.

We unload the boot and plate up the scrumptious-looking contents of the Tupperware boxes, adding our creations to the cakes and cookies that have already been brought over by villagers who promised to bake for the stall.

As we work, I keep sneaking a look around for Jack, my heart beating uncomfortably fast. Selena's sure to look stunning, as usual. But it's still quite early – not even nine yet. A whole hour before the fete kicks off. All the same, my eyes seem irritatingly programmed to flick around the green every few minutes.

The dancing competition is scheduled to start at one-thirty, so Prue probably won't make an appearance until after midday.

'Is Jack bringing your mum over later?' I ask Layla.

'Yes, he is. Mum was having a big wobbly about the whole thing when I left. I could swear she'd had a whisky, although obviously she denied it.'

'Oh, poor Prue,' I murmur. 'I wonder if we're doing the right thing, encouraging her to be brave? It takes real guts for her to do this.'

'I know.' Layla frowns. 'But I'm frightened, Holly. Honestly, if that bloody Ribena just *dares* to upset Mum today . . .'

I smile encouragingly. 'With you fighting Prue's corner, she's sure to be fine.' I look around, half-expecting to see a scary, wart-nosed hag hovering close by. 'Is Robina here?'

Layla glowers over at the far side of the green. 'Over there with her scabby dog. She's due to work on the refreshments stall with Lucy Feathers apparently, according to Ben. Although Lucy's obviously not here yet.'

I glance over and see a tall, thin woman with slate grey hair straggling down her back, wrapped in an enormous purple mohair cardigan. She seems to be trying to get to grips with the coffee urn. Her dog, a chocolate brown Labrador with a lovely shiny coat, looks far from scabby.

'I'm sure Jack will make sure your mum's okay.'

Layla grunts, still glaring over. If looks could kill, Ribena would be stretched out cold under the refreshments table. 'It's hard to believe that *she* was Mum's rival in love.'

I stare at her in surprise. 'Robina was in love with your dad?'

Layla nods. 'She was going out with Dad, but then he met Mum in New York and that was it. She's had the knives out for Mum ever since.'

'But that was over thirty years ago.'

'I know. Talk about bitter and twisted and bearing a grudge. She's never married and she obviously blames Mum for stealing the love of her life. Which she absolutely didn't, by the way. Jack says Dad finished with Ribena long before he got together with Mum.'

'And she's the reason Prue won't venture into the village?' I murmur, trying to fathom how an inoffensive-looking woman in a fluffy, hand-knitted cardigan could possibly account for Prue feeling she had to cut herself off from the community for years. 'What on earth did Robina *do*?'

Layla shook her head. 'No-one will talk about it to me, especially not Mum. Even Jack won't tell me anything. But I know it was something horrible that Mum can't forgive.'

We exchange an anxious look.

'Mum only agreed to be a judge today because Jack said he'd be by her side all the time.' She grins. 'He also said she could pass for a glamorous forty-nine-year-old in the dress she was wearing, which I think might have swung it.'

I smile, thinking how clever of Jack.

'Ooh, that's an interesting look.' Layla grins broadly at me. 'Do you fancy my brother by any chance?'

My heart gives a huge jolt.

'*No!*' I exclaim in horror, silently cursing Layla's sharp observation skills. 'He's really nice, though,' I add quickly, hoping Layla will put my very red face down to the shocking nature of her question.

There's a hint of smugness in her smile. 'Sorry. My mistake. It's just your face went all sort of soppy for a second there.'

I make various grunts of disbelief to assure her she's got it completely wrong, and bury myself in yet another box of cookies.

'It's a shame, though,' she says pensively. 'Because I'm fed up with that annoying drip, Semolina-what's-her-face, being at the house all the time. I can't *wait* for Jack to give her the old heave-ho.'

'Maybe he won't,' I say carefully, pretending to search through a bag.

Layla snorts. 'Look, that woman smells of complete desperation. *Not* an attractive scent. She won't last, believe me.'

'He might be in love with her, though,' I argue, while at the same time feeling ridiculously heartened by the knowledge that Layla would rather *I* was Jack's girlfriend than Selena. 'And if that's the case, you'll just have to get used to her.'

She looks at me as if I know nothing. 'Jack might fancy her but he's not *in love* with her. Have you *seen* the way she minces across the grass in her sky-scraper heels? She keeps banging on and on about how she *simply adores* the countryside, but I think it's all a load of bullshit to keep Jack.' She shakes her head firmly. 'No, he'll twig and then she'll be history.'

I don't say a word, but my foolish heart soars with hope that she might be right.

'Oh God, speak of the devil, she's actually here.' Layla nods over to the far side of the green. And sure enough, there's Selena ensconced behind a stall, chatting up a couple of customers. I can hear her high-pitched squeal of a laugh from here.

At ten, people start to pour in through the entry gate, and immediately we're doing a roaring trade in Victoria sponges, raspberry and white chocolate cupcakes, and iced gingerbread men. Layla keeps looking over at the refreshments stall.

'Robina's ears must be burning,' I laugh, trying to lighten the mood. 'Does she know you've got your evil eye on her?'

'Actually, I'm looking at Lucy. When the queue dies down, I could go and talk to her if you want?' She flashes me an innocent look, knowing fine well my response would be, *Like hell you will!*

'Lucy Feathers?' I swing round towards the refreshments stall, and manage to lock eyes not with Lucy but with the scary Robina. I've no idea how long she's been looking over, but it's fairly obvious she has either me or Layla firmly in her sights. There's a brooding intensity to her stare. No wonder poor Prue is spooked by her. I swallow hard and look away.

Ben appears, rubbing his hands together and greets us both

warmly. He has that slightly detached, adrenalin-pumped look of one who's ultimately responsible for the event's success.

'Hello, girls. Doing a roaring trade, I see. Brilliant! The village hall roof will be all the better for your efforts.'

'Double chocolate cookie on the house?' Layla holds out a paper plate.

'Better not.' He pats his stomach. 'Got to think of your health and your waistline when you get to seventy-two – and I plan to make it to ninety and beyond!'

I smile, thinking how energetic and lively he is for someone of his age. I can certainly see what Ivy might have seen in Ben. Anyone would be proud to have his genes . . .

Catching myself daydreaming, I quickly rein myself in. Okay, Ivy liked Ben. I know that from reading her diary and from things Ben has told me about her. But being lovers is a very long way from being friends, as I know only too well . . .

Ben takes my hand. 'So glad to see you becoming part of our little community here, Holly, even if it is just for a little while. Although to tell you the truth, I'm secretly hoping you'll decide to stay for good in Moonbeam Cottage. What do you say, Layla?'

Layla grins. 'Yes. She has to stay. If she leaves, I'll have to look after Ivy Garden all by myself.'

We laugh and I glance at her in surprise. It was just a throwaway remark, of course, but I'm almost sure she meant it. It gives me a warm feeling inside. When I leave, it will make all the difference in the world knowing Ivy Garden will be in Layla's safe hands.

'So, Layla,' says Ben. 'You wanted to meet my friend, Lucy?'

Layla glances guiltily at me. 'Er, yes, that would be great.'

He peers over at the refreshments stall, rubbing his hands together. 'Right, well, she's due a break at twelve so I'll get her to come over.'

When he's gone, Layla gives me an excited thumbs up.

I don't feel quite so upbeat. How on earth am I supposed to broach the subject of Ivy and Ben? Lucy was Ben's girlfriend when they attended Ivy and Peter's dinner party, and even though they probably split up years ago, no-one ever wants to find out that a former boyfriend had been at it with someone else while he was going out with you.

When Lucy comes over, I'll just have to play it by ear, but I already feel a bit nauseous at the very thought. If it was up to me, I might have chickened out. But I know Layla won't let the opportunity pass.

Lucy comes over soon after twelve.

'Hi, I'm Lucy Feathers,' she says with a pretty, dimpled smile, running her hands through her mane of springy blonde-grey hair. Her blue eyes are kind, etched with fine lines, and I guess she's maybe a decade younger than Ben, in her early sixties. 'And you must be Layla. And Holly?' She smiles sadly. 'I was *so* sorry to hear about Ivy,' she says, touching my arm. 'How are you coping?'

She looks genuinely upset, which makes me quite emotional. I smile and tell her I'm getting there.

'I hadn't seen Ivy for years,' she says. 'We lost touch when I got married and moved away to Cirencester. But I have such fond memories from when I lived here all those years ago.'

I swallow and take my courage in both hands. 'Ivy actually mentioned you in her diary.'

'Really? Oh, wow.' She laughs. 'I hope it's flattering.'

'It is.' I glance at Layla who's watching us intently. 'She describes the night you and Ben went to a dinner party at her house, when Peter was still alive. There was another couple there . . . Mr H and Penelope?'

Lucy frowns, thinking back.

Then she laughs. 'That would be Hamish Hornchurch and his wife, Penny. Gosh, I haven't thought about them for years. Lovely couple. Scottish. They'd only just moved down to live in Appleton the week before the dinner party. I remember Ivy made a point of inviting them along that night, to make them feel welcome. They'd moved in next-door to the Chickens, so the four of them arrived at Ivy's together, I remember. We all got on really well. It ended up being a great night.'

I exchange a quick look with Layla.

Ivy's mystery man definitely wasn't Mr H, then.

According to Lucy, Ivy hadn't even met Hamish Hornchurch until the night of the dinner party, so he could hardly have been her mysterious lover.

So that was both Henry Chicken and Mr H crossed off Ivy's dinner party guest list.

That just left Ben . . .

'I remember Ivy really pushed the boat out with the menu that night,' Lucy recalls. 'What was it, now? Venison? No, *quail*! That's right. We had quail and a glorious dessert.'

I smile. 'Crêpes Suzette.'

'Yes!'

'Had you and Ben been going out for very long?' Layla asks, and I shoot her a warning look.

'Me and Ben?' Lucy laughs. 'Oh no, we were never boyfriend and girlfriend.'

'Really?' Layla inches slightly forward in her excitement at this news. 'So did Ben have his eye on someone else, then?'

'Layla!' I jump in, alarmed. 'That's a bit too personal.' I glance apologetically at Lucy, shaking my head as if to say, *Teenagers!*

But Lucy smiles broadly. 'Funny you should say that but—'

'Oh my God, what's wrong with Mum?' gasps Layla, staring past me.

I swing round to look. With all our focus on Lucy, I hadn't even noticed Prue's arrival.

I spot her hurrying towards the fete entrance, making much better progress than Selena, who's in hot pursuit a yard or two behind but hampered by her spindly heels digging into the grass.

Selena sees us and veers over, arriving at the cake stall pink-faced and out of breath.

'Jack just arrived with Prue,' she pants, 'but she'd forgotten her anxiety tablets so he had to go back to the house, and he left me in charge.' She breaks off and takes a huge breath, grasping her heaving chest. 'But then that lanky grey-haired woman came over and Prue got all upset and ran off. Can you go after her, Layla?'

Layla glances at me in alarm. 'Mum will never talk to *me*. Will you go, Holly? She likes you.'

We all stare over. Prue's at the entrance, battling through a small crowd to get out, obviously desperate to put as much distance as possible between her and the public, but particularly Robina.

'What the *hell* did that skanky witch *say* to her?' demands Layla.

'She didn't say anything.' Selena shudders. 'It was just the *look* on her face.'

I take Layla's arm. 'Look after things here. I'll go after her. Don't worry, she'll be fine.'

'Thanks, Holly.' Relief washes across her face as I race off after Prue.

THIRTY-TWO

I find Prue in Ivy Garden.

She's sitting bolt upright on the tree stump, hands tucked under her thighs, staring into the distance. Tear tracks mar her perfect make-up. When she sees me, she holds out her arms in a helpless gesture, her face full of anguish. 'Oh, Holly, it was dreadful. I should never have let Layla persuade me to do this. I've made a complete and utter fool of myself.'

I sit down on the mossy ground beside her and take her hands. She's trembling.

'Prue, you were very brave coming here today,' I tell her gently. 'I know it was the last thing you felt like doing, but Layla's really proud of you. I expect Jack is too. Did Robina threaten you in some way?'

Prue shakes her head sadly. 'It's stupid, I know, but when she started walking over towards me, I thought I was going to faint. I haven't seen her for years, not since—' She breaks off and swallows hard.

'Not since?' I prompt softly.

Prue shakes her head.

'You can tell me. It won't go any further and maybe I'll be able to help.'

Still she hesitates, although I sense she wants to trust me.

I repeat in a whisper, 'You haven't seen Robina since . . .?'

Prue clears her throat. 'Since . . . since she labelled me a whore. She put up posters of me in just my underwear all over the village.' She swallows and tears well up. 'The posters said I was unfit to be a mother to Jack and Layla.'

I stare at her, shocked.

'She was right, of course,' Prue whispers. 'I didn't deserve to be a mother. Not then. William had just died and I went completely off the rails. Layla was just a baby and poor Jack had to be a mum to her and a virtual carer to me, because I just went totally to pieces.'

'Oh God, poor you.' My heart goes out to her. 'But it wasn't your fault, Prue. It was no-one's fault. Obviously you weren't yourself.'

She's staring sadly into the distance. 'But it *was* my fault. All of it. I should have found the strength to cope. Other people do. But instead I let the situation get on top of me and we all suffered.'

'So what actually happened?' I ask her gently.

I don't want to pry but it might help her to get everything off her chest. How terrible that she's been blaming herself and holding on to all this guilt for so long. I know from my own experience that talking about the bad stuff, getting it all out in the open, can make you feel a hundred times better. Talking to Connie about Mum and Dad's accident made all the difference in the world to me. I'm determined I'll never bottle things up like that again.

Prue gives a shaky sigh. 'William's death was so sudden. It knocked me sideways. It felt like my whole world just ground to a halt. Except I couldn't afford to give in to the overwhelming grief because I had Jack who was thirteen at the time, and I was pregnant with Layla.' She smiles grimly. 'Those pregnancy hormones probably didn't help my state of mind one bit. There were times I honestly thought I was going insane. I can barely remember Layla's birth. My sister came up to be with me and completely took over, apparently, demanding all the pain relief available because she was so worried the birth might tip me over the edge.'

'That must have been so bittersweet,' I murmur. 'William gone and you giving birth to his child. I just can't imagine . . .'

'Later, I started drinking to numb the pain. I made myself stay completely sober while I was weaning Layla, but once she started taking a bottle, I fell off the wagon completely and was drinking an embarrassing amount of gin every night after the children had gone to bed. It was the loneliness and because I missed William so desperately. And it was so hard trying to make my benefits stretch so that the kids didn't go without.'

'Your benefits?' I asked, surprised. 'Didn't William have life insurance, then?'

She shook her head. 'The silly man kept putting it off, never imagining he was going to fall off his perch so suddenly. Every penny he earned went into the upkeep of Rushbrooke House, so there was no personal pension plan or insurance or savings of any kind. A house like this just *eats* cash. All the same, I had no idea he was so disorganised financially.' She laughs sadly. 'I used to tell him he never stopped surprising me – in a good way. Little did I know he was saving the biggest shocks till last!'

'So along with everything else, you had no money? What on earth did you do?'

She shrugs. 'I did the only thing I knew I could do well. I started auditioning for dance roles in the London theatres. I had a friend in Stroud who was kind enough to babysit for me and I stayed the occasional night in London, when I was trying to get work, with an old friend from college days. But of course I was kidding myself. Theatre hours are so ridiculously unsociable. It would never have worked, even if I'd managed to get a job.' She sighs. 'So Carol – my London dancer friend – suggested I lower my sights and go down the same route she had.'

'Which was?'

'The men's clubs. Exotic dancing.'

I nod, trying to look as if I found this a completely logical thing to do. 'At least it would be regular money.'

'It was *very* good money. I found that, with the tips I was getting, I only needed a few nights a month to make a real difference to our income.'

'Who took care of Jack and Layla?' I ask.

'Well. I had to drive them all the way down to my sister's and she'd have them overnight. I'd then get the train up to London, go to work, stay over at Carol's, then get the train back to collect the kids next day. It was exhausting but at least I was able to put food on the table and pay the bills.'

'But then Robina found out how you were earning a living?'

Prue nodded. 'She'd always hated me, ever since William fell in love with me in New York. When we were married and I moved into Rushbrooke House, she started spreading rumours about me to anyone who would listen. She implied I'd lived a high old life in New York, sleeping around to get the good jobs, and while William's friends, once they knew me, didn't believe her, there were plenty of others who did. Especially the older generation. They took all the tales of sleazy goings-on on board and whispered behind my back. It was horrible. But then, of course, I managed to play completely into Robina's hands by starting work as an exotic dancer after William died. It must have been a red letter day for her when she found out what I was doing to earn a crust!'

'So she stuck up posters of you all around the village?' I whisper, horrified that anyone could have so little compassion for someone in Prue's vulnerable state.

'Yup! She managed to get her hands on a photo of me with very little on, except for ear-rings and a saucy smile, and she got the image printed on a big poster with the words, "Fit To Be A Mother?" emblazoned underneath it. Then she had dozens of copies run off and presumably in the dead of night, stuck them on all the lampposts and the shop windows, and posted one through every door in Appleton!'

'Phew! Now that's dedication to a cause,' I breathe, shaking my head in horror.

Prue's mouth quirked up at the side. 'You're telling me.'

'And did she have any *friends* left after that little stunt?'

'God knows.' Prue sighs heavily. 'I went into the village that morning and saw all the posters, and it felt like the end of my world all over again.'

'I'm not surprised,' I murmur. 'What an utter cow!'

'Having my shame announced to the whole world like that – all the people I knew in the village – was just . . . horrible.'

It's all so hard to take in.

Prue obviously went to hell and back after her husband died. It was almost impossible to imagine this proud and elegant woman working as an exotic dancer. It would have crucified her, I'm certain, but she did it all for the sake of her children. And then a scorned woman took out her anger on Prue – and basically sentenced her to a life in hiding, unable to rise above the shame and humiliation, terrified to face the woman who hated her enough to wreak such a nasty revenge. Prue already felt she'd failed as a mother, and to have it so cruelly stated for the whole village to witness must have done huge psychological damage.

Damage that Prue was even now failing to move on from . . .

'If it had just been me, it wouldn't have mattered. But what my *babies* had to go through, especially Jack. I'll never forgive myself.' A tear leaks out but she leaves it unchecked. 'The thing is, in a way I felt I deserved people's censure. Robina was saying I was a bad mother, and I actually agreed. I was so ashamed of the direction my life had taken, I just gave in and hid from the world.'

'You were much too hard on yourself,' I murmur, squeezing her hands gently. 'As far as I can see, Jack and Layla don't seem to have been scarred by this in any way. You're their mum and they love you, full stop. It was just a horrible, horrible time after your husband died. Everyone reacts differently. But you're strong and you can get through it. You can't let someone as small-minded and pathetically vengeful as Robina hold you back.'

She stares at me sadly. 'I know I've got to be braver, but over the years, it's just seemed easier to let my world shrink to the size of a pea and allow Jack to carry on being the man of the house, like he did when his father died. I despise myself for relying on him so much and I really want to change things but I'm frightened I won't be able to. I look at you and what you've been through, losing your parents so young and then your lovely Ivy.' She gazes at me, her eyes brimming with tears. 'You're an inspiration to me, Holly. Really you are.'

I feel the hot sting of my own tears. *I inspire Prue?* I'd never have believed it. Almost as touching is that she seems to have dropped the deafness act and is now calling me Holly instead of Polly!

'You can rise to the challenge, Prue. I know you can.' There's a lump in my throat. 'Why don't we go back to the fete and show Robina you absolutely refuse to be bullied any longer?'

She gives me a watery smile but I can sense the struggle going on inside her. 'I'm not sure I'm cut out to be as brave as you, Holly.'

'You took your first step today,' I remind her. 'Okay, you might have faltered a bit, but next time, you won't.'

Prue takes a paper hanky out of her pocket and delicately blows her nose.

'We can help you,' I tell her firmly. Then I remember with a little shock of dismay that I won't be here in Appleton for much longer. But I draw a deep breath and say determinedly, 'Jack's brilliant. And Layla's definitely got your back. She's a force to be reckoned with, that girl.'

'Very true.' Prue smiles fondly. 'It's funny how a crisis like this can actually bring you closer. Layla's been really lovely with me.' Glancing down, she whispers, 'I'm not sure I deserve it, though.'

'Hey, that's nonsense,' I chide her gently.

She looks up, her eyes full of pain. 'But I'm much too hard on her. I'm *terrified* she'll get in with the wrong crowd and go down the same slippery slope that I did, and I just couldn't bear that. So I nag her. Constantly. Instead of making allowances for the fact that she's a teenager with hormones.'

'And she bites back.' I smile. 'You do realise that just makes you a typical family?'

She acknowledges this with a tiny laugh.

'Are you talking about me?' Layla herself appears through the gap, and beside me, Prue jumps nervously. She laughs at her over-reaction, slapping her hand to her chest.

'Lucy Feathers is looking after the cake stall, Holly,' Layla says, before turning to Prue. 'Are you all right, Mum?'

Prue reaches out for Layla's hand. 'Yes, love, I think I am. In fact, I think I might be ready to go back to the fete.'

'Yeah?' Layla's eyes open wide. 'You ready to kick ass?' she says in a terrible phoney American accent. 'Show that evil witch you're the boss?' She holds out her hand, her mum takes it, and Layla hauls her to her feet.

Prue's laugh sounds strained. 'Well, I might not go that far, darling daughter. On the other hand, I'm sort of thinking Robina's been queen of the castle for far too long now . . .' She links Layla's arm – very bravely, I think. (Almost as brave as her decision to face Robina again.) Layla flinches away slightly at the unfamiliar contact but decides to allow it, and we prepare to head back to the fete.

Prue stops at the gap in the hedge and takes a deep breath. 'Ah, the scent of those lilacs! You know, this garden really is magical. When I arrived less than half an hour ago I was a complete mess, yet now, I'm thinking: *Why have I wasted all this time allowing Robina to bully me?*

'Quite right, Mum. Way to go!' cheers Layla.

'Thank you, Layla.' Prue turns to me with a smile. 'Of course, it might have nothing to do with the lilacs. I have a sneaky suspicion it was your lovely pep talk that worked the magic, Holly.'

'Hmm.' I pretend to weigh it up. 'No, definitely the lilacs.'

Smiling, we slip through the gap in the hedge and start walking in the direction of the village green.

'Speaking of scents,' says Layla. 'You know that smell of freshly mown grass that everyone goes barmy over?'

'Ooh, yes. I love it,' says Prue.

'Well.' Layla pauses dramatically. 'That scent is *actually* the grass yelling for help because you're attacking it.'

I laugh. 'You just made that up.'

'No, I didn't.' She stares at me indignantly. 'It's a chemical reaction, if you must know. It's the plant trying to heal itself. A customer at the garden centre told me.'

'Fascinating,' breathes Prue, still holding on to her daughter's arm for dear life.

'I know.' Layla grins. 'So basically, every time you cut the grass, you're *actually* committing GBH.'

THIRTY-THREE

As we draw nearer the colourful crowd on the green, the fairground music grows louder and the scent of warm caramel drifts up my nose.

I can sense Prue's anxiety levels rising.

As we pass through the entrance, I glimpse Lucy Feathers laughing with Ben behind our cake stall. In all the panic over Prue, I'd forgotten about Lucy and how our conversation about the night of the dinner party had ended on a cliff-hanger. She was on the point of telling us about Ben's love life.

My insides shift uneasily.

Do I really want to find out what Lucy is going to tell us?

I glance at Layla and know I have no option. My partner in crime is like a dog with a bone. She's definitely not about to let it go.

It's time to face the truth.

With Mr H eliminated from our enquiry on the grounds he'd just moved to the area from Scotland, with his wife Penelope, it looks as if we finally have our answer.

Ivy's mystery man has to be Ben . . .

I watch him now, telling a story, using his hands liberally to illustrate it and making Lucy crease up with laughter.

A warm, tingly feeling spreads through me.

Could he really be . . .?

'Right, I must be brave,' announces Prue beside me, clearly in the process of psyching herself up. 'I need to do something symbolic.'

'Like punch Ribena's lights out?' suggests Layla hopefully.

'No. Like . . . having a go on the helter skelter!' Prue glances at her watch. 'Come on. We've got time before the dance contest starts.'

She lets go of Layla's arm and starts marching over, and after a brief look of disbelief at one other, Layla and I start hotfooting it after her. Prue is staring straight ahead, avoiding catching anyone's eye, and I can only guess how terrified she must be feeling at that moment.

I climb to the top with her, and Layla says she'll catch her at the bottom.

Once up there, though, Prue starts to have second thoughts and I can tell the stress of the day is really getting to her. There are bright spots of feverish colour in her cheeks and she seems restless.

We keep letting other kids and parents brush past us while Prue takes big breaths to calm herself.

Down below, Layla is hiding her worry at the delay by shouting encouragement, which is actually the last thing Prue needs, as it means an interested crowd of people are lingering to watch the entertainment.

'Come on, Mum. I'll catch you!' Layla keeps yelling. 'Just be brave and do it!'

Behind Prue, I'm frantically drawing my finger across my throat and waving my arms to shut her up.

Finally, Prue turns to me and says, 'Bugger Robina Worsley. I'm going to do it.' She arranges herself on the mat and pushes herself off.

When I reach the bottom myself, several people have followed

Layla's lead and are still clapping and whooping at Prue's triumph, although they probably aren't quite sure why. I give her a little sideways squeeze and she beams at me.

As we cross the grass to the marquee where the dance competition is being staged, I hold my breath as we drew near Robina's stall. Prue, as she passes, turns to her tormentor, nods at the helter skelter, and – without slowing her stride – says airily, 'You should have a go, Robina. Exhilarating. And you know what? I wish I'd done it years ago.'

I sneak a look at Robina's face, pleased to note that Prue seems to have stunned her into silence. There's a ripple of laughter from the folks around us, and Layla remarks with a hint of pride, 'I guess you're not the only one who can't stand her, then, Mum.'

Jack has arrived – just in time to witness the impressive spectacle of his normally inhibited mother throwing off her fears in public. He wraps an arm round her and hugs her so tightly, she jokingly complains he's blocking her airwaves. I watch them, my heart swelling with emotion.

Then Layla murmurs in my ear, 'Let's go and talk to Lucy again.'

So, with legs as weak as water at the prospect, I leave Prue to get ready for the judging in the marquee, with Jack for support, and follow Layla over to our cake stall.

And Lucy.

She beams at us. 'I saw your mum come down the helter skelter, Layla, so I'm assuming she's okay now?'

We assure her that she is. Then Layla, wincingly direct as ever, says, 'So you were telling us about Ben that night at Ivy's dinner party?'

Lucy looks confused for a second. Then she laughs. 'Oh yes, you thought we were going out together?'

'And you weren't?' asks Layla.

'No, just really good friends. We still are.' She leans closer, her eyes full of mirth. 'Actually, I'll let you into a little secret. All this

303

happened years ago, and I've been happily married to Terry for over thirty years now. But way back then, I thought Ben was lovely, and at Ivy's that night, I was half hoping something might happen between us.' She gave an odd little laugh. 'But then he made his big announcement, which sort of put paid to any romantic hopes I might have had. You can maybe guess what it was?'

Layla and I shake our heads.

My heart is beating so fast I can hear it drumming in my ears.

'That was the night he chose to come out,' she says, lowering her voice confidentially. 'He'd been hiding his sexuality for a long time and it was a really emotional night. For everyone.' She smiles fondly over at Ben. 'Yes, that was quite an evening. A great deal of alcohol was consumed and I remember Ivy going in search of more supplies at one point.' She smiles, remembering. 'She was convinced there was a magnum of champagne in the garage so she went off to find it and didn't reappear for ages. We all kidded her that she must have conked out and had a little sleep somewhere. Mind you, we were all pretty much out of it. I remember my hangover lasted the best part of three days!'

THIRTY-FOUR

'But I *mean* it, Holly. You can't give up the search. Just because
it turns out your granddad isn't Ben.'

Layla is adamant we have to continue looking for Bee.

And me? I think I've had quite enough of having my hopes
raised then seeing them crash to the ground, thank you very much.

Layla sighs, her frustration rising at my lack of response during
the short drive back to Moonbeam Cottage. 'We need to read the
diary again and hunt for more clues. There *has* to be something
in there that we've missed. Something that would crack the case!'

'Fine.'

The fete is over and we've packed up the stall, Layla keeping
up a constant stream of cheerful chatter, obviously intended to
buoy up my spirits.

But it isn't working.

I feel strangely dead inside. And hopeless. Like there's no point
to anything any more.

Our hunt has led us up a blind alley. All along, I've been trying
to protect myself from the inevitability of being crushed by telling
myself: *Of course Ben isn't likely to be my granddad! I'm being
swept along by Layla's enthusiasm, that's all!* But underneath the
surface bravado, my subconscious was clearly entertaining a

different idea. I'd been pinning all my hopes on Ben without even realising it.

The numbness I'm feeling is weird.

Since Ivy died, I've felt a whole exhausting array of emotions: shock, grief, fear, hope, despair. And anger. It's been simmering away inside me ever since I found the diary and realised Ivy had kept so much from me.

But I haven't experienced this odd numb feeling since the days immediately after Ivy died. It's probably my body protecting me from the stab of disappointment I felt when Lucy Feathers made it clear Ben could never have been Ivy's secret lover.

I suppose it's a bit like an anaesthetic. But what will happen when the numb feeling wears off?

We reach the gate of Moonbeam Cottage.

'Shall I come in and we can start reading through the diary again?' persists Layla. 'At least, *you* can read it. Out loud. My stupid dyslexic brain would be stumbling on forever trying to decipher it.'

Dazed, I vaguely register that she's branded her brain stupid, but I haven't the energy to correct her.

'I'm tired, Layla. I just want to go to sleep.'

She opens her mouth, presumably to suggest another line of attack. But the look on my face silences her.

'Okay.' She hesitates. 'See you tomorrow, then?'

I nod, just so I can escape.

Inside, I go through the motions of making tea, then I sit staring into space in the living room, until the contents of my mug are cold and the room grows dark. The numbness is starting to wear off and a weight of grief has settled over me.

I tried to pretend otherwise, but I'd really bought into the idea of a lovely granddad I'd never known existed becoming part of my life and being over the moon to find out he had a grand-daughter he never knew about.

And I'd so wanted it to be Ben.

His kindness and gentleness, I'd thought, would surely mean he wouldn't reject me when I broke the news that I was his grand-daughter.

I even kidded myself at one point that I felt a connection with Ben at a deeper level. But in the end, it had been my imagination playing tricks on me. Ben was, after all, a red herring. A lovely man. But at best, a nice friend.

I climb the stairs on autopilot, undress slowly and lie in bed curled on my side, staring at the bedside clock. Time will ease the ache of disappointment. But right now, the feeling of alone-ness has never felt so raw . . .

Next morning, a rap on the door arouses me from a half-slumber.

I squint at the clock. It's just after nine-thirty. Who would be up and about at this time on a Sunday morning?

The events of the day before at the fete start barrelling into my head, one image after another, in quick succession. Layla and I finally chatting to Lucy Feathers. Prue bolting from the event and me running after her. Our heart to heart in the secret garden. And finally, the crushing realisation that we've been way off the mark thinking Ben could be Ivy's mystery lover.

A dull lethargy settles over me. It's sure to be Layla at the door. She's not going to give up on the mystery until she's finally cracked it, but do I really have the energy to face her right now? She'll be on at me to read through Ivy's diary all over again, looking for more clues. But I've been through it with a fine-tooth comb plenty of times already, and I'm certain I haven't missed a thing.

I collapse back on the pillows, wondering if I can perhaps not answer the door. But then, knowing Layla, she'll just keep on knocking in her youthful enthusiasm, and I'm not sure my aching head can stand it.

So I pull on my short summer robe and run downstairs bare-foot. When I pull open the door, my heart leaps into my mouth.

Jack.

Pulling the skimpy robe tighter, I try to smile while fervently wishing I'd at least pulled a comb through my hair. I feel vulnerable enough this morning without having to face Jack looking as if I've spent the night in a hedge.

In contrast, Jack looks groomed and business-like in a charcoal grey suit, white shirt and pale blue tie. I breathe in his familiar cologne and my insides roll over. The man is utterly gorgeous. All I want to do is sag against the doorpost and just gape at him.

Does Selena know how lucky she is?

What a bloody idiot I am to have fallen for a man who is *so* out of reach and unavailable!

He says hello, his eyes sweeping briefly over my half-dressed form. 'Sorry. I didn't mean to disturb you,' he murmurs in the deep, velvety voice that does seriously disturbing things to my person. He glances at his watch as I blush to the roots of my haystack hair. 'I'm doing a day at the office and I'd forgotten that most normal people don't actually get up at the crack of dawn on a Sunday.' He smiles lazily.

'It's fine. Honestly,' I mumble, my brain having turned into marshmallow. 'I – er – was about to have breakfast. Would you like some?'

He looks a bit surprised. 'No, thanks. I'll grab a Danish on the way.'

I feel my blush deepen. 'What I meant was, would you like to come in?' In a rush, I add, 'I'll just slip out of these things and I'll be with you.'

A second later, I realise how that must have sounded.

Oh God, I've just invited him in for a naked fry-up. No wonder he seems lost for words.

In the brief silence that follows, his eyes lock on to mine and the air between us seems suddenly super-charged with emotion. He takes half a step towards me, gazing at my mouth, and my knees turn to cotton wool.

His blue eyes are hypnotic, and the way he's looking at me is causing my heart to bound around in my chest like a novice trampolinist.

And then I gulp.

It's a dismayingly loud, cartoon-style gulp – like Sylvester dreaming he's swallowing Tweety Pie – and my nervous laugh breaks the spell between us.

Jack clears his throat. 'I need to get on. But actually, the reason I'm here is to invite you to dinner.' He names a day the following week. 'Are you free?'

Dinner?

With Jack?

My heart beats a little faster. 'Er, yes. Absolutely.' I give a self-conscious laugh. 'Although I probably should have said, "Let me check my diary," so you'd think I was leading a really exciting life, going out every night, instead of . . .' I trail off.

'Instead of living in the tedious back of beyond where the sheep outnumber the humans?' He's smiling but there's a slight edge to his tone. 'I guess we still haven't convinced you that the countryside is the best place to be.'

'Have you been trying, then? To convince me?' I ask, boldly.

He glances down at his shoes, saying nothing, and something leaps inside me.

But when he looks up again, he's smiling. 'Anyway, if your diary permits, Prue would love to see you on that night. It's a special occasion, apparently, but she's being very mysterious. She says she has an announcement to make.'

'Oh. Right. How intriguing.' I try to match his broad smile, even though my heart just did a disappointed dive when it became apparent this wasn't dinner-for-two he was suggesting, but a family occasion. Still, at least I'll get to spend an evening in Jack's company. Perhaps Selena is busy that night.

'Yes, of course, I'd love to come.' I pause, then enquire airily, 'Who else will be there?'

'Mum, obviously. Layla, if we can pin her down. And Selena.'

Marvellous!

Frowning, he murmurs, 'Actually, Mum specifically asked if Selena could be there.'

Better and better!

Instead of glowering and gnashing my teeth, I force a sweet smile. 'How lovely.'

When he's gone, I wander through to the living room and flump down. My phone, on the sofa next to me, is far too tempting. Picking it up, I dial Ivy's number.

I can't pour my heart out to my grandma the way I always used to.

But hearing her voice is the next best thing . . .

Autumn

'An autumn garden has a sadness when the sun is not shining'
– Francis Brett Young (*Cold Harbour*)

THIRTY-FIVE

The day of Prue's dinner party rolls around.

I stare at my outfit laid out on the bed.

I'm really conflicted about going – and it's nothing to do with the streaks of paint I've managed to get in my hair from giving the living room a final coat of magnolia. On the one hand, I will get to see Jack. And poor pathetic no-hoper that I am, I can't stop the butterflies at the very thought – even though I know Selena will be there, lording it over me, pouting her bee-stung lips at Jack and feeling him up at every available opportunity. And no doubt declaring her undying love for cow dung.

I know I can't compete with Selena in the catwalk stakes, so I've decided to dress down in my skinny jeans and a fine black sleeveless polo neck, which showcases my sun-tanned arms and shoulders but not much else.

I've spent the time since the fete finishing the painting in the cottage. I phoned Prue and told her I had flu and was too unwell to garden, which served a dual function: it meant I had a good excuse to avoid Layla and her irritating inability to let things lie, and it made me focus on the practicalities.

For the past few months, I've been in cloud cuckoo land, imagining I was about to discover family I never knew about.

But after the fete, I realised what an idiot I'd been. This sort of thing – a granddad emerging from the woodwork – only ever happened in fairytales. I'd allowed myself to get completely carried away by Layla's naïve optimism – but the truth was, we'd got precisely nowhere.

In fact, I was even worse off than I was before I found the diary.

I'd allowed myself to hope and now that hope had been utterly dashed.

The only glimpse of sunshine this week, funnily enough, was Sylvian calling round the previous day.

After our disastrous 'date', I hadn't seen him at all, so when he showed up at the cottage, my first thought was that he might be there to try and talk me into a threesome or something equally dubious.

But the news he had was amazing.

He'd had an email from the organisers of the short story competition, saying that Layla had been short-listed! As I'd been so encouraging of her writing, Sylvian thought I should be the one to break the good news to her. He gave me a copy of the email and it's now tucked in my bag, ready to take over to Prue's. The thought of sharing the news with Layla is the one thing that's stopping me from phoning Prue and pretending I still have flu.

It's early September and there's a definite chill in the air, so I put on a belted wool jacket and knee-length boots for my scurry through the woods to Rushbrooke House.

At the cottage door, I glance down at my plain outfit.

Then on an impulse, I throw off the jacket, run upstairs and ditch the black polo neck in favour of a plunging lace-effect top in palest pink.

Watch out, Selena! I might be down but I'm not out!

Taking the short cut to Rushbrooke House through Ivy Garden, I squeeze through the hedge and make for the path through the woods. Then my eye catches something that makes me stop in

314

amazement. The love seat – which the storms had broken in two – has been mended and is now back in its old place over by the hedge.

A lump rises in my throat as I brush off some leaves and sit down on it. Jack must have fixed it for me. I can't think who else could have done it so beautifully. He's such a lovely man . . .

With my eyes misted over, my progress along the narrow path through the woods is a little hazardous. But finally, I arrive at Rushbrooke House.

Layla greets me at the door. 'Wow. I didn't know you actually *had* boobs,' she says really loudly, just as Jack walks into the hall.

Colour races into my cheeks. 'Thanks, Layla. I *think*.'

I exchange a slightly awkward grin with Jack.

'My little sis is nothing if not direct,' he says. 'You look lovely, Holly.'

My stomach swoops deliciously at the warmth in his tone. He looks utterly gorgeous in slim black jeans and a pale shirt that brings out the blue of his eyes. And for a long moment, as we look at each other, it's as if no-one else exists apart from the two of us . . .

'Jack? Where are you, darling?' Selena clatters into the hall on her sparkly heels, and the spell is broken. She drags him off into the kitchen to open the champagne, while I pull myself together and take the opportunity to talk to Layla.

After Josh's horrible betrayal and her fall-out with Anne-Marie, she's been looking peaky and under the weather, while trying to pretend that she's fine. But when I tell her that her story has been short-listed and she's in with a good chance of winning the competition, her face lights up in sheer wonder. A happy tear rolls down her cheek and she doesn't even dash it away.

'I can't believe it, Holly. Is it really true?' She grabs the email and reads it, her eyes round with excitement.

'It's really true. You've got talent, Layla.' I smile at her fondly. 'Didn't I tell you?'

She laughs. 'And me who can't even spell properly!'

'Dyslexia doesn't have to hold you back. You've proved that a hundred times over.' I pause. 'Can I have a hug, please?'

She laughs and flings her arms around me, and I'm crying happy tears myself over her shoulder, knowing how much she deserves this.

'When are you going to tell your mum and Jack?' I say as we repair our eye make-up before joining the others.

She looks anguished. 'What will they think?'

'They'll think you're amazing,' I laugh. 'And if *you* don't tell them, *I* will.'

Prue greets me with a big hug, which takes me completely by surprise. In fact, she seems like a different person. She's more relaxed than I've ever seen her, her eyes shining, the life and soul of the party and pouring drinks for everyone.

'Telling that Robina to fuck off is the best thing she ever did,' murmurs Layla, watching me observing Prue.

'Layla! Wash your mouth out,' I hiss. But I can't help smiling because she's right. The transformation is incredible.

'Attention, please!' Prue tinkles a knife against her glass and everyone turns. 'I have an exciting announcement to make.'

'You're having a helter skelter installed in the garden!' shouts Layla, and everyone laughs.

Prue smiles and pulls Layla close. 'No, my darling daughter, although it's a lovely idea! And speaking of lovely ideas –' She glances around the table and holds her glass up in a toast. 'Here's to Rushbrooke House Luxury B&B!'

'Yay!' calls Selena, also raising her glass.

I look at Prue, along with everyone else, waiting for an explanation.

Her eyes are gleaming with excitement. 'So I've decided it's time to sell the cottage in the woods and plough the money into renovating Rushbrooke House, with the aim of taking in paying guests to keep our heads above water!'

There's a stunned silence from everyone except Selena, who seems to be taking it all in her stride. Then everyone is talking at once, and Prue is telling Jack that the best thing about it is that he can give up his daily London commute and start making furniture instead.

'Obviously, I can't do it all on my own. I need a project manager,' Prue says with a secretive smile. 'And dear Selena, with her huge talent for interior design, is the perfect person for the job!' I stare in shock, as my stomach falls down a lift shaft. 'Thank you, Selena, for agreeing to come on board!'

Everyone clinks glasses and I try to join in. Even Layla seems to think it's a great idea that Selena will be masterminding the project for Prue.

My cheeks ache with trying to look pleased. I feel like exposing the witch as a total fraud but I can't do that to Prue. She might well be great at the job she does – and who am I to stamp on Prue's excitement?

We sit down to dinner and I'm trying not to look at the way a triumphant Selena is clinging like a limpet to Jack. She winds herself around him and stays pretty much glued to his side for the entire meal, even swapping places with Layla so she can fondle his thigh under the table and stare up at him adoringly at every possible opportunity.

I can't help noticing that Jack takes it all in his stride and doesn't resist in the slightest.

Prue has made a hearty beef stew with a lovely rich gravy, but bits of meat keep getting stuck in my throat. Try as I might, I'm finding it impossible to look upbeat sitting opposite the pair of them.

Jack's warm reception when I arrived raised my hopes to the sky. But now, watching Selena kiss him on the cheek, I'm sliding down into a horrible pit of despair. I might be mistaken, but Jack seems to be avoiding my eye now.

Several times, I catch Layla watching me. At one point, she

does a sneaky fingers-down-the-throat gesture, aimed at Selena, which makes me feel slightly better.

But not much.

The plain fact is, Selena is never going to let go of him and Jack isn't exactly complaining.

And that leaves me precisely nowhere.

A huge lump lodges in my throat and I have to fight really hard to stop the tears from springing up. Luckily, Layla is telling everyone about being short-listed in the short story competition and they're all turning their delighted attention on her. Only Jack catches me sneaking out my hanky. I turn away and dab my nose, pretending I've got a sniffle.

I decide that as soon as the dinner is over, I'll make my excuses and leave.

But in the meantime, I can't stand to watch Selena claiming ownership of Jack – and pretty much the whole Rushbrooke family, now that she'll be working so closely with them all. I excuse myself and escape to the loo.

Dropping the lid, I sit down gingerly, my head in my hands. I really shouldn't have had that champagne because the alcohol is making me even more emotional than I otherwise would be.

What a bloody mess!

When I emerge a few minutes later, Jack is standing in the hallway, examining the label on a bottle of wine.

'I've been meaning to thank you,' I burst out.

'Thank me?'

'For fixing Ivy's love seat.' I smile. 'I'm assuming that was you.'

He nods. 'It was a pleasure to do it. For you.'

I swallow hard, my knees trembling at the tender way Jack is looking at me. If he keeps it up, my already shaky composure is in danger of dissolving completely. 'Well, thank you. I really appreciate it.'

'Are you okay?' he asks gently, and I manage a watery smile.

'Fine, thanks. I'm – er – just feeling a bit weird at the thought of going back to Manchester. You know, selling Moonbeam Cottage. Leaving Appleton for good.'

He nods, glancing down at his feet. Then he looks up, an intense gleam in his eyes. 'I'll really miss you.'

My heart does a gigantic leap of joy and I stare at him word-lessly, my head in a spin. *He'll really miss me?*

He smiles into my eyes and I long to reach up on tip-toe, loop my hands round his neck and kiss him; feel his skin, the silkiness of his hair and his mouth against mine – and show him exactly how much I'm going to miss him. I want this desperately, with every fibre of my being, More than I've ever wanted anything before in my life.

But there's Selena.

A chill descends on me. It's as if the September sun has been eclipsed, even though I can see it through the window, shining in a sky the colour of the forget-me-nots I planted the other week with Layla.

I almost smile at the irony.

Forget-me-not.

I've grown so close to Layla and Prue and Connie – *and Jack* – but once I've gone back to Manchester, I can't guarantee they won't forget me.

How long will it be before I'm just a pleasant but faded memory to them all?

'Look, I know you're set on going,' Jack says brusquely. 'But are you sure I can't tempt you to stay?' His whole demeanour has changed. The intensity of his eyes searching my face makes my heart leap with longing.

I stare up at him, my heart beating wildly, then suddenly his mouth is on mine and we're kissing with such savage passion, I feel like I'm floating a foot above the ground. I stumble back against the wall, feeling the urgent weight of him against me, all rational thought flying out of my head.

Being so close to Jack is everything I ever thought it would be

– and more – and my head spins like a fairground ride, as all kinds of feelings course through me.

Then just as suddenly as we crashed together, Jack breaks free, gasping and putting me away from him, gripping my arms so tightly, I wince.

'Sorry. I can't—' He lets go of me and steps back, running a hand through his hair, his blue eyes a shade darker, his face etched with anguish.

'I know you can't,' I whisper.

He's thinking of Selena.

I picture her slender beauty. How could I ever measure up by comparison? And now that she'll be helping Prue with the B&B project, she's almost part of the family already . . . It would be truly unbearable for me to stay on in Appleton, with Jack so far beyond my reach.

I swallow hard, fighting back the tears. 'Good try at convincing me,' I quip, attempting a smile. 'But my mind is made up. I'm going back to Manchester.'

'Layla will be heartbroken.' His smile is strained. 'Although naturally, she'll pretend she isn't. And Mum credits you with turning her life around. I don't know what you said to her in Ivy Garden that time but it made a real difference.'

'She just needed to get her confidence back. Start believing in herself again. It was Ivy Garden that worked the magic, not me.'

He looks at me so affectionately that perversely, I feel like screaming with frustration. I need to leave Appleton as soon as possible because the thought of staying here, drowning in unrequited love, forever hoping, is totally unthinkable.

I love Jack with every ounce of my being, but he isn't free to love me back.

My mind really *is* made up. I'll contact the estate agent in the morning.

Then I'll head back to Manchester on the next available train . . .

THIRTY-SIX

It's been a strange few days.

By the time I got back from Prue's dinner celebrations, I'd already made my plans. It was time I left Appleton because nothing good could come of me staying on here any longer. But the thought of saying goodbye to everyone filled me with dread. The only solution, I decided, was to slip away quietly without telling anyone. It was probably the coward's way out, but in my fragile state of mind, I wasn't sure I could cope with leaving any other way.

I would phone Connie when I got back to Manchester and explain everything. Perhaps she would even come and visit me in the city some time. And I'd be in touch with Layla, too. I'd really miss her and I wanted to keep in touch to find out how she'd fared in the writing competition.

I told Prue that, regretfully, my work on the cottage was taking up so much time, I wouldn't be able to do any more gardening for her at the moment. She was perfectly fine about it, saying that with the renovations she had planned, the whole place was going to be a mess for months on end anyway.

I'd done one last weeding session for her, and as I was leaving, she looked at me fondly, gave me a big hug and said, 'Please don't be a stranger, Holly.' She then made me promise to pop over for tea the following week, and not knowing what else to say, I agreed. I felt terrible, knowing that by then I'd be settled back into my life in Manchester.

As I walked back through the woods, I felt choked. I'd grown so fond of Prue over the last few months. Having made the decision to leave, I was realising just how many lovely friends and acquaintances I'd made in the short time I'd been there. I'd been dreading spending time here, all alone, and had regarded it as something of a nightmare. But it hadn't turned out like that at all.

Even the open countryside doesn't hold the fear it once did.

Thanks to unburdening myself to Connie that time, and my therapeutic walks out into the countryside, I've slowly grown accustomed to the wide open spaces. Instead of allowing the bad associations to envelop me, I've learned to focus on the hedgerow scents, the gentle sound of the sheep and the good feeling of exercising in the fresh air.

There's so much I'll miss about the countryside when I leave. Moonbeam Cottage. The golden silence of a hot summer's day in Ivy Garden. Colin the cockerel's regular early morning rehearsals. (Yes, even him.) And the way the stars seem so close at night, you feel you could almost reach up and touch them.

And I'll miss the people most of all. Especially Jack.

My heart twists painfully.

But Jack, of course, is the reason I can't bear to stay . . .

I board the local bus with a heavy heart.

As we drive slowly through the village and out into the open country, the lump in my throat feels as big as a golf ball.

But by the time we arrive in Stroud what seems like hours later, after meandering through so many Cotswold villages I've lost count, I'm starting to think rather fondly of the quick and efficient public transport services in Manchester.

It will be good to get home.

At the station, I buy myself a magazine and settle myself on a bench to while away the twenty minutes till my train arrives.

Moonbeam Cottage is now in the hands of a cheery local estate agent. She smiled and said she doubted it would be on the market for long because properties like this one were snapped up before you could say, *Location, location, location!* I tried to look delighted but it was hard.

So now all I have to do is wait for her phone call telling me I've received an offer on the cottage. I'm trying not to think about how I'll feel when that happens.

I'm so deep in thought, at first I fail to notice someone waving at me from the road on the other side of the fence and shouting my name.

When I finally glance up, my mouth falls open in amazement.

It's Layla, holding a helmet, astride a motorbike being driven by Tom! To my astonishment, the angular, black and blonde look has gone and her hair is now a lovely gleaming dark brown. All over.

She slides off the bike and runs over to the platform entrance, where I join her. 'I can't *believe* you were going to sneak off without telling us!' she says. 'What's going on?'

I smile sheepishly. 'Sorry. I felt really bad. But I couldn't bear having to say goodbye to everyone.'

'By "everyone", you don't really mean everyone, do you?'

'Er, well . . .'

'Some people you'll miss more than others,' she says cryptically. 'And some*one* you'll miss most of all?'

I laugh uncertainly. Does she mean Jack? How did she know . . .?

'I'm not daft,' she points out calmly.

'You're definitely not that. And yes, you're absolutely right. There *is* someone I'll miss desperately.' I grin. 'How on earth will I cope without dear Selena in my life?'

We both snort with laughter.

'So will you miss *me*?' she says off-handedly, as if she doesn't really care about the answer.

I smile fondly at her, eyes suddenly blurry with tears. 'What do *you* think?'

She laughs. 'I think you probably can't wait to see the back of me and my smart comments. Correct?'

'Amazingly, no.'

We smile a little awkwardly at each other.

'Oh, bugger. Come here,' I say, reaching out to her and drawing her into a huge hug. Her hair smells of fresh air and lavender, and the rich colour really suits her. I swallow hard on the big lump in my throat, knowing I'll miss her so much.

Her own cheek feels suspiciously wet.

'So. You and Tom, eh?' I tease when we draw apart. 'I thought he was too geeky for words?'

She gives a wicked smile. 'You'd be surprised. Apparently you can be a bit of a geek but really sexy at the same time.'

I pretend to look shocked.

'But don't tell Mum I said that,' she warns. 'And absolutely *don't* tell her about the bike. She'd have a hairy fit if she knew.'

I laugh. 'You'll have to tell her some time.'

'I will. She keeps saying we need to talk more. So I'll start educating her about motorbikes!'

She glances over at Tom and he waves at us.

'Right, I'd better go. Have a safe journey and please stay in touch!'

'I will. And keep writing! Keep me posted about the short story competition.'

She darts back to Tom, dons her helmet and climbs on the back of the bike.

As they ride off, she's making a frantic 'phone me' signal . . .

THIRTY-SEVEN

'She sounds like a right cow!' says Vicki, plonking her wine glass on the side table.

It's a girls' night in at my place and I've had enough to drink to start really opening up about my time in Appleton.

Beth grins. 'An *evil bastard* cow, you mean!'

We all explode with laughter.

Vicki and Beth are truly the best thing about being back home.

I've missed them both so much; the daft banter, the laughter, the support. In that sense, I've slipped right back into my cosy life in Manchester, as if I've never been away. They spotted almost immediately that I was hugging a secret – and it didn't take them long to wheedle it out of me because girls just seem to know when their best friends are in love. They laughed their socks off when I told them about Sylvian's tantric meditation and were gobsmacked when they heard about him wanting me to join his love nest down in Cornwall.

On the subject of Jack, they agreed wholeheartedly. They thought he sounded gorgeous.

'But what I don't understand is why Jack's with that evil bastard cow, Helena,' says Beth as she and Vicki stumble down the stairs to their waiting taxi. 'You're a thousand times nicer.'

'It's Selena,' I call after her, laughing.

'Never mind,' shouts Vicki, her voice growing distant. 'We'll find you a man. Pub. Friday night. Take care, love.'

I close the door and wander through to the living room, still smiling.

As I clear away glasses and stack the dishwasher, I try not to think about Jack, but of course it's impossible.

It's mid-November now, more than two months since I left Appleton. At first, I was full of resolve, determined to plunge right back into my old life. I'd go back to work at the café but I'd start looking at the possibility of going to art college, once Moonbeam Cottage was sold.

And I've tried. I really have. I spent a whole Sunday online looking at colleges and trying to decide what would be best. Should I try to stay local? Or should I have an adventure and move away somewhere completely different; start a whole new chapter? I have no ties any more, so the world is, as everyone says, my oyster.

Then I realised that the college I kept going back to – the one that made my heart beat a little bit faster – was so close to Appleton, it was laughable. I abandoned the search at that point. I was clearly in no fit state to make important decisions about my future when my subconscious was hell bent on pushing me towards Jack!

I climb into bed and settle back against the pillows.

I miss my life in Appleton.

There, I've finally admitted it.

I miss Connie. I miss Layla. I miss Moonbeam Cottage and hopping over the road to Ivy Garden. I miss the stars at night and the barnyard smells and the clean air. And if I had to choose between Colin the Cockerel and the crashing of a bin lorry as my alarm clock, I'd pick Colin every time.

I even think wistfully of Prue. She was so excited about her plans for the B&B, and I find myself longing to know how the renovations are going at Rushbrooke House. It's hard to think of

Selena being there, right at the centre of things, while I'm here, hundreds of miles away.

I've spoken to Connie and Layla on the phone and they keep trying to persuade me to go down for a visit. Connie says I can stay in the flat above the deli-cafe any time I'm in the Cotswolds and I know she means it. But the truth is, I'm scared to go back. I'm afraid I might get down there and find myself tempted to stay. But that would be impossible. Being so near to Jack, and yet so far, would be pure torture.

I need to move on, not remain stuck in the past, dreaming and hoping. I learned that lesson the hard way, getting all caught up in a sentimental, yet ultimately fruitless search for Ivy's secret lover, in the vain hope I might be part of a family again.

When I look back at my search for Bee, with an enthusiastic Layla at my side urging me on, it's with an odd sort of wistfulness. Of course I'm gutted that we never got to the bottom of the mystery. But Layla and I were a team, and I will always remember those times with affection.

Ivy's diary is now in my bedside cabinet and I still think about the night of her dinner party all the time, wondering . . .

But I've made peace with the idea that Ivy's secret died with her.

For whatever reason – and I'm certain she felt she was acting out of love for me – she never told me who my real granddad was. And I'm learning to live with the fact that I will probably never know.

I snuggle down and switch off the light.

I can never go back to Appleton.

Moving on. That's what I need to do.

It's late November and the call I've been expecting and dreading at the same time finally comes through. The estate agent says she has good news. She finally has a buyer who's prepared to meet the asking price.

I've been holding out for a sum that I knew was probably a little too high. I told myself it was because I needed the money to secure my future, but deep down I knew that really, it was because I didn't want Moonbeam Cottage to sell.

But now I have an offer I can't refuse.

My head is all over the place when I return the estate agent's call.

I tell her that before I can make a decision, I need to see Moonbeam Cottage for one last time . . .

Winter

'If winter comes, can spring be far behind?'
— Percy Bysshe Shelley

THIRTY-EIGHT

I step off the train at Stroud in the late afternoon, smiling wistfully at the memory of a tall nun barging into me the last time I was emerging from the station. Then I catch the bus to Appleton.

It's the first week of December.

Every one of the pretty Cotswold villages we drive through is aglow with little signs that Christmas is on its way – from the twinkling window decorations to the imposing trees on the village greens, sparkling with multi-coloured fairy lights, and the little rows of shops hung with the jolly, decorative touches that proclaim the festive season is upon us once again.

I've been trying hard not to think about Christmas this year, but the time has come when it's impossible to ignore.

Finally, we arrive in Appleton and I get off the bus outside the village store with my backpack and make my way slowly along the main street to Moonbeam Cottage.

The store is in darkness but the lights are on in the flat above. I smile to myself, thinking about Sylvian. I did like so much about him – his giving nature, peaceful aura and his almost total lack of ego. I still meditate when I felt the stress beginning to take over. But communal living? I think it's fair to say we didn't have that much in common in the end!

I reach the gate and glance over at Ivy Garden. I'll go over there tomorrow, in the daylight. Make sure everything is okay. Maybe the winter jasmine will be flowering . . .

My heart squeezes painfully.

Then I stop and look more closely. Is it my imagination, or is there a sort of glow visible in the gathering gloom, through the winter-sparse hedge? Quickly, I cross the road and slip through the gap.

The garden looks the same as the last time I saw it, except for a rustic wooden table, flanked by two chairs, where Ivy's old bench used to be. On the table sits an ornamental lantern with a candle glowing inside it.

I barely have time to wonder what's going on when I hear a rustle in the trees as someone approaches through the woods.

That someone stops just inside the clearing.

'Holly. You're here,' says a familiar male voice.

I've heard that voice in my dreams, both waking and sleeping, many, many times over the past few months.

I swallow hard. 'Hello, Jack.'

He walks towards me, into the centre of the clearing, and my heart gives an enormous leap at the sight of him. He's wearing the same jeans and lumberjack boots he was wearing when I found him chopping down Ivy's tree that time, with a thick black casual jacket today to keep out the winter chill. He gives me a broad smile and my heart flips again. I smile back at him, feeling like I've never been away.

'I hear you might have a buyer for Moonbeam Cottage,'

'You know about that?' I say, surprised.

He nods. 'We're using the same estate agent to sell the cottage in the woods. I've been following your progress. I heard that Moonbeam Cottage was under offer, and I was pretty sure you'd be back in Appleton.'

I smile up at him, loving the thought that he'd cared enough to keep a check on Moonbeam Cottage. 'What made you think I'd come down here?'

He shrugs. 'Just a feeling. I know how much the place means to you.'

I nod, still amazed that Jack is actually here. What were the chances I'd bump into him as soon as I stepped off the bus? Sylvian would say it wasn't a coincidence because there *were* no coincidences in life . . .

Jack moves away from me and, for a terrible moment, I think he's leaving. But he lingers at the edge of the clearing, reaching up into the branches of a tree.

'When I told Layla you might be back, she wanted to do something to welcome you.' He chuckles softly. 'She has an agenda of course. She thinks she can persuade you to stay.'

I watch him as he fiddles with something on one of the branches. I can't quite see in the soft glow of the single candle. But frankly, it's so good to see Jack again, he could be watching paint dry and I still wouldn't be able to take my eyes off him.

He turns and gives me the familiar quirky smile that always melts my heart. 'Technical problems,' he explains. 'But never mind, I'll sort it later.'

'I love the table and chairs. Did you . . .?'

'Glad you approve. They were a labour of love.'

Our eyes meet and hold for a heartbeat longer than necessary, and my pulse starts to race.

'What are you doing now?' he asks. 'I don't suppose you've got any food in if you've just arrived?'

'Er, no, I haven't even been back to the cottage yet.'

'Then why don't I introduce you to a nice country pub I know? To see if I can help Layla's cause and tempt you to stay.'

I laugh and open my mouth to say it will have to be a *very* good pub in that case. But I catch the searing intensity in his eyes as he looks at me, and the words choke in my throat. A little quiver of longing ripples through me.

I can't help it. I'd planned to act so cool if I happened to bump into Jack. But it seems I completely forgot to inform my body of this . . .

'A country pub sounds lovely,' I tell him, finding my voice.

He smiles. 'Great. Let's go. My car's on the road.'

I slide into the passenger seat and we set off. He turns up the heat, which feels delicious after my slightly chilly train journey, and we drive along in silence for a while. Then I pluck up the courage to ask about Selena.

Jack glances over. 'She went back to London. For good.'

'Oh?' My heart soars to the rooftops of the houses we're speeding past. 'Why?'

He smiles ruefully. 'It – um – turned out that Selena and a building site weren't really a match made in heaven after all. Her Jimmy Choos kept getting mud on them.'

'Ah. Well, yes, they would.'

'You were Mum's first choice, by the way, but she knew you were leaving, so . . .'

'Really? Prue wanted *me* to help her with the building project?' I can't believe how delighted that makes me feel.

'Yes. You still could, of course.' He turns and I catch his grin in the passing headlights. 'But that would mean you'd have to stay.'

I smile happily back at him. Right this minute, I really can't think of anything I'd like more.

Then I tell myself to slow down. Just because Selena is off the scene (*OMG, OMG, OMG!*), that doesn't mean I necessarily have a chance with Jack. There's no point being here if all I'm going to be doing is wishing and hoping that one day everything might come right for me with Jack (if the wind's in the right direction and porkers take flight and Selena stays in London, et cetera, et cetera).

It's hard to be sensible, though, when I'm sitting so close to him in the warmth of his car and there's a tension in the air that I'm daring to imagine is not coming entirely from my side.

When we draw into the car park of The Stoat & Weasel, Jack is a proper gentleman, making sure I've got my coat and bag, and shepherding me into the warmth of the country pub. His hand at my waist makes me feel all tingly inside.

Normally I start getting twitchy if a man is overly protective of me, but with Jack, it's completely different. I love his thoughtfulness. I sit at our table by the roaring log fire watching him at the bar, ordering our drinks and food, and my heart contracts with longing. I still can't believe I'm back here in Appleton, with Jack. It's like a dream come true.

He returns to the table and elects to sit beside me on the banquette, instead of opposite, which is lovely because it feels so much more intimate. Our shoulders keep colliding and the feeling of his muscled, jean-clad thigh casually nudging mine is making my heart skitter about so much, I can barely concentrate on what he's saying.

I want to hold on to the moment. Because sitting here beside Jack feels like all my Christmases rolled into one.

'It's great to have you back, Holly,' he says with a smile. 'I'm glad I beat Sylvian to it.'

I glance at him, puzzled. 'Sylvian?'

'Selena said she bumped into him after you left. He told her he'd been in touch with you to invite you down to Cornwall and you were thinking about giving your relationship with him another chance.'

'*What*?' My face must be a picture. The last time I spoke to Sylvian was when he called at Moonbeam Cottage to give me the email about Layla being short-listed in the writing competition. I haven't heard a peep from him since.

He frowns. 'He wasn't in touch?'

'No. Never. I can't believe Selena would make something like that up.'

Well, I can, actually. I can *totally* believe it. Selena always had it in for me, right from day one. I suppose she thought she'd ruin

335

my chances with Jack if he thought I was getting back with Sylvian. What a cow!

Jack sighs. 'It's probably my fault. Selena must have guessed how I felt about you.' He smiles ruefully. 'I tried to hide my feelings. I knew it was hopeless because you seemed to be so set on leaving Appleton.'

I smile happily up at him. 'And I thought it was hopeless because Selena was in the picture.'

'She shouldn't have lied like that.'

'No, but I can sort of understand.'

Sitting here with Jack, hearing him say he liked me all along, I can afford to be generous about Selena's blatant lies!

'She lied because she sensed there was something between you and me.'

He nods slowly and turns, smiling into my eyes. 'And she was right. Wasn't she?'

'Oh, yes,' I murmur.

We lock eyes and he moves closer to me, sliding his arm round me and drawing me closer.

'One shepherd's pie and one quail,' says a voice, and we turn as the waitress sets down our food.

Laughing, we unroll our cutlery from the paper napkins.

The moment might be ruined but my heart is still banging fit to burst out of my chest.

'Quail,' Jack says, looking at my plate. 'Do you know, that's something I've never tasted. I've always thought of it as quite exotic. I'm more a chilli con carne sort of bloke.'

I smile into his gorgeous blue eyes. 'You can try mine if you like. It's not that exotic.'

As I say the words, a memory knocks at my brain.

Ben in the café talking about Ivy's fateful dinner party, remembering they ate quail that night. And my response: *That was quite exotic for Ivy!*

Ivy liked plain dishes, mainly because she *couldn't* cook! She could bake up a storm but she never had any talent for conjuring up extravagant main courses.

Like quail.

So if Ivy didn't cook the meal that night, who did?

Peter?

But theirs was the sort of marriage where the man went out to work and the woman stayed at home and did the domestic chores. Ivy said Peter never lifted a finger around the house. It's a bit of a stretch to imagine him donning an apron and rustling up haute cuisine for a party of eight.

What if the dinner was made for them? What if it was supplied by a local caterer?

Jack nudges me. 'Everything okay?'

'Pardon? Er, yes . . . sorry, something just occurred to me. Something really important.'

Oh my God, I have to make a phone call. Now.

I turn to Jack, excitement bubbling up through my dismay. 'I'm so sorry, but I think I'm going to have to go.'

THIRTY-NINE

Jack drops me at the deli-café and says he'll sit in the car while I chat to Connie. He seems to understand the urgency and brushes off my apologies. I can only hope and pray he'll be waiting for me when I come out . . .

I'd made my phone call to a startled Connie, who luckily was still clearing up in the deli-café. After she heard what I had to say, she was desperate to see me.

In the car on the way back, I told Jack it was too complicated to explain what was going on, but if my hunch was right – and I'd cracked the mystery – I'd tell him everything later. It wasn't ideal, especially since we had to slightly rush our meals as I was so keen to get to Connie. But Jack seemed to understand.

I knock on the door of the deli and, after a minute, a light goes on in the back.

My heart lurches in my chest. Soon, I'll know the truth. But what if I'm wrong? Just thinking this makes me feel sick with nerves.

Then I have another thought that ramps the nerves up a hundred-fold.

What if I'm right?

Connie looks at me for a second through the glass, a strange expression in her eyes. Then she rushes to unlock the door.

'Hi.' She sounds breathless. 'Come in.'

I follow her through to the little back room, feeling sick with anticipation, and we sit down on two orange plastic chairs.

Connie hitches her chair so she's opposite me, sitting on the edge of it as if she's as nervous as I am. 'You know, don't you? You've worked it out.'

I swallow hard. 'I think so. But how do *you* know?'

She shakes her head quickly. 'I only found out recently, but I couldn't say anything to you because I was sworn to secrecy.'

I nod slowly. *Right, here goes.*

'So your grandfather started up the deli-café years ago and originally it was a bakery?'

She nods. 'But as a spin-off, he started delivering desserts and cakes for parties. Then he went into business with a local chef and began catering for full-scale dinner parties.'

My heart is pounding in my ears.

'Your grandfather was there the night of Ivy's dinner party, supplying the food?'

'Yes.' She shuffles forward and grabs my hands.

'And he is Ivy's mysterious Bee?'

She nods, pink-cheeked with excitement.

'Why did Ivy call him Bee in the diary?'

'He always got called "Beaky" because of his, er, *handsome* nose, remember?' She smiles and touches her own nose. 'Ivy shortened it to Bee as a sort of codename.'

I shake my head in amazement. It's all just as I thought when I saw my plate of quail! No wonder Layla and I had been unable to track down Ivy's mystery man. We were only considering the dinner party guests, but Bee wasn't a *guest* at the dinner. Bee was the *caterer* that fateful night!

'So basically,' squeaks Connie, 'My granddad is your granddad, too!'

I laugh, barely able to take it all in. I'm searching Connie's face for little signs that we're related, and I feel sure that's what she's doing, too. It's funny but the first time I met her, I had a feeling I already knew her. I'd brushed it off, of course, but maybe at some level I was actually recognising the family connection?

I shake my head in wonder. 'So did your family know all along about your granddad's affair with Ivy?'

'No, Granddad kept it a secret all these years. For Ivy's sake. My grandma died young, way before Granddad got to know Ivy. But Ivy was still married to Peter, you see, so no-one could know. And after your mum was born, Ivy was forced to play happy families with Peter for the sake of appearances. Sometimes people can be very cruel. Especially in a close-knit community like this one.'

I nod, thinking of poor Prue being taunted all those years by Robina Worsley.

'So did Peter find out that Mum wasn't biologically his?' I ask.

'No, I don't think he ever knew.'

'And when did you find all this out? Did you know when I first arrived in Appleton in April?'

'No. I heard you talking to Layla one time about needing to find your real granddad and that the only clue to Ivy's secret lover was in her diary that you'd only just discovered. It was after you met Ben in the café?' She leans forward and presses my knee. 'Sorry, I didn't mean to listen in. And I should never have told my family about your search.'

I shake my head. 'Don't worry about that.'

'It was only after I mentioned you were back in the village and had found Ivy's diary that Granddad confessed everything to us at dinner, one night soon after. But he said that on no account were we to tell you about him. Not because he didn't want you to find him – but because he'd made Ivy a promise before she died that he would only ever admit who he was in relation to you, if you yourself came to him and asked for the truth.'

I smile sadly at her. 'I don't know why Ivy never told me the truth herself. I was really angry with her when I first found out there was this whole side to her life I never knew about.'

Connie shakes her head. 'You shouldn't be mad at Ivy. She was only protecting you. You know how people gossip. She must have thought it was for the best you didn't know about the affair. Either that, or by the time she decided you ought to know the truth, maybe she was worried the revelation after all that time would destroy your relationship. And you know how very precious you were to her.'

I nod, tears springing to my eyes. It all made sense.

'You must know that anything Ivy did, whether it seems wise or not, was because she really, really loved you,' says Connie, squeezing my hands.

'I know.' I smile at her through my tears and my heart suddenly takes flight.

Oh my God, I have a granddad! And Connie and her mum and dad. And probably other relatives, who I don't even know about yet!

'So what relation are we to each other?' I ask Connie, feeling suddenly shy.

She thinks hard. 'I'm not sure. Your mum was my mum's half-sister, I guess, so does that make us *half-cousins*?'

'Cousins twice removed?' I grin. 'Or something like that.'

We look at each other and squeal in unison.

Connie stands up and holds out her arms. 'Whatever the title, we're family. And that's what matters,' she says, drawing me into a hug that somehow turns into a weird sort of dance as we jig excitedly from side to side.

When we break apart, Connie holds my shoulders and looks me straight in the eye. 'Now, would you like to meet him?'

My heart lurches. 'Of course I would!'

'You've already met, you know.'

'I know. In the café when you introduced us.'

She shakes her head. 'Before that. He was there, in the church, for Ivy's funeral. He gave you his handkerchief.'

'Oh my God,' I breathe, remembering that terrible day and

how my legs almost gave way. He helped me to a chair and gave me the hanky. 'I've still got it somewhere. Your granddad was so lovely to me.'

She smiles and squeezes my arm. '*Our* granddad.'

I nod, unable to speak. It all still feels so utterly unreal.

'He is lovely,' Connie says. 'I know I'm biased but he is officially the kindest, funniest, cleverest granddad alive. So aren't *you* the lucky one!'

We laugh and I ask her when I can meet him.

She grins. 'Right now. If you like. They're waiting upstairs.'

'*Really?* But how . . .?'

'As soon as you phoned, I rang Mum and told her they had to get themselves over here as soon as possible. Dad drove like the wind, apparently, to arrive before you.'

I nod, feeling suddenly overwhelmed by what was to happen. I was about to meet my granddad. I wanted so much for him to like me. But what if . . .

'Okay?' she checks.

I nod, my heart beating very fast. 'Okay.'

Connie disappears upstairs and, seconds later, she walks into the room with the tall and distinguished man I remember from the funeral.

'Holly,' she says. 'Meet your granddad, Rex.'

His eyes are so warm when he smiles at me – with just a trace of sadness in them, I guess because he sees Ivy in me – that any worries I had simply melt away.

I hold out my hand and he takes it in both of his. 'Holly,' he murmurs. 'You can't imagine how much I've longed for this moment, my dear.'

'Me, too.' I'm smiling from ear to ear and so is he, and the suspicion of a tear in his eye is no doubt reflected in my own.

'You're so like Ivy,' he muses. 'Those expressive eyes. Your voice. And you have her great inner strength and determination, I can tell.'

'Sit down, sit down,' fusses Connie, and we smile at her and take the seats she and I were sitting in, opposite each other.

'I saw you that day on the station platform,' he says, and I stare at him in surprise.

'She was waving me off, back to Manchester. I had a feeling she'd spotted someone . . .'

He nods. 'There was something in her eyes that day, when she looked at me. I knew she was going to tell you the truth at last.'

'And she almost did,' I recall. 'But I had to get on the train and she missed her chance. So she was planning to tell me everything? About you?'

'She was.' He smiles wistfully. 'But then all through the autumn she wasn't herself. She kept getting cold after cold. I knew something wasn't right because she'd always been so strong and healthy. She never got the chance to tell you before . . .'

He breaks off and I see tears of grief in his grey eyes. I shuffle my chair round and take his hand.

'We used to have little trips away, you know.' A smile breaks through as he turns to me. 'They were the best times, when we didn't have to pretend we were just friends so that the people we knew didn't discover our secret.'

'So you're Olive!'

He looks puzzled. 'Well, not last time I looked, my dear!'

I laugh. 'No, she kept going to see her old school friend, Olive, who strangely enough, I never, ever met. She was meeting *you* . . .'

He nods, his eyes twinkling at the memories.

I have to ask him. 'Why didn't she tell me sooner? If she had, you and I could have met and . . .'

He sighs. 'She dreaded your reaction. She'd kept the truth from you for all those years, afraid you'd judge her harshly for the affair. How could she tell you now and risk alienating you?'

I nod, absorbing his words. 'So how did you meet?'

'Well, my wife, Izzy, died when my daughter was very little – and I met Peter and Ivy soon afterwards and we became friends.

I lived above the shop here at the time. I hated the way Peter treated her.' He shakes his head, still visibly upset all these years later.

'You were Ivy's refuge. I'm so glad you were there for her.'

He smiles at me. 'We've so much to talk about, you and I. We were the two people who loved Ivy the most.'

I nod and a single tear rolls down my cheek.

'I wanted to tell you who I was that time Connie introduced us, but of course, I couldn't. Ivy had made me promise to wait until you came to me. So all I could do was hope that you'd find a clue among her possessions that would eventually lead you to me.'

'Thank goodness for the diary. I think she must have known I'd find it and eventually put two and two together.'

He pats my hand. 'And a lovely bit of quail helped you solve the mystery! That will forever be my favourite food.'

We laugh and he says, 'Now to important matters. What are you going to call me?'

'Oh, I'm not sure. What would you prefer?'

'Anything you like, my dear. As long as it isn't "that silly old duffer".'

Connie comes in at that moment and joins in the laughter.

We decide on 'Rex' for now, with the option of 'Granddad' when it feels right.

Connie says she has a feeling that won't be too far off, and I think she's probably right . . .

FORTY

After Connie's mum and dad come down to join the gathering, and we've all chatted for a while, Rex wants to know if I'll accompany him over the road to Ivy Garden.

I tell him I'd be delighted, if they could just give me a little time to talk to Jack, who I'm hoping against hope is still waiting for me outside.

Connie says she'll make some tea for everyone and they'll join me outside in half an hour.

She winks at me as I leave. 'What a day you're having. Go for it, girl!'

I dash outside but Jack's not in the car, so I guess he must be in Ivy Garden. I really hope he is.

Please be there, Jack! Please be there!

To my relief, when I look through the hedge, there he is, lounging on one of the wooden seats, feet up on the table, hands thrust in the pockets of his jacket against the cold night.

I hesitate, though, before stepping through the gap.

Before I go to Jack, there's something I must do.

It's time . . .

Taking my phone out of my pocket, I trawl through my contacts and find Ivy's number. For a long moment, I stand there, psyching

347

myself up to do it. It's a huge deal for me. But I always knew the time would come . . .

A part of me can't quite believe what I'm doing when I hit 'delete'. But there, it's done.

I put my phone back in my pocket and draw in a huge lungful of air. Then I breathe out slowly. How do I feel?

Actually, I'm okay.

'Hey, there,' Jack says, getting to his feet, when I join him in the clearing. 'Everything all right?'

'Everything is great,' I tell him, happy but slightly dazed from everything that's happened over the past few hours.

'Do you want to tell me?'

'Later.' I smile shyly up at him, desperately hoping we can pick up where we left off in the pub – that moment before the waitress arrived when Jack's hand was clasping my waist and we were about to kiss.

He nods. 'Okay. Well, I've got a surprise for you.'

'Another surprise?' I laugh. 'I'm not sure I can cope!'

'It was Layla's idea, but it wasn't working earlier.'

He walks over to the same tree he was standing by earlier, does something I can't quite see in the gloom – and suddenly, the whole place lights up like a winter wonderland.

I gasp at the sight.

Soft white lights hang low in the trees all around the little woodland clearing. It's so perfect, it actually brings tears to my eyes.

'It's beautiful,' I breathe, staring around me in amazement. 'I can't believe you did this for me.'

We look at each other across the clearing.

'I'd do a lot more than string up a few lights,' Jack says softly. 'If it meant you would decide to stay.'

My heart leaps with hope. I swallow, unable to drag my eyes away from his, but at the same time, half-expecting Selena to suddenly emerge from the bushes and totally sabotage this moment for me.

I take a step towards Jack, hardly daring to believe this is real, and he does the same.

And then somehow, I'm in his arms, and his mouth comes down on mine and the whole world disappears.

It's just us now. Jack and me. His kisses are hard and determined, and a primitive beat of desire pounds through my whole body. I kiss him back, my face wet with tears, all the despair of those heartbreaking months of longing pouring out of me, letting Jack know just how much I want him.

Finally, we break apart, gasping, although Jack keeps me grasped firmly against him as if he's never going to let go.

'Tell me what happened at the café,' he says.

'Later,' I whisper, not wanting to interrupt the moment – not even to tell him something so incredible that I still can hardly believe it myself. 'I promise.'

Groaning, he pulls me closer and bends to kiss my neck, keeping his mouth there as I run my hands through the dark silkiness of his hair, my head spinning with the joy of finally being able to love Jack after needing him for so long.

Later, he draws the two chairs together and we sit beneath the magical fairy lights of Ivy Garden, smiling at each other, unable to let go even for a second. He tells me he thinks he fell for me at our very first meeting outside Stroud railway station, with me being all snappy and disapproving of his drunken state. I tell him that I was closer to being locked up in jail than I've ever been, because I could have cheerfully murdered Selena for monopolising his attention.

This exchange takes longer than you'd imagine, interrupted as it is by a long, passionate kiss that fizzes through my whole body and makes me wish we could go back to Moonbeam Cottage immediately.

'So,' Jack says at last. 'Tell me your news.'

'Okay. But first, can I ask you a personal question?'

'Go on, then.'

I clear my throat. 'What are your views on polyamory?'

He stares at me. Then he chuckles. 'Christ, you're not going to tell me you've got three husbands already!'

I feel myself blushing, rather liking the implication that he might want to be husband number four.

'No. It's just . . . well, I couldn't be with a man who thought it was perfectly acceptable to live in a commune and have sex with whoever took his fancy that particular day.' I shrug apologetically. 'It's just not me.'

He laughs. 'And it's not me, either, I'm happy to report. What the hell put that idea in your head?'

'Oh, nothing. Just checking.'

'You're a funny one,' he says, but his eyes are so full of love, I can tell that, in this case, being funny is a good thing.

'I have a feeling you're going to keep on surprising me,' he says.

I smile happily. 'I'll certainly try my best.'

'And by the way,' he growls, pulling me closer. 'Forget polyamory. I happen to be a *huge* fan of one-on-one.'

'Well, that's a relief,' I giggle, my body melting deliciously at the very thought of this.

There's a rustling in the trees behind us and torchlight shines into the clearing.

'Come on, Mum,' says a familiar voice. 'Keep up. Or we'll be having to get you down to the motorised scooter shop.'

Layla!

I hear Prue's laugh. 'Don't be so cheeky, young lady. *You're* not the one who walks into the village and back most days. I'll have you know I've never been fitter!'

'Don't the fairy lights look amazing? Ooh, look, she's here!'

Jack chuckles. 'Family. Who'd have them?' Then he realises what he's said and tightens his arm around me. 'Sorry.'

I smile up at him. 'You don't have to be sorry. Because here comes *my* lot!'

Right on cue, Connie squeezes through the hedge, followed by her mum and dad, and Rex.

Jack stares at me. 'They're your family?' he asks, just as Layla bounds over to say hello.

I nod. Then I turn to Layla. 'Thanks for my surprise.' I wave at the lights in the trees.

'You're very welcome. Do you want another surprise?'

'I'm not sure,' I laugh. 'Do I?'

She nods eagerly. 'I just heard that I came second in the short story competition – and they had hundreds of entries!'

'Wow, Layla, that's awesome!' I pull her into a delighted hug.

'I know. Mum and Jack are sending me on a writing course and I've started my first novel!'

'I can't wait to read it. Actually, I've got a surprise for you, too.'

'Ooh, what is it?'

'The answer to the mystery we tried so hard to solve.'

Her eyes lights up. 'You mean . . .?'

'Yes. Layla, meet my granddad!'

She spins round. 'What, *Rex*? Well, bugger me! You're Ivy's secret lover?'

'Secret lover?' repeats Prue, bemused.

Everyone laughs, including Rex, who puts an arm around Layla and remarks, 'You can always trust this girl to say it as it is. Cut through the cow pat, as it were. She's assisted me at that garden centre of hers on many an occasion.'

'Rex. Wow!' Layla is still taking it in. 'Good result, Holly.'

'We brought champagne to celebrate,' says Connie, holding up a bottle in each hand.

'Oh, how lovely,' says Prue. 'Now, will someone please tell me what on earth is going on here?'

Jack puts his arm around Prue and says, 'How about we all go back to Rushbrooke House out of the cold? My baby sis has made mince pies.' He smiles wickedly at Layla. 'I realise that sounds like a threat, but they actually taste quite good.'

351

Everyone is in agreement and Prue starts leading everyone back through the woods. Jack slips his hands round my waist and we stand for a moment in the clearing, in among the magical festive fairy lights.

'What a day you've had,' he murmurs.

'Thanks to you.'

'Me?'

'Well, if you hadn't taken me to the pub, I'd never have ordered quail. And I'd never have had my light bulb moment about Ivy and Rex.'

'Good old Ivy! She certainly kept that one secret. Although I think she'd be delighted at how it's all turned out for you.'

I nod, my eyes filming with bittersweet tears.

And I also know she'd have been over the moon that Jack and I are finally together.

'Rex seems like a really good guy,' says Jack into my hair.

'Well, I'm sure he is,' I joke, trying to pull myself together. 'He *is* related to *me*, after all, and I happen to be perfect!'

He chuckles. 'Okay, I'll give you that one. Since I do actually agree with you.'

He bends to kiss me again, then he stops. 'So can I assume you've decided to stay in Appleton?' He's smiling but there's a touch of uncertainty in his expression.

'Are you asking me to?'

He nods slowly, gazing into my eyes and turning my knees to jelly.

I smile happily up at him. 'Then I'm definitely staying.'

He searches my face for a second, as if he can't quite believe I'm real. Then he pulls me closer for the millionth kiss of the night. And this time, I have no worries – like I did with Sylvian and his kundalini antics – that Ivy might be looking down on me disapprovingly.

In fact, I'm quite certain she's cheering . . .

ACKNOWLEDGEMENTS

Thanks to my wonderful editor, Phoebe Morgan, for her endless encouragement, patience, hard work and great insights – and to the brilliant teams at Avon and HHB, who all continue to make this 'job' of mine a delight.

Thanks also to my lovely family and fantastic friends for all their support. I really couldn't do it without you!

Two ex-friends.
One Christmas to remember . . .

A funny, heartwarming read – the perfect
book for fans of Jenny Colgan and
Lucy Diamond.

Can Izzy sort the wheat from the chaff
and the men from the boys?

When Izzy Fraser's long-term boyfriend walks
out on her, she decides to take matters into
her own hands . . . with unexpected
consequences!

Lola Plumpton can't believe her luck.
Until, of course, her luck runs out . . .

A warm and cosy festive tale you won't
be able to put down.

Wedding season isn't always smooth sailing . . .

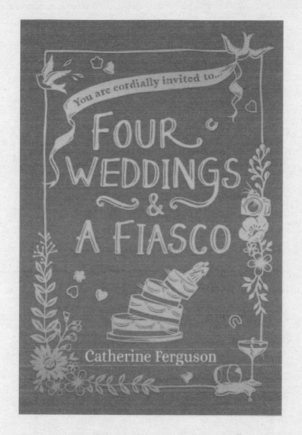

A funny, feel-good read about weddings
gone wrong . . .